One man has seen the danger in the undersea volcano reaching toward the surface of the Atlantic: American geophysicist Benjamin Meade, whose lifelong study has shown him the threat that R-Nine presents to the world's future.

In Britain, a young scientist may hold the knowledge necessary to save a starving, freezing population, but Marjorie Glynn has lost battle after battle for funding geothermal power stations to supply her Biosphere Brittania.

In Parliament the representative for the Coal Miners Union holds power over all energy research funding: Seamus MacTiege can see only the opportunity to seize Britain by the throat and hold the government hostage to its need for power and heat.

As the crisis escalates, and the climate becomes worse and worse, it will take the personal courage of a few dedicated individuals to turn the politicians from their madness.

Books by Richard Moran

Cold Sea Rising
Dallas Down
The Empire of Ice
Earth Winter

THE
EMPIRE
OF
ICE

Richard Moran

TOR®

A TOM DOHERTY ASSOCIATES BOOK
NEW YORK

THE EMPIRE OF ICE

Copyright © 1994 by Richard Moran

Cover art by Tim Jacobus

A Tor Book
Published by Tom Doherty Associates, Inc.
175 Fifth Avenue
New York, N.Y. 10010

Tor® is a registered trademark of Tom Doherty Associates, Inc.

ISBN: 0-812-53009-8
Library of Congress Catalog Number: 93-43241

First edition: February 1994
First mass market edition: February 1995

Printed in the United States of America

0   9   8   7   6   5   4   3   2   1

For my daughters, Jody and Emily.

ACKNOWLEDGMENTS

I created the heroine of this book using as a model my aunt, Marjorie Louise Heffernan Glynn, a woman who faced many challenges in her life and emerged from the wilderness with her faith, kindness, and joyous heart intact. Marjorie passed away in October 1993, leaving a great void in the lives of many.

I would first like to thank Mrs. Phyllis Cleave of Bromley, Kent, England, without whose hundreds of hours of expert research I could not have written *The Empire of Ice*. Phyllis never failed to answer the myriad questions about Britain with which I deluged her, tracking down the most obscure facts about everything from Parliament to the depth of the English Channel. Phyllis is a wonderful lady, a gifted researcher, and a treasured friend.

I also wish to express my appreciation to Dr. Alice S. Davis and Dr. Randy Koski of the U.S. Geological Survey in Menlo Park, California. Drs. Davis and Koski generously took time out from their busy schedules to aid my geological research, and to review the manuscript to insure the accuracy of the science I present in these pages.

Special thanks to my neighbor and friend, Mel Orton, who contributed his vast knowledge of aeronautics. A former radio operator on a scout observation plane, Mel began his career in the air flying reconnaissance missions off the USS *Arizona*.

As always, I am indebted to Glenna Goulet, my sounding board, my friend, and the lady who prepares my manuscripts. I could not do a book without Glenna.

Finally, I wish to thank my fellow novelist, B. Stuart of San Francisco, for her continuous encouragement and support. B. is at once a multitalented writer, a keen student of the human condition, and my dearest friend.

Had the fierce ashes of some fiery peak
Been hurl'd so high they ranged about the globe?
For day by day, thro' many a blood-red eve,
The wrathful sunset glared . . .
                    Tennyson (1809–1892)

MID-ATLANTIC
●●●●●●●●●●●●●●

12:53 a.m.—February 3, 2000
British Fuel Reserves—18 Days

EVEN THOUGH HE'D BEEN probing the guts of the earth for half his life, geophysicist Benjamin Franklin Meade felt very small and very vulnerable as he stared at the live television pictures of the fiery submarine volcano rising through the depths of the North Atlantic three miles off the starboard side of his ship.

The geothermal power of the earth's interior was a force awesome beyond imagination. He could still remember that moment when he was nine years old reading a geology text in his room at night. He'd suddenly realized with a shiver that only a few miles from his bed a hot spot, a hellish cauldron of molten magma and superheated gases, churned below Yellowstone Park.

The hair had risen on the back of his neck at the thought that a human body exposed to such heat would vanish in a millisecond, like an ant in a forest fire.

Ben had grown up fascinated with the inner workings of the planet and determined to become a geologist. He'd studied hard, taking every science course he could at his small Cody, Wyoming, high school, and won a full scholarship to study geology at Stanford.

During his four years at Stanford, Ben came to understand that the planet's geology, oceans, and climate were all inter-related. If he wanted to realize his dream of harnessing the heat energy of the earth's interior, he would have to become not only a geologist but an oceanographer and climatologist as well.

After college he went on to the Massachusetts Institute of Technology, earning a Ph.D. in geology and master's degrees in oceanography and climatology. Six months out of MIT he started his own company, Meade International, now the world's foremost developer of geothermal energy.

Yet he wasn't out here in the middle of the Atlantic on his research vessel, the *Abyss*, to investigate a geothermal site. He was here because the continuously erupting volcano would soon push its fiery peak up through the surface of the freezing sea.

The earth's newest island was about to be born, and even before it emerged from the womb of the sea it had begun to change the weather of the world.

The suddenly active volcano was designated R-9 on sea-floor charts. It was part of the Mid-Atlantic Ridge, one segment of a forty-thousand-mile-long system of midocean ridges that circled the earth.

Split along its crest by a gaping volcanic fissure, the ridge is part of a geological "Spreading Center," a great cleft in the earth's crust through which molten magma rises continuously from the planet's fiery mantle to become new ocean floor on both sides of the fracture. As the new land formed beneath the sea, North and South America were slowly moving farther away from Europe and Africa.

Oceanographers began a systematic echo-sounding study of the ridge in late 1971. By bouncing a narrow acoustical beam off the outcroppings below and measuring the time the echo took to return, the scientists were able to draw a topographical map of the seafloor features.

The researchers discovered that along most of the length of the ridge, magma was rising slowly through the fissure and the ridge remained eight thousand to ten thousand feet beneath the waves. Yet one part of the submarine rise stretching from 46 to 52 degrees northern latitude was far different.

Here, midway between Newfoundland and Northern France, a five-hundred-mile-long range of volcanic mountains towered above the ridge. The submarine volcanoes were huge, rising six thousand feet through the black icy depths to within two thousand feet of the surface. The summit of one peak, R-9, was only seventeen hundred feet below the waves.

The ship's phone rang, and Ben turned from the monitor and picked up the receiver.

"Yeah?"

"I'm in the galley," Captain Mel Sanderson said. "You want anything?"

"Depends on how long you've been there."

"What the hell's that supposed to mean?"

"The way you graze a galley, I figure if you've been in there more than five minutes there's nothing left but Brillo pads. And those have probably been gnawed on."

"You've just insulted a man surrounded by knives. How'd you like to start life over as a eunuch? Little squeaky voice, be kind of cute."

"I'd rather have a sandwich. Roast beef."

"What do you want to drink?"

"Coffee. Black."

"You've been gulping down coffee for the last two days. All that caffeine, you're going to be whizzing around down there like Rocky the Flying Squirrel."

"Coffee, Mel."

"All right, all right. About ten minutes."

Ben grinned as he hung up. Sanderson had captained the *Abyss* on geothermal explorations all over the world and through the years Ben had come to regard the gruff, good-natured old sea dog as his best friend.

He yawned and turned his attention back to the monitor screens before him. Although a Soviet acoustical survey during the early eighties seemed to indicate the mid-Atlantic volcanoes were rising, the evidence was largely ignored. Most oceanographers simply concluded that an equipment malfunction had given a false reading of the height of the volcanic peaks.

Then, in 1989, British oceanographers mapping the ridge were startled to discover that R-9 had now risen to within nine hundred feet of the surface, with the volcanic peaks to the north and south only two hundred feet lower.

The British geophysicists involved in the study attributed the sudden rise of the volcanoes to an abnormal upwelling of molten materials through the fracture cleaving the Mid-Atlantic Ridge. Such periods of heightened volcanism were always short-lived, the British scientists insisted, and the chain of volcanoes could be expected to return to a dormant stage within a relatively short time.

Twenty-four-year-old Ben Meade wasn't so sure. Still a graduate student at MIT, he'd managed to secure a berth on a French research ship sent out to study the rising volcanoes during the summer of 1990. The thrill of his life had been to dive to the seafloor in the French submersible *Archimede*.

The three-man crew aboard the submersible had gathered lava samples from the slopes of R-9 during the dive and when Ben returned to Boston he brought several pieces of the rock home with him.

While the typical Gallic bureaucracy slowed the French research to a snail's pace, Ben began testing the R-9 lava the day he got back. When he released the results of his research late that fall, his findings startled the scientific world.

He pointed out that the composition of the lava from R-9 was far different from that usually found along the ridge. While mid-ocean ridge basalts were normally lower in dissolved gases and alkalies, the samples from R-9 were rich in both alkalies and volatiles. Such an alkaline content was the chemical signature of magma that had risen suddenly from great depths.

Ben also argued that the sheer volume of the material being erupted—enough magma to raise the volcanic peaks eight hundred feet in the past eighteen years—was far too great to be attributed to the spreading center alone.

Taken together, the two pieces of evidence could mean only one thing: the North Atlantic volcanoes were sitting atop a titanic, previously unknown hot spot, a megaplume of superheated magma rising from far down in the earth's mantle.

Similar hot spots had formed the island of Iceland eight hundred miles to the north, and the Hawaiian Islands chain in the Pacific. Fed by the immense reservoir of molten magma generated deep within the planet, the discharge potential of the Mid-Atlantic hot spot was virtually incalculable.

While most magma plumes had to burn their way through the lithosphere, the sixty-mile-thick hard outer layer of the earth, this hot spot had risen directly beneath the great cleft of the Atlantic spreading center. Here there was zero lithosphere, and molten materials were feeding directly from the mantle up into the magma chambers beneath the volcanoes.

Ben went further, predicting that the entire five-hundred-mile-long chain of volcanoes would reach the surface within fifteen years, with the largest of the peaks, R-9, breaking through the waves by the year 2000.

A furious controversy erupted over Ben's conclusions. Only a handful of scientists agreed with his prognosis, with most oceanographers clinging to the original hypothesis that the rise of the volcanoes was more likely a result of a temporary increase in volcanism along the spreading center. There was little chance R-9 or any of the other peaks would reach the surface within the next thousand years.

Ben shrugged and went back to his studies. Time would tell who was right. And time did tell. By the fall of 1997, R-9 had built itself up to within one hundred feet of the surface.

Then the volcano suddenly stopped spewing out magma. Instead, great plumes of mineral ash and volcanic gases laden with water vapor, carbon dioxide, hydrochloric acid, and sulfur dioxide began jetting from the submerged peak. Bursting through the shallow water above the summit, the ejecta drifted east on the winds toward the British Isles.

Hydrochloric acid dissolves in water and it soon rained out of the atmosphere. But the sulfur dioxide reacted far differently. Gradually the gas converted into sulfuric acid and condensed into a mist of fine particles. These sulfate aerosols reflected the sun's radiation, cooling the atmosphere.

Temperatures in England and Ireland began to plunge. Yet the loss of sunlight was not the only reason the climate of the British Isles was getting continuously colder.

The phone rang again and Ben started. Maybe he had been drinking too much coffee. He snatched the receiver off the hook. "Yeah?"

"We don't have any roast beef," Sanderson said.

Ben sighed. "Tell you what, Mel. Surprise me."

"I think Cookie hid a salami around here but I can't find it. If I go wake him up and ask where it is, he'll serve me runny eggs for the next month, spiteful little bastard that he is."

"So far you've told me I can't have roast beef and I can't have Cookie's hidden salami. What can I have?"

"Ham. Canned. We've been out here so long we're out of everything else."

"Ham will be fine. And stop bitching. You're a ship's captain. You're supposed to be at sea."

"So are turtles and seals. But even they return to land once a year. You know, to propagate the species."

"The thought of you propagating has just ruined my appetite, Mel."

"I'll bring the sandwich down anyway. If you don't eat you'll die, and you haven't signed my last paycheck yet."

Ben hung up and rose to stretch his aching muscles. He could see the three-quarter moon through the starboard porthole and he walked over and stared out at the luna-lit sea. The *Abyss* was anchored in the middle of the Gulf Stream, the warm-water current that rose in the Caribbean and flowed up the east coast of the United States.

A virtual river in the sea, a hundred miles wide and a thousand feet deep, the great current turned east off the coast of Canada and became the North Atlantic Drift, an immense flow containing a hundred times more water than all the rivers of the earth combined.

For millions of years, the prevailing easterly winds had picked up heat from the tropical current and warmed the air above the British Isles. No more. The chain of volcanoes centered on R-9 had risen directly in the path of the current and was now diverting the warm water to the southeast. Satellite tracking showed the river in the sea had begun circling back toward the Americas.

The heat carried across the sea by the North Atlantic Drift had always given England and Ireland a temperate climate, and few people realized the islands were located between 50 and 60 degrees north latitude, farther north than any part of the United States but Alaska.

Climatologists calculated that the loss of tropical heat from the warm current had by now lowered mean temperatures in England and Ireland as much as ten degrees Fahrenheit.

The scientists warned that if R-9 reached the surface and began erupting ash and sulfur dioxide directly into the atmosphere, the volcanic debris and gases would block enough solar radiation to drop the air temperature over the British Isles a further ten degrees.

Although Ben had continued to monitor the data on R-9 at least once a year during the nineties, his geothermal work around the world demanded most of his time and energy. It wasn't until the midocean volcano suddenly started erupting magma again three months ago that he'd turned his attention back to R-9.

He'd spent hours poring over the latest oceanographic readings. The data confirmed that while the chain of volcanic peaks to the north and south of R-9 seemed to have quieted down, R-9 itself was still steadily rising toward the surface of the sea. The next day he'd arranged for the *Abyss* to pick him up in New York and go on station above the fiery submarine mountain.

Ben left the porthole and wearily sat back down before the monitors. Six years before he had pioneered the use of ARCS, Autonomous Remotely Controlled Submersibles, in underwater geological research. He now had two of the twenty-foot-long unmanned vehicles circling the upper slopes of R-9.

One carried television cameras and powerful lights to illuminate the volcano at great depths. The other was outfitted with sophisticated electromagnetic sensors that measured gravity readings beneath the seafloor.

When molten magma rises through the earth's crust it gives off a lower magnetic reading than the dense surrounding rock. The sensors detected the differences in gravity and relayed the information to computers aboard the *Abyss*.

The gravitational readings on the monitor to his left began to change and Ben stared intently at the numbers. The rise of magma up into the central vent of the volcano was accelerating.

He looked over at the television screen and watched as fresh magma erupted from a fissure near the summit of the submarine mountain. Water pressure formed the lava into pillow-shaped boulders that rolled down the slope out of range of the ARCS's lights.

Ben turned as the cabin door behind him opened and Mel Sanderson squeezed his six-foot, two-inch, 220-pound frame through the bulkhead, letting in a blast of freezing air behind him.

"I hope you're hungry, considering I just froze my ass off getting down here to feed you," Sanderson said, putting a tray of sandwiches and coffee down on the console next to Ben and blowing on his cold hands.

The captain was a barrel-chested man with a lion's mane of white hair, flushed cheeks, horn-rimmed glasses, and a deep booming voice. "You scientists do eat occasionally, don't you?"

"I hunger after knowledge. It's my life."

"Yeah. Here's your coffee."

"Thanks. It's the only thing keeping my eyes open."

"You ever going to bed? It's one in the damn morning. You've been in here for almost three days straight."

"The eruptions have been getting stronger for the past sixty hours now, Mel. I've got to keep an eye on the ARCS monitors."

Sanderson peered over Ben's shoulder at the television screen as a tongue of lava squeezed from a vent on the volcano's flank, like toothpaste from a fiery tube. "How long before the peak emerges?"

Ben munched his sandwich reflectively. "Depends. A week or two if she keeps erupting at her present pace. But if there's a sudden surge of magma up through the cone, the summit could reach the surface within hours."

"That's something. A brand-new island forming right before our eyes. This ever happen before? I mean in modern times."

Ben nodded. "Yeah, the Mid-Atlantic Ridge suddenly spewed up an island off Iceland thirty-seven years ago, back in sixty-three. They call it Surtsey. It's already about half covered with vegetation. Seabirds have nested there for years."

"So you think R-Nine is going to replace Surtsey as the newest island on earth?"

"Yeah, I do, Mel. The electromagnetic sensors are showing a huge pool of molten material within the base of the volcano. It's all going to vent, got to."

"If we've got an island coming up under us, might be a good idea if we moved the *Abyss*, don't you think?"

"We're ten miles south of the summit, but yeah, it might be prudent to slide off a ways. Just so long as we stay within a twenty-five-mile radius. Any farther out and I'll lose contact with the ARCS."

A radio speaker in the corner of the cabin suddenly crackled to life and the two men heard a voice with an English accent request a weather report from ships to the west.

"Sounds close," Ben said.

"She is. That's the *QE Three*. I've been monitoring her radio traffic for the past day. She's crammed to the rails with British immigrants fleeing to Canada. Mostly people taking along too many personal possessions to go by air."

Sanderson walked over to the porthole and stared out across the dark sea toward the approaching superliner. "She's about fifteen, twenty miles to the east and coming our way fast."

"I assume her captain knows there's a shipping advisory out to keep at least five miles away from R-Nine."

"Yeah, he knows, all right. But from what I've been hearing on the radio, he intends to steam as close as he's allowed.

The passengers on board have been waiting the whole voyage to see the ash and smoke erupting out of the sea."

"How the hell did the *Queen* get out of Southampton? I thought the English Channel was frozen over."

"It is. The Royal Navy had to clear a sea lane through the floes with an icebreaker."

Ben leaned forward toward the monitor. "That's strange."

Sanderson turned from the window. "What's strange?"

"The summit's suddenly gone quiet. No smoke, and the magma's stopped venting."

"That mean the eruption's over?"

Ben turned to the screen monitoring subterranean gravitational readings. "Can't be. The electromagnetic sensors are still showing magma rising from that huge pool under the seabed. There's enough molten rock down there to build three islands. I don't like it."

Sanderson walked over and looked from one screen to the other. "Maybe the magma's coming up somewhere else."

"No. The plumbing's plugged up. Either an internal earthquake collapsed the main vent or seawater got in and hardened a block of magma before the mountain could spit it out."

"That bad?"

"It means the pressure's building within the cone. It also means I'm going to be sitting here all night again watching the screens until the vent clears."

"Want me to spell you for a while?" Sanderson asked.

Ben leaned back in his chair and stretched his arms above his head. "Yeah. I could use a ten-minute run on deck. You got someone on the bridge?"

"Tony Albano. Not that there's much to do up there while we're just sitting here."

Ben rose. "Better get steam up and pull the sea anchors in."

"Goin' to get hot around here, huh?"

"When the pressure gets high enough inside the cone, she's going to blow superheated gases, magma, and steam straight up through the sea, like a huge depth charge going off."

Ben put on his heavy parka and went out on deck. The usual fresh salt smell of the sea was masked by the rotten-egg odor of the hydrogen sulfide gases seeping up from the submarine volcano off in the dark to starboard.

The cold felt good to Ben after his long hours in the over-warm control center and he leaned on the rail and stared out in the direction of R-9.

In his mind's eye he could see the volcano emerging from the waves, magma spewing from its pocked summit and great Niagaras of seawater cascading down its steaming sides.

It was incredible to contemplate what this one lone volcano in the middle of the North Atlantic was doing to the climate of the British Isles. The eruption couldn't have come at a worse time, following hard on the heels of the catastrophic meltdown of the British nuclear reactor at Windscale in 1995.

The meltdown had killed thousands, and completely shut down nuclear power in Britain. With oil becoming increasingly expensive, England soon found itself facing an energy crisis that worsened as temperatures began to drop.

In the spring of 1997, Richard Booroojian, one of Britain's foremost geologists and an old friend of Ben's, had asked him to come to England to help conduct a search for geothermal energy beneath the British Isles. During his exploration of the mid-Atlantic rift, Ben had found evidence that a perpendicular fracture zone extended far to the east. The fracture passed beneath Ireland and on under the Irish Sea northwest of the Isle of Man. The most promising site to drill into the rift zone proved to be the area where the Irish Sea met North Channel, an arm of the Atlantic separating Ireland and Scotland.

Ben had brought in a Meade International rig and built a platform. He had just started sinking an exploratory well when an acrimonious debate over energy policy erupted in Parliament.

It was pure politics. The rabidly radical Labor Party was headed by Seamus MacTiege, a former head of the National Coal Miners Union. MacTiege saw geothermal power as a direct threat to his miners' livelihood, and his own power base.

MacTiege had made some back-room deals and swung enough votes his way to force Parliament to withdraw funding for the North Channel geothermal project. Ben had packed his maps and scientific gear and gone home mad.

That decision to halt the geothermal work was now going to cost England dearly, he thought, heading for his cabin. Ben changed into his thermal sweatsuit, then returned to the wind-swept deck and began limbering-up exercises.

He started with deep knee bends and felt a muscle tighten in his left calf. I've been out on this ship too long, he thought. Too much time sitting on my ass watching the damn monitors.

As he started to jog around the deck he could feel a stiffness in his back from the constant cold and dampness of the ship. I'm out of shape, he thought.

In truth, at thirty-four, his six-foot, four-inch, 205-pound frame was well muscled, and he kept in condition even out in the middle of the Atlantic with a daily regimen of jogging and exercise.

He spent a lot of time outdoors in his work and his dark blue eyes had the faraway look of a man used to gazing at distant vistas. The sun had lightened his brown hair and there were the first inroads of gray around his temples.

Ben rounded the stern and started up the port deck of the *Abyss*, his breath turning to clouds of freezing white vapor every time he exhaled.

Off to the east he could see tiers of lights bunched on the horizon. The *QE 3*, he thought. I bet she's got a beautiful big gym on board. I could use a long soak in a Jacuzzi.

By the time he'd circled the deck again, the lights were closer. Mel was right, the huge liner was coming their way fast. He was on his third lap when the captain suddenly burst out of the control center door, a plume of steamy heat flaring out behind him. "You'd better get back in here, Ben. All hell's breaking loose below."

Ben dashed into the cabin behind Sanderson and stared at the television monitor. The underwater cameras were focused on the southern slope of R-9. As the two men watched, boulders of red-hot pillow lava shot out into the water from a new vent near the summit of the volcano. Then the mountain seemed to shudder.

Suddenly an entire shoulder of the volcano gave way and millions of tons of rock and magma slid toward the bottom. From the newly exposed rock below, a stream of super-heated water and gases jetted out horizontally into the surrounding sea, like a sudden break in a steam boiler.

Ben turned to Sanderson. "She's going to blow, Mel. Better get us the hell out of here."

Sanderson picked up the bridge phone. "Tony, this is the captain. You got steam up yet?"

"Yes, sir."

"Rudder hard right. All engines full ahead."

"The sea anchors are still out, Captain."

"Get some men out there with axes. Cut 'em, damn it. I want to see a wake in two minutes."

"Yes, sir."

Sanderson turned back to Ben. "How much time have we got?"

"You got a crystal ball?"

"Crystal ball, my ass, what happened to your scientific calculations?"

"You don't calculate when a volcano's going to blow, Mel, you guess." Ben looked at the gravity monitor. "The electromagnetic imaging is showing the magma's risen near the summit again. She could go any minute."

Captain Sanderson paled and rushed over to the porthole. "Son of a bitch, the *QE Three* is still headed straight for R-Nine. On her present course she'll steam within five miles of the summit."

The men felt the *Abyss* suddenly lurch forward as the mate on the bridge jammed the engines into full speed ahead.

"Get on that damn radio, Mel. Tell them to turn her off ninety degrees. Fast."

Sanderson slammed out the door for the bridge. A minute later Ben heard his voice on the speaker. "Research Vessel *Abyss* to the *Queen Elizabeth*. Come in, please."

"*QE Three* here. Go ahead, *Abyss.*"

"This is Captain Mel Sanderson. Put me through to your bridge immediately."

"Yes, sir. One moment, please."

"Bridge, here. Second Officer Jenkins speaking. What may I do for you, Captain Sanderson?"

"You can listen real good. We're approximately fifteen miles southwest of your position. You are steaming into dangerous waters."

There was a moment's pause, then, "I have you in my glasses, Captain. What's the problem?"

"The submarine volcano directly ahead of you is going to erupt any minute."

"Jolly good. The passengers have been complaining they haven't seen any of R-Nine's famous ash columns."

"You don't understand, Jenkins. This is not just another discharge of ash. A major magma eruption is coming. You've got to turn the *Queen* south immediately."

"I'll have to get the captain, sir."

"You don't have time to—shit," Sanderson swore as the British officer cut him off.

Ben rose from the console and crossed to the porthole. The *QE 3* was off their port stern now as the *Abyss* steamed south. Unless the huge liner turned, she'd pass within five or six miles of the submarine volcano within minutes. He hurried back to the monitors.

The summit of R-9 was beginning to crumble. Great slabs of lava were breaking away and sliding down out of range of the underwater lights from the ARCS cameras.

The speaker in the corner crackled again. "This is Captain Fitzhugh. Who am I speaking to?"

"Captain Sanderson, Research Vessel *Abyss.*"

"What's all this about turning the *Queen* south, Captain Sanderson?"

"There's going to be a major magma eruption from R-Nine any minute, Captain. You've got to put your rudder over hard. I advise you turn ninety degrees south immediately."

"Are you mad?" Captain Fitzhugh sounded incredulous.

"We're doing over forty knots. If I made a turn like that I'd put my port rail under water."

"If you keep on your present course, you could lose your ship," Sanderson said.

"Nonsense. What evidence do you have that this will be anything more than another discharge of ash and gases? That's all R-Nine's been doing for the past two years."

"Stubborn son of a bitch," Ben exploded, stabbing at the intercom.

"Yeah, Ben?" Sanderson said.

"Patch me through to that British captain, Mel."

"Good luck."

There was a second or two of static, then the line cleared. "This is Dr. Benjamin Meade, Captain Fitzhugh. I'm a geophysicist aboard the *Abyss*."

"What is this all about, Dr. Meade?"

"Captain, there's only time to say this once. I am looking at a screen monitoring the submarine slopes of R-Nine. Magma is rising rapidly within the cone. Sometime within the next few minutes, there's going to be a huge eruption. If the *QE Three* is anywhere near when she goes, tons of twelve-hundred-degree magma could come raining down on your ship."

"I simply cannot turn the *Queen* that fast, Dr. Meade. Good God, man, I've got passengers lining the port rail waiting for a look at the ash column as we pass. If I suddenly throw my rudder hard aport, I'm going to lose several hundred people overboard."

"Get on your loudspeaker, order the passengers inside, and turn your ship, Captain."

"Do you know for certain that volcano's going to erupt before we're past?"

Ben looked at the monitors. The two pictures were beginning to flutter as shock waves from the magma moving up through the cone sent vibrations through the water around the ARCS.

"She's going to blow, Captain. Whether in one minute, five minutes, ten, I don't know."

"In ten minutes we would be several miles on the other side," the captain said.

"How many people do you have on board, Captain?"

"Passengers and crew, three thousand six hundred fifty-four."

"You willing to risk that many lives you can make it?"

The British captain hesitated, then "No, no I'm not. Hold on, please." The radiophone went dead a moment, then Fitzhugh came back on. "I've ordered the crew to get the passengers inside. We've begun our turn. I can't put the rudder hard over until we have everyone off the decks."

"We'll keep you advised, Captain," Ben said. He hit the button for the bridge phone. "Better keep a line open to the *Queen*, Mel."

"Right."

Ben turned back to the screens. The pictures were jumping all over the place as continuous shock waves radiated out into the sea from the awakening volcano. He knew they were going to lose the cameras any minute. Once that happened, they'd be blind.

A minute went by, two. The ARCS were intermittently losing the picture as fierce tremors shook the submarine slopes. Then the volcano abruptly quieted and the camera steadied. An ominous column of black smoke and ashes began to rise from the summit.

Ben picked up the bridge phone. "This is it, Mel. Better tell that British captain to button up his ship."

"Right. *Abyss* to *QE Three*."

"This is Captain Fitzhugh."

"The eruption's imminent, Captain. I advise you to close your watertight doors and have fire crews at their stations."

"Will you stand by, Captain Sanderson?"

"Of course. Good luck, Captain."

Ben stared transfixed at the monitors. The column of smoke and ashes had become a great plume seething furiously toward the surface. A vent suddenly split open on the upper slope and huge bubbles of sulfuric gases boiled out in a fusillade of sooty effervescence.

The entire peak was now shaking violently. A second fissure tore open near the summit and through the quickly blackening seawater Ben could see the red of molten magma pouring from the wounded rock.

A moment later the top of the mountain began to bulge outward. Then the volcano sent a salvo of fiery boulders hurtling through the depths toward the ARCS, and the two cameras suddenly went dead.

Ben tore out of the control center and ran forward up the deck, climbing the icy steps to the bridge three at a time. Captain Sanderson was scanning the sea behind them with a pair of night-vision binoculars. First Mate Albano was gripping the wheel with white-knuckled hands, peering back over his shoulder every few seconds.

"Has the *Queen* turned?" Ben asked.

"Yeah, some, but she's going too fast to stop her forward progress. Even if that British captain throws his rudder all the way over, he's still going to deflect into the sea within six or seven miles of R-Nine," Sanderson said, handing Ben the glasses.

Ben brought the binoculars up to his eyes. The *Abyss* was steaming away south at twenty knots and the column of smoke and ashes rising from the volcano was already almost twenty miles off their stern.

He focused on the base of the plume. The surface of the sea had turned into a maelstrom of violent waves and the waters were beginning to bulge upward from the tremendous pressure of gases and volcanic debris surging up from below.

He swung the glasses toward the lights of the *QE 3*. The bow of the liner was turning south toward the *Abyss*, but she was still on a course that would bring the great ship dangerously close to R-9.

"Turn, damn you, turn."

Sanderson shook his head. "She can't, Ben."

The seconds ticked by. The *Queen* was within seven miles of the volcano now, six and a half, six.

Then a muffled roar began to build in the distance and a moment later the ocean behind the *Abyss* suddenly became part of the sky. The sound of the eruption was deafening, a thunderous pandemonium of exploding gases and shattering rocks that devoured every other sound of wind and water across the face of the mid-Atlantic.

Shock waves tore into the *Abyss*, heeling the ship far over to starboard and sending the three men on the bridge careening into the bulkhead.

Tony Albano let out a scream and grabbed his right arm. The shattered end of his ulna bone had punctured an artery and blood was spurting out. Sanderson crawled across the pitching deck and ripped off his belt to use as a tourniquet.

Ben ached all over as he pulled himself up toward the shattered stern windows of the madly rolling ship. A pyroclastic dome of glowing gases and red-hot magma fragments hung over the sea behind them, turning the night into day.

Where R-9 had erupted beneath the waves, a titanic mushroom of fiery magma and flaring gases towered thousands of feet above the surrounding sea. A roll of the ship brought the binoculars sliding across the deck and Ben bent and grabbed the glasses.

He swept the sea to the east and found the *Queen*. The great liner was rocking madly in the grip of huge waves radiating out from the epicenter of the eruption. Water was streaming off the twin funnels and the radio mast, and he knew the first shock wave must have blown the liner far over on her side. Anyone who'd been out on deck was now lost in the sea.

He snapped the glasses up. The red-hot magma ejected thousands of feet above the Atlantic had reached its apex and was falling again, like an umbrella of fire descending on the maddened waves below.

As Ben watched, the flaming debris began to rain down on the *Queen*. He sucked in his breath as glowing house-sized boulders struck the tossing liner, starting a huge fire amidships.

He focused the binoculars on the doors of the main salon. Passengers were streaming out onto the deck to escape the inferno within, only to have their clothes catch fire from the magma particles raining down outside.

"Sweet Jesus, no, no!" The cry caught in Ben's throat as he watched a mother and two small girls, their hair on fire, leap from the rail into the freezing sea below. Scores of passengers were throwing themselves into the ocean now as the fire spreading across the deck forced them overboard.

Toward the stern he could see crew members frantically trying to launch a lifeboat full of passengers. The boat was halfway down the side of the *Queen* when a huge wave rolled the ship, putting the lifeboat under water. When the *Queen* righted herself, the boat was empty.

The fire had now raced the length of the *QE 3*, turning the great ship into an immense steel torch, a funeral pyre blazing on the surface of the tortured Atlantic. A moment later the flames reached the liner's fuel tanks and a blinding explosion threw Ben to the deck a second time.

As he fell, a barrage of jagged steel fragments raked the *Abyss*, breaking out the remaining bridge windows and peppering the bulkheads with shrapnel.

"God Almighty, what was that?" Sanderson screamed into the din, still cradling the groaning mate on the deck.

"The *Queen*," Ben shouted, pulling himself slowly back up above the rail.

Sanderson cupped his hands around his mouth. "We've got to get the lifeboats out."

Ben looked at the captain and slowly shook his head. There was no need for lifeboats, no need at all.

The sky was darkening quickly as the remaining volcanic gases dissipated in the cold Atlantic air. Ben brought the binoculars to his eyes once more and searched the sea in the fading light. The *QE 3* had disappeared.

Where the great ship had flamed against the horizon a moment ago, an angry black cloud hovered over the watery grave of the *Queen*, the billowing plume greasy with the residue of fuel vapors and incinerated human flesh.

Slowly the prevailing winds gathered again and began to sweep the cloud east across the cold sea, taking the ashes of 3,654 men, women, and children back toward the ice-ringed British Isles they had departed two days before.

Aldergrove Royal Air Force Base, Northern Ireland

4:56 a.m.

THE TITANIC THUNDERCLAP OF sound born of the eruption of R-9 radiated out over the North Atlantic in an ever-widening circle, exploding through the freezing air at 1,130 feet per second.

No nuclear detonation, no fusillade of artillery or hail of bombs in all the wars of man had ever been one hundredth as loud. Not since the eruption of the Indonesian volcano Krakatua in 1883 had such a sound been heard on earth.

Eight minutes after the eruption, the birthing scream of R-9 cracked across a Greek freighter a hundred miles to the west, breaking out the bridge windows and throwing the terrified crew from their bunks.

Forty-five minutes later it engulfed a Russian fishing fleet six hundred miles to the east, drowning out the noise of the huge winches drawing in bulging nets of cod. Convinced they had just heard one of their trawlers blow apart, the fleet began frantically searching the swirling mist for survivors.

The sound wave reached western Ireland at 4:25 A.M. The volcanic thunder had dimmed on its eight-hundred-mile passage across the sea, but still it was loud enough to wake thousands of Irishmen from Blacksod Bay down the coast to Dursey Head.

Fourteen minutes after crossing the Irish coast, the sound burst through the sprawling Aldergrove Royal Air Force Base outside Belfast in British-occupied Northern Ireland. In the RAF operations center, thirty-two-year old Wing Commander Peter Atkins had night duty.

The terrorists of the Irish Republican Army had blown up a hangar on the base the month before and Atkins's first thought was that the British installation was again under attack. He immediately put the base on full alert.

Two minutes later, the direct phone line to RAF headquarters in Whitehall, London, rang. The young night-duty officer picked up the receiver. "Operations, Wing Commander Atkins here."

"This is Air Vice Marshal Croft. What the devil's going on up there, Atkins? Our status board here is showing Aldergrove on full alert."

"I'm not sure what's afoot yet, sir. There's been a tremendous explosion somewhere in the area. Whether it was in Belfast or here on the base, I don't know. I thought it prudent to go on alert."

"I can't fault you for your caution, Atkins, but the sound you heard was an explosion almost twelve hundred miles to the west. Mid-Atlantic, to be exact."

"Good Lord, sir, that can't be. What on earth could make a sound that would travel that far?"

"R-Nine, that volcano our meteorologists have been watching. It erupted through the surface of the sea about an hour and a half ago. Our science adviser here tells me it was the loudest noise heard on earth in over a century."

"A volcano! Are you sure, sir?"

"Yes, we have satellite confirmation. It was just as loud the other side of the pond. I'm told there were hundreds of policemen tearing all about New York convinced a building had blown up somewhere in the city."

"Certainly scared me, sir. Very well then, I'll stand down the base."

"The fighter pilots can go back to bed but I'll want the Nimrods in the air."

"Long-range reconnaissance, sir?"

"Yes. An American research vessel on station near R-Nine has radioed that the *QE Three* was steaming past when the volcano erupted."

"Was the *Queen* badly damaged then, sir?"

"I'm afraid it's far worse than that, Atkins. The Americans report the *QE Three* went to the bottom with all hands."

The young wing commander sucked in his breath. "Good God, sir. There were no survivors at all?"

"There's little chance, I'm afraid. Still, we'll want our long-range Nimrods out there to have a look."

"I'll get them up immediately, sir."

"There's one other thing, Wing Commander. Be damn sure the Nimrods stay well north of the border with the Free State on their flight out. I don't have to tell you how sensitive the Irish are about the sovereignty of their air space these days."

"They've been getting more belligerent by the week, sir. One of their jet fighters actually buzzed our helicopter base at Londonderry yesterday."

"It all traces back to Windscale, doesn't it?" Croft sighed.

"Yes, sir. If war does come, it will be Windscale to blame."

Labeled "England's Chernobyl" by the tabloids, Windscale had been the worst nuclear accident in history. Built originally in 1959, the ancient reactor on the coast of Cumbria in the north of England had long been accused of leaking radioactivity into the neighboring Irish Sea.

Dublin had asked time after time through diplomatic channels for assurances that the reactor problems at Windscale be given top priority. The British responses had been continuously evasive and pro forma.

As it turned out, the leaks were nothing, stray shots before a war, compared to the meltdown that began on a beautiful spring day in 1995. There were strong winds from the east that morning and they carried the radioactive clouds across the sea and over Ireland.

Before dawn the next day, the winds shifted and left

Wales, Devon, and Cornwall in England bathed in a radioactive dew.

In the weeks that followed, thousands died from lethal doses of plutonium, strontium 90, and cesium 137. Physicians warned that over the next ten years, hundreds of thousands more would succumb to heart and lung diseases, nervous disorders, digestive-tract ailments, and thyroid-gland cancer.

The Irish government, enraged that British indifference to the early warnings at Windscale had now resulted in thousands of Irish deaths, severed all diplomatic relations with England the day after the disaster.

A resurgent Irish Republican Army, regarded for decades by the Irish people and the world as little more than underground terrorists, suddenly gained new respectability. The IRA found ready recruits now, especially in the counties where the death toll from nuclear fallout had been highest.

Sinn Fein, the IRA's political front, became a force in Irish politics again for the first time in seventy years, inflaming anti-British sentiment further with an endless litany of past English sins against Ireland.

In almost every local election since Windscale, Sinn Fein candidates either gained office or made such a strong showing at the polls that their opposition saw the way of the wind and hastened themselves to pay lip service to Ireland's increasingly strident nationalism.

In the turbulent years since Windscale, Anglo-Irish relations had continued to deteriorate as misunderstandings, distrust, and increasingly militant positions on both sides combined to stir up ancient animosities between the neighbor nations.

"We came close to war with Ireland in 'ninety-eight," Croft said. "I shouldn't like to see things go to the brink like that again."

"You mean when our fishing fleet and those Irish trawlers exchanged small-arms fire off Iceland?" Atkins said.

"Yes. I still think it was wrong of us to send warships up there just to protect our fishing rights. It only provoked the Irish to send out their own gunboats."

"It was a near thing all right, sir."

"Damn near. If the coming of the winter storms hadn't forced both navies to retreat to their home ports, it might have meant war then and there."

"I'll have the squadron leaders map a flight plan well north of the border, sir," Atkins said.

"Do keep your radio traffic down as well, Wing Commander. Having one of our reconnaissance squadrons circling out to their west is bound to make the Irish nervous."

"Very good, Vice Marshal. We'll keep the flight under tight wraps."

Atkins would hardly have been so confident of his security had he known that Irish intelligence had an operative working as a snowplow driver at the sprawling base. As soon as the squadron of Nimrods rolled out of their snow-covered hangars, the driver slipped off the airfield and called his contact fifty miles to the south in the Irish Free State.

All along the border, Irish Army units went on alert. As the RAF reconnaissance planes took off and headed west toward the Atlantic, Irish antiaircraft guns swiveled on their mounts, their long barrels following the English planes.

Stanraer Peninsula, Scotland
••••••••••••••••••••••

5:05 a.m.

THE GREAT WOLF BEELZEBUB was eating a barn cat, a fine fat gray Maltese, when the sound wave from R-9 cracked across the Stanraer Peninsula facing the ice-bound North Channel between Scotland and Ireland.

Instantly the huge animal was on his feet, his turning ears and burnt-ocher eyes probing the dark snowy moors around him. The roaring was coming from far off, from somewhere beyond the western horizon.

Beelzebub had grown used to the sounds of civilization since his capture in northern Canada two years before. The winter of 1998 had been harsh and to supplement his diet of moose and snowshoe rabbits the wolf had taken to raiding human settlements around Yellowknife on the shores of Great Slave Lake.

Classified as incorrigible, Beelzebub had been trapped and was hours away from being destroyed when King Charles and his two sons stopped in the town on a royal visit to Canada.

The English princes had been horrified to learn the wolf was about to be killed. They begged their father to intervene, and Beelzebub had shortly been on his way to the Glasgow Zoo.

The wolf's confinement in Scotland was filled with the noise of car horns and machinery and yelping children. He had learned to ignore the cacophony of man. The hubbub was annoying, at times unsettling, but the sounds did not convey a danger.

The sound that had interrupted his meal of cat meat was different. This sound had triggered a memory cell stored in his genes millions of years before he was born.

Beelzebub did not know what had caused the sound. Nor did he know why it made him instinctively look toward the sky and sniff the cold air. He knew only that his world would soon change in a terrible way, and that the danger would come from the west, from the direction of the sound.

Restless now, Beelzebub picked up the remains of the cat with his sharp canine teeth and began to trot across the moors toward the deep ravine where the rest of the pack was hiding.

He covered the ground quickly, for he was an immense animal. While the average gray wolf measured three feet at the shoulders, four feet in length, and weighed one hundred pounds, Beelzebub in maturity stood almost four feet tall and stretched five feet from his nose to the base of his tail. With a full belly, he weighed over two hundred pounds.

During his long days in the Glasgow Zoo, the huge animal had drawn morbidly fascinated crowds to the wolf compound. A local country vicar had observed the relentlessly pacing beast's black color and his demonic eyes and dubbed him Beelzebub, a biblical name for Satan. The name was to prove most prophetic.

The wolf had no way of knowing that the sound that had so unsettled him had come from the very source of his freedom. When R-9 began diverting the warm Gulf Stream two years before, temperatures in the British Isles began to drop precipitously and great blizzards drove in off the suddenly colder North Atlantic.

During one of the worst of the storms at the end of the past winter, an ice-encrusted tree had toppled over against the fence of the wolf compound, flattening the wire mesh almost to the ground.

Beelzebub had seized the moment, leading the three bitches and twelve yearling cubs inside on a daring escape through the suburbs of Glasgow. For several weeks they had raided farms in the Scottish countryside, stealing in at night to take chickens, ducks, goats, pigs, and sheep.

When the snow finally melted in June, vengeful Scottish farmers who'd lost livestock to the wolves formed hunting parties to track down the canine killers. Beelzebub and his pack had been driven steadily south into Dumfries and Galloway.

One of the bitches and five of the yearlings fell to the hunters during the wolves' retreat, most shot from helicopters as they crossed open fields. Yet Beelzebub had come to maturity evading hunters in Canada, and his cunning and instincts had saved the majority of the pack from the guns of the humans.

The wolves had managed to reach the relative safety of the wild west coast of Scotland where tracking was difficult and deep canyons and caves hid them from scouting planes.

The pack had subsisted on the game birds still plentiful last summer, avoiding the isolated farms and villages in the countryside. Gradually, the numbers of their pursuers had lessened as the hunters returned home to their farm work.

Then, in late August, with the Gulf Stream no longer warming the British Isles, the temperature had begun to drop steadily. By mid-September, gales off the North Atlantic were scourging the countryside with freezing rain. Game had quickly disappeared, flying south to the temperate lands around the Mediterranean or burrowing underground.

The wolves had grown thin and hungry. Their normal caution lessened, and they scouted for food ever closer to human settlements. They began hunting cats and smaller dogs, often snatching domestic pets off the very doorsteps of their owners.

On one such hunting foray in the city of Girvan on the west coast of Scotland, a terrified housewife had snapped a

picture of Beelzebub as the great wolf tore apart her fox terrier in the backyard of her home.

The picture the woman snapped had appeared in the local
paper the next day. The wire services soon picked it up, and
the following morning the photograph of a blood-smeared
Beelzebub devouring the small dog had filled the front
pages of three London tabloids.

Millions of people all over Britain were outraged by the
grisly picture of the fiendish-looking wolf feeding on the
tiny terrier. Phone calls and telegrams flooded government
offices. If the wolves were bold enough to steal pets off doorsteps, children would be next. The government must do
something immediately. The next day, Whitehall ordered
the army to begin a systematic hunt to eradicate the murder-
ous wolves.

The pack had been pushed steadily south along the ice-
choked Firth of Clyde by five hundred soldiers from the 2nd
Battalion Scots Guards.

A month ago the deepening snows had forced the wolf-
hunters from the field. But by now the line of soldiers behind
them had the wolves trapped out on the southern tip of Stanraer Peninsula facing North Channel.

There was little to eat in this gale-scourged place, but for a
chance meal like the stray barn cat Beelzebub now carried
back to the pack.

The other wolves were pacing the snow restlessly when
Beelzebub reached the ravine. They, too, had heard the ominous sound in the dark sky to the west. Still, they were starving, and when Beelzebub dropped the half-eaten cat carcass
in the snow they forgot their anxiety for the moment and
dove for the meat.

There was only enough for a morsel for each of the
wolves, and several of the younger animals got none at all.
The hungry yearlings began to whimper for food, food Beelzebub could not provide. To escape the begging cries, the
great wolf turned and trotted down to where the ravine
mouth opened onto the icy shore of North Channel.

The twenty-five-mile-wide waterway between Scotland
and Ireland was frozen solid and the three-quarter moon

shone on a field of pack ice that stretched toward the horizon as far as the great wolf could see.

The night before Beelzebub had caught the faint but unmistakable aroma of roasted mutton coming from somewhere across the ice to the southwest. Only humans cooked flesh, he knew that. And where there were humans, there was death for wolves. Yet there was nothing to eat here on this barren shore, and the pack was near starvation.

He turned toward the ravine and let out a long howl. One by one the other wolves approached out of the dark, their snouts low and their tails between their legs in submission. Wherever he led, they would follow.

Satisfied, the great wolf wheeled and headed out at a trot across the floes of North Channel, the nine surviving members of the pack close behind.

Somewhere across this vast wasteland of broken floes before them was meat, food, life.

LONDON
● ● ● ● ● ● ● ● ●

5:16 a.m.

IN THE MOMENTS BEFORE the phone rang, thirty-one-year-old Marjorie Glynn was dreaming she was far away on the soft pink sand of a Caribbean island, the sun warming her tanned skin and the turquoise sea breaking in perfect waves a meter beyond her toes.

The freezing blizzards and unrelenting demands of her work in Britain were 6,500 kilometers across the sea. The hardest decisions she would face all day were what book to read next and should she have lobster or filet mignon for dinner.

Every time she came up to London, it seemed, she dreamt of this warm paradise free of the cold and cares of England. She supposed it was because the bonds loosened when she came to the city to shop and see old friends, and forget for a few days she was the head scientist on the most important project in the weather-scourged country.

Biosphere Britannia was the focus of her life. The huge glass-enclosed miniearth she had helped design was crucial to the very survival of the British people. Yet there were times, like this week, when she simply had to get away, when she had to be a woman instead of a scientist, if only for a few days.

In London she actually wore dresses and did her hair and felt feminine. And dreamt of the island in the Caribbean where there were only endless sunny days of peaceful bliss.

It had been snowing when she went to bed last night in the apartment she'd so infrequently visited over the past couple of years. For a long time she'd stood in her dark bedroom in her neck-to-ankle flannel nightgown and stared out at the swirling flakes.

The snow fell silently between the four-story Georgian buildings facing Clabon Mews and piled three feet deep on the cobblestones below. The storm had brought London traffic to a standstill and there was no sound in the night save the muffled bark of a dog somewhere down the block and, far off, the metallic scraping of a snowplow clearing King's Road.

She had gone to bed aching to be away from the cold and the snow that never seemed to stop. She'd willed herself to dream of her island in paradise again, and it had worked. She'd made it back.

How good the sun felt baking her back. She took a sip of the tall frosty drink in the sand beside her hand. It was a rum something. Good. Full of fruit and a tiny parasol. She brought the parasol up to her eye and squinted. It was pink. With toothpick ribs. It made her laugh. And laughing made her feel good, a carefree young woman again instead of the always serious—half the time screaming at a subordinate—Dr. Marjorie Glynn.

Her laugh grew longer, louder. An abandon enveloped her like a narcotic cocoon. She couldn't stop laughing. The world was warm, the world was fun, the world was—

The phone rang, echoing shrilly through the dark quiet of her Belgravia flat, invading the dream womb. Marjorie fought not to hear it, to get back to the island where it was all right to let go, all right to laugh.

She could still see the pink sand, at the vortex of the now swirling dream. She concentrated, willing herself back. She was almost there. It was going to be all right. The phone rang a second time and the dream shattered.

Awake now, she lay there feeling angry and empty. The fuzzy warmth of the dream seeped away into the cold dark of the bedroom. A third ring. Damn it!

She reached for the phone on the bedstand. It wasn't there. Instead her hand brushed a smooth icy surface. She shot straight up in bed at the sound of the glass of a picture frame smashing on the hardwood floor.

Then she remembered she wasn't in her bedroom in the habitat wing at Biosphere Britannia, she was in her apartment in London. The picture she had just knocked over was her favorite photograph of her parents. It had been taken in the garden at their farm in Scotland and it was so *them*.

Her father, the graying country squire, was kneeling in his tweed jacket scratching George the spaniel's ear while her mother looked down fondly at them, pruning shears in one gloved hand and a pink rose in the other.

Damn it. Where the bloody hell is the lamp? Think. The other side of the bed. She rolled across and groped in the dark. Her hand found the shade. She felt down the fabric toward the rim. The switch was at the lamp neck just below. Suddenly her fingers wouldn't go any further. The switch was an inch away and she couldn't extend her arm to reach it.

The phone rang again.

I'm losing my mind. Then she realized the shoulder of her nightgown had bunched under her body as she'd rolled over. The taut flannel was holding her arm back. She jerked her upper body hard. She knew it was a mistake the instant she did it. Her fingers were still extended. As her shoulder came free, her hand shot forward like a javelin, knocking the lamp off the night table.

The lamp smashed against the floor at the precise moment the phone rang for the fourth time. The two noises together produced an endless instant of shattering sound so intense she could feel it in her teeth.

For a long moment she remained totally motionless, stunned, her arm still out in the empty air. The lamp had been hand-painted Chinese porcelain. From Harrod's. The first thing she'd bought for the apartment. A hundred and fifty bloody pounds, when she was earning ninety a week. *Damn it, damn it, damn it!*

A fifth ring echoed through the cold bedroom. Half a ring as the answering machine picked up the call. "Hello, this is Marjorie Glynn. I'm unable to take your call at the moment . . ."

She crawled across the bed and swung her feet to the floor. "Ooww, bloody hell." She reached down and felt the sliver from the broken picture glass sticking out of her right instep.

"If you'll leave your name and number at the beep—"

She remembered now. She'd called her parents the night before from the wing chair near the window. The combination phone-answering machine was on the floor beside the chair.

"—I'll return your call as soon as possible."

She oriented on a crack of street-lamp light slitting through where the drapes met and began to hop on her left foot toward the sound of her recorded voice.

Hop, hop, hop.

A beep sounded, followed by the voice of Richard Booroojian, chief geologist at Biosphere Britannia. "Hello, Marjorie, this is Richard. Sorry to ring up in the middle of the night but we have a code red. It's happened."

She could see the shadowed silhouette of the chair now, and below it the blinking red light on the answering machine.

Hop, hop, hop. She was there. Her fingers closed on the machine, then the phone receiver. "Richard, hello."

"Marjorie?"

"Ooww, damn it." Her right foot had brushed the hooked rug in front of the chair as she'd sunk down next to the phone, driving the sliver in deeper.

"Marjorie? Are you all right? What's happened?"

"I stepped on a piece of glass. Feels like I've got a bloody railroad spike in there."

"Glass? Are you bleeding?"

Of course she was bleeding, for God's sake. She could feel the warm wet stickiness between her toes. She had probably bled all over the damn rug as well. "Never mind my foot, Richard. What's going on?"

"Are you sure? Do you want to get off and get a bandage or something? You could ring me back."

"Richard, I've just been yanked out of a perfectly wonderful dream, smashed my favorite picture of my parents, destroyed a hundred-and-fifty-quid lamp from Harrod's, and crippled myself. All to get to this bloody phone. Now what the hell's happened?"

"It's R-Nine, Marjorie. There's been a titanic eruption. The summit's risen through the surface of the sea."

Instantly she forgot the dream, the wreckage around her bed, her bleeding foot. "When?"

"About three hours ago. I've just had a call from NERC."

Marjorie slumped against the base of the chair. NERC was the Natural Environment Research Council, the British agency monitoring the loss of solar radiation as R-9 sent volcanic clouds over England. "How bad was the eruption?"

"On a scale of one to ten, it was a fifty. NERC estimates the eruption equaled the magnitude of Toba."

Marjorie shuddered at Booroojian's mention of the volcanic eruption on the Indonesian island of Sumatra 73,400 years before. Paleogeologists studying the ancient caldera, the huge basin-shaped depression left when Toba blew itself apart, estimated that the prehistoric volcano had ejected 2,800 cubic kilometers of material into the air.

The supereruption was like eight thousand Mount Saint Helenses going off at the same time. Climatologists calculated that the immense volume of ash and gases spewed into the stratosphere had brought on a volcanic winter, with global temperatures plunging perhaps ten degrees Fahrenheit.

The volcanic clouds had circled the earth for as long as fifteen years, and many scientists believed that the Toba eruption had speeded up glacial cooling, precipitating an ice age.

It suddenly occurred to Marjorie that even if the magnitude of the R-9 and the Toba eruptions were roughly the same, there would be a profound difference in the climatic changes caused by the debris clouds from R-9.

Toba was located on the equator, and the volcano's ash and gases had spread equally over both the Northern and Southern Hemispheres. R-9 rose through the Atlantic far north of the equator, at almost 50 degrees north latitude, and the prevailing winds would keep the ash and gases almost entirely over the Northern Hemisphere.

The earth was about to become two different worlds, with the Northern Hemisphere freezing beneath volcanic clouds while the weather in the Southern Hemisphere remained largely unchanged.

Marjorie got a grip on herself. "Do you have satellite coverage yet?"

"We should be getting a live transmission any moment now."

Marjorie sawed her bottom jaw back and forth in frustration. This was it. The titanic eruption they knew was coming. The volcanic blast that would send England into another ice age. And she was stuck in London. Blind.

No, wait. There was her IBM Imager 3 in the spare bedroom. She'd used it to monitor the ecosystems in the Biosphere before her quarters in the habitat were finished. She hadn't even turned it on in almost a year, but as far as she knew it was still hooked up to the Biosphere systems.

"Richard, look, I've got an Imager here. Do you think you can patch me in?"

"I can try. What's the access code?"

Access code? Damn. It's been a year. How am I supposed to remember . . . then it hit her. She used the same code for everything; computers, the automatic teller at the bank, the combination lock on her bike. It was the six numbers of her birth date.

"Ten, fifteen, sixty-eight. But don't try it yet. I have to go turn the Imager on."

"All right."

Marjorie put down the receiver and felt along the floor to the wall behind the chair. The door to the hall was at the end of the wall. There was a light switch next to the door.

Hop, hop, hop. The wall was cold. Hop, hop. Her fingers felt the fluted wooden surface of the doorjamb. She began to circle her hand on the wall a foot from the jamb. Round once, round twice. There. She'd found the switch. She pushed the button and the room flooded with light.

She squinted and turned her foot up to examine the cut. The bleeding had stopped but there was dried blood from her ankle down between her toes. It was all over the hem of her nightgown as well, and there were several smears on the rug in front of the wing chair.

She hopped back to the phone. "Richard."

"Yes, I'm still here."

"Give me another minute. The Imager's in the next room. I'll have to take the phone with me."

The receiver in one hand and the phone in the other, Marjorie started back across the bedroom. Hop, hop, hop, hop. She was at the door.

Richard's puzzled voice came from the receiver. "Marjorie, are you all right? What's that thumping sound?"

She leaned against the jamb and brought the receiver up. "I'm hopping. That sound is me hopping."

"Hopping?"

"Normally at five in the morning I dance madly about the apartment, Richard. It's my personal pagan ritual to welcome the sun. But I've cut my foot. Remember?"

"Your foot? God, I'd forgotten. How is it?"

"It hurts."

"Mercurochrome's the thing, Marjorie. You want to swab it well. Ignore it at your peril. You'll wind up with a nasty infection."

"Later, Richard. At the moment it's taking all my energies to get to the bloody Imager."

Two hops and she was at the door to the spare bedroom. She opened the door and turned on the light. She hadn't been in here in a long time and she'd forgotten how bare the room was. The Imager was against one wall. There was nothing else in the bedroom but an old dresser she kept her summer things in.

Hop, hop, hop, hop, she reached the computer. *Where is the on/off switch? Lower left under the screen*, she thought. Yes, there it is. She turned the machine on. Nothing.

"Richard, the Imager won't turn on."

"Is it plugged in?"

"Plugged in?"

Jesus. She got down on all fours and looked under the metal stand. The plug was lying in a clump of dust and lint.

She could just make out the edge of the outlet behind one of the table legs. She reached under as far as she could, grabbed the plug, and felt for the outlet. A fingertip found the two small slots and she fed the prongs of the plug into the slits.

Her father had told her a thousand times beginning at age three, *hold the plug by the plastic, not the prongs.* Zzzttt. She saw the blue-white sparks at the same instant she felt the current race up her arm. Her head jerked up and smashed into the underside of the metal stand above. A loud clang reverberated like a dinner gong through the stark room.

From the receiver on the floor behind her, she could hear Richard's faint voice. "Marjorie, are you all right? What's that clanging sound?"

Sucking on her singed finger, she didn't know whether to laugh or cry. Here she was, a lionized scientist, a confidante of the prime minister, stuffed under a table with her nightgown riding up over her bare arse, a bloody foot, a singed finger, and, in a moment she was sure, a monstrous headache.

She allowed herself a small whimper, pushed the plug the rest of the way in, and backed out from under the stand.

The Imager was on, thank God for that at least. She picked up the receiver and stood. "Ooww, damn it!" She'd forgotten her wounded foot.

"It's on, Richard."

"Marjorie, what on earth's going on there? It sounds like a street brawl."

"Punch in the goddamn access code."

"I must say, Marjorie, you are testy in the morning."

"Richard . . ."

"All right, all right, here we go."

Marjorie looked around for the straight-backed chair she always sat in when she used the Imager, then remembered she'd brought it into the dining room the last time she'd had friends over for dinner.

She let out a resigned sigh of the damned and shifted her weight to her left foot, keeping just the toes of her injured foot on the floor for balance.

A moment later the screen flickered and Richard's oval face came on the screen, his glasses low on his nose and his thinning dark hair ruffled as usual. Behind him she could see the computers and monitors of the Biosphere's communications center.

"How's the transmission? Are you getting a clear picture?" he asked.

The IBM was old. There were vertical lines slowly crawling up the screen. But it was good enough for now.

"It's all right, Richard. When are we going to get the NERC coverage?"

"Should be any minute now. Apparently the Royal Navy's latched onto the feed and NERC's having a problem getting it back."

Marjorie glanced toward the window. The shade was up and she could see the snow falling through the diffused glow of the street lamp down the block.

"How's the Biosphere been holding up to the storm? If we get an ice buildup again, we'll have shattered glass all over the place, just like the last blizzard."

"I had men up there clearing the snow yesterday afternoon. We probably got six more inches during the night, but I can't do anything about it until the sun comes up. It's dangerous enough for the workers, much less sending them up in the dark."

Marjorie frowned. They should have anticipated the buildup of snow on the Biosphere. When the chain of Atlantic volcanoes first started diverting the warm waters of the North Atlantic Drift, the British Isles had felt the effects within months. England and Ireland were as far north as Labrador in northeast Canada.

In the British Isles, a plethora of plants and trees thrived, and food crops nourished man. In Labrador, only sparse tundra and snowbound coniferous forests could exist, and the land was all but uninhabited. It had always been the North Atlantic Drift that made the difference in climate from one side of the sea to the other and kept England and Ireland green.

Now the British Isles were getting inexorably colder. A preliminary study by NERC scientists back in 1997 warned that mean temperatures would continue to drop as the mounting sulfate aerosols in the stratosphere reflected more and more sunlight and the rising Atlantic volcanoes increasingly diverted the warm current from the west.

As if reading her mind, Richard said, "We should have planned for blizzard conditions back when we got that first NERC report."

"Hindsight is always twenty-twenty, isn't it, Richard?" Marjorie said, not a little defensively. "Where's that bloody satellite feed?"

"Patience, old girl."

The NERC study had predicted that future summers would be short and chill, while blizzards would rage through freezing winters lasting seven or eight months. Growing seasons would become too short and cold to raise crops, and England and Ireland would have to import most of their food.

Prime Minister Butler had appointed a board of England's top scientists to plan some way to deal with the increasingly hostile environment. Marjorie was one of England's foremost molecular biologists, with graduate degrees from Oxford in both botany and zoology. She had been one of the first scientists named to the panel.

Arguments over what to do had raged for months, but in the end the scientists all agreed there was only one answer; if the land surface of the British Isles were becoming uninhabitable, science must create artificial environments where life could continue to exist.

In less than three months, Marjorie and her colleagues had designed Biosphere Britannia, a glass-enclosed ten-acre mini-world that mimicked the geological, biological, and chemical cycles of the original biosphere, the earth itself.

The scientists had originally planned the Biosphere to be

self-supporting. Everything the inhabitants ate, drank, and breathed would be recycled. Intensive agriculture within the huge greenhouse would produce more crops on one acre than had been raised on fifty acres outside.

Marjorie had been given the responsibility of selecting the plants and animals that would be raised in the Biosphere. For months she had flown all over the world, searching out species that would contribute most to the environment of the miniworld while taking up the least space.

In the spring of 1998 the first Biosphere Britannia rose above the Kent countryside. Others were planned outside Birmingham, Liverpool, Glasgow. By 2005, scientists envisioned Biospheres around every town and city in Great Britain. The entire population would soon live and work under the huge pyramids of glass.

Richard's voice interrupted Marjorie's musing. "The NERC's picture's coming in. I'm going to switch you over."

Marjorie watched him type a command into the computer keyboard before him. The Imager screen flickered and cleared, and a live television picture of the mid-Atlantic appeared before her.

The three-quarter moon was still well above the horizon as the satellite camera peered down from its geostationary orbit 870 kilometers above the sea. To the east, Marjorie could see long ocean swells rolling across the surface below, their white-capped crests reflecting the lunar light.

But to the west she could see nothing. It was pitch-black, as if a curtain had been pulled across the sea. Then, as she watched, the entire sky to the west suddenly lit with red, white, and orange flares that reminded her of the fireworks displays the Americans always shot off on their Independence Day.

"Major eruption," Richard said. "God Almighty, look at that."

Volcanic gases flared thousands of feet into the night sky, illuminating the ocean surface for hundreds of kilometers around. Now Marjorie could see an immense cloud bank of ash and black smoke rolling across the sea like a nightmarish tidal wave tens of thousands of feet high.

The front edge of the debris cloud ran north to south for hundreds of miles and Marjorie's gut tightened at the thought of what would happen when the towering wall of ash reached land.

A second eruption sent a fusillade of red-hot magma into the air, and for an instant Marjorie caught a glimpse of a pillar of flaming gases and fiery pumice rising from the volcano itself.

Booroojian had seen it too. "R-Nine's down there at the eight-o'clock position," he said.

"Can you get a close-up of the summit?" Marjorie asked.

"Yes, I think so, if I can center the camera on that last eruption."

Marjorie could hear the clicking of computer keys through the receiver as Booroojian punched in the command. As the camera zoomed in on a close-up of the sea around the volcano, Marjorie suddenly spotted a small oblong cluster of lights glowing against the dark sea not far from the fiery column.

"Good God, is that a ship down there?"

"It's an American research vessel, the *Abyss.* Ben Meade's boat. You remember him."

"Yes," Marjorie said. "I remember Dr. Meade."

"He's been out there for the past three months monitoring R-Nine. As we now know, he was right that a Toba-sized eruption was coming."

"You needn't rub it in, Richard."

"Merely pointing out a fact, Marjorie, old girl," Booroojian said as the ship below slipped out of view of the camera. A moment later, the satellite eye focused on the swirling column rising from R-9, then began to pan down toward the base.

"What's the altitude setting here?" she asked.

"Five thousand feet and descending," Booroojian said. "Forty-five hundred, forty-four, forty-three . . . look out, it's getting hot."

Instinctively, Marjorie flinched back from the Imager as a salvo of smoking magma boulders rocketed into view from below, leaving vapor trails behind as they flashed across the screen.

Several long seconds passed as the camera continued to pan down. "Thirty-one hundred, three thousand, twenty-nine hundred," Richard singsonged.

The entire screen was now a hellish picture of erupting magma, blazing gases, and violently swirling black ash as the camera closed in on the volcano below.

"Twenty-six hundred, twenty-five, that's as close as I can get."

At that moment, an immense discharge of flaming gases jetted skyward, burning away the shroud of volcanic smoke and ash. For a few brief seconds, the surface below was visible.

Marjorie stared transfixed at the picture on the screen. She was only dimly aware of Richard's voice shouting into the phone. "Do you see it? Jesus, Marjorie, do you see it?"

"Yes, Richard," she whispered, her lips barely moving. "I see it."

Centered on the screen before her, the glowing volcanic peak of R-9 rose above the churning sea, the crater at its summit a yawning mouth of molten red magma and flaring gases. From all sides, white-crested waves smashed against the steep slopes, their frothing crests turning to steam as the seawater struck the 800-degree lava walls.

R-9 was now an island, the highest peak in the 800 kilometers long volcanic chain that had risen to dam the warm North Atlantic Drift. The great river in the sea would never again bathe the British Isles with its tropical heat. From this day forward, the subarctic cold that had gripped the islands the past two years could only grow longer and more bitter.

Yet what worried Marjorie most of all was the ash and sulfur dioxide R-9 was spewing into the air above the Atlantic. Biosphere Britannia was heated by solar energy, and the pyramid itself was made of thermal glass. It could survive cold, but only so long as the sun continued to shine and provide the artificial environment with solar energy.

For the past two years, the stratosphere above Britain had become increasingly laden with ash and volcanic gases. Still, the solar panels heating the Biosphere were state-of-the-art, able to maximize even weak sunlight.

Staring at the continuously erupting volcano on the screen before her, Marjorie knew that the volume of sulfate aerosols in the stratosphere would soon escalate out of sight, cutting off even this limited solar radiation. Oil was now far too expensive to use, and the Biosphere had been forced to rely on backup coal furnaces to heat the interior on dark stormy days.

Marjorie sagged. "What now? We're about to lose the last of our solar energy, and with the fuel crisis in this country, we'll be far down on the priority list for more coal."

"Ben Meade."

"What?"

"You asked what we do now. Where do we get the energy to keep the Biosphere going? There is only one answer, Marjorie. Geothermal. And that means Ben Meade."

"Richard, I don't disagree, but we've been through this. Seamus MacTiege has threatened to cut off the funding to run the Biosphere if we attempt to start up the North Channel project again. And he's got the votes in Parliament to do what he says."

"I hate to say this, Marjorie, but you've been letting MacTiege intimidate you ever since this all began. Ben Meade predicted as far back as 1990 that R-Nine would reach the surface. He warned us that a supereruption as bad as Toba was coming, and that the trade winds would carry the ash and gases east over England."

Marjorie fidgeted. "I'd like to remind you, Richard, that while it turns out your friend Meade was right, a lot of respected vulcanologists and oceanographers were saying the opposite; that R-Nine had stopped rising two years ago."

"That's a cop-out, Marjorie, and you know it. You simply haven't had the guts to stand up to MacTiege."

Marjorie stamped her right foot down in frustrated anger, forgetting the sliver still embedded in her instep. "Oowww, bloody damn hell."

"Your foot?"

"Yes, my damn foot. I hate this night. I hate that goddamn

volcano. I hate the awful cold and the bloody snow that never stops." Even as she ranted, Marjorie knew that what she really hated was her weakness in giving in to the bully MacTiege.

Not that she hadn't tried at all. When she'd been helping design Biosphere Britannia, she'd realized geothermal was the perfect energy source for the pristine miniworld they were building.

She'd gone to Parliament with a request for the research funds Richard needed, and she'd cheered from the sidelines as Ben Meade began to sink the first exploratory well up in North Channel.

Yet when it came time to push through the far more costly bill for full development of geothermal, she'd run smack into the stone wall of Seamus MacTiege and his radical Labor Party.

MacTiege had immediately recognized the threat that geothermal posed to his power base. If the immense energy resources of the earth's molten interior could be harnessed, there'd be no need for coal, and MacTiege and his miner-based party would soon find themselves irrelevant.

When Marjorie threatened to take her request for geothermal funding directly to the British people, MacTiege had offered her a deal. He would back financing for Biosphere Britannia; in return, Marjorie was to drop development of geothermal.

At the time, Marjorie needed all the support in Parliament she could get, and she'd agreed. She'd made a deal with the devil, and now it had come back to haunt her.

She took a deep breath. "Do you think Meade would come? After all, when Parliament suddenly withdrew that funding, we left him high and dry up there in North Channel."

"I spent three months on the *Abyss* with Ben sounding the seafloor under North Channel for geothermal formations. He's absolutely first-class. He'll come."

"How long do you think it would take him to get here?"

"He's got a catapult plane on board. He could be in Ice-

land in four or five hours and catch a commercial flight out
of Reykjavik."

"There's still the matter of paying Meade International to
undertake the project. As I recall, sinking even a single well
will cost several million pounds."

"That's your department, Marjorie. I suggest you take it
up with the prime minister."

For a moment Marjorie hesitated, unsure whether to send
for Meade. Then the monitor screen suddenly went almost
completely scarlet as an immense bloodred column of sear-
ing gases and fiery magma exploded into the ash-choked
sky above R-Nine.

"The magma reservoir below the seabed has to be immense," Richard said. "There must be several square kilometers of debris being ejected."

Marjorie stared at the hellish scene on the monitor. The
pillar of flaming magma was feeding a mushrooming cloud
of black pumice and ash that was already broiling east toward England.

She suddenly had a chilling mental picture of the volcanic
debris and gases cutting off solar radiation to Biosphere Britannia and smothering all life in the miniworld she had
worked so hard to create.

"Get Ben Meade over here, Richard," Marjorie said. "I'll
call the prime minister. Without geothermal energy, every
plant and animal in Biosphere Britannia will be dead within
weeks."

MID-ATLANTIC
●●●●●●●●●●●●●●●●

8:50 a.m.

BEN MEADE SLOSHED A triple shot of Cutty Sark into his chipped coffee cup and propped the almost empty Scotch bottle against a rail post on the starboard side of the violently tossing *Abyss*.

Dawn had broken two hours before but only now was a sliver of pale sun able to filter through the ash clouds to the east, slitting beneath the layer of volcanic debris that hung over the sea like an immense black umbrella.

The sudden emergence of the volcanic island twenty miles off the starboard rail of the ship had turned the surrounding sea into a maelstrom. White-crested rollers pushing east before the winds were now breaking off the steaming shores of R-9 and doubling back toward the *Abyss*.

An ash-blackened wave rose as the ship rolled and swept the Scotch bottle off the deck. To Ben's liquor-soaked mind, it was as if R-9 had sent the wave to snatch the bottle, and it infuriated him.

"Goddamn you, you whisky-stealin' bastard," he screamed drunkenly at the volcano smoking furiously on the horizon.

He'd been drinking steadily since R-9 had incinerated the

Queen, and the 3,654 human beings aboard. Now he was drunk enough to hate the volcano as if it were an intelligent force, a being capable of thought and malice.

"I'll be back here with a goddamn laser cannon, you hear me," he slurred. "The biggest laser I can find. I'll blow your rock ass to smithereens."

As drunk as he was, the absurdity of threatening a volcano suddenly struck him and he began to laugh, then cry at the same time. He sank down next to the pitching rail, the tears clearing tracks down his ash-layered face.

Captain Mel Sanderson popped out of the door to the wing bridge above and looked down at his boss. He'd only seen Ben like this once before, years ago when he'd caught his wife and his brother in bed.

Ben was a lot of things; decent, generous, loyal, an internationally famous earth scientist consulted by presidents and prime ministers. But he had a weakness; he kept things in, bottled up his emotions until the pressures were so intense he suddenly blew. When that happened he was dangerous, to himself and anyone who'd wronged him.

Jesus, five years ago he'd almost killed his brother. Not that the cuckolding bastard didn't deserve killing. That wouldn't have helped Ben, though, if he'd ended up doing twenty years to life in the Wyoming state pen.

Sanderson shook his head and descended the steel stairs to the lower deck. Ben was half sitting, half sprawled against a rail post. As the captain approached, Ben's chest began to heave and he rolled on his side and vomited into the sea.

"You're a fucking mess, Ben, you know that?"

"Screw you."

"C'mon. I'll get you cleaned up."

"Get away from me, you fat old bastard."

"Look, I don't give a shit whether you lie here all day drinking and puking. But I'm holding a call for you on the bridge. You want to take it or not?"

"Who is it?"

"Guy named Booroojian. Richard Booroojian. He says it's real important."

"Booroojian?" Ben's Scotch-soaked brain swirled. He knew a Booroojian, but he couldn't connect him.

"Where's he calling from?"

"England."

"England?" Then, dimly, the name registered. Richard Booroojian. English geologist. That geothermal survey of the North Channel seafloor a couple of years ago.

"You say he's still on the line?"

"Yeah, but I don't think you're in any condition to talk to him right now. I'll tell him you'll call him back."

"Bullshit. Help me up."

"Ben—"

"You won't help me, I'll get up myself." Ben began to hoist himself up the rail, then his feet went out from under him and he pitched toward the sea.

Sanderson lunged forward, grabbed Ben around the chest and frog-walked him across to the bridge stairway. "Jesus, you stink."

"I love you too."

Shoving from behind, Sanderson managed to get Ben up the steep stairs and into the bridge. The ship's carpenter had only enough glass on board to replace half the windows blown out when R-9 first erupted, and sections of plywood now filled every other window frame.

"Whata ya doin', Mel, panelin' the place?" Ben slurred, an idiotic grin on his face as his mood swung from depression to euphoria.

"Yeah, I'm making it into my personal den," Sanderson said, plopping the drunken scientist down in the chair in front of the radiophone.

Ben swayed in the chair. "Who'd you say was callin'?"

Sanderson rolled his eyes. "Jesus. Booroojian. Richard Booroojian. From England."

"Oh yeah . . . Booroojian," Ben said, picking up the receiver. "Hello, Richard . . . how's merry ole England?"

Sanderson feigned disinterest, his back to Ben as he picked up a pair of binoculars and studied R-9 smoking in the distance. Still, he was listening. Ben might not remember the call when he sobered up. He might want to know what the hell he'd said.

"Yeah, Richard . . . 'course I saw the eruption. Jesus, whata ya think I'm doin' out here . . . humpin' mermaids?"

"Ben!" Sanderson said sharply.

"Whatsa matter . . . it's my ole buddy Richard."

Sanderson shook his head and turned away again.

"What? 'Course I know the *Queen's* gone," Ben slurred. "I saw . . . Jesus . . . when the magma hit her she went up like a torch. In minutes . . . minutes . . . she was burnin' bow to stern. God Almighty . . . I'll never stop seein' it. Never."

Sanderson lowered his binoculars. Tears were streaming down Ben's face now. "The *Queen* turned into a floating hell, Richard . . . women and kids on fire . . . the flames every-where . . . people leaping into the sea. And then . . . *kaboom* . . . the fuel tanks went . . . the *Queen* blew into a million pieces. And there was nothing we could do . . . nothing."

Ben listened for a moment, then said, "Yeah . . . yeah . . . I know . . . I know . . . we're all sorry, Richard. That won't bring 'em back, will it . . . Jesus, the poor goddamn kids."

The largest wave in a set of seven rolled the *Abyss* far over on her side and Ben almost fell from the chair. "Look, Rich-ard, it's rough out here . . . what the hell do you want?"

A pause, then, "Yeah, I still got a catapult plane on board. Why?"

Sanderson put the binoculars down and turned toward Ben, listening openly. He had a feeling Ben was about to vol-unteer for something he couldn't handle right now.

"Hell, I told you and Marjorie what's-her-name R-Nine would erupt like Toba did. I warned you. Didn't I? Now you want me to bail your ass out."

Silence again, then Ben sighed deeply. "All right, all right, I'll come. But not for you. I'll come 'cause I owe England. I should have warned the *Queen* off sooner . . . I owe England three thousand lives."

Sanderson suddenly understood why Ben had gotten so thoroughly drunk. He blamed himself for what had hap-pened to the *QE 3*. The captain shook his head; he should have known that was it.

Ben slammed down the receiver and got unsteadily to his feet. He lurched across to the stern bridge windows and stared down at the deck below.

"Get someone out to fuel up the catapult plane, Mel. I got to fly to England."

"You're not flying anywhere. You're drunk."

"Get me a pot of coffee. I'll be fine. Fine, fine, fine."

"No."

"How'd you like to get your ass fired off this ship?"

"If you want to can me when you've sobered up, that's your right. But I'm not letting you fly drunk. You'll kill yourself."

"I'll fuel the damn plane myself," Ben said, starting for the bridge door.

In two large strides, Sanderson was across the bridge, blocking the exit. "You're going to your cabin to sleep it off, Ben."

"Damn it, you son of a bitch, I'm the boss around here."

Sanderson swung his balled-fist up from his side, catching Ben full in the face between his nose and his cheekbone. The captain put his entire two hundred twenty pounds into the punch, and Ben went down like a sack of rocks. He was out cold before he hit the deck.

Sanderson bent and grabbed Ben's arms, then pulled him across the bridge and through the door to his cabin. He got his friend up on the bed and covered him with a blanket. Then he went back to the bridge, called the third mate, and ordered the catapult plane fueled.

When Ben woke up he'd be one mad son of a bitch, and this time nothing would keep him from flying to England.

LONDON
•••••••••

SEAMUS MACTIEGE WAS BORN to the wife of an unemployed laborer in a cold-water flat in Newcastle upon Tyne in the late winter of 1939.

At the moment of his birth, the toothless seventy-year-old midwife in attendance had cut the umbilical cord and cackled to his semiconscious mother, "You've popped out a gargoyle, deary. He's got a face like a stonemason chiseled 'im."

Not a few of those who recognized the leader of Britain's Labor Party as he and his dog Alfie hurried south on foot across Blackfriars Bridge this cold February morning would agree that with his squashed-tomato face and bulging eyes the man did indeed resemble a medieval waterspout.

MacTiege never knew his father, who'd been called up to serve in World War II, and killed in 1942 at the Battle of El Alamein in North Africa.

His mother had taken to the gin bottle soon after, and when she wasn't being abusive to her son, one of the string of soldiers and sailors and lorry drivers who found her bed would take over for her, cursing and backhanding the boy from the family's tiny boarding-house room in their lecherous heat.

Despite having no father, and an indifferent whore for a mother, the young MacTiege might have had a chance at normal feelings and relationships had he not found a small stray dog rummaging through the garbage in the alley behind their house when he was seven.

All the tenderness and affection bottled up in the boy he gave to the dog, sharing with the curly-haired mongrel his food, his bed, his every thought.

Six months later, the son of the titled owner of the largest coal mine in Staffordshire had sped his gleaming Jaguar coupe down the street where MacTiege lived. The boy had just thrown a stick into the street for his dog to retrieve when the Jaguar screeched past his boarding-house.

Lord Binksley's son was slumming, showing his new dancer girl friend Newcastle upon Tyne's seamy section of Elswick. One hand and both eyes of the young fop were busy beneath the dancer's short dress and he wouldn't have seen a horse ahead much less a small dog.

The boy watched in helpless horror as the Jaguar crushed his dog into the cobblestones. His tormented scream brought the car to a halt and the young lord and the leggy dancer got out and walked back to click their tongues over the mound of bloody fur lying in the filthy street.

A month before, the boy had walked two kilometers out to Lord Binksley's estate to cadge free food at the nobleman's annual picnic for his miners. He had seen the son there, and stared in awe at the young man's fine clothes and confident bearing. For weeks he had dreamed of being rich and wearing a suit and tie, of being like the man who had just killed his dog.

The young nob had handed the stricken boy a pound and steered the dancer back to his car, the two giggling at their naughty deed as they slammed the doors and raced away.

The weeping boy laid the mangled body of his pet in an empty whisky case and buried his little dog in a vacant lot down the street. As he pushed in the dirt, he was seized by a hatred of the privileged class that would consume him the rest of his life.

The death of his dog closed a door forever in the seven-year-old's forming mind. His mother, her men, the noble-man's son he had come to admire, every human that touched his life had caused him only pain and cold aliena-tion. From that day on, Seamus MacTiege trusted no one, be-friended no one, loved no one.

Yet this man who could not love his fellow man loved ani-mals with a passion. Time and again growing up, he went without meals to buy food for the homeless scraggly cats and dogs he found slinking through urban alleys, and his home now was more often than not a refuge for some re-jected pet.

MacTiege reached the Southwark bank of the frozen Thames and paused for the morning paper at a weather-beaten kiosk.

"Good morning, sir," the rheumy-eyed newsvendor said through the small window, the fumes from his charcoal heater billowing out around the ragged muffler that wrapped his head and neck.

"Good morning," MacTiege said, as always making a pre-tense of rummaging through his overcoat pocket for change.

As always, the vendor held up a hand sheathed in a soiled glove from which the tips had been cut to allow him to fin-ger coins. "No, no, Mr. MacTiege, I wouldn't hear of it. You're for us working blokes, that's all the pay I need."

MacTiege accepted the small daily rite of obeisance with his customary nod, and continued on his way. Alfie lifted his leg, urinated on a light pole, then hurried to catch up.

Man and dog were a block away from the Labor head-quarters when a snowplow approached down the street from the other direction, the huge blade in front curling a hardened crust from the pavement before it. The driver spot-ted MacTiege ahead and leaned out of the glass cab to shake a conspiratorial fist of recognition at the great friend of the working man.

"Give 'em hell, Mr. MacTiege. You got the vote of the GMWU," he yelled out, assuring the Labor leader of the support of the once most conservative General and Munici-pal Workers Union.

MacTiege returned the fisted salute with a wave of his

cane. It pleased him, as much as anything could, to be recognized on the street, albeit those that shouted friendly greetings were almost always members of the working class. The damn toffs would as soon see him dead.

He pushed back the cuff of his glove and looked at his watch, then picked up his pace. He had a nine-thirty interview with a writer from *Forbes*, the American business magazine. The Americans, he'd found, were habitually punctual, a trait he prided himself on as well.

MacTiege and Alfie reached the Labor headquarters and took the elevator up to the top floor of the sixty-story building. The Labor leader exchanged perfunctory "good mornings" with the staff members he passed in the hall and paused before his secretary's desk.

"Good morning, sir," the prim spinster said, handing him several telephone messages.

"Morning, Mary," MacTiege said, leafing through the slips. "I'm expecting a writer from *Forbes* magazine this morning."

"He's waiting in the reception room."

"I'll buzz you when I'm ready," he said, heading for the tall, ornately carved oak doors to his sanctum.

Alfie trotted ahead into the office, crossing to a dog-hair-covered oval rug before the fireplace, where he circled twice before settling down facing the hearth. MacTiege followed, turning on the gas flames that immediately licked up around the fake logs.

He stroked the dog fondly for a moment, then went to his desk and buzzed his secretary. "Send in that chap from *Forbes*, will you, Mary?"

"Very good, sir."

A moment later the door opened and a thin, sandy-haired man in his early thirties entered and started across the room. "Good morning, Mr. MacTiege. Mark Klein from *Forbes*. It's good of you to see me."

Klein was wearing a hand-tailored dark gray pin-striped suit, starched robin's-egg-blue shirt, regimental tie, and highly polished black wingtips. MacTiege was acutely aware of the stark contrast between the writer's fashionable attire and his own off-the-rack brown suit, plaid tie, and white cotton shirt his housekeeper had indifferently ironed as she watched a soap opera on the telly.

The day after he'd been elected to Parliament four years ago, he'd actually gone to a tailor and had three expensive suits done up, along with monogrammed shirts and silk ties. But he'd felt stiff and awkward in the finery, like another man might feel in a rarely worn tuxedo.

Worse, the miners and union members he represented seemed to resent his new look. Men he was around every day suddenly wouldn't meet his eye. The week after he'd gotten his new wear, he'd given the suits and shirts to the Salvation Army and gone back to his department-store garb.

MacTiege came around his desk and shook the writer's extended hand. "My pleasure, Mr. Klein. I always have time to be interviewed by such a prestigious publication as *Forbes*. Please sit down."

Klein eased down into the ersatz Louis Quatorze chair and stole a glance around MacTiege's huge and stunningly garish office. Like the chair, the other furniture were wrongly scaled reproductions of period pieces.

The imitation-leather Victorian couch and armchairs sagged from use. The side tables, bookcases, and a large breakfront across the room looked as if they had all been spray-shellacked in some factory.

A tangle of plastic banana plants and stamped-out ferns from Woolworth's mobbed the corners of the room, their leaves such an unnatural green hue they offended the plant-loving Klein. Yet it was the walls that set his teeth on edge.

The walls were covered in a vertically striped red, white, and blue wallpaper that gave him the unsettling and vaguely sticky feeling he was sitting within an immense, hollow candy cane.

MacTiege followed Klein's eyes. "Rather patriotic, don't you think?"

"I beg your pardon?"

"The wallpaper. Had it done to remind me of our Union Jack."

Klein shifted in his chair. "It does bring your British flag to mind, doesn't it? Yes indeed, red, white, and blue."

The dog rose from his place before the fire and ambled over to sniff the newcomer.

"Well, hello, Alfie." Klein bent to pet the mongrel. "There's a good dog."

MacTiege's eyebrows arched. "How did you know his name?"

"I daresay several million Americans still remember his name, Mr. MacTiege. You made the front page of *The New York Times* when you saved his life."

Klein clicked open his briefcase, pulled out a manila folder, and searched through the papers inside. "I have the story here in your bio file," he said, handing a yellowed clipping across the desk to MacTiege.

Despite himself, a thin smile spread over MacTiege's face as he read the headline aloud: " 'British Labor leader risks life to save stray dog.' I say, that's a bit rich. It was such a small thing. I had no idea the American media picked the story up."

"With all respect, sir, I disagree it was a 'small thing,' as you put it. You showed great physical courage. It was, what, five years ago? You must have been about fifty-five."

"Fifty-six."

"Fifty-six. Yet you took on two hulking thugs half your age."

"They were dock workers, actually," MacTiege said, remembering the day. He'd been on his way to address a Labor rally in the wharf section of Liverpool when he came across two longshoremen whipping a large black mongrel with thick lengths of hemp from a cargo net.

The starving beast had stolen a sandwich from one of the men, and they obviously had every intention of beating the dog to death.

MacTiege had snatched the frayed rope away from the man closest him and lashed the two back away from the bleeding, half-dead animal. Taken by surprise at first, the longshoremen had rallied, coming at MacTiege from both sides.

The Labor leader had grown up in the tough streets of Els-wick and he hadn't forgotten how to fight. Despite his age, he was in good physical condition and he'd put up a spirited battle.

When the two brutes found they couldn't beat him with their fists, one of them grabbed a cargo hook from a nearby crate and swung it viciously at his face. MacTiege had dodged to the side a split second before the steel struck, but still he caught the hook just above his left collarbone.

The sharp point severed his subclavian artery and a tor-rent of blood erupted out over his face and body. A woman passing by let out a scream and ran for the police, frighten-ing off MacTiege's attackers.

When the police and the ambulance arrived, he had in-sisted they take the injured dog along to the hospital. A week later, man and dog emerged from Liverpool's Red-court Hospital weak and sore, and thereafter inseparable.

MacTiege had named the mongrel Alfie, after the father he'd never met. Alfie was his closest friend and faithful con-fidant, and he rarely went anywhere without the big black dog.

"Well then, Mr. Klein, shall we get on with your inter-view?" MacTiege said as Alfie wandered back and circled down again before the fire. "Where would you like to begin?"

Klein took out a yellow legal pad and a pen. "How did you get started in the labor movement?"

MacTiege leaned back in his chair and stared at the ceiling for a long moment. "I suppose I would trace that moment back to a mine accident in 1960. I was just an ordinary coal miner at the time. Then one day an explosion of coal dust trapped me and sixty other blokes a mile underground. It looked like the end for all of us."

"How did you get out?"

"By not losing our heads. Later, I was credited with keep-ing the chaps calm, convincing the other miners we'd make it through somehow. Frankly, most of the chaps were half out of their minds, afraid of death, terrified they'd never see their families again."

"But you weren't afraid?"

"Oh, I was scared all right. It was pitch-black and hard to breathe, and we had hardly any water to drink. But I had a big advantage that kept me from panicking, as some of the others did."

"What advantage?"

"I didn't have a family, Mr. Klein. No one. Death didn't hold the terror for me it did for the men with wives and children. I was able to keep my senses about me. I requisitioned what food and water we had and parceled it out so all got a fair share."

MacTiege allowed himself a small smile. "I even organized sing-alongs to keep the chaps' spirits up. I must tell you, I despised sing-alongs then, and do to this day."

"How long were you trapped down there?"

"Six days, all told. When we were finally rescued, the other miners made rather a fuss over what I'd done. A week later I was made a steward in the National Union of Mineworkers. After that, I simply kept climbing the ladder."

Klein glanced at his notes. "Your rise through the NUM leadership was quite rapid during the sixties and seventies, Mr. MacTiege. This was also the time, of course, when radical unions were gaining unprecedented power in Britain."

MacTiege bristled. "If by 'radical' you mean favoring extreme change, than I accept the label. Nevertheless, when most people hear the term they immediately conjure up visions of wild-eyed bomb-throwers. The Labor Party and the many unions we represent are for social justice, Mr. Klein. I hope you will make that point in your story."

"I'd be glad to quote you, sir. I believe you were elected president of NUM in 1979."

"That's correct."

"The same year Margaret Thatcher became prime minister."

"Yes, the Iron Maiden and I took office within weeks of each other," MacTiege said wryly.

"I believe Mrs. Thatcher said at the time that British unions had become, quote, 'virtually a state within a state, dictating their terms to the government and people of the country.' "

"I don't remember her exact words, but that sounds like her."

"Obviously she struck a chord with the people, Mr. Mac-Tiege, because a conservative revampment soon took hold in Britain," Klein said, "a political shift that lasted well into the nineties."

"Right up until Windscale, Mr. Klein. That unprecedented disaster exposed the Tories for what they are—a party of the privileged. Their lax nuclear regulatory policies benefitted big business, and ultimately cost the lives of thousands of innocent British and Irish people."

"Certainly Windscale cost the Conservatives their control of the government in the general election of 1996," Klein said. "Yet it was the Social Democrats, not the Labor Party, that won that election."

MacTiege shrugged. "There was still some residual distrust of Labor in 'ninety-six, I won't deny that. Yet we elected over thirty new Labor members to Parliament that year."

"Including yourself."

"Yes. I ran for a seat from Warrington, an industrial city in Lancashire. If memory serves, I won with a plurality of ten thousand votes."

Klein looked through his file. "It was shortly after the election that the chain of mid-Atlantic volcanoes began to rise and climatic conditions started to deteriorate in Britain."

"Yes, the weather has become our most bitter enemy."

"Yet it has also swelled the ranks of NUM with new miners."

"I don't know where you're leading, Mr. Klein. Yes, the terrible cold has quadrupled the demand for coal to fire the furnaces of Britain. We now have almost a million members in NUM."

"And tens of millions of pounds in union dues to fund Labor candidates running for office. Is that not true?"

"I resent the implication."

"I've done my homework, Mr. MacTiege. Within the past

two years, the Labor Party has elected almost sixty new members of Parliament. Ninety percent of those elections were funded with NUM money."

"Contributing to the campaigns of politicians who support your view is neither illegal nor immoral, Mr. Klein."

The American writer flashed a thin smile. "Apparently, enough of those politicians not only shared your views but were grateful enough for your support to elect you leader of the Labor Party eighteen months ago. You've had a meteoric rise to power, Mr. MacTiege."

"If you're implying I bought the leadership, you're dead wrong. Before I came along, Labor had been floundering. The party had put forward no clear direction for this country. I offered programs and solutions people could grasp onto and believe in."

"Those solutions, sir, advocate a host of radical new social policies and political powers that have been labeled undemocratic. Rather harsh terms have been applied to you, not only by your fellow countrymen but by libertarians within the European Community and the United States."

"Say it!"

"I beg your pardon, Mr. MacTiege?"

The Labor leader came out of his chair. "Say it, damn you. Fascist! They're calling me a fascist."

"That word has been used to describe you, yes," Klein said, alarmed at MacTiege's suddenly mottled red face.

"Let the bloody Tories and the industrialists and the titled toffs call me a fascist," MacTiege spat. "The term is a mark of their fear, their loathing of my rise from the coal pits to the leadership of the Labor Party."

"I have no doubt there is some personal animosity involved," Klein managed weakly.

"All that I have done, all that I propose to do, is for the good of the working man, the millions of poor bastards struggling to feed their families and pay the rent on the pittance they earn in wages."

"I think part of the criticism of you has to do with the autocratic manner in which you rule the Labor Party."

"I won't deny I run things with an iron hand. It has to be

that way. If I didn't maintain discipline, keep the lads in line, the monied class and their Social Democrat lap dogs would soon find a way to exploit any weakness and destroy all I believe in."

"And what do you believe in, Mr. MacTiege?"

"Change, Mr. Klein," MacTiege said, regaining his composure as he sank back into his chair. "Fundamental change. England must forsake the dangerous path of high technology and science that brought on Windscale. We must return to an economy and a way of life based on coal."

"You can't mean that, Mr. MacTiege. Coal was the fuel of the nineteenth century."

"It can be the fuel of the twenty-first century as well. Coal can heat homes and fire factory furnaces. Coal can be synthesized into chemicals, drugs, fibers, food flavorings, perfumes, preservatives, and countless other products we once imported."

MacTiege threw up his hands. "Besides, what choice have we? After Windscale, nuclear power is out of the question for Britain. Most of our North Sea oil wells and pumping stations have been destroyed by sea ice, and we can't afford to import oil any longer. The British Isles have enough coal reserves to last us a century or more. We must use what we have. We must go back to the old ways."

"You have said that Britain must eschew futuristic technologies. Does that mean you are against the development of Biosphere Britannia?"

MacTiege paused. He had visited the glass-domed mini-earth Marjorie Glynn had built in Kent and seen for himself the possibilities it encompassed. Glynn advocated a brave new world of intensive agriculture and nurturing human habitats.

He could live with the concept of the Biosphere itself. What he could not accept was Glynn's plan to develop non-polluting light industry within her miniearths, factories powered not by coal but by the geothermal energy that lay under North Channel.

Glynn was a direct threat to the coal-based economy he envisioned, and he was determined to stop her.

"Biosphere Britannia is a hypothetical concept," he said. "It is unproven. We cannot risk the entire future of our country on the whimsical theories of some young scientist, however well-meaning Dr. Glynn may be."

"I have one final question, Mr. MacTiege," Klein said. "The meteorologists are predicting the immense clouds of ash and smoke from R-Nine will descend on Britain the day after tomorrow, blocking almost all solar radiation from reaching the ground. Temperatures will plummet even further, and the demand for coal will soar. Are you prepared to supply that demand?"

"The National Union of Mineworkers and the Labor Party will take whatever steps necessary to insure the well-being of those millions of workers we represent. Beyond that, Mr. Klein, I am not prepared to go."

The American packed his notes in his briefcase and came to his feet. "Thank you for your time, Mr. MacTiege."

The Labor leader rose behind his desk. "You're welcome, Mr. Klein. Please give my best to your publisher at *Forbes*."

Klein nodded. "Goodbye, then."

As the door closed behind the writer, MacTiege reached for the phone. The time was ripe for his checkmate move.

"Yes, sir?" his secretary answered.

"Ring up Roscoe Phelps at the TUC."

"Very good, sir."

MacTiege replaced the receiver. He had handpicked Phelps as general secretary of the Trades Union Congress. The staunch union man would not hesitate to call the general strike MacTiege was about to ask for.

He had already worked out the details. He would instruct Phelps to call a news conference for later today. With the television cameras rolling, the general secretary would insist that workers needed an immediate twenty-percent wage increase to compensate for the rising costs of food and fuel brought on by the worsening weather.

Unless the TUC's demands were met immediately, miners, snowplow operators, railway workers, air traffic controllers, and hundreds of thousands of other workers would go out on strike effective at midnight tomorrow.

The strike would shut the country down, and leave Britain facing the prospect of running out of fuel in the midst of the coldest winter since the last ice age.

If the government called out troops to break the strike, the Trades Union Congress would send a million workers out to confront the soldiers. Blood would redden the snow-covered streets.

MacTiege's pale eyes glowed with a grim determination. He had Prime Minister Butler by the short hairs. If the PM gave in to the TUC's call for exorbitant wage increases, it would bankrupt the already tottering British Treasury.

If Butler resisted the demand, the strike would go on until the capitalist-based economy collapsed in ruins.

Either way, upheaval was coming, and with it would come Seamus MacTiege's great chance to take power at last in Britain.

ENGLISH CHANNEL
••••••••••••••••••••

12:15 p.m.

THIRTY-FIVE-YEAR-OLD channel pilot Ray Bauer stared through the snow-encrusted bridge windows of the *SS Isle Sainte Marie* as the small freighter ploughed southeast through the thick ice floes layering the surface of the English Channel.

Five hundred yards ahead of the ship, a Royal Navy ice-breaker cleared a path through the icefields, its reinforced bow rising rhythmically to crush the snow-covered sheet before it.

Earlier in the winter, the *Isle Sainte Marie* had been trapped in the English port of Dover by the icing over of the Channel. When the Royal Navy announced two days ago that an ice-breaker would lead a convoy across to France, Bauer had been hired by the French owner to pilot the ship home to Calais.

This was the last time a shipping lane would be opened until the following spring, and three other small freighters and a Dutch motorized barge followed in the wake of *Isle Sainte Marie*, all anxious to gain the coast of the Continent before the Channel became impassable again until spring.

Bauer punched a request for a position fix into the *Isle*

Sainte Marie's satellite-fed navigation computer, then turned from the screen and smiled at his seven-year-old son Ian standing beside him. "We're right over it now, son."

The red-haired, freckle-faced boy pressed his nose against the cold bridge window and stared down at the ice-choked seawater passing beneath the black-hulled ship. "Ain't it somethin', Dad, to think there's trains speedin' along down there under the sea?"

The *Isle Sainte Marie* was directly above the "Chunnel," the thirty-four-mile-long tunnel complex that had been completed under the English Channel back in 1993.

The first physical link between England and the Continent since the last ice age twenty thousand years before, the Chunnel consisted of two larger tunnels carrying trains north and south, with a third service tunnel between them.

The three main tunnels were linked by smaller cross tunnels every 1,230 feet. One-third of the way out from each shore of the Channel, huge crossover caverns had been excavated where the running tunnels met.

Each large enough to house a cathedral, the caverns held diamond switches that allowed disabled trains to change from one tunnel to another. To keep the air pressure even in both train tubes, a series of pressure relief ducts arched over the service tunnel from one running tunnel to the other.

The tunnels under the frozen English Channel were the longest in the world. Twenty-four hours a day, a hundred high-speed trains sped in both directions, carrying passengers and freight between terminals at Folkestone in England and Coquelles in France. From these points, the trains connected to rail systems that now linked the British Isles to every country in Europe.

Bauer smiled at his son. "Speedin' is right. Them trains cross under the Channel in twenty-six minutes flat."

"When will we be back here, Dad? I mean right under here where we are now?"

Bauer glanced toward the icebreaker ahead. The Royal Navy ship was making good progress through the floes. "Unless we run into thicker ice, we should be in Calais around four. Then I'll have to do the paperwork once we dock."

"How long will that take?"

"Couple of hours maybe. Them frogs got to stamp every-thing two, three times before they figure it's official. Soon's I'm done, we'll rent a car and drive to Coquelles. I'd say we'll be in the middle of the Channel around seven o'clock."

The boy's face shone with excitement. "It's hard to think this very night we'll be down there, Dad. I bet it'll feel like we're in a submarine."

Bauer tousled his son's red hair. "The compartments on them shuttle trains are sort of like long halls you park your car in. They're clean and shiny and they got plenty of win-dows, but the tunnel walls are so close speedin' by that you don't see much. I don't want you to be disappointed."

A look of wonder played on the boy's face. "Oh no, Dad, there's no chance of that. I'll be thinkin' all the time we're in the Chunnel about all the water and ice and fish and such above our heads."

"There'll be rock and earth over us too," Bauer said. "The Chunnel's down under the seabed, don't forget."

The boy was fascinated. "It must have been something, diggin' it. I shouldn't like to have done that, under all that mud and water."

"Nor I, son. A score of men died pushing those tunnels through the chalk."

The boy straightened and glanced out over the ice to the west. In the distance he could see what looked like a jagged white plateau rising above the floes. "There's another one of them icebergs, Dad. Big one."

Bauer picked up a pair of binoculars and studied the mas-sive ice three miles off the starboard bow. The berg was over thirty feet high and perhaps three miles across.

"It's good sized, all right. One of that lot that drifted down from the Arctic last spring."

"How come it didn't melt last summer?" the boy asked.

Bauer laughed. "It's a short memory you've got, Ian. We hardly had a summer. It never got above sixty degrees. What with fog half the day and the air temperature that low, a berg that size could last for years."

"Do you think it could drift into Dover? Smash up the port?"

Bauer shook his head. "Oh, I wouldn't worry about that, Ian. I've passed that same berg a dozen times crossin' the Channel before the sea froze. It hasn't moved in months. It's hard aground, no doubt."

The boy looked worried. "Aground? You mean the berg's scrapin' the bottom of the Channel?"

Bauer nodded. "The thing to remember, Ian, is that when you see a berg, you're only lookin' at maybe ten percent of her. Near ninety percent is underwater."

The youngster studied the huge table of ice. "Suppose it starts movin', Dad? Couldn't the underside scrape away the sea bottom and crush the Chunnel?"

"The Chunnel's a hundred and fifty feet beneath the sea-bed, Ian. I doubt the bottom of the berg could slit open the chalk that deep."

A strong gust of wind suddenly swept in from the west, lashing the bridge of the *Isle Sainte Marie* with freezing spray from the open lead behind the icebreaker. "Radio says there's a gale comin' in," Bauer said. "The winds'll probably close the ice behind us again in a couple of hours."

"We're not going' to get frozen into the floes out here, are we, Dad?"

"I shouldn't worry about that, Ian. We'll be in Calais long before the worst of it hits."

As the small convoy of ships steamed toward the French coast, the gale working up the English Channel steadily built in force. The storm coincided with a flood tide, raising the Channel waters and the ice floes on the surface almost ten feet above normal.

The huge iceberg young Ian Bauer had worried about began to creak and groan as the rising seas made it more buoyant and the winds pushed ever harder against its steep ice cliffs.

Slowly, imperceptibly at first, the plateau of ice began to move. The thinner floes splintered before it as the huge berg advanced, its ice keel gouging out a trench 105 feet deep in the chalk seabed below.

MID-ATLANTIC
•••••••••••••••••••

12:45 p.m.

THE EXPLOSIONS GOING OFF in Ben Meade's head grew louder the closer he came to full consciousness and he ground his teeth and let a moan from his soul well up through his sinuses and out his nose.

"Ohhh, God."

"God won't help you. You're a sinner. You're being punished." The gruff voice of Mel Sanderson assaulted his tender eardrums.

"I don't need a sermon this morning, Mel."

"This afternoon. You've been out for something like twenty-eight hours."

"What?"

"What do you expect when you go without sleep for three days and then drink a quart of Scotch? You smell like a squid that's been lying on the beach for a couple of weeks. I'm going to have to burn my sheets."

"Your sheets?" Ben opened one eye. "What am I doing in your day cabin?"

"I dragged you in here. I've been checking every couple of hours to see if you'd come around. You remember anything?"

"The seductive golden glow of Scotch swirling in my cup."

"Yeah, you got seduced right out of your goddamn skull. You were shitfaced."

An ear-splitting detonation thundered somewhere off above the sea, the sound wave echoing through the steel-walled cabin, and Ben suddenly realized the explosions he'd heard weren't in his head.

It all came flooding back to him now; the titanic eruption of R-9 and the sight of the *QE 3* blazing like the head of a torch jutting through the sea.

Sanderson crossed the cabin and stared out a porthole. "R-Nine is waking up again," he said, a vermilion glow from the erupting volcano washing his face.

"Any sign of survivors from the *Queen?* Lifeboats? Flares?" Ben asked.

"You know better," Sanderson said softly.

"I know I know better. I just thought . . . shit, I don't know, a miracle."

"No miracles, Ben. No flares, no boats, not even a piece of flotsam. The *Queen* blew apart like a damn bomb going off. I doubt there's a piece of her left bigger'n my fist. And if there is, it's at the bottom of the sea."

"Speaking of fists," Ben said, yawning his jaw back and forth. "It feels like someone cold-cocked me."

"Me. You needed help going beddy-bye."

Ben winced as he moved his jaw too far. "Ooww, damn it. You son of a bitch, I'm going to be slurping pabulum for the next week."

"You scientists are too delicate. I gave you a little tap, was all."

"Yeah, well, the next time we hit port and I catch your ass all beered up in one of those topless joints you hang out in, I'm going to tap you asleep."

"I do not hang out in topless joints. I happen to enjoy interpretive nude dancing."

"The only thing you're interested in interpreting is a big set of jugs. You're a tit freak, Mel. Probably the result of being weaned too early."

"I can't tell you how I appreciate these little insights into my character. You plan on hoisting your ass out of my bed anytime soon?"

Ben swung his feet to the floor and cradled his head in his hands. "Ring the galley for me, will you, Mel? Have them send up some coffee. And a bottle of aspirin."

Sanderson picked up the phone. "You better have some food with that."

"Yeah, all right. Steak. Steak and eggs."

"I told you the last time, all we have left aboard is ham. Canned."

"All right, all right, ham. Ham and eggs."

"No eggs."

"Jesus, I don't care, just get me some food, will you?"

"My, we're touchy today," Sanderson grinned as he picked up the phone.

Ben rose and lurched across the tossing cabin to the small head. He splashed cold water on his face, then groaned as he surveyed his blotchy face and bloodshot eyes in the mirror. "Booze," he said to his reflection. "When are you going to learn, asshole?"

"The catapult plane's all fueled," Sanderson said when Ben came back. "Not that you can take off anytime soon. Not the way the *Abyss* is rolling."

Ben looked blank. "What are you talking about, the plane's fueled?"

"I knew you wouldn't remember."

"You love this, don't you?"

Sanderson laughed. "You had a call from some guy in England named Richard Booroojian yesterday morning. You were drunk out of your mind at the time, but you insisted on talking to him."

"And?"

"You said something about warning him and some woman named Marjorie that R-Nine was going to erupt. Then you promised him you'd fly to England."

Ben couldn't remember a word of the conversation with Booroojian, but he had no doubt why the English scientist wanted him in England. With the huge heater hose of the

North Atlantic Drift severed and the volcanic clouds from
R-9 about to envelop England in cold, the British needed
geothermal energy more than ever now. They needed him.

"You were heading out the door to fuel the plane when I
put your lights out," Sanderson said.

Ben shook his head sheepishly. "I guess I owe you one."

"You might say that."

"I'm going down to shower and change. Have someone
bring a tray to my cabin."

"Careful on deck," Sanderson said. "The footing's treach-
erous as hell out there."

Ben opened the cabin door and stepped out onto the wing
bridge. "Jesus," he said under his breath at the sight of the
ash-cloaked *Abyss.* From bow to stern, eight inches of gray-
black pumice and volcanic powder covered the decks. The
ash was everywhere, coating portholes and masts, piled in
deep drifts against bulkheads and machinery.

He paused for a moment and stared out across the sea toward R-9. Though the volcano was at least thirty miles
away, he could see glowing red magma flows streaming
down the near slopes.

As he watched, a violent eruption sent a plume of fiery
magma and superheated gases into the freezing air and the
summit suddenly appeared against the scarlet sky.

R-9 now towered at least five hundred feet above the Atlantic waves, and the volcanic peak was building ever higher
as magma continued to pulse up from the hot spot deep beneath the seabed.

For several more minutes he watched the pyrotechnics
lighting the horizon, then shook off his foreboding and
made his way carefully down the ash-coated bridge stairs toward his cabin.

He took a long hot shower, then shaved. The quart of
Cutty Sark he'd consumed left his hands shaky and he
nicked himself several times, cursing every time another cut
reddened the shaving cream.

You're an alcoholic, Meade, admit it, goddamn it, he told his
reflection in the mirror. *No more booze. You can't control it any-*

more. One of these days, you're not going to have Mel around to put you to bed.

As he was dressing, the cook arrived with two ham sandwiches, a microwaved potato, a pot of coffee, and a bottle of aspirin. He wolfed the food down, gulped four aspirins, then turned on his computer and hooked up via cellular modem to his data base in Wyoming.

Meade International owned a chunk of G-Sat, a privately funded geological research satellite sent up in the midnineties. An infrared scanner aboard the G-Sat continuously probed deep beneath the land and sea below, mapping out mineral deposits and geothermal fields around the world.

Ben programmed in orders for a multiorbit satellite scan of the geothermal reservoir under North Channel, directing the data be forwarded to him in England. Then he called up local weather coverage from a National Oceanic and Atmospheric Administration Nimbus 9 meteorological satellite in geostationary orbit southwest of Iceland.

A moment later the monitor flickered and an infrared image of the North Atlantic came on the screen. The towering clouds of ash, pumice, and smoke from R-9 were warmer than the surrounding air and appeared as a huge orange-red blotch over the blue-green ocean below.

The trade winds blowing to the east had already carried the volcanic debris a third of the way toward the British Isles. Ben studied the thermal map for several minutes more, then shut down the computer. He threw some underwear and socks in a canvas valise, grabbed his leather flight jacket, and headed for the bridge.

Captain Sanderson was studying diesel fuel consumption figures on a clipboard in his hands when Ben opened the bridge door. He eyed Ben's valise suspiciously. "Goin' somewhere?"

"England. You said the plane was fueled."

"Yeah, she's fueled. But you can't take off in these seas. The swells are running twenty-five, thirty feet. You don't time it just right, you'll catapult your ass straight into the side of a wave."

"It's my ass, and my ass is heading for England. Now."

"Ben . . ."

"I'll need the extra gas tanks. Topped off."

"They're already on board. Full as I can get 'em."

"I got enough fuel to reach Iceland?"

"Yeah, but you better not do any sightseeing along the way. You got maybe an extra hour of fuel, hour and a quarter tops."

"No problem. Flying east I've got the trade winds behind me."

"We've been kickin' around together a long time, Ben. Do me a favor. Wait until morning. From the weather reports, the seas'll be down by then."

"I can't wait, Mel."

"For God's sake, why?"

"The ash clouds. I've got to beat them to England. When the volcanic fallout from R-Nine starts coming down over there, there'll be no way to land a plane. It could be days before aircraft can get in or out."

"The clouds are between us and Iceland. You can't fly through that stuff. The ash would clog your carburetor in minutes."

"I won't have to fly through it. I've just called up a satellite shot of the cloud. So far it extends from latitude fifty degrees north up to about sixty degrees."

"Which is the latitude you have to cover to reach Iceland."

"Let me finish, will you? The fallout's blowing east from R-Nine. When I take off, I'll circle the volcano to the west where the skies are still clear, then head due north. When I reach sixty degrees latitude, I'll turn east and fly north of the ash all the way into Iceland."

"Jesus, that will add three, four hundred miles to your flight. You'll be on fumes by the time you reach Reykjavik."

Ben shrugged. "I've got to make this flight, Mel."

"Still blaming yourself for what happened to the *Queen*, aren't you?"

Ben looked at him sharply, then turned and stared out the bridge window toward R-9. "If I'd have warned off that British captain just ten minutes sooner—"

"Stop it, Ben. Jesus, everything was happening at once.

Ten minutes, twenty minutes, he was steaming so fast it wouldn't have made any difference."

"Yeah."

"Damn it, if that captain hadn't been so intent on giving his passengers a close look at R-Nine, the *Queen* would be docking in Quebec about now."

"Let's drop it, Mel."

Sanderson threw up his hands. "Sure, I'll drop it, but you won't. You gotta wear a hair shirt. You gotta risk your neck flying to England to atone. Shit."

Sanderson whirled around and punched the ship's intercom button. "Kaneko. Get aft to the catapult. On the double." He turned back to Ben, his face red. "You insist on flying off a ship rolling in thirty-foot seas, who the hell am I to stop you?"

"Calm down, Mel."

"Up yours. C'mon, hero, let's get this over with."

Ben grinned and followed Sanderson out the bridge door. Mate Rich Kaneko met them at the catapult. Kaneko was the machinist on board. He'd been an aircraft mechanic before he'd signed on the *Abyss,* and Ben had entrusted him with the maintenance of the ship's scout plane.

When the *Abyss* was anchored above a submarine geological site, Ben often used the prop plane on reconnaissance flights over the surrounding sea. The aircraft's belly was crammed with sophisticated electronic gear that monitored the ocean floor as Ben flew over.

"What do you think, Rich," Ben said, "can I get off tonight?"

Kaneko arched his eyebrows. "Was me, I wouldn't chance it."

"That's encouraging."

"You asked."

"Forget it, Rich," Sanderson said. "He's made up his mind."

Kaneko shrugged. "Something to tell the grandkids about."

"You mean if I make it." Ben grinned.

"Actually, Ben, it would make a better story if you didn't."

Ben and Sanderson broke into laughter as Kaneko reached down and hoisted one end of a long thin rectangular crate at his feet. "Someone give me a hand loading the cartridge."

Kaneko slid a six-foot-long, five-inch-diameter blank cartridge out of the crate and Sanderson helped him load it into a piston chamber on the catapult assembly. When the cartridge was fired, it would drive the piston forward, activating a wire pulley system.

The plane sat on a four-foot-wide V-shaped carriage attached to the pulley wires. When the blank went off, the wires would yank the carriage forward down twin sixty-foot-long greased tracks and catapult the aircraft out over the sea.

Timing was crucial. Ben would have to throttle up and then release the brakes at exactly the right instant. If he didn't have the RPMs built to takeoff speed, or the engines suddenly cut off, he'd drop into the waves like a stone.

It took the men another twenty minutes to warm up the engines, do a systems check, and clear the volcanic powder from the wings and fuselage. Kaneko brushed off the carriage tracks and lubricated the two steel ribbons with a fresh coat of grease.

Ben inspected the pontoons beneath the plane's belly and wings, searching the metal skin for dents or cracks. After each reconnaissance flight, the pontoons allowed him to land in the sea beside the *Abyss*. A derrick on deck then lowered a cable over the side and hoisted the plane back aboard.

When he reached Iceland, he'd lower the plane's retractable landing gear housed within the pontoons and put down at Reykjavik Airport. The capital of Iceland was a busy hub for transatlantic flights and he figured he'd have no trouble getting a seat on a passenger jet into London.

Captain Sanderson picked up the deck phone and ordered the helmsman to head the *Abyss* into the wind. The maneuver would give Ben an extra ten knots of wind behind him as he took off.

"We're as ready as we'll ever be," Ben said. "I'd better get off before R-Nine erupts again and fouls the engines."

Kaneko stepped forward and offered his hand. "Good luck, Ben. Keep her nose up, huh?"

"You bet, Rich. Thanks."

Sanderson's worried face reflected his deep concern. "You stubborn son of a bitch, you gotta do this, don't you?"

Ben craned his neck toward the dark, glowering sky. "Like I said, Mel, I have to beat those clouds to England."

"Remember what I said about the gas. You've got just enough to reach Iceland. If the fallout's been blown north of sixty degrees latitude, turn around and come back."

"You got it."

Sanderson embraced Ben in a bear hug. "I love you, you crazy bastard."

"It's not a physical thing is it, Mel? I mean, we have been out here a long time."

"Jesus, get off my ship."

Ben grinned. "I love you too. See you in England."

"What?"

"Didn't I tell you? I'll need you up at North Channel. As soon as I take off, chart a course for Iceland. By the time you dock, the skies over England should have cleared enough for you to fly in."

"The last minute, you always spring these things on me at the last minute."

"I love surprises," Ben said, then climbed the catapult assembly and pulled the door of the plane closed behind him. For several minutes he listened carefully for any indication the twin props might be running rough.

Satisfied the engines were firing perfectly, he ran his eyes over the gauges before him, tested the controls, then gave a thumbs-up signal to Sanderson and Kaneko standing off to one side.

Ben turned his attention to the sea, watching the wave tops rise and fall beyond the deck of the rolling ship. It was like going up and down in an elevator, and he knew choosing exactly the right moment to fire the explosive cartridge would mean trusting the feeling in his gut as much as his eyes.

The time to take off was when the *Abyss* was in the bottom of a wave trough so that by the time the plane shot down the catapult tracks and crossed the edge of the deck the ship would be rising again above the waves.

Ben let the *Abyss* roll a few times more, getting used to the rhythm of the swells, then he revved up the engines and rested a finger on the firing button. He concentrated on the sinking feeling in his stomach as the ship descended. A second passed, two, three.

Now! He simultaneously released the brakes and hit the button and a loud explosion behind sent the plane rocketing down the tracks. A wall of saltwater spray blowing off the angry swells engulfed the cockpit as he shot out over the sea.

Ben eased the stick back and pushed the throttles full forward. For a moment he was flying blind as the wind-whipped spray pelted the windshield. He hit the toggle switch for the wipers. The first swipe of the blades cleared the glass and his heart leaped into his throat. He was too low, only a few feet above the wave tops.

The extra fuel on board had made the plane heavier than he'd anticipated. *Don't yank the stick back and stall her*, he reminded himself. Slowly he eased the controls toward him, bringing up the nose. It was going to be all right. He was going to make it.

Then dead ahead he saw the cross sea. The huge set of white-crested swells were an aberration, rogue waves generated by volcanism erupting through the submerged slopes of R-9. The foaming wave tops were rolling toward him at least thirty feet above the surrounding water.

"Oh, shit." Ben gripped the stick with both hands. He'd have to pull back hard, take a chance the engines wouldn't cut out. The angry blue-green wall of water was two hundred yards ahead, then a hundred. He closed his eyes and yanked back the stick with all his strength.

He could feel the nose shoot up, then the entire plane shook violently as the pontoons below the belly and wings knifed into the summit of the leading swell. For the longest moment of Ben's life, the plane hesitated, the pontoons submerged three feet into the wave top.

Then the bullet-shaped floats shot through the back of the wave and he felt the plane lift free. Quickly he gained altitude, the foaming Atlantic swells blurring below. He leaned back in his seat and let out a long slow breath. Despite a temperature of barely 35 degrees in the cabin, he was sweating profusely.

He circled back and flew low over the *Abyss*, dipping his wings at Sanderson and Kaneko waving from the deck below. Then he banked the aircraft and began to climb, circling west twenty miles off the black smoking slopes of R-9.

At eight thousand feet the volcanic clouds parted and he could see the fiery crater at the summit. Geysers of burning gases and white-hot magma were erupting hundreds of feet above the hellish pit, while to the south a huge river of molten rock was boiling over the lip of the cauldron and flowing down the volcano's flanks toward the sea below.

For several long moments Ben stared down at the awesome display of the power of nature, then finally pulled his eyes away and turned on the plane's Global Positioning System. The GPS was linked by radio to a navigation satellite that continuously fixed his exact latitude and longitude. He couldn't afford any navigation mistakes on the flight to Iceland. If he were off just half a degree, he'd run out of fuel before he reached land.

Flying at twenty thousand feet, the plane would glide down for several miles after the engines coughed and quit. He'd have maybe five minutes to contemplate his life before he knifed nose first into the depths of the unforgiving ocean below.

CALAIS
•••••••

5:20 p.m.

RAY BAUER HANDED THE packet of ship's manifests to the bored official in the harbormaster's office in Calais and turned to his son with a smile. "There, that didn't take long, did it now?"

"Can we go now, Dad?" Ian asked impatiently. "Can we go rent the car?"

Bauer steered the seven-year-old for the door. "How about some supper? You must be hungry; we haven't had a bite since breakfast."

"A candy bar will do me, Dad. I'm not much for this frog food. All that wine sauce, it don't taste like Mum's cookin'."

Bauer laughed. "It's a meat-and-potatoes man you are. Let's have some chips at least. And a soda."

"Can we eat it in the car, Dad?"

"You're just dyin' to get into the Chunnel, aren't you, boy? All right then, chips and Cokes to go. Mind you, don't tell Mum what I fed you for supper."

Forty-five minutes later, Bauer nosed their rented Renault into line at the Coquelles Shuttle Terminal eight miles south of Calais. He looked up at an electronic schedule board above the ticket booth four cars ahead.

"We're in luck, son. There'll be a train in about half an hour."

Ian sucked the last of his Coke through a chewed straw. "How long does it take to drive all these cars and trucks onto the train?"

"Oh, they're superefficient, ya know. The last time I was here, I shouldn't think it was more'n fifteen minutes from the time the train pulled in till we was rollin' into the Chunnel."

The seven-year-old looked at his watch. "That's forty-five minutes. In fifteen more we'll be under the middle of the Channel. You don't think that big berg's moved, do you, Dad?"

Bauer smiled. "It's a terrible worrywart you are. I'm sure that ice ain't moved a bloody inch."

But the berg had moved. The furious gale sweeping in from the Atlantic was pushing the ice up the Channel at almost a mile an hour.

Deep below the surface, the keel of the berg was slicing open the seafloor like a plough furrowing a field, its forward edge of iron-hard ice heading straight at the busy Chunnel dead ahead.

LONDON
• • • • • • • • •

6:05 p.m.

BRITISH PRIME MINISTER ALDIS Butler ignored his dinner of
lamb chops and buttered potatoes as he sat at the dining
room table at Number 10 Downing Street scanning the banner headline in the *Evening Standard*.

SUBMARINE VOLCANIC ERUPTION SINKS QE 3. 3,654 LOST AT
SEA.

As horrible as the news was, he knew the smaller headline
below portended far more dire days to come. NEW ATLANTIC
ISLAND EXPECTED TO CHANGE EUROPEAN WEATHER.

Butler tossed the paper on the table. "Expected to change,
my bloody ass," he mumbled to himself. If the secretary of
state for the environment were even half right, what was
coming would be nothing less than the most precipitous
drop in temperatures since the last ice age.

Butler had been in Riyadh, Saudi Arabia, the morning
before trying to talk King Faisal into lowering oil prices
when news of the eruption of R-9 and the loss of the *QE 3*
reached him.

He'd never forget the slight but unmistakably malevolent
grin that had crept over the face of the tall, hawk-nosed

Faisal when he'd learned the titanic eruption would send temperatures plummeting in the British Isles.

England would now be even more desperate for fuel to heat homes and factories. The Arab king had England by the neck, and he knew it.

His talks with the Saudis were critical and Butler hadn't arrived back in London until the next day. He'd immediately begun making condolence calls to the families of the passengers on the QE 3, then taped a reassuring television address to the country for the evening news. Afterward he conferred via videophone with President Herbert Allen in Washington and the German and French leaders.

In between there'd been frantic staff briefings and a call from Marjorie Glynn, head of the Biosphere Britannia project. Glynn's news that an American geothermal expert was on the way to England was the one spot of good news he'd had all day.

With British pleas to the Arabs for cheaper oil falling on deaf ears, the nation would now need an alternative source of energy more than ever. He'd readily agreed to Glynn's request for funding to restart drilling operations at North Channel, despite he wasn't sure yet which budgetary barrel he'd scrape to get the money.

With one thing and another, he hadn't had a moment to breathe since he'd stepped off the plane and his exhaustion showed in the deep lines in his distinguished sixty-four-year-old face.

Two soft raps on the dining room door interrupted his sour musing.

"Come."

"Good evening, Prime Minister."

"Evening, Smythe-Bruce," Butler said to his private secretary, a reed-thin man with an acne-scarred face and a bobbing Adam's apple. Owen Smythe-Bruce was obsequious to those in power and overbearing to those beneath him. Never married, his job was his entire life, and he guarded his privileges and perks with a fierce territorialism.

"Your Cabinet will assemble at six-thirty, sir," Smythe-

Bruce said, crossing the room with quick mincing steps that always reminded Butler of a mouse nibbling cheese.

"The whole mob?"

"No, sir. Several of the ministers are abroad. The chancellor of the exchequer and the secretaries of state for defense, energy, and the home department will be here. The secretary of state for the environment has already arrived."

"Tanner?" Butler glanced at a Chippendale grandfather clock in the corner. It was just after six. "Bit early, isn't he?"

Smythe-Bruce spread his hands palms up. "Rather, sir. He arrived twenty minutes ago and I could not dissuade him from rushing into the Cabinet Room with several aides. They've brought along slides and charts and Lord knows what else. It looks like a classroom at Eton in there."

Butler nodded. "Sir Geoffrey was quite beside himself when he rang me up. Warned we were all going to freeze in our beds."

"In my experience, these weather chaps are terrible alarmists, sir. Always predicting gales and blizzards that never seem to come off."

"Yes, well, any word what that press conference at the Trades Union Congress is all about?"

"No, sir, not yet. One of the ink-stained lads from Fleet Street has promised to call me as soon as it's over."

"Whatever General Secretary Phelps has to say, I don't think we'll like it."

"Phelps is nothing more than a mouthpiece for Seamus MacTiege, sir. There's no one in Britain doesn't know it."

Butler frowned. "If the polls are right, come the next election MacTiege will be forming the first Labor government in decades. We've got to turn this thing around, damn it, we can't have a scoundrel like MacTiege running Britain."

"He's worse than a scoundrel, sir. He's a bloody fascist. 'MacHitler,' as the tabloids like to headline."

As always, the thought of Seamus MacTiege in power agitated Butler and he rose and began to pace the room. "Can you imagine what it would mean to have MacTiege as prime minister?"

"God save us," Smythe-Bruce said.

"There'd be no one else to. And we thought the Tories were bad. I'd sooner have Thatcher back for another twelve years than have MacTiege as PM for twelve months."

Butler had helped form the Social Democrat Party in 1975 as a moderate alternative to the right of center Conservatives and the leftist Labor Party. He'd become prime minister following his party's election victory in 1996.

The same year, Seamus MacTiege had been elected to Parliament. Yet it wasn't until the former coal miner took over leadership of the Labor Party eighteen months ago that the Social Democrats realized this strange and strident outsider from Newcastle upon Tyne represented a very real political threat.

"MacTiege would still be sitting in some dusty office in Birmingham if it weren't for Windscale," Smythe-Bruce said down his nose.

Butler paused before a window overlooking the garden and stared out at the dormant rosebushes. Even today, four and a half years after the meltdown of the Windscale reactor, Englishmen and Irishmen continued to die from the lingering effects of radioactive poisoning.

"You lost family, as I recall, Smythe-Bruce."

"Yes sir, an aunt and two cousins in Devon."

"I'm very sorry."

"I've thought about it, sir. Perhaps they were lucky to go so quickly. A month, it was. It's the ones that linger on that suffer most."

Butler nodded wordlessly. "If it comes to war with Ireland, the casualties could dwarf Windscale. Every time we get another bellicose letter from their Defense Ministry, I think of that line, what is it, 'envy of the dead'?"

" 'Pity is for the living, envy is for the dead,' " Smythe-Bruce furnished.

"Yes."

"It's almost inconceivable," Smythe-Bruce said. "War with Ireland."

Butler turned from the window, his face stony. "Inconceivable? Good Lord, man, if you look at your history, we've been at war with them for centuries. Hardly a generation has passed since Henry the Second invaded Ireland in 1171 without Englishmen and Irishmen slaughtering each other. What the bloody hell do you think's been going on in Northern Ireland the past thirty years?"

Smythe-Bruce was taken aback by the emotion in the voice of the normally controlled Butler. "I meant a war between national armies, Prime Minister. Surely that would be a different thing from the terrorism in Ulster."

Butler flung himself down into a chair. "Men get killed by artillery shells and planes instead of sniper bullets and car bombs, is that what you mean?"

"No, sir. I was referring to the fact that we are dealing with an elected government in Dublin, responsible people, not IRA murderers who strike in the dead of night and hide in cellars."

Butler let out an exasperated sigh. "Are you unaware, Smythe-Bruce, that Sinn Fein, the political arm of the Irish Republican Army, is now the strongest party in Ireland? Thousands more flock to their banner every month."

"Yet the Fine Gael party still controls the government in Dublin, sir. From the diplomatic correspondence, Prime Minister O'Fiaich doesn't want war any more than we do."

"You're right there, Smythe-Bruce. She's a good woman, from what I know of her. Only met her once. Still, it's a question of how long she can hold out against the IRA saber rattlers. If she falls . . ." Butler left the sentence unfinished.

To have continued would have meant revealing to Smythe-Bruce the most closely held British secret since the Second World War. Only cabinet-level ministers and senior military officers knew that most of England's armed forces existed only on paper.

In the first months after the mid-Atlantic volcanism sent winter temperatures plummeting, the government had realized the futility of trying to maintain even a moderate-sized standing army and navy.

The snow-clogged roads forced the bulk of the troops to hole up in idle garrison duty, ice-covered runways kept RAF planes confined to their hangars, and the frozen seas trapped the ships of the Royal Navy in port.

With Windscale reparations to Ireland costing billions of pounds and tax revenues drying up as the worsening climate decimated the economy, England could no longer afford to feed, clothe, and house hundreds of thousands of idle men.

Whitehall made the decision to cut the armed forces down to a skeletal force of fifty thousand active duty personnel. Barely a third of these would be combat troops.

Still, the English lion could not present itself toothless to the world, and the demilitarization was kept secret from even the country's closest allies. While individual units were quietly mustered out, their barracks and equipment were maintained in place by small caretaker units. Specially trained radio operators even kept up what passed for normal communications between the mothballed bases and naval installations.

The paring down had taken eighteen months and had been so successfully disguised that the rest of the world continued to believe Britain's armed forces stood at nearly a quarter million men.

In fact, though the Irish didn't know it, they now had a larger and better equipped army than Britain. It was one of Prime Minister Butler's greatest fears that Irish militants would discover the truth and exploit England's weakness with a massive uprising in Northern Ireland. If that happened, there was little Britain could do to prevent a takeover.

"I'd best prepare for the meeting," Smythe-Bruce said. "With your leave."

The prime minister waved a hand and the secretary turned and left the room. Butler sat back at the table, stared at his cold dinner a moment, then pushed the plate away. War looming, the fuel-starved economy in shambles, and now the climate to get even colder.

"I should have stayed in the bloody Navy," the prime minister mumbled to himself, then sighed and dug into the pile of official papers on the table.

Fifteen minutes later he strode into the Cabinet Room, nodding to the ministers as they rose in deference. "Good evening. I'd like to start with a moment of silence in memory of the thousands of souls lost aboard the *QE Three*."

The ministers bowed their heads around the long, rectangular Cabinet table, then Butler sat down. "There will be a period of national mourning, of course. I have directed the Navy to make all attempts to recover bodies, although from the circumstances described to me it is unlikely we will find many."

"Had we no way of predicting this volcano would erupt, sir?" the chancellor of the exchequer, Malcolm Fulbright, asked, looking pointedly at the secretary of state for the environment.

Sir Geoffrey Tanner bristled. "Until early yesterday morning, R-Nine was thirty meters below the surface. At that depth, the volcano did not pose an immediate threat to shipping."

"Or so you thought," Fulbright said.

"We were hardly as cavalier about the danger as your tone implies, Malcolm. Damn it all, we did send out an advisory for vessels not to steam within five kilometers of R-Nine. That distance provided a safe margin when the volcano was only sending up ash and smoke."

"Gentlemen, this is all fruitless speculation. We have more urgent matters on the agenda," Butler said impatiently. "Geoffrey, I want to know what this volcanic eruption is going to do to our weather."

"The past three years have given us only a taste of what's coming, Prime Minister. As we're all painfully aware, ever since the volcanism along the Mid-Atlantic Ridge began diverting the bottom waters of the North Atlantic Drift back in 'ninety-seven, air temperatures in these islands have been dropping precipitously."

"Surely it can't get any colder." Malcolm Fulbright shook his head. "Good God, who would have dreamed the bloody Channel and the Irish Sea could freeze over?"

"That is only a portent of things to come," Tanner said. For the next ten minutes, he used the charts his aides had set up behind his chair to point out the changed course of the

North Atlantic Drift, and the path of the ash- and gas-laden winds over Britain.

Finally he paused and looked around the table. "I must tell the Cabinet that if my climatologists are right, from this day forward Britain will be entirely surrounded by sea ice up to five months of the year."

There was a shocked silence in the room.

"We've been able to open shipping lanes in the Channel with icebreakers," the prime minister said finally. "Surely we can continue this."

"That is highly unlikely, Prime Minister. Not only will the floes thicken, but there are dozens of icebergs that drifted down from the Arctic last spring and never melted. My computer projections forecast the winds from the west will drive more and more of these large bergs into the Channel."

The secretary of state for defense shifted uneasily in his chair. "What are those projections based on, Sir Geoffrey?" James Litchfield asked.

"The decline in warmth from our two principal thermal benefactors, the North Atlantic Drift and the sun," Tanner said. "The loss of warmth from the ocean current has lowered the mean temperature in these islands some ten degrees. That heat loss alone is enough to allow the formation of winter sea ice."

The Cabinet members shifted uneasily in their chairs.

Tanner picked up a fact sheet from among the papers before him. "According to preliminary satellite observations, the volcanic clouds now approaching Britain contain enough debris and gases to block out fully ninety percent of the solar heat normally reaching the ground. This will lower temperatures a further ten degrees."

"How long will these volcanic clouds block out our sunlight?" Ralph Merriweather asked.

"There is no way of knowing," Tanner said. "The hot spot beneath R-Nine is one of the most volcanically active regions on earth. The eruptions could continue for months, years, decades."

Merriweather took off his thick bifocal glasses and tiredly massaged the bridge of his large aquiline nose. "Have you considered, Sir Geoffrey, what a twenty-degree drop in temperature will do to our agriculture?"

Tanner nodded dejectedly. "Over the past three years we have seen the worsening cold and the loss of solar radiation make growing crops in England and Ireland increasingly difficult. Come the spring, farming as we know it will be literally impossible. Agriculture in the rest of the Northern Hemisphere will be affected as well, of course. Several of our top climatologists have told me every country in the northern latitudes will soon be plunged into a volcanic winter."

Merriweather was red-faced now. "I don't give a pig's ass about other countries. I want to know what foodstuffs we can still raise here. Good God, we can't import every morsel we eat. There's not the money, there's not the means."

"Our growing season will be too short and too cold to continue cultivation of the grains, fruits, and vegetables we plant now," Tanner said.

Secretary of State for Energy Nanette Dupont stared across the Cabinet table at Tanner, a look of disbelief on her attractive face. "We are facing famine, then, Sir Geoffrey."

Tanner nodded a silent yes.

"There is one hope," Prime Minister Butler said.

"And that is?" Fulbright said.

"Biosphere Britannia."

"That huge greenhouse we funded three years ago?" Merriweather scoffed. "You propose to feed these islands from a greenhouse?"

"Not a single biosphere, Ralph, but hundreds of them," Butler said evenly.

Secretary for Defense Litchfield pushed himself back in his chair. "Assuming we can raise enough food within these biospheres to feed the country, Prime Minister, what about sheltering the population? The past three years have proved our present dwellings are woefully inadequate. And now the climate's to get even colder."

"Each biosphere will have a human habitat as well as an agricultural wing," Butler said. "From what I've seen of the plans, there will be room for housing, shops, even light industry."

"We'll have to provide these biospheres with heat and power," Ralph Merriweather said. "Where's the energy to come from?"

"Oil's out of the question," the chancellor of the exchequer said. "Our North Sea field has virtually ceased to exist. Drilling platforms, pumping stations, even the seafloor pipelines have been smashed to pieces by drifting icebergs. And we can't afford to import a tenth of the oil we need, even if we could get the tankers through the ice surrounding these islands."

"What about nuclear power?" Merriweather said. "From what I understand, it supplies most of the energy needs of France."

Fulbright shook his head and frowned. "Frankly, I'm astonished you'd even make the suggestion. After Windscale, the people won't hear of building any more nuclear plants on British soil. No, gentlemen, I see no other alternative to coal."

"Then you'll see Seamus MacTiege sitting in this chair." Butler bristled. "No, there is one other answer to our worsening energy crisis: geothermal."

"We've been down that road, Prime Minister," Nanette Dupont said. "Seamus MacTiege blocked funding for geothermal two years ago. What makes you think he won't do the same thing again?"

"I don't intend to go to Parliament, Nan, not at first in any case. As prime minister, I have enough discretionary funds to at least get the North Channel project restarted. If we can actually begin producing energy up there, MacTiege will not find it so easy this time to stop Parliament from financing further development."

"Even if we succeed in bringing geothermal energy on line, there is still the astronomical cost of constructing hundreds of these biospheres to consider," Fulbright said. "Surely it will run to hundreds of billions of pounds."

"I have only the cost of raising the first Biosphere Britannia to go by at the moment," Butler said. "However, if we extrapolate the figures, building hundreds of these mini-earths will take approximately the same percentage of our gross national product as did the waging of World War Two."

"Then we face rationing, food lines, shortages of all kinds," Fulbright said.

"Let me be clear, gentlemen," Butler said. "Sixty years ago we were attacked by the Huns and forced to fight for our very survival. Today, it is the forces of the earth itself that are marshaled against us. We will either triumph, or Britain will become a frozen, underpopulated land as impotent in the scheme of international events as Siberia or Greenland."

The Cabinet Room door opened and Smythe-Bruce hurried across and handed a note to the prime minister. Butler's face paled as he scanned the paper. Slowly he crumpled the sheet into a tight ball and looked up at his ministers. "I have just been informed that the Trades Union Congress is threatening to call a general strike. Coal miners, factory workers, public employees, they'll all walk out at six o'clock tomorrow night unless the government agrees to an immediate twenty-percent wage increase."

A chorus of angry indignation swept the room. "We all know Seamus MacTiege is behind this, the bloody bastard," Sir Geoffrey Tanner exploded. "He'll drive the country to ruin."

"We ought to hang the ugly beggar," James Litchfield thundered, smashing his fist down on the Cabinet table.

"Enough of that," Butler said, his voice calm despite the rage and fear boiling inside him. He turned to Secretary Dupont. "What are our fuel reserves, Nan?"

"Seventeen days, Prime Minister," Dupont said softly. "If the strike takes hold, by February twentieth there won't be a lump of coal or a drop of oil left in England."

COQUELLES, FRANCE
● ● ● ● ● ● ● ● ● ● ● ● ● ● ● ● ● ● ● ●

6:50 p.m.

GALE WINDS WERE LASHING the Chunnel terminal at Coquelles with almost horizontal sheets of snow, obscuring the
entrance to Running Tunnel North two hundred yards
ahead down the track.

A French traffic-control officer, his blue uniform plastered
with snow, fought to stay on his feet as he waved the rented
Renault onto the top level of the last car on the double-deck
shuttle train.

Seven-year-old Ian Bauer looked around excitedly as his
father followed three other cars and a van onto the shuttle.
"It's like a long room in here," he said to his father, rolling
down his window and craning his neck out to inspect the
beige interior of the gleaming rail car.

Waist-high handrails were fastened to each side of the
shuttle beneath large windows set three feet apart. The Renault's tires rested on diagonal yellow nonskid strips that
ran the length of the sixty-foot-long rectangle. The space was
brightly lit by twin rows of foot-square lights recessed into
the low ceiling above.

"Prepare for departure," an electrified voice advised in

French from a speaker midway down the shuttle, repeating the caution in English and German.

"Here we go, son," Ray Bauer said.

A moment later the wide auto entrance door behind them shut and the shuttle train began to move forward down the seamless tracks. Ian watched the snow swirl against the windows, then suddenly there were curving walls close beyond the glass.

The boy turned bright-eyed to his father. "We're in the Chunnel, Dad."

Twenty miles out from the French coast at Coquelles, the fierce gale winds continued to push the iceberg northeast through the Pas de Calais, its immense bulk smashing steadily through the floes before it.

One hundred and five feet below the seabed, the frozen keel of the berg sliced deep through the sediment layering the dark floor of the Channel.

The submerged bow of the ice was now within a hundred yards of Running Tunnel South, the first of the three Chunnel tubes. The weight of the huge plateau of ice above crushed the seabed downward as the berg advanced, splitting open the chalk layer below it. A latticework of rapidly widening cracks reached ever closer to the long concrete cylinder dead ahead.

At His Majesty's Coast Guard station in Dover, the radar supervisor on duty paused before the station of the technician monitoring the Pas de Calais. "Everything all right?" Lieutenant George Russell asked of the young radarman on duty.

"Quiet as a morgue, sir."

"Yes, I expect that small convoy to Calais this afternoon will be the last shipping until the ice breaks up next spring."

"If then, sir. That big berg out there could go aground again and block the shipping lanes right through the summer."

"Let's hope not," the lieutenant said, turning to continue his rounds. He suddenly stopped and looked down at the radar screen. "What do you mean, 'go aground again'? Isn't it still fast off Hastings?"

The radarman pointed at a large white blip the sweeping radar radius had just left behind on the screen. "No, sir, the gale's broken it loose. The berg's drifting up through the Pas de Calais."

Though he wasn't sure why, Russell felt a sudden pang of trepidation. "Why didn't you notify me?"

"I didn't see the need, sir. There's no ships out there it could harm, and it's well away from land."

The lieutenant watched the radar arm sweep around and again leave the white blip of the berg behind on the green screen.

What the radarman said made perfect sense. There was nothing out there the berg could threaten. Still, an ominous foreboding nagged at the corners of Russell's mind.

"Very well, then, Higgins, carry on," he said. "Would you fancy a cup of tea?"

"That I would, sir." The radarman smiled. "I'm still half frozen from my drive to work. The bloody heater in my car couldn't keep up with that cold gale wind."

Russell turned for the station's small kitchen. "I'll put the kettle on then."

Out in the Channel, the berg had now split open the seafloor to within yards of Running Tunnel South. Tons of foaming seawater were plunging into the deepening fractures in the chalk floor of the Channel, cascading down on the suddenly exposed concrete tube of the tunnel below.

Lieutenant Russell poured boiling water into the porcelain teapot in the radar-station kitchen. He couldn't shake the nagging feeling that there was something about the drifting iceberg he should remember. It'll come, he told himself as he put the pot, two cups, and sugar and cream containers on a tray and turned for the radar room.

There was nothing, nothing at all out in the Channel for the berg to threaten, he reminded himself as he crossed the threshold. All ships were now safely in port, their cargoes transferred to freight trains for transport through the Chunnel.

Thank God for the Chunnel. If it weren't for the rail tunnels under the sea, England would have only an air link to the rest of Europe.

Russell suddenly stopped in midstep, the tray of tea things slipping from his hands to crash loudly to the floor beside him.

Radarman Higgins snapped his head around. "You all right, sir?"

"The Chunnel," Russell said, white-faced, dashing across the room to the radar screen. "How high is that berg?"

"High, sir?"

"Yes, from the waterline up."

Higgins looked at the calibrations at the side of the screen as the radar arm swept around again. "Approximately thirty-one feet, sir. Why?"

"Because only one-ninth the total height of a berg shows above water."

"You mean to say there's two hundred and seventy feet of ice beneath the sea?"

"Yes. And the Channel's only one hundred thirty to one hundred eighty feet deep through most of the Pas de Calais. That berg's slicing open the seafloor at least ninety feet below the bottom."

Russell jerked the phone off its cradle on the console before Higgins and rang the station operator. "Lieutenant Russell here. I have a Code Red emergency. Put me through to the Chunnel operations center in Folkestone immediately."

"Operations, Timmons here," a voice answered a moment later.

"This is Lieutenant George Russell at HM Coast Guard headquarters, Dover."

"Yes, Lieutenant."

"You've got to shut down the Chunnel immediately, Timmons. Halt the trains going in."

"What's this all about?"

"There is a huge iceberg moving up the Pas de Calais. It's going to pass directly over the Chunnel."

"Look, old chap, I don't see what all the fuss is about. The Channel's been full of floes and great chunks of ice for the past two winters."

Russell felt his jaw clench in frustration. "This is not a 'chunk' of ice, Timmons. It's a bloody iceberg several miles across. From what's sticking up, there's got to be nearly two hundred and seventy feet of it beneath the waterline."

"That's hardly possible," Timmons said. "The Pas de Calais isn't that deep."

"That's exactly my point. The bottom of the ice must be tearing open the seabed as the berg drifts ahead."

The reality of what was happening suddenly struck the operations chief. "Dear God."

"You've got to shut her down, man. Don't let another train in."

Timmons's eyes darted to the large digitized operations board on the wall. There were two trains in the Chunnel, each longer than eight football fields. A freight train was in the Running Tunnel South and a car shuttle just out of Coquelles was headed north toward Britain in the parallel tube.

"Which direction is the berg coming from?"

"The west," Russell said.

"That means it'll pass over Running Tunnel South first," Timmons said. "How close is it?"

"The top of the berg is perhaps a quarter mile away. But it's what's below water we've got to worry about. If there's a submerged bow out ahead of it, the ice could be literally within yards of the Chunnel."

Timmons's forehead broke out in a cold sweat. "I'll get back to you, Lieutenant," he said, slamming the phone down in its cradle to break the connection, then immediately picking it up again. He dialed the trackmaster at the Folkestone Chunnel entrance.

"Trackmaster here."

"This is Timmons in operations. Stop all trains immediately. No more through until you get the all clear from me."

"Stop the trains? This time of day, we'll have the rails jammed all the way back to London."

"Can't be helped. Just do it."

Timmons picked up the direct phone to his counterpart across the Channel in France. "Coquelles operations," a voice with a heavy French accent answered.

"Jacques, is that you?"

"Yes, hello Robert."

"Jacques, we have an emergency," Timmons said, telling the Frenchman of the huge iceberg headed for the Chunnel.

"I wish you'd called ten minutes ago," Jacques said. "We've just had a full passenger-car shuttle go in."

"At least they're in the northbound tube, Jacques. It's Running Tunnel South that will take the ice first."

"My board shows a freight train from Scotland nearing the middle of the tunnel," Jacques said. "Maybe we should radio him to stop and back up to Folkestone."

"No, that would take too long. We've got to get him out fast. I'm going to order the engineer to increase speed. It's the only chance he's got."

"Very well, Robert. Keep me advised."

Timmons put down the phone and hurried over to the communications set that would patch him through to the engineer on the freight train in Running Tunnel South.

"Engineer here."

Timmons recognized the voice. It was old Bill Munson. "This is Timmons in Folkestone operations. That you, Bill?"

"Aye, it's me."

"We've got rather a problem, Bill. What's your speed?"

"I ain't breakin' no limits, gov'nor. I'm right at a hundred and twenty kilometers an hour."

"You don't understand, Bill. I want you to pour it on. Give her everything she's got."

"What?" the engineer said suspiciously. "Last time you rang me up, you said I was goin' too bloody fast. You certain this is Timmons?"

"I assure you it's me, Bill. I haven't time to explain, but we want to clear the Chunnel as quickly as possible. What's your top speed?"

"Jesus, I don't know. Depends on the load. I got eighty cars behind me. Maybe I can get her up near a hundred and fifty kilometers an hour."

"Do it."

Four miles ahead of the freight train, torrents of muddy seawater were steadily washing away the earth and rocks surrounding Running Tunnel South. Within moments, a hundred-yard-long section of tunnel was undermined.

The terrible sounds of steel rings stretching then snapping echoed down the inside of the tunnel as the tube sagged into the sudden vacuum below it. Unsupported by the seabed, the concrete cylinder couldn't hold together and a fifty-foot length of tunnel suddenly collapsed downward.

A flood of freezing seawater rushed into the cylinder of air, splashing madly back from the curving walls and racing down the tunnel in both directions.

In the Folkestone operations center, the tunnel failure alarm went off, its piercing scream echoing shrilly off the close walls. Timmons stared up in horror at the board as the location of the tunnel break flashed on the control screen. The failure was at number 17 milepost. Seawater was coming in ahead of the train!

For a moment, Timmons couldn't tear his eyes away from the board. The small bulbs marking quarter-mile lengths of tracks were blinking off one by one. He suddenly realized the circuits were shorting out as the seawater coursed down the tunnel toward the train now just two miles away.

Timmons chewed the inside of his cheek. Should he tell Bill? Tell him he had only seconds to live? No, Jesus, the old man would spend the last moments of his life suffering the horror of what was coming. Let it be sudden.

"You've got a vacation due you, don't you, Bill?"

"What's this, you want to talk about my vacation? I thought there was a problem with the tunnel."

Timmons gripped the edge of his desk, fighting to keep his voice normal. "It's going to resolve itself, Bill. Where are you going on holiday?"

"Greece. Me and the missus is takin' the Orient Express all the way."

Two more bulbs went out. The water was a mile and a half from the train now.

"Greece is it. Sunshine and ruins."

"They can shove them marble columns up their arses. It's the sun I want. At my age, the cold gets right inside your bones."

Three more bulbs went dead. The rushing wall of water and the speeding train were now three-quarters of a mile apart.

"You're not so old, Bill," Timmons said, his voice beginning to break.

"Horseshit. I'm sixty-four and feelin' every day of it."

There were only two bulbs still burning now.

"You may be sixty-four but you're the best engineer on the Chunnel run, Bill."

"I hold my own, I'm proud of that. I haven't missed a day in . . . what's this? There's something in my lights up the track."

The last bulb went out and Timmons closed his eyes.

"It's water," Bill screamed. "Jesus God, the tunnel's flooded ahead."

Timmons could hear a hellish roaring sound building in the background.

"Bill . . ."

"Not like this . . . Dear God, not—"

Bill's scream was cut short by the sound of the locomotive's windows smashing inward as the wall of water racing through the tunnel exploded against the front of the train. For an instant, there was the hellish noise of metal and fiberglass tearing apart, then the radiophone went mercifully dead.

A second alarm went off almost at once and Timmons

snapped his reddened eyes back up at the control board. The seawater was beginning to leak into Running Tunnel North through the pressure relief ducts, twenty-four-inch-wide tubes that connected the ceilings of the two main bores.

He looked at the train locater screen. The passenger-car shuttle from Coquelles had just passed the midway point in Running Tunnel North. The train would be sprayed by seawater as it passed beneath the pressure ducts, but the tunnel itself would flood behind the shuttle. They still had a chance.

Timmons put through a call to the engineer on the shuttle. Nothing. The line was dead. The water had probably leaked into the service tube between the two main tunnels and knocked out the radio relay.

He knew Running Tunnel North would flood within minutes now. Once the deluge began, it would be a race up the tracks between the shuttle and the water surging through the tube behind it.

Ian Bauer pointed through the windshield of the Renault at the tunnel walls passing by in a blur as the shuttle sped toward England at over seventy miles an hour. "The train sure is a tight fit in here, Dad."

His father smiled. "Yes, they've engineered it close all right. Every inch more space they bored through the seabed meant tons of rock and earth they had to cart out. They designed the trains to take up nearly all the tunnel as they go through."

The train passed under a pressure relief duct and Ian suddenly started as the curving wall outside seemed to gleam for a moment in the lights of the passing shuttle. "Dad, I think there was water coming down the wall back there," he said, turning in the seat to stare through the rear window.

"It's just your imagination, son. The lights play funny tricks in here. The Chunnel's perfectly waterproof."

"Yeah, I guess so, Dad," the boy said. He turned around in the seat and glanced back toward the shuttle window beside the car. For a moment he stared at the glass, then he turned back to his father, his seven-year-old eyes big and round.

"It's not my imagination, Dad. Look."

Ray Bauer sighed and humored his son, leaning past the boy to look at the window. In an instant the half smile froze on his face. There was water streaking down the outside of the window. A couple in the car ahead of them had seen it too. They climbed out of their Volkswagen and approached a window just as the train sped under another duct. Water hit the outside of the glass with a loud slap and the two jumped back in fright.

Passengers in the other cars began to get out to see what the commotion was about. A fat woman in a checkered coat and snow boots suddenly noticed the water streaking down the windows and screamed. "Oh God, the tunnel's flooding. We're goin' to drown like rats."

Ian started to open his door but his father reached out a restraining hand. "No, son. Stay in the car. Whatever's comin', we're safer in here."

A half mile behind the shuttle, the wall of Running Tunnel North burst inward and a deluge of freezing seawater raced up the tunnel behind the train. The incredible pressure of the sea above shot the water down the concrete tube as if it were a blast from a huge hose.

The flood built to twice the speed of the train and within moments the wall of water slammed into the back of the shuttle. The train lurched forward down the tracks, pitching the passengers who'd left their cars against the floor of the shuttle.

Ray Bauer pulled his son across the seat and held him tight against his chest. "I love you, Ian," he yelled against the roaring of the water behind them.

Rivulets of seawater were now running down the windows but the clearance of only inches between the train and the tunnel walls kept most of the flood back behind the last car.

In the operations center, Robert Timmons stared up at the control board in disbelief. He could tell by the bulbs blinking out that the tunnel was flooding right behind the train. But the train hadn't been stopped. He glanced at the speed indicator. Jesus, the shuttle was going almost 120 miles an hour.

Then it hit him. The huge jet of water behind the shuttle was driving the train forward like a high-pressure hose blasting debris through a pipe. His eyes darted to the position monitor. The train was only three miles from the Chunnel exit at Folkestone.

When the shuttle came out the tunnel mouth, there'd be no way the engineer could stop it, not with the tremendous water pressure driving it forward from behind. Timmons picked up the phone and stabbed at the buttons.

"Trainmaster."

"This is Timmons. Get on the loudspeaker and order everybody away from the entrance to Running Tunnel North. Tell them to drop everything and run as fast as they can."

"It'll take a few—"

"Now, damn it. The shuttle from Coquelles will be through in less than a minute. It can't stop. It's going to fly out the Chunnel mouth at over a hundred and twenty miles an hour."

"Bloody hell. He'll never be able to stop her before the Folkestone curve. She'll leave the tracks."

"I know," Timmons said, lowering the phone. "I know."

The shuttle was a mile from the tunnel entrance now and beginning to hydroplane as a tongue of water from the huge jet behind snaked under the carriages. The top of the cars scraped the tunnel ceiling, slicing open a long crack in the metal.

Ray Bauer clutched his terrified son to his chest as water cascaded down on the windshield of the Renault. He suddenly felt the angle of the tracks increase upward. He'd ridden the shuttle enough times to know they were about to reach the exit at Folkestone.

Thank God, we'll be out in a minute, he thought. Then he re-

membered the sharp bend in the tracks beyond the station.
Sweet Jesus, they'd never be able to stop in time. He suddenly realized they were sitting four feet from a full tank of gasoline.

He snaked his hand down into his pocket and felt for the small seaman's knife he always carried. If the tank exploded when they hit, he wouldn't let his boy burn to death. He'd end it quickly for Ian.

At the Folkestone tunnel entrance, train crews and rail workers were fleeing the northbound track as the loudspeaker warning was repeated over and over. "Evacuate the rail area immediately. Evacuate the rail area immediately."

In the operations center, Robert Timmons stared at the locater board. The train was only half a mile from the tunnel entrance now. He tore his eyes away and raced across the operations center to a window overlooking the tunnel exit.

For a long moment the swirling snow blocked his view. Then the wind shifted and he stood transfixed as a huge spray of water erupted from the mouth of Running Tunnel North. A split second later the shuttle rocketed out, seawater streaming off its sides as it roared through the station complex at over 110 miles an hour.

Long strips of metal were torn from the sides of the train as it ricocheted off the lip of the station platform. Then the last rail car cleared the entrance and a torrent of seawater jetted out behind, the pressurized stream arcing out a quarter mile into the rail yard.

Tracks and parked rail cars flew into the air as the huge hose of freezing water scoured the yard, washing away anything in its path. Timmons felt the building tremble as a wave of water surged across the terminal complex and slammed into the first floor of the operations center.

The shuttle raced on down the tracks, released from the terrible pressure of the water behind it but still unable to stop. Timmons watched a blizzard of sparks shoot up from the train's wheels as the engineer jammed the brakes on full.

The Folkestone curve was only two hundred yards ahead

down the tracks. The shuttle was slowing, but not enough. Timmons sank his teeth into his bottom lip, tasting blood. She wasn't going to make it.

A hundred yards now. The rail cars were beginning to telescope into each other as their locked steel wheels screeched against the tracks below. Fifty yards. The last two cars suddenly jumped the tracks, snapping their links to the train ahead and careening off into the deep snow bordering the right of way. They rolled over once, twice, then came to a stop on their sides fifty yards from the tracks.

The rest of the shuttle raced on down the track, heading into the curve at over eighty miles an hour, the remaining rail cars leaning outward as they hit the sharp bend. A moment later the locomotive left the tracks, pulling the cars behind off after it.

The shuttle smashed into the concrete embankment flanking the curve in a raucous cacophony of screaming metal and shattering concrete. The violent sound wave shot back across the rail yard, vibrating the window glass before the horrified Timmons.

Then the gas tanks on the smashed cars inside the train began to explode and the twisted wreckage of the shuttle from Coquelles disappeared beneath a towering ball of fire.

LONDON

● ● ● ● ● ● ● ● ●

9:15 a.m.—February 5
British Fuel Reserves—16 Days

MARJORIE GLYNN SLAMMED HER palm against the steering wheel of her Morris Minor car in mounting frustration as the traffic on the snowy approaches to Heathrow Airport came to a dead stop for the tenth time in the last few minutes.

"Bloody fools. Where do they think they're all going?"

Richard Booroojian stared out at the bumper-to-bumper line of cars and buses. "Anywhere, so long as it's south. When that berg crushed the Chunnel last night, the panic really set in. The only way out now is by plane."

"Did you see the television coverage from Folkestone?" Marjorie asked. "The BBC had a live camera right there at the tunnel mouth."

"I watched for a while, then I turned it off. All those burned bodies twisted up in the wreckage of that train."

"At least a few survived."

"Yes, I saw that before I turned the telly off last night. I don't know how anyone could have lived through the hammering they must have taken when those last two cars flew off the tracks."

"I was watching as I dressed this morning," Marjorie said. "They found two more survivors just after dawn, a young red-haired boy and his father. The newsreader said they'd suffered deep cuts and fractures, but they were both going to make it. I cried watching them being loaded into an ambulance."

"England's going to need more miracles like that when the ash clouds arrive tomorrow," Richard said. "It's hard to believe it could get any colder, but it will."

"The hoarding's already started," Marjorie said. "There've been long lines in front of every butcher shop and greengrocer we've passed this morning."

"It will get worse," Richard predicted. "If you think it's been bad the past three years, just wait. In a week you won't be able to buy a warm coat or a pair of mittens."

"We can manufacture clothes, and with rationing we should have enough food to make it through to spring," Marjorie said. "It's our fuel reserves I'm worried about. Things were bad enough and now the miners and the other unions are threatening to walk out on strike."

A chauffeured Bentley cut them off and Marjorie hit her horn in fury. "Bloody bore."

Richard jabbed a finger at the $120,000 car ahead of them. "The rich won't waste any time getting out."

"And taking their money with them."

"Our economy is going to be a shambles, Marjorie. Capital dried up, factories without fuel, the best minds in technology and commerce fleeing to the Commonwealth countries and America."

The wind parted the swirling snow for a moment and Marjorie spotted the turnoff for Heathrow ahead. "There it is, thank God."

The two fell into melancholy silence the rest of the way to the parking garage at Heathrow. Marjorie locked the Morris and they walked through the tunnel into the main terminal.

There were long lines in front of every airline counter. The normal airport mix of business and holiday travelers had been replaced by a motley throng of anxious evacuees. As they shuffled slowly forward, the refugees pushed along cardboard boxes and shopping bags hastily crammed with clothes and keepsakes from their homes.

Children with frightened eyes clung close by their parents, some kneeling to console cats and dogs whining from their travel cases.

A woman in a soiled cloth coat and rubber boots cut in front of Marjorie and Richard as they walked toward the arrivals board. Marjorie bumped into the woman and a loud chime sounded incongruously from a large Leatherette sack slung over her back.

"Mind where you walk," the woman scolded. "You might've broken Granddad's clock."

Richard cocked an eyebrow at Marjorie as the woman wandered toward the Quantas Airlines counter, muttering grumpily about "clumsy nobs."

"It's a wonder she isn't taking her bed with her," he said.

"Where do you suppose she's going?"

Richard shrugged. "Probably has relatives somewhere abroad. Canada perhaps, or Australia."

"God, it's depressing," Marjorie said. "How many thousands, millions like her will flee England?"

"I shouldn't give up on our countrymen yet, Marjorie. There's still Biosphere Britannia. There's still hope that people can live in England and Ireland, no matter how hostile our climate becomes."

"Quite right, Richard, but nothing will be possible without geothermal power. And that means all our eggs are in the basket of Dr. Benjamin Franklin Meade. Did you say he called you from Iceland?"

"Yes, he's on flight eight twenty-seven." Richard looked up at the arrivals board. "His plane's late. Won't be landing for another hour."

"I'm not surprised, with all this snow. Well, I could do with a cup of coffee."

"And a sandwich," Richard said. "I'm famished."

They waited twenty minutes until a table was finally available in a small cafe halfway down the concourse.

"Tell me about Benjamin Franklin Meade," Marjorie said after they'd ordered. "You worked with him up at North Channel two years ago. What's he like?"

"He's quite a fascinating fellow, actually," Richard said.

"Grew up mucking about in the geothermal hot springs around his home in the American state of Wyoming. That's what got him interested in geology."

"Wyoming. 'Where the buffalo roam, and the skies are not cloudy all day,' " Marjorie singsonged. "Is he one of those laconic Westerners, then? 'Howdy, ma'am, help you down off your horse?' "

Richard laughed. "Hardly. He's terribly sharp." A perplexed look came over Booroojian's face. "Except the other night when I called him. The radio transmission was abominable, interference from all the volcanic debris in the air, I suppose, but there was a moment or two when I could have sworn he was drunk."

"Drunk?"

Booroojian shrugged. "It was my imagination, I'm sure. Ben was awfully upset about the loss of life on the *Queen*; that could have been it."

"What's his mind like?" Marjorie asked.

"He's a brilliant earth scientist, a Ph.D. geophysicist cross-trained in oceanography and climatology."

"And he's a millionaire."

"Many times over. His company, Meade International, is the most successful developer of geothermal power in the world."

"Married?"

Richard grinned. "I was wondering when you'd ask that."

"Really, Richard. I'm curious, is all."

"He's divorced. Touchy subject with Ben, by the way."

"I don't imagine it will come up," Marjorie said defensively. "My interest in Benjamin Meade is as a geophysicist. Period."

"Of course. Still, he is a rather handsome chap, you know."

Marjorie snatched a breakfast roll and winged it at Richard's head.

Forty minutes later the two heard the announcement of the arrival of Icelandic Airlines flight 827 from Reykjavik. "He'll have to clear customs," Richard said. "Might as well have another cup of coffee."

As they walked toward the customs area, a man at the TWA counter began yelling at the ticket clerk. "You've got to get me on that flight," he screamed in a Midwestern American accent. "You're all going to freeze to death. Not me, damn it, I'm not one of you. I want off this fucking island."

"Yankee charm," Marjorie said dryly. "I hope he's not a foretaste of what we can expect from your Dr. Meade."

"Ben's flying in, Marjorie, not out."

Ten minutes later Richard pointed to a tall, sandy-haired man in jeans and a leather flight jacket emerging from the customs exit. "There he is."

At six feet, four inches, Benjamin Franklin Meade towered above most of the other passengers. Yet it wasn't just his height that made him stand out from the crowd. Even from a distance, Marjorie could sense the man with the high forehead and intense blue eyes had a powerful presence about him.

Meade spotted Richard, flashed a wide, even-toothed grin and started toward them.

Marjorie stared transfixed at the reaction of the people between them. Meade didn't push, or jostle, or shout a warning to get out of his way, yet the throng in his path parted like the Red Sea before Moses.

Richard laughed. "I'd almost forgotten. No one I know crosses a room like Ben Meade."

The man had an immanence like a physical force, Marjorie thought, a crackling field of energy that people could sense coming on the backs of their necks.

At the same time, Ben was no more aware of his effect on people than a browsing bull notices the grasshoppers scrambling out of the way of its massive muzzle.

Marjorie burst into laughter as a fat man in a deplorable wig was swept suddenly through an open ladies' room door by the surge of people getting out of Ben's path.

Ben stopped before them, a quizzical grin on his face. "Hello, Richard." He looked at Marjorie. "You going to let me in on the joke?"

"How are you, Ben?" Richard grinned, shaking hands.

"This merry lady with me is Marjorie Glynn, head of our Biosphere Britannia project."

Ben hadn't expected the director of Biosphere Britannia to be so young. Early thirties, he guessed. He'd had a mental picture of a scientific spinster, a fifty-year-old woman with thick glasses, a pinched mouth, and her hair in a bun.

Instead Marjorie was pretty, with wide-set green eyes, a strong but feminine nose, and wavy auburn hair. She was wearing a forest-green wool suit under her camel-hair overcoat and a single strand of pearls at her neck. Class, he thought.

Marjorie regained control. "I'm terribly sorry, Dr. Meade, but you see—"

A shriek from the ladies' room interrupted her. It was followed by a high-pitched woman's voice. "Get out of here at once, you huge pervert."

"Madam, I assure you—" The fat man came flying back out the door, minus his hairpiece.

"And take your hedgehog with you." The wig came sailing out, catching the red-faced fat man full in the chest.

Marjorie collapsed in laughter against Ben. The ludicrousness of her position, roaring into the chest of a man she'd just met, only made her laugh the harder.

Ben's back was to the scene in front of the ladies' room. He had no idea what Marjorie was laughing at. He looked at Richard. "You two been having cocktails?"

"Isn't she fun?"

"I am not fun," Marjorie managed, still laughing as she pulled back from Ben.

"I'm sorry to hear that," Ben said.

"I mean I don't normally greet people howling like a hyena," she said, wiping the laughter tears from the corners of her eyes.

She put out her hand. "Shall we start over? I'm very pleased to meet you, Dr. Meade."

"Call me Ben," he said.

"Ben, then. And I'm Marjorie."

"If you'll give me your claim check, Ben, I'll retrieve your bags," Richard said.

Ben hoisted the valise in his hand. "This is it, Richard, underwear and socks. I wasn't expecting to come to England. All I had on board the *Abyss* were jeans and workshirts, and most of those are mildewed."

Marjorie smiled. Here was a man who could afford a closet full of hand-tailored suits and he traveled about with only a small kit of underthings. She liked that about him.

"Well, shall we go, then?" Richard said. "We have a lot to talk about. And I know Marjorie would like to show you around Biosphere Britannia."

They passed a bar on the way out and for a moment Ben had an intense desire to make some excuse and dash in for a couple of quick belts. *Knock it off, asshole,* he chided himself. *Your drinking days are over.*

As they drove out the entrance to Heathrow, he glanced through the window at the towering snowbanks flanking the road. "I'm amazed you can still get around over here with all the blizzards you've had already this year."

"Plows have kept most of the main highways open in London and the other major cities," Richard said. "But out in the country the roads drift over faster than they can be cleared. Many of the smaller towns and villages are completely cut off."

"Even the trains have trouble getting through," Marjorie added. "There hasn't been any service north of Birmingham for the past month."

"How do you get food and fuel to the towns that are isolated?" Ben asked.

"Helicopters fly in emergency supplies," Richard said. "But most of the daily staples, groceries and coal and the like, are brought in by homemade snowmobiles."

Ben turned in the seat and looked at Booroojian. "Homemade?"

"Yes. Mechanics out in the country have become quite adept at converting cars and lorries. They take off the wheels, attach skis in front and usually rig up some sort of tread drive behind."

"No doubt you'll see a lot of them on your way up to

North Channel," Marjorie said. "Snowmobiles are the only
way you can get around Scotland these days."

"What kind of shape is my drill platform in up there?"
Ben asked.

"From what our people on the ice tell me, it's come
through remarkably well," Richard said. "Some metal machinery parts have snapped in the extreme cold, hydraulic
lines have frozen, things like that. Still, the platform itself is
fifty feet above the sea. The ice floes have had very little effect."

"I've ordered my new laser drill tower and two big steam
generators flown in from Wyoming," Ben said. "I'm also
transferring my best people to the project."

"When will your equipment and men get here, Ben?"
Marjorie asked.

"If the weather holds, they'll fly into Heathrow sometime
before dawn tomorrow."

"I'm afraid they may not be able to land in Britain, Ben,"
Richard said. "The unions are threatening a general strike.
There's a good chance the air traffic controllers at Heathrow
will walk out at six tonight, along with all the other unions in
the country."

"Wonderful," Ben said. "I've got sixty tons of machinery
and seventy-five engineers and roustabouts waiting to
board a cargo jet in Wyoming. What the hell do I do now?"

"You could have them land at Charles de Gaulle outside
Paris," Marjorie suggested. "From there your men and
equipment could be transported up to Calais and brought
across the Channel on an icebreaker."

Ben nodded. "I guess that's the best we can do."

The traffic was lighter heading away from the airport and
twenty minutes later they reached the outskirts of London.
Ben hadn't been in the British capital since shutting down
North Channel two years before and he was shocked at what
the freezing weather had done to the city.

Despite the fact that snow had been falling for several
hours, only the main arteries were plowed. The side streets
were lined with white hillocks covering cars that were obviously going nowhere until the snow was cleared.

Everywhere, piles of refuse and overflowing garbage cans stuck up through the white blanket, and down one alley Ben spotted a pack of dogs tearing at what appeared to be the corpse of a huge rat.

The buildings that had looked so elegant and well cared for on his last trip were now showing signs of decay and abandonment. Windows were dirty, and where panes had broken squares of cardboard had been taped behind the cracked glass. Doors once glossy with varnish and paint were now dull and peeling, and on almost every block there were buildings with entryways gaping open and fingers of snow reaching in across hall floors.

Richard followed Ben's eyes. "I'm afraid quite a few people have abandoned London, Ben," he said. "The rents are terribly expensive, and we've had almost thirty percent unemployment since oil prices went out of sight."

"Where'd they go?" Ben asked.

"To the smaller cities and towns. They're isolated by the snow out there, but the rents are half or less what they are in London."

"Many have immigrated to Canada, Australia, New Zealand," Marjorie added. "Quite a few have gone to America as well."

Ben stared at the few pedestrians they passed struggling along the drifted sidewalks. The people looked numb, deep inside themselves, hope gone from their eyes. Marjorie stopped at a light and there was suddenly a man at Ben's side of the car.

He was wearing a filthy overcoat several sizes too big and only his eyes were visible beneath the thick scarf wrapped several times around his neck and head. He tapped on the glass and held a hand out beseechingly, his dirt-caked palm visible through a jagged tear in his glove.

Ben rolled down his window. A blast of freezing air swept in, followed by a foul stench from the long-unwashed beggar. " 'Ave ya got a few shillings to spare, gov'nor? I've 'ad nothing to eat all day."

Ben fished out his wallet, then suddenly remembered he had only U.S. currency on him. He turned to Richard in the back seat and passed him a fifty-dollar bill. "Here, all I've got is American. Let me have twenty pounds."

Richard made the exchange and Ben put the money in the beggar's hand. "Get yourself some dinner. And a new pair of gloves."

"God bless ya, gov'nor, God bless ya," the beggar said, stepping back as the light changed and Marjorie started the Morris forward.

She glanced sideways at Ben. He had a heart. He was turning out to be far different from the rich, overbearing American she had thought she'd meet.

"Unfortunately, there are thousands like him on the streets of London," Richard said dejectedly. "The worsening weather has cost Britain four hundred thousand lost jobs in the greater London area alone over the past three years. God only knows what the eruption of R-Nine will now do to the climate."

"The climate's not the only thing we have to worry about Richard," Ben said. "There's going to be a hell of a psychological effect on people when the light begins to change color. There could be widespread panic."

"The color of the light? What are you talking about?" Richard said.

"Solar light, Richard," Ben said. "When that ash cloud arrives tomorrow, the sun will turn blue."

IRISH SEA
••••••••••

11:10 a.m.

A LIGHT SNOW WAS falling out on the broken ice floes crusting the Irish Sea as the great wolf Beelzebub climbed the side of a jagged pressure ridge and stared through the falling flakes at the ship frozen into the ice a mile away.

The other wolves were tired after a long hunt for food the night before and most were dozing away the day in the leeward shelter of the ridge, their bodies covered with mounds of snow that rose and fell rhythmically with their slow breathing.

Only Beelzebub was alert, his eyes searching the deck of the ship for the human that often walked there. Two nights before, the pack had trekked for almost ten miles across the ice before discovering the lingering scent of roasted mutton was coming from this rusting freighter.

Beelzebub did not consider it strange that this ship should be here, motionless in the grip of the ice, miles from the nearest shore and even farther from a harbor. To the huge wolf, this was simply another human habitat.

He had circled the vessel warily, keeping several hundred yards away in the predawn dark, the rest of the pack close behind him. Satisfied there were no humans out on the ice, the great wolf had led the way closer to the ship.

The wolves were only twenty yards away when one of the yearlings nearest the stern suddenly stopped, sniffed the air, and bounded ahead. A moment later the rest of the pack heard the young wolf tearing at what could only be food.

In seconds the other wolves had been beside the youngster, digging frantically into the snow-covered mound of garbage piled beneath the rust-streaked stern of the vessel. The remnants of pork and beans, vegetables and canned meats were all frozen solid, but the starving wolves had chewed it with little trouble, their sharp canine teeth slicing through the icy fibers.

Beelzebub had hung back, suspicious this might be a trap, that humans were lying in wait with their killing sticks. For several minutes his eyes had remained glued on the moonlit deck above. He'd seen no movement, and the only scent of a human had been the one he'd already detected coming from the ship. Finally, he too trotted forward to feed.

When dawn began to pink the eastern horizon a half hour later, the pack had eaten every scrap they could find. A brisk wind had risen, layering the animals' thick fur with blankets of blowing snow as Beelzebub led them away to find a place to hide during the day.

Two hours afterward, the great wolf had been watching the ship from the pressure ridge when he saw a human come out on deck, walk to the icicle-draped rail directly above the place where the wolves had found food, and throw something over the side.

The human had started to walk away, then stopped suddenly and looked down at the ice. For a long moment he stared at the feeding place, then he walked along the deck and descended a set of rickety stairs to the floes.

For a moment Beelzebub stirred restlessly, an instinctive fear rising in him that the human would find the tracks of the pack. Then the wind ruffling his fur reassured him their tracks would be covered by now by the blowing snow.

The man had walked back to the feeding place and kicked at empty cans and frozen scraps of burlap sacks the wolves had dragged out onto the ice from the garbage piled against the side of the ship.

Then he had turned and looked out over the floes, as if searching for something. For several minutes the man stood there, just looking. Finally, he shook his head and climbed the stairs again to the deck of the ship.

Beelzebub had watched all day and seen the man appear on the deck several times. Each time he had been alone, and the great wolf smelled no other human scent. Then, just before the sun set, the man had come out again and lowered something on a long wire over the garbage dump.

When dark came Beelzebub could see the thing was a light, and it lit up the side of the ship and the garbage and the ice for several yards around. Now, the wolves no longer dared to forage there, and two of the bitches howled their frustration into the whistling wind.

That night, the pack had searched the floes for food, but none was to be found, although they trotted back and forth for many miles around. At dawn they had come back to their icy lair hungry and tired.

Beelzebub knew the pack would have to feed again soon. The intense cold and their long trek in search of sustenance had sapped their energy.

In this landscape of ice and snow, there was food in only one place. Even as the wolves had searched the floes the night before, they had again caught the smell of mutton roasting aboard the ship.

Beelzebub had a great fear of humans, for many of them had the killing sticks that had taken so many of the pack the summer before. Yet it was now a matter of survival. The pack must eat or they would perish.

The stairs leading down to the ice had no lights to give away his presence, and, but for a weak bulb above one of the doors, the deck was also shrouded in darkness.

The great wolf yawned, the slanting rays of the sun glinting off his huge yellow teeth. Tonight, in the dark before the moon rose, he would hunt aboard the ship.

London
●●●●●●●●●●

12:06 p.m.

"I'VE GOT IT," RICHARD Booroojian said in triumph from the back seat of the Morris as Marjorie Glynn guided the small car carefully along a snowy two-lane road in Kent. "I knew I'd read of the blue-sun phenomenon occurring before and it's suddenly struck me what caused it."

For over an hour now, Richard had refused to let Ben tell him why the sun would turn blue, preferring to puzzle out the answer himself.

Marjorie glanced at Booroojian in the rearview mirror. "Well, let's have it, then."

"Lakagigar volcano in Iceland," Richard said. "It spewed up an enormous volume of gases when it erupted in 1783, producing a blue haze that lasted for weeks."

"There was a difference," Ben said, turning to face Booroojian. "The Laki blue haze was the result of fluorine in the volcanic gases. We know it was fluorine because over a quarter of a million cattle, sheep, and horses died of fluoridosis after grazing on the grass near the volcano."

"Is there fluorine in the volcanic clouds from R-Nine?" Marjorie asked.

"Traces, probably," Ben said. "But that's not what will

cause the sun to appear blue tomorrow. When the debris clouds reach Britain, ash particles in the air will scatter the sun's longer red wavelengths and the light will become richer in shorter blue and violet wavelengths."

"Presto, chango, the sun turns blue," Booroojian said.

Ben nodded. "The effect will be especially pronounced at sunrise and sunset when the light will be almost a blue-green."

"I'd better have the media warn the public it's going to happen," Booroojian said. "After the continuous blizzards and arctic cold of the past two years, half the population is on the verge of a nervous breakdown as it is."

"I think that's a good idea," Ben said. "Despite the scientific explanation, no one alive has ever seen a blue sun. It could freak out a lot of people."

"There it is, Ben, Biosphere Britannia," Marjorie Glynn said, pointing through the windshield toward a huge step pyramid rising above the leafless treetops ahead. "We'll be there in about five minutes now."

Ben stared up as the pyramid took shape through the slackening storm. The lower half of the Biosphere's steep sides was dusted with snow. Above, though, the winds had swept the inclines clear and he could see the large triangular panes of glass that formed the sides of the towering greenhouse.

He whistled softly. "What is it, three, four hundred feet high?"

"Three hundred and seventy-five," Marjorie said.

They rounded a bend in the road and Biosphere Britannia came into full view ahead. The Biosphere looked from a distance like a Mayan temple made of glass and for a long moment Ben stared silently at the eerie sight of the immense pyramid rising above the snowy English countryside.

Five hundred yards from the main colossus he could make out a second glass pyramid, somewhat smaller than the first but still huge against the horizon. The two triangular towers were connected by a long rectangular glass structure with sloping sides.

"God, when you described the Biosphere to me I had no idea it was that large."

"The Biosphere covers ten acres of land," Marjorie said. "Altogether, there are a hundred and sixty-three million cubic feet of space enclosed inside."

"That's got to be the biggest damn greenhouse in the world," Ben said.

Marjorie laughed. "You could call Biosphere Britannia a greenhouse, Ben. But we like to refer to it as a sealed ecosystem."

"It's a miniearth really," Richard Booroojian said. "That's why we named it after the biosphere, the envelope of air, water, and land in which living things exist on this planet."

"I remember reading about the project when you first started construction," Ben said. "What was it, three years ago?"

"We began erecting the space frame in 'ninety-seven," Marjorie said. "It took almost eight months for the steel and cement and all that, then another four months to set all the glass in place."

"The physical structure was a piece of cake compared to collecting all the plant and animal species for the five separate ecosystems," Richard said. "Marjorie trekked from the American desert to the Amazon Basin bringing back everything from land tortoises to Brazil nut trees several hundred feet high."

"There are over a thousand different species of animals alone," Marjorie said. "I often think the Biosphere's more an ark than anything else. *Ark Britannia*, a ship of glass adrift on a sea of ice."

Ben looked at her incredulously. "A thousand species. Where do you find the room, the food for all those animals?"

Marjorie smiled. "A thousand species sounds like a lot, but I'm counting the fish and insect families as well. Then there are several thousand varieties of plants, grasses, and so on. You probably won't even notice some of the smaller lifeforms, not at first anyway."

"I take it you're a biologist," Ben said.

"Molecular biologist, actually," Marjorie said. "I started

out studying to be a medical researcher, then fell in love with zoology. I still intend to get into DNA research someday."

Richard gestured to the left. "That series of arched vaults connected to the south end of the Biosphere house the intensive agricultural biome. Just beyond is our food-processing plant. The white-domed building on the right is the human habitat."

"That's where you live?" Ben said.

"Yes, all the Biosphereans have apartments there. There are also workshops, a library, a gym, research facilities, and computer and communications equipment."

Five minutes later, Marjorie parked the Morris in front of the Biosphere and the three crunched through the snow to the main entrance. Richard punched a series of code buttons into a panel next to the entry and the large glass door opened.

A young, straw-haired guard rose from behind a desk to one side of the fieldstone-floored foyer. "Good afternoon, Dr. Glynn, Dr. Booroojian."

"Hello, Mickey," Marjorie said. "This is Dr. Meade. He'll be staying with us here a while."

"You've had a call from your laboratory in Wyoming, Dr. Meade," Mickey said, handing Ben a telephone message.

"Thank you," Ben said. He read the note, drew his lips into a hard line, and put the paper in his pocket.

"Dr. Meade is to have full access privileges to all the facilities, Mickey," Marjorie said.

"I'll see to it, Dr. Glynn."

Richard looked at his watch. "If you'll excuse me, I have to give a lecture in the amphitheater in twenty minutes. I'll be speaking on soil erosion, Ben, if you'd care to come along."

"Soil erosion? I know I'll be sorry, Richard, but I think I'll stick with Marjorie. Maybe you could tape it for me and I could listen as I nod off tonight."

Booroojian laughed. "Enjoy your tour. I'll see you both at dinner."

"Come along then, Ben," Marjorie said. "We'll have to get sanitized before we can enter the Biosphere itself. We can't risk foreign organisms hitching a ride into the environment on our bodies or clothes."

Ben followed Marjorie into a rectangular room off the foyer. The ceiling and walls of the room were faced with bright white tiles. At the far end, dozens of small shower heads protruded from the gleaming squares. A head-high opaque partition divided the shower area in half.

"Why don't you take the right side there, Ben? Just hang your clothes on the hook and Mickey will have them cleaned and ready when you leave."

"What do I wear in the meantime?"

Marjorie swung back the sliding doors on a long closet beside the entrance. There were several dozen bright red coveralls on hangers inside. She eyed him speculatively. "A large, I'd guess," she said, pulling a set of coveralls from the end of the line and handing it to Ben.

He draped it in front of him. "Looks right. At the risk of being indelicate, what about underwear?"

Marjorie laughed and opened a drawer built into the wall beside the closet. "Waist size?"

"Thirty-four."

"There you go," she said, handing him a pair of blue shorts.

Ben fingered the material. "These are made out of paper."

"Naturally. They're disposable. All the same, they're as comfortable as cloth."

Ben turned the shorts around and looked at the other side. "Where's the—"

"Fly? There isn't any. They're unisex shorts, silly man. If you have to pee you simply push up the leg."

"Jesus."

Marjorie took out coveralls and a pair of underwear for herself and walked to the left shower area. "See you in a minute," she said, pulling the neck-high door shut behind her.

Ben shrugged to himself, went into the right cubicle, and stripped down. "What about towels?" he asked, avoiding looking to his left. At six-feet-four, the level of his eyes was well above the partition.

Marjorie laughed. "We don't need them. It's not a water shower. It's a mild germicidal spray. Harmless to humans but murder on bacteria. It will dry on your body."

Ben heard a hiss as Marjorie turned on her shower. He shrugged and turned the handle built into the tile. Instantly a fine mist from the multihead shower sprayed him directly in the face. "Oww, damn it." He grimaced, his eyes burning as he danced away from the medicinal-smelling vapor.

"God, that stuff stings your eyes."

"Lord, I'm sorry, Ben, I should have warned you to shut your eyes. It'll pass in a moment."

He rubbed his lids, blinked several times, squinted, then opened his eyes again. Without realizing it, he had made a half turn to his left as he pulled away from the spray. He was facing the partition, looking directly across at a stark-naked Marjorie Glynn.

She had her eyes closed, her hands back behind her neck holding her hair up to the spray. He should have turned away instantly, he knew. He wanted to, out of decency, out of embarrassment. But for a moment he couldn't tear his eyes away. He'd been at sea for three months, almost a thousand watery miles from the nearest woman. And her body was beautiful.

She had firm melon breasts with perfect pink nipples. Her flat stomach flared down into firm thighs that framed a triangle of auburn pubic hair. She turned, revealing her little round bottom, her smooth cheeks curving down to long shapely legs.

Ben groaned inside and yanked his eyes away, intensely aroused and at the same time ashamed he'd looked at her. What could he do? He hadn't meant to look. Jesus, he had an erection.

"You okay?" Marjorie asked from the other side of the plastic. "Get the mist out of your eyes?"

"Yeah," Ben managed, his voice husky. He cleared his throat. "Yeah, I got it out."

He heard Marjorie shut off her vapor shower and he closed his eyes again and faced into the nozzles, relieved the hospital-hall odor of the medicinal spray was stilling his overactive libido.

Finally his erection subsided and he turned off the shower and reached for the paper shorts Marjorie had handed him. Then he pulled on his coveralls and stepped out of the cubicle. Marjorie was sitting on a stool putting on disposable paper slippers. She handed a pair to Ben. "These should fit."

Ben slipped his feet into the slippers. "Fine."

"Good," she smiled. "Ready for your tour?"

"Lead on," he said, fighting unsuccessfully not to picture her body beneath her coveralls.

Marjorie opened a door opposite the one they'd come in and Ben followed her out into a large intersection of corridors. A domed skylight above flooded the area with light.

"This way, Ben," Marjorie said, starting down a hall to their right.

Halfway down the corridor, Ben heard the distinct sound of a rooster crowing. He stopped and looked around. "Can't be."

Marjorie smiled. "But it is. A rooster. We have a complete farm in the agricultural biome Richard pointed out. It's through that double door. Everything's on a miniature scale, of course, but we have chickens, goats, pigs, even pygmy cattle."

"How do you feed a menagerie like that?"

"We raise crops. Feed for the animals and grains, fruits, and vegetables for ourselves. We have a virtual year-round harvest of wheat, rice, sorghum, soybeans, peas, potatoes, tomatoes."

"It sounds like you Biosphereans dine well."

"We do. I'll show you the farm on the way back. First, I want you to see the Biosphere itself."

At the end of the corridor they came to a head-high cylindrical door. Marjorie pressed a button on the wall and the door swung open to reveal a tunnel beyond. Five feet down the tunnel was a fine mesh screen curtain.

"It's an air lock between the Biosphere and the human habitat," Marjorie explained.

"What's the screen for?"

"To keep the insects in. We have bees, butterflies, spiders, ants, termites, beetles, scorpions, and several hundred other species."

"I can see bees and butterflies," Ben said. "But what the hell do you want scorpions for?"

"Because they are part of the desert ecosystem," Marjorie said, parting the screen curtain. "They feed on other anthropoids like ticks, mites, and centipedes, and that helps keep the insect population under control."

"You've anticipated everything."

"Everything but the eruption of R-Nine," Marjorie said soberly.

A moment later they passed through a second screen and Marjorie opened an airtight door beyond. Light suddenly flooded into the tunnel and Ben had to squint as he followed Marjorie through the entry.

As his eyes adjusted to the brightness, he became aware they had entered a huge open space. Then his vision focused and he stood awestruck as his eyes swept the incredible vista of rain forest, grasslands, swamps, and desert that stretched within the immense cathedral of glass before him.

To his right, several acres of jungle climbed the side of a man-made hill that rose toward the apex of the main pyramid far above them.

Directly in front of the tunnel entrance, one side of the pyramid was joined to the huge rectangle of glass he had seen from the road. A shrub-dotted grassland almost a quarter mile long sloped gently away under the high glass roof.

At the far end of the grassland he could make out desert sand dunes and huge rock formations clustered under the second, smaller pyramid.

Ben suddenly became aware of a humid warmth bathing his skin, and a rain-forest smell of rotting vegetation and tropical flowers mixed in a strange sweet odor. From the jungle came the sounds of chattering birds. As he watched, a rainbow-hued parrot winged from one treetop to another, a bright red berry in its beak.

"My God, Marjorie," Ben said softly. "It's like entering Eden."

"Yes, it is a paradise, but a practical paradise," Marjorie smiled. "I designed the Biosphere to be self-supporting. All the life-forms we brought in were chosen to react symbiotically with each other. Every plant and animal in here plays a part in supporting the environment as a whole."

"What about that macaw up there?" Ben challenged, pointing at the brightly colored parrot that had resumed its flight through the jungle. "How does a bird contribute to the life cycles in here? Besides lending the jungle a touch of beauty?"

"Its beauty is a bonus, Ben. I chose that particular species because it doesn't fully digest the berries and other fruits it eats. The seeds survive in its digestive tract and the macaw disperses them all over the jungle in its droppings."

"Like a little winged farmer." Ben smiled.

"Yes, except that a macaw eats far less than a person. The whole idea behind Biosphere Britannia is to test the theory that controlled environments like this can support human populations."

"Why not just make the whole thing a farm?" Ben asked. "What do you need with a jungle and a desert and all these other ecosystems?"

"Do you remember Richard calling the project a 'mini-earth'?"

"Yes."

"Well, that's exactly what it is. I've designed Biosphere Britannia to mimic as many of the earth's biological, geological, and chemical cycles as possible. To do that I had to re-create the five basic ecosystems that make up the planet's biosphere: desert, rain forest, savanna lands, marshes, and ocean."

Ben looked around. "You've got an ocean in here?"

"Yes, only the size of a small lake, but an ocean all the same. C'mon, I'll show you."

As they started across the grass of the savanna, a herd of animals Ben had never seen before dashed from behind a clump of scrub trees and bounded away toward the distant desert.

"What on earth are those?" Ben asked, watching the

graceful animals leap a small stream a hundred yards away.

"Pudus, tiny deer from Chile," Marjorie said. "Their browsing keeps the grasses clipped, and at the same time their droppings fertilize the soil. Every once in a while we harvest the herd and have venison in the mess, although I don't eat it myself."

"Hard to eat a cute steak, huh?" Ben grinned.

Marjorie laughed. "Something like that."

They climbed a low rise and Ben caught sight of the miniature sea ahead. He guessed it to be about four acres in area, stretching from the base of one of the glass walls to the edge of the grasslands.

At the fringe of the far shore he could see ducks and geese feeding in a marine marsh fed by a stream tumbling down a hill behind. On the other side, wavelets lapped against a sand beach dotted with coconut palms. Fifty feet from the beach, a coral reef stretched across the sea parallel to the sandy shore.

"Is it salt water?" Ben asked.

"Of course it is," Marjorie said, miffed at the question. "Everything I've done here is true to nature down to the last detail. Our small sea has exactly the same salinity as the Atlantic or the Pacific."

"I didn't mean to imply—"

"There are over a hundred species of saltwater fish swimming around in there," Marjorie charged on. "If the salinity isn't just right, the whole thing would soon turn into a huge bouillabaisse with waves."

"Okay, okay, it was a dumb question."

Marjorie grinned. "Sorry. I do get a bit hot at any suggestion that the ecosystems in here are not exactly as they exist outside. That marsh over there, for instance, was brought in intact from the Florida Everglades. Frogs, turtles, crabs, even the microorganisms in the soil are in the same proportion as they would be in the wild."

"It must have taken an immense effort to put all this together," Ben said, watching a green turtle push itself up the beach at the far end of the small sea.

"Details, Ben, millions of details. Everything from making

sure the leaf litter in the bottom of the stream was edible for fish to selecting a species of hummingbird with the right-shaped beak to pollinate the different flowers we brought in."

She pushed back her auburn hair impatiently. "I went half mad searching out a termite species that could break down the tough savanna grasses yet didn't have an appetite for the sealant around the panes of glass."

Ben's eyes held Marjorie's. "And you loved every minute of it, didn't you? The research, the discoveries, the creation of a virtual world within a world."

Marjorie smiled. "We've just met. It's not fair you know me so well already."

"I know myself. We're both earth scientists. We get a rush from nature, from knowing its secrets, from finding ways for people to live on this planet without continuously gobbling up its resources. It sounds corny, but it's true."

Ben turned and surveyed the wide expanse of grassland between the rain forest and the desert. "You plan to bring whole populations into these biospheres?"

"Yes. We believe a biosphere this size can house and feed five thousand people. This is only the prototype, of course. We intend to build biospheres around our cities large enough to support populations of a hundred thousand each, eventually."

"Around the cities? Then people would live in the biospheres and go out to work?"

"At first. But in time we hope to convert much of our economy to low-pollution light industry that can be carried on in structures attached to the biosphere."

"What sort of jobs are you talking about?"

Marjorie's face became animated. "Computer design, genetic engineering, medical research, education, financial services, food production. Ben, we could create millions of jobs for everyone from scientists to businessmen and farmers."

Ben stared across the sloping grassland toward the dun sand dunes of the distant desert. "I know you're developing intensive agriculture, Marjorie. But are you sure you can feed hundreds of thousands of people with what you grow in a single Biosphere? When I picture a farm, I see fields of crops stretching to the horizon."

"I think I can best answer that question by taking you on a walk, Ben," Marjorie said. "I want to show you the bounty of nature."

At the fringe of the tropical rain forest, Marjorie led Ben through a thick belt of vegetation, pointing out ginger, banana, papaya, apple, coffee, and tea plants.

"Is that sugar cane?" Ben asked, pointing at a stand of green stalks in a clearing.

"Yes," Marjorie said. "I'm afraid even Biosphereans have sweet tooths." A few yards farther on, a path led into the dense jungle and Marjorie impulsively reached down and grabbed Ben's hand.

"C'mon. I can't wait for you to see the rain forest."

Her fingers were callused in his. He liked that. It meant she wasn't one of those desk-bound scientists spinning theories on computer screens. She was like him, hands-on. He could see her at work, planting trees, carting coral down to the small sea, milking goats.

And there was her enthusiasm for the project. It was spontaneous and infectious. They ducked under a tree limb overhanging the path and his nose brushed against her hair. She smelled fresh and clean. A feminine smell, unmasked by the perfume or powder so many women wore.

God, she's got it all, he thought. *She's smart and sexy and full of life.*

Marjorie named the plants they passed as they hiked into the rain forest. "There's a guava tree," she said, pointing at a small evergreen beside the trail.

"The fruit looks like pears," Ben said. "What's it taste like?"

"That particular variety has a sweet, musky flavor. We have another species from South America that tastes like strawberries."

"What are those?" Ben asked, looking up at a pod-laden tree.

"Cacao trees," Marjorie said.

"For hot chocolate in the evenings?"

"Yes, we do refine chocolate from the kernels in our food processing plant, but the cacao also has a high food value. It's chock full of protein, carbohydrates, and fat."

Ben shook his head. "Damn, it sounds like you can eat half the jungle."

Marjorie laughed. "We could, literally. Still, food isn't the only reason I've brought in the rain forest. Every plant that produces food must also have enough chloroplast in its leaf area to fix a maximum amount of carbon out of the air. All these trees and shrubs return oxygen to the atmosphere within the Biosphere."

A reddish-brown animal the size of a large rabbit darted across the trail in front of them and disappeared in the dense bush on the other side.

Ben cocked an eyebrow. "You do have the strangest-looking creatures in here, Marjorie."

"That was Forgetful. He's one of my favorites."

"And what manner of beast is Forgetful?"

"An agouti. They're forest dwellers from the tropical Americas. I call him Forgetful because he often buries seeds then forgets where he's hidden them. The seeds germinate and before long a tree begins growing."

"Another little farmer."

"Yes, except he eats different foods than the macaws."

Ben suddenly felt water drops on his face and neck. He looked up just as a shower began over the forest. "It can't be."

Marjorie laughed and pulled him under the shelter of the broad leaves of a banana tree beside the path. "It'll pass in a few minutes."

"Rain?" Ben peered up in disbelief at the clouds gathered in the apex of the pyramid. "You've got rain? Inside?"

"I told you this was Oz."

"How the hell—"

"It's a simple matter of physics, really. I began by dropping the floor line of the Biosphere three hundred feet from the higher rain forest to the lower desert."

Ben flicked a rivulet of rain drops from the ridge of his

eyebrow. "I noticed the difference in elevation when we first came in."

"Well, the slope drives convection currents that pick up heat from the desert and carry the hot air over the ocean where it absorbs moisture. Soon after clouds form and accumulate above the forest."

"And you get rain."

"Not quite yet." She pushed the foliage apart and pointed to a set of huge drumlike metal canisters suspended on cables high above the jungle.

Ben studied the machinery. "Are those condensers?"

"Exactly. They cool the moist air rising from the sea and before long we have rain."

Ben shook his head. "This really is a miniearth. You even have weather in here."

The shower trailed off and Marjorie stepped back on the path. "My favorite place in the world is around the bend ahead. Mind the puddles."

Fifty feet up the path, Ben could hear the sound of water splashing on rocks. A moment later Marjorie led him off the track and down a moss-covered incline to the foot of a waterfall cascading over a small cliff.

"Tranquility Falls," Marjorie said, her eyes glowing. "This is where I come to renew my spirit."

The waterfall was but twelve feet high, and the little river that plunged over the man-made precipice only four feet wide and eighteen inches deep. Yet to Ben the sparkling cascade and the deep green glen bordering the clear pool at its base were an idyllic place, limitless in its beauty and in the pervasive sense of peace it imparted.

"You're more than a scientist, Marjorie," Ben said. "Only an artist, a dreamer of beauty, could have created this."

"What a lovely thing to say."

Ben stared at her, seized by the animation in her face, the creator in her. He couldn't remember ever wanting a woman more. It wasn't just lust. She was the essence of woman, at once life-giving and sexually alluring. He wanted to possess her, to devour her body with kisses, inch by inch, from her nose to her toes.

Their eyes met and Marjorie was startled by the desire in his look. She was suddenly aware of how alone they were. And that he was very near her. The hairs prickled on the nape of her neck as she sensed the sexual voracity raging within him.

"Stop looking at me like that."

"Like what?"

"Like you want to rip my clothes off."

Ben felt like the time in third grade when the teacher had caught him deliberately dropping his crayon on the floor so he could bend way down and look up Ilona Cesta's dress. His first instinct was flustered denial. "You assume a lot from a look."

"You have one of those faces."

"What faces?"

"Easy to read; like a book."

"Really. And you read in my face that I wanted to tear your clothes off. Did my face tell you where I'd start? Sometimes I rip off a woman's earrings first, you know. Other times—it's a mood thing, really—I start with the socks."

"Good try, but it won't work. There's guilt written all over your puss."

Ben retreated. "I will admit to one slightly lecherous thought. I've been at sea for three months. What do you expect?"

"Professional behavior. I thought I'd be working with the world's foremost geothermal scientist, not some scourge-of-the-pond horny toad."

"And I didn't expect to be working with some lock-kneed professional virgin."

"I am not a professional virgin."

"Pardon me, amateur virgin."

A loud rasping noise suddenly boomed down from the steep roof of the Biosphere above them and the two whirled toward the sound of glass breaking somewhere over the jungle. A moment later they heard something heavy falling into the trees at the edge of the forest.

Marjorie rushed up the hill beside the waterfall. "Bloody hell," she said, staring at the wall of the pyramid sloping up above the trees. "There's been an ice slide down the north side. We've lost a whole section of glass."

Ben climbed the hill and stood beside her. He could see snow blowing in through the house-sized break in the steep expanse of glass above. "This happen often?" he said.

"Yes," Marjorie said, putting aside her pique at his lecherous stare. "Three or four times already this winter."

Ben sensed their argument was over. "Looks like you've lost some plants," he said, pointing at a huge mound of ice and snow that had fallen in and flattened a section of shrubbery at the fringe of the jungle.

Marjorie shivered as a blast of cold air swept down from the jagged hole above. "We're going to lose more if I don't get that roof fixed. We'd better go back. I have to get a repair crew up here."

Ben stared up at the canopy of glass as they hurried out of the rain forest and started across the grassland. "How much of your heat are you getting from solar?"

"When we first built the Biosphere, we could count on converting about seventy percent. Then last winter the snows started getting heavier and the average fell to below fifty percent."

"I don't have to tell you that after that immense cloud of ash and volcanic gases drifts over tomorrow you can just about forget solar altogether."

Marjorie pointed up at rows of immense grow lights suspended beneath the glass. "As you can see, we're able to supply our own light. It's the energy to power those lamps and heat the Biosphere I'm worried about."

"What do you supplement the solar with?"

"We have coal-burning furnaces in a separate building outside."

"Kind of ironic, isn't it, burning a polluting fuel like coal outside to heat the inside of a Biosphere that couldn't exist without clean air."

Marjorie stopped and looked up at him, anguish in her face. "What choice have we, Ben? We're about to lose solar, and with the astronomical price of oil we'll have to rely more and more on coal for our energy."

"If Parliament had approved funds to develop geothermal two years ago, you wouldn't have an energy crisis today," Ben said.

"You must have been furious with me when I withdrew my support for the geothermal bill."

"You were not exactly on my Christmas-card list."

"Please understand, Ben, I had no choice. If I'd continued to advocate developing the North Channel project, Seamus MacTiege would have cut off every shilling in support for the Biosphere."

"You had your priorities, I had mine."

"What do you want me to say? That I should have fought MacTiege? That I'm a coward for caving in?"

"I don't want you to say anything. But I have a point of view too. Jesus Christ, I had months of time and several million dollars in Meade International money invested in the project when Parliament pulled the rug out from under me."

"If you feel that way, why did you come back?"

"Like I told Richard, I figure I owe England."

"I thought we owed you; several million dollars you said."

"The money's not important."

"Really? Then what do you care about?"

"The truth for one thing. That's something you British have been playing fast and loose with lately."

"I beg your pardon!"

"Do you remember that telephone message I got when we arrived at the Biosphere?"

"Yes, I recall Mickey handing you a note."

"It was from my satellite research center in Wyoming. Before I flew off the *Abyss*, I had my people begin a multiorbit scan of the seafloor under North Channel."

"I thought you did that three years ago."

"No, your own Department of Energy people did the satellite surveys. I was only given the geological data on specific locations. It was all very hush-hush."

"They kept the surveys secret? But why?"

"Because the geothermal reservoir of superheated water and steam is far larger than the British government has let

on. It extends over a hundred and twenty miles to the southwest of the drill platform."

"To the southwest! But that would mean the geothermal
pool runs under Irish territorial waters."

"Exactly," Ben said. "Half the energy we need to keep
Biosphere Britannia alive belongs to the country Windscale
almost wiped off the face of the earth."

DUBLIN
● ● ● ● ● ● ● ●

3:46 p.m.

WHEN GENERAL SEAN MCCORMICK walked into the office of
Irish Prime Minister Bernadette O'Fiaich, he carried in one
hand a dossier on the British Army in Northern Ireland and
in the other a single red rose, its petals still chill from the
thermos canister in which it had been shipped from Brazil
by his arms agent the evening before.

The minister for defense laid the files on the prime minister's desk and with a flourish presented her the rose, in lieu
of a kiss which they would share later.

Bernadette O'Fiaich pressed the flower beneath her large
nose and inhaled its essence, her face transformed from the
countenance of a troubled chief of state it had been before
McCormick entered to the softened look of a lover.

"If you don't beat all, Sean," she smiled fondly, forgetting
in her rapture to draw her upper lip down over her horsey
teeth as she usually did. "Dublin's buried to the eaves in
snow, there's hardly a green thing growing in all of Ireland,
and you waltz in here with a fresh rose. I don't suppose
you'll be telling me where you got it."

"A man must have his secrets, Taoiseach," he said,
using the Gaelic word for "prime minister." "If you knew

every little thing about me, you'd lose interest soon enough."

The forty-five-year-old McCormick had light blue eyes, a dimpled chin, and the manner to churn a spinster's heart, which was how he got his job.

As a government minister, he regularly briefed the prime minister. As Sean McCormick, he regularly shared her four-poster bed.

McCormick made himself comfortable in a chair before the prime minister's antique walnut desk. "How fine you look this morning," he said, a small smile playing at the corners of his mouth. "I take it you slept well, then."

"You know perfectly well how I slept, you wicked man," she smiled, the affection welling up in her as she looked at his face. There were terrible moments every few weeks when Bernadette O'Fiaich woke up soaked in sweat in the middle of the night, struggling to deny to herself that she loved this man more than her God.

The Right Honorable Ms. O'Fiaich had been a nursing nun for twenty years before the radioactive cloud from the meltdown of the British reactor at Windscale descended on Ireland.

It had been a time of terrible panic at the hospital where she worked in Louth, the county on the east coast of Ireland that bore the first brunt of the deadly wind that blew across the Irish Sea from Cumbria. The civil defense sirens had screamed all that first night as doctors, nurses, and staff tore through the hospital corridors rushing patients out to evacuation ambulances and buses.

The terminally ill patients in intensive care, and those on respirators and heart-lung machines, could not be moved, and when the mother superior announced she would remain behind to ease the suffering of her doomed charges, Bernadette had volunteered to stay with her.

Eighteen hours later, the electricity from the unattended power station ten kilometers away had suddenly gone off, and patients on the life-support machines had begun to die. The mother superior had raced off in a small car to see what could be done at the station. She never came back, and they found her body months later, decomposing behind the wheel of her car mired to the doors in now dry mud.

At the hospital, all the patients had died but one, a small boy with viral pneumonia who'd been on a ventilator. Bernadette had managed to keep him alive with bottled oxygen, but she'd known they'd both die from radioactivity if they stayed where they were. She'd strapped a canister of oxygen to a wheelchair, and set off pushing the boy down the road before her.

She'd fully expected them both to die along the way, but the worst of the radioactive cloud had drifted past a distance away, and later that day an Irish Army helicopter, its pilots wearing protective suits, spotted Bernadette and the boy on the road below and lifted them out to a hospital in Dublin.

One of the pilots had snapped a picture as the helicopter lowered toward the road. The next day the photograph of Bernadette pushing the boy in the wheelchair appeared on the front page of the *Irish Times*, her eyes sunken and rimmed with black from lack of sleep, and her white nun's habit now a frayed shroud of dust from the road. That afternoon, the international media had picked up the story.

Overnight, Bernadette O'Fiaich, a studious and painfully shy nun who'd hardly been noticed before beyond a grateful nod from one of her patients, had suddenly become a heroine, not just in Ireland but around the world.

Hospitalized herself for treatment of radioactive poisoning, she'd made light of all the fuss. Her own recovery had been slow and the doctors had told her she could expect no more than five or six more years of life.

Bernadette had kept her prognosis to herself, and when she'd left the hospital three months later, she'd pronounced herself fully cured, for it would have disheartened tens of thousands to know the truth.

"You've got half the Fine Gael members of Parliament out there waitin' to see you this morning, Taoiseach," McCormick said, rolling his eyes toward her outer office. "That volcanic cloud comin' at us has 'em all bleatin' like frightened sheep."

Bernadette was the leader of Fine Gael, the most liberal of

the Irish political parties, which also included the Fianna
Fail, the Workers Party, and the Sinn Fein, the political front
for the outlawed Irish Republican Army.

She put the rose in a pitcher of water on the table behind
her. "The truth be known, I'm as frightened as them, Sean.
Do you know what's going to happen to Ireland's weather?"

"I have an idea, to be sure, Taoiseach. But I'm a military
man, not a scientist."

"I'll tell you, then. More than half of our farms have failed
in the three years since we started losing the warmth of that
current out in the ocean. But at least we could still import
enough feed to raise livestock; sheep and pigs and the like.
Now the climatologists tell me it's to get so cold the animals
will freeze to death in their barns. God save us, farming's
done in Ireland."

"It's fuel I'm worried about," McCormick said. "The people are freezin' in their homes as it is. And half the factories
have shut 'cause the oil to run them costs more than they
make."

Bernadette shook her head. "The feeling's come over me
lately, Sean, am I the one should be prime minister now?
There's others with more government experience."

"That may be true, Taoiseach, but none the people love
more than you, and surely none they trust as much. Terrible
times are comin'. The people will need a prime minister they
believe in."

Bernadette O'Fiaich's rise to the highest office in Ireland
had been propelled by Windscale. A month after she'd left
the hospital in the summer of 1995, the prime minister had
summoned her to his office in Government Buildings on
Upper Merrion Street and offered her a Cabinet post as minister for health and social welfare.

She'd demurred at first, for although the Church had provided a university education, and she'd had long and wide
medical experience, Irish politics was a rough-and-tumble
business, and she was still, in her heart, a simple bride of
Christ.

Yet, there were tens of thousands of Irish victims of Windscale, and as far as she could see little was being done to help

them recover. With the Pope's blessing she'd shucked her reticence and her nun's habit, and accepted the post, taking with her from her convent past a naïve idealism, her religious faith, and, at age thirty-eight, her intact virginity.

No longer a nun, she'd kept her faith, but lost her idealism to politics, and her virginity to the man sitting before her.

"That's kind of you to say, Sean," Bernadette said, coming around her desk. Although they had long had an agreement not to display physical affection in any public place, no matter they were alone, she hugged him roundly and kissed his cheek.

Sean scowled and pulled away. "Enough of that, Taoiseach. You know how I feel about such goin's-on not at home. It ill befits your office."

"I may be prime minister, Sean, but I'm a woman as well, and I'll thank you for a kindness in my own woman's way," she said, hurt as usual by his coldness. He could give a compliment but not himself, she thought, retreating to her chair.

"Now, now, you needn't take offense, me Bernie girl," he said, attempting to mollify her.

"Sometimes I find myself wondering, Sean," she said, her pique tugging at the veil through which she saw him. "Is it Bernadette or the Taoiseach you're courting?"

"That's a cruel thing you say." He screwed his face up in wounded protest. "If there's little romance in me this miserable snowy mornin', the reason's before you," he said, sweeping a dramatic hand over the dossier he'd just placed on her desk. "The baby killers are making suspicious moves again."

She knew, of course, he meant the British Army in Ulster, at whose hands his wife and two young sons had died in February 1996. Carol Ann McCormick was from County Derry in Northern Ireland, and she'd driven across the border with her boys to visit her sister's family in Ballykelly.

The night she'd arrived, IRA terrorists had detonated a bomb at the Droppin' Well pub in Ballykelly, a gathering place for off-duty British troops. Twelve young soldiers had died on the spot and another thirty were seriously injured. The British had set up roadblocks around the city.

Mrs. McCormick and her two young sons had the terrible misfortune to be driving in the same model and color two-door Vauxhall Astra that the terrorists had reportedly escaped in. When she'd been slow to stop at an army barrier, the car had been riddled with machine-gun fire by nervous British soldiers. Sean McCormick's wife and young sons had died instantly.

Bernadette had been in the convent with Sean's sister Kathleen. When she'd read in the *Dublin Times* of the terrible deaths of Kathleen's sister-in-law and nephews in Derry, she'd gone to the funeral to pay her respects, slipping quietly into the back of the church.

Kathleen had shown her a picture of Sean once, and Bernadette had immediately recognized him by his curly hair and dimpled chin. What she hadn't expected was the intense physical attraction she'd felt on seeing his face, a tide of desire that so overwhelmed her it had taken Bernadette five Hail Marys in quick succession to regain her composure.

Then he'd risen to give the eulogy, standing ramrod straight in his dress uniform of an Irish Army lieutenant general, and she'd sat spellbound by his wonderful face and the loving words with which he remembered his family.

After the funeral, she'd approached Sean at the cemetery gate to offer her condolences. He'd recognized her name and told her that Ireland needed more heroines like the new minister for health and social welfare.

Sean had asked her to walk with him, and, during the hour-long stroll that followed, he'd told her that she was a great source of comfort to him, and he hoped he'd see her again.

Bernadette had thought of him often during the next six months, although her work with the victims of radiation poisoning from Windscale had kept her in her office twelve and sixteen hours a day.

"Are you at least going to look at it, then?" Sean prompted, arching his eyebrows at the dossier on her desk.

"In a moment. I was just thinking of the first rose you gave me. Do you remember?"

Sean's face softened and he nodded. "I brought it to your door the first time I took you out. The June after we met."

"It was August."

"August, then. I took you to dinner, then a play at the Abbey Theatre."

"Yes, that's right," she said, every moment of their first evening together still vivid in her memory. After the theatre they'd wandered through the Front Square at Trinity College talking of Irish history and literature.

He'd recited snatches of poems he remembered from his school days, and found stray reasons to touch her hands, her arms, her face. When they'd finally said good night sometime after midnight, Bernadette had gone to bed with the intoxicating notion he was attracted to her, despite the fact that with her large nose, horsey teeth, and several facial moles she considered herself the least comely woman in Dublin.

"The next morning I took you to Mitchell's Cafe on Grafton Street for buns and coffee," Sean said. "I recall it as if it were yesterday."

Bernadette felt a rush at his mention of Mitchell's Cafe. It was there he'd held her hand for the first time over the crisp white cloth of their corner table.

Afterward, as they'd meandered down the wide thoroughfare of Grafton, he'd impulsively whisked her onto narrow Harry Street and there, in the doorway of a still shuttered rugby pub, delivered the first romantic kiss of her life.

Her first instinct had been to stiffen in his arms, for she wasn't over being a nun, and in many ways never would be. Yet her need for physical affection and intimacy, so long bottled up by the cork of the Church and her own pious self-denial, could not withstand his nearness, his searching lips, his breath upon her neck, and she'd abandoned herself to his embrace.

They'd spent the entire day together exploring Dublin, although they were as often in each other's arms as walking. By the time he'd suggested they spend the night together at his apartment, Bernadette was in love and as willing to accompany him to hell as to the heaven he proposed.

She was a nurse and familiar, of course, with a man's

body. But not what that body felt like warm next to her, over her, in her, and the hours of first passion they'd shared were leagues beyond the fantasies that had come to her in her teens and twenties lying in her convent bed, at once aroused and dreading tomorrow's confession to the priest.

Today, after nearly four years, his touch still made the down rise on the nape of her neck, and every time they made love was like that first night in his apartment.

Despite the fact that he often hurt her, as a moment ago, somehow she could never stay angry long, and she relented now as she looked across her desk at his wounded face. She'd learned to take this business about the British Army always at the door with a grain of salt, but he had a fragile ego she must take care not to bruise.

"What is it this mornin', Sean? Another of your intelligence reports warning the British are about to invade?"

"You won't be such a doubtin' Thomas after you've read what's in there," he said, roughly shoving the dossier across the desk. It drove him mad when she got that "humor the lad" tone in her voice.

Bernadette sighed and opened the folder. Inside were several computer printouts of readings from radar scopes, along with analyses of the sighting written in the terse style of the Irish Army. On one sheet were columns of letters and numbers headed: time, direction, aircraft.

"What am I looking at?"

"Radar reports of British military air activity in and out of Northern Ireland over the past three days."

Bernadette studied the reports. "What I know of radar readings you could put in a thimble. Still, it looks to me like most of these planes have been flying west out over the Atlantic, then coming back. Is that correct?"

"Basically."

"What kinds of planes are these?"

"RAF Nimrod MR."

"MR?"

"Maritime reconnaissance. Long-range stuff."

Bernadette put down the dossier. "Have you been listening to the news at all the last few days?"

"Of course."

"Then you know when that volcano erupted in the mid-Atlantic, it sunk the *QE Three*. Isn't it possible these maritime reconnaissance planes are on a maritime reconnaissance mission? They're probably out there searching for survivors."

Sean reddened. "Damn it, I knew that'd be your reaction. The British planes are on a rescue mission, nothing else."

"It stands to reason that's what they're doing."

"The *QE Three* blew apart, for God's sake, disintegrated. There'll be no survivors. The bloody Brits are usin' what happened to the *Queen* as an excuse."

"An excuse for what?"

"To fly near our coasts. Those MR's have got sophisticated cameras and military intelligence experts on board."

Bernadette threw up her hands. "They're spying on us, is that what you're saying, Sean?"

"Don't you see? What happened to the *Queen* gives them a reason to send them planes out. 'Oh, we was only tryin' to rescue our darlin' people out in the cold ocean,' they'll say. The bloody bastards, them planes flew within five miles of one of our artillery regiments in Donegal near the Ulster border."

Bernadette's stomach tightened. Donegal was the northernmost Irish county, a constant flashpoint of conflict with the British across the border in Ulster.

The animosity between Catholics and Protestants in Ulster had become inevitable when Ireland was partitioned by the Anglo-Irish Treaty of 1921. The twenty-six counties of the west and south, holding the great bulk of the land and people of Ireland, became the overwhelmingly Catholic Irish Free State.

The six counties of northeast Ireland, with two-thirds of its inhabitants Protestant descendants of English colonists, remained part of the United Kingdom as the quasi-independent state of Ulster.

Then, in 1972, mounting violence between Ulster's half a million Catholics and one million Protestants forced the British government to suspend the Parliament and assume all security powers in Ulster.

Most of the killing was carried out by members of illegal paramilitary forces on both sides. The Protestant murderers were usually Loyalist vigilantes that were vehemently anti-Catholic and favored the union of Ulster with Britain.

The Catholic killers were either members of the anti-Protestant Irish Republican Army or the even more savage Irish National Liberation Army.

"I've told you a dozen times, Sean, I don't want our military anywhere near the border."

"They're on maneuvers, Taoiseach. You authorized it yourself."

"So I did. A training exercise, you said. I should have known training to you means pointing guns at the British."

"It's them that's occupyin' our northern counties. If they'd get their limey asses out of Ireland, the troubles'd all be over."

Bernadette blew out her cheeks and rolled her eyes back in her head. Reunification with Ulster, if it came, would require years of delicate negotiation. Up until 1995, most rational Irishmen accepted that.

Then came the meltdown at Windscale. Within weeks, the radioactive wind from the English coast had killed forty thousand Irishmen and poisoned the counties of Louth and Meath so badly they would be uninhabitable for centuries to come.

As the newly appointed minister for health and social welfare, Bernadette had repeatedly begged Britain for money and medicine to tend the tens of thousands of Irish victims, only to be answered with bureaucratic stalling and, increasingly, silence.

Whitehall had pleaded that England had over three hundred thousand victims of her own to tend, and that the Treasury would have to examine each foreign claim individually, a process that could take years.

Bernadette had one card left to play; the Americans. In March 1996, she'd flown to New York where she was greeted at Kennedy Airport by eighty thousand Irish American sympathizers. At a thronged news conference later at City Hall, she'd brought out blown-up pictures of the victims of Windscale.

American television cameras zoomed in for close-ups of hideous burns and lesions caused by the radioactivity. Bernadette accompanied the pictures with an eloquent speech describing the suffering of tens of thousands of innocent Irishmen who'd lost their health, their homes, their very reason for living.

When she finished, there were tears in the eyes of half the hard-boiled newsmen, and a tidal wave of rage and indignation swept the United States at England's refusal to help the Irish victims of Windscale.

Boycotts of British goods were announced in a dozen American cities, and even the President abandoned his neutrality and issued a strong statement urging England to reconsider its position.

By the next day, Canada and the other Commonwealth countries had come out in support of the righteous cause of Bernadette O'Fiaich. Faced with boycotts and international condemnation, Whitehall capitulated.

Before the week was out, an Irish reparations bill was rushed before Parliament. After a tumultuous debate in the House of Commons, a consensus was finally reached and the British government announced a payment of ten billion pounds would be made available immediately to the victims of Windscale. Parliament also agreed that a joint team of Irish and English arbitrators would negotiate further compensation.

Bernadette had returned from America hailed by the media as the Irish Joan of Arc, the principled and fearless woman who had forced the British to their knees.

Despite the reparations, the hatred of the English that had simmered in the Irish soul for centuries continued to boil. Sinn Fein, the political arm of the terrorist Irish Republican Army, organized huge protest rallies that drew thousands, then hundreds of thousands.

In the general election two months later, almost a hundred Sinn Fein candidates were elected to the Dail Eireann, putting enormous pressure on the liberal Fine Gael government. When Sinn Fein demanded that Ireland arm herself against a British attack from Ulster, the government had no choice but to acquiesce.

The alternative would have been to turn over the reins of power entirely to Sinn Fein and this the moderate prime minister refused to do, reasoning that it was wiser to give the radicals the bone of a bigger army than the body politic of Ireland.

In the months that followed, Dublin carried out a rapid mobilization, calling up thousands of reserve forces. The United States and the Common Market countries of Europe refused to help Ireland arm herself, but Dublin had no trouble buying tanks and missiles from China and Brazil.

By the spring of 1997, Ireland had fielded a new armored brigade with over four hundred heavy tanks and eight thousand men. It had bankrupted the Irish Treasury to build the force, but the buildup satisfied the Sinn Fein. The Irish Army was now powerful enough to bloody the nose of the British lion should it stick its greedy paw across the Irish border.

The following fall, the rising chain of volcanoes along the Mid-Atlantic Ridge began diverting the warm waters of the North Atlantic Drift. By December, fierce blizzards were scourging Ireland, closing roads and factories. Tens of thousands were suddenly unemployed, swelling the already bulging ranks of Irishmen thrown out of work by skyrocketing oil prices and the economic aftereffects of the Windscale disaster.

With the country on the brink of economic ruin, the Irish people began to turn away from the strident rhetoric of the Sinn Fein. People were freezing in their homes; thousands were a sack of potatoes away from starvation. What was needed now was a leader to give Ireland not bullets but bread.

The leaders of the Fine Gael Party summoned Bernadette O'Fiaich. It was Bernadette who'd succeeded in winning reparations from Britain when all else failed, Bernadette who'd brought relief to the thousands of victims of Windscale.

If anyone could lead Ireland out of her vale of sorrows it was her, and in the spring of 1998 the courageous former nun from Louth was elected prime minister of Ireland.

For her first appointment, she had named Sean McCormick minister for defense, the post he'd requested, despite howls from the opposition that a stridently nationalist army general with no political experience was wrong for the job.

She'd paid no attention to the objections, for she not only loved Sean, she trusted him. Besides, she'd needed someone working with her she could confide in.

If she'd had it to do again, she would have offered him a different position, for his vehemently anti-British sentiments often made life difficult for her.

And now here he was at her again with his silly tale of British spy planes. Damn his ego, there were times when she'd had all she could take of his saber rattling.

"I see no cause for alarm in these reconnaissance flights at all, Sean," she said calmly. "If you wish, I'll make some inquiries through the usual informal channels."

"And you'll get the usual informal lies back," he said, rising angrily and snatching the dossier back off her desk. "You've a terrible problem, Taoiseach. You trust too much."

"And you too little, Sean."

"Tell me that after you've buried your babies," he threw at her, then spun on his heel and stalked from the prime minister's office.

For a long time Bernadette sat motionless in her chair, wondering what Sean would say if he knew he'd soon be burying her. For the past several weeks she'd been experiencing shortness of breath and constant fatigue, and two days before a hospital checkup had confirmed her heart was dangerously weak.

The stress of her office would soon kill her, her doctors warned. She must resign, and enter the hospital for an operation.

She'd refused, and sworn the physicians to secrecy. Ireland needed her more than ever now. She'd carry on as long as she could, and leave the rest up to God.

She hadn't told Sean her heart was bad. She wasn't sure

whether she kept the truth from him out of fear it would pain him, or fear it would make him leave her.

Bernadette rose with a sigh and crossed to the window to look out at the driving snow. God in heaven, would the icy gales never stop? Why couldn't Sean understand it was not an attack by British troops but an assault of volcanic ash and arctic cold that Ireland had most to fear.

NORTH CHANNEL
• • • • • • • • • • • • • • • • • • •

7:35 p.m.

"BONKERS BRIAN" WAS NOT the least crazy, even though he lived alone on a small, battered freighter frozen into the middle of the ice of North Channel, and had long conversations with a statue of Saint Patrick regular as clockwork twice a day.

When the little freighter had first become trapped by the pack ice that now joined England to Ireland, a British air-sea rescue helicopter had spotted the vessel, and dropped down to investigate.

The pilots found only Brian aboard, who told them the four other crewmen had already taken knapsacks of provisions and walked the twenty kilometers across the ice to the Irish shore.

As for himself, he was staying put, for the vessel was the property of the Donegal Shipping Company, Limited, a fine firm with which he'd been employed since he was a boy, and he meant to guard the ship against thieving salvagers until the ice melted next summer and he could steam her free.

When the English airmen warned he could freeze or starve to death way out here so many miles from the nearest inhabited land, he'd taken them below and showed them a bunker full of coal, and a cargo hold crammed with canned goods he explained he'd been ferrying from Buncrana in the north of Ireland to Schull at the country's southern tip.

He'd be warm and well fed, content as Paddy's pig, Bonkers Brian had insisted with a strange, cackling laugh, no matter if the blizzards blew all the winter long, and he had no visitor save the occasional hardy gull come to pick the garbage he tossed out on the ice.

The British airmen had exchanged looks of raised brows and cocked eyes that confirmed silently to each other the man was daft, then shrugged, wished Brian well, and took off again in their helicopter.

Thereafter, every few weeks, the same pilots, or another crew in their coastal squadron, would land with a bottle of Scotch or a case of Guinness for the grizzled Irish freighter captain they'd derisively named Bonkers Brian. Soon, the "crazy Irishman" became a favorite topic of conversation, and the butt of many jokes back in the airmen's mess.

Brian always welcomed the British visits, and he flattered the pilots with many questions about their lives, the goings-on at their home bases, morale in the British armed forces, scuttlebutt young soldiers loved to gripe about, especially when they could get things off their chests by telling this daft Irishman who likely didn't understand half of what they said, and had no one to tell if he did.

But Brian did have someone to tell. After every visit by a British helicopter, he would sit down in his warm cabin before a statue of Saint Patrick and tell the small wooden figurine all the English pilots had to say.

Over the months, Brian told Saint Patrick about British troop strengths, the movement of units, shortages of aviation fuel, the unavailability of spare parts, the scaling back of pay and benefits to British forces that had sapped morale, and many other interesting military matters he had gleaned from his visitors.

Anyone peeping in his cabin window would have confirmed the judgment of the helicopter crews that Brian was quite mad to be talking such to a statue. Of course, if they had heard Saint Patrick talk back, in a military vernacular, they might have suspected that Brian was not only not bonkers, but not a sea captain, and not even a sailor, but an Irish spy camped out on Britain's frozen doorstep.

Major Brian Finigan, Irish Army Intelligence, talked quite often to Saint Patrick, for inside the statue were both a transistorized microphone and a receiver that gave him instant two-way communication with headquarters in Dublin.

There were several other things about the icebound freighter that were not what they seemed. The rusting mast that tilted with the ship toward the shores of Scotland contained a sophisticated radar within its hollow tube that fed images to a computerized radar screen disguised as an old broken television in the crew's mess.

Each day Bonkers Brian spent many hours before the radar, noting the types and number of British aircraft that passed over flying between Britain and Northern Ireland. The major had several other duties on board each day. He had to check the sonar devices that extended down into the freezing black water beneath the ice to listen for the sounds of any British submarines passing beneath the thick floes.

If the British had bothered to check their maps, they would have noted the curious fact that the rusting freighter was frozen into the ice directly above the main undersea phone cable between England and Ulster, and Bonkers Brian daily checked his instruments to insure the Irish tap was working, feeding British conversations through the line that led southwest under the floes to the shore of the Irish Free State.

The entire operation was the brainchild of General Sean McCormick, and through the electronic eyes and ears built into the rusting, icebound freighter, and the information Bonkers Brian culled so disarmingly from his English visitors, McCormick had gained a most thorough picture of the current infrastructure of the British military.

It was Bonkers Brian who first learned, in a conversation with a Royal Air Force lieutenant quaffing his third pint of bitters, that while Whitehall continued to insist officially that RAF strength remained equal to that during the Falklands

War, the truth was only a handful of planes could now get into the air.

There were practically no spare parts obtainable anymore, aviation fuel was harder to find than hens' teeth, and there were neither the personnel nor the snowplows available to clear British military airfields, ninety percent of which were now abandoned under towering snowdrifts.

The phone tap on the underseas cable to Ulster had provided General McCormick the startling disclosure that British troop strengths in Ulster were at most one-quarter what the British ministry of defense claimed them to be.

Nevertheless, McCormick had made clear in a recent coded message to Major Finigan that he was gravely concerned that should hostilities break out between Ireland and England, the British might attempt to rush reinforcements from their own shores across the ice of North Channel to Northern Ireland.

Finigan had assured the nervous general that he would keep a sharp eye on the radar scanning the ice to the east. Truth be told, though, he was not as concerned the British would attack as was his superior in Dublin. He'd rather come to like the English airmen who dropped in on him by helicopter, and he hoped in his heart he would not someday have to go to war against these fine young flyers.

On February 2 they had even surprised him with a leg of mutton, the first fresh meat he'd had in months, and the generosity of the RAF pilots had touched him deeply. That very night, the smell of roasted mutton filled the little freighter, and wafted away on the westerly wind blowing toward Scotland.

Brian had gone to bed feeling content. Then, just before dawn the next morning, he'd woken in a drenching sweat, for he'd dreamt he'd heard the howling of banshees. Although he was a grown man, and an Irish Army officer to boot, the tales of his sainted grandmother when he was a child had instilled in him the haunting superstition that the female spirits of Gaelic folklore were somehow real, and that their wailing foreshadowed death. The dream left him shaken.

Later that morning he had been emptying the garbage over the side as usual when he'd suddenly noticed the contents of the dump below were strewn across the ice. When he'd descended to the floes to investigate, he'd found that something had dragged cans and torn sacks twenty yards and more from the side of the ship.

Wind-driven snow had obliterated the tracks of whatever animal had foraged in the dump, and he could see no sign of life when he'd looked out over the floes. To spook him even further, as he'd searched the ice he'd had the distinct feeling he was being watched.

Brian had climbed the hand-built stairs of the freighter and downed two stiff shots of Scotch to calm his nerves. Then he sat down in the coal-fire-warmed galley to think. There was no sound save the wind whistling through the frozen rigging above, and the calls of a flight of gulls passing over.

Gulls. He considered the possibility. Occasionally the birds dropped down to scavenge through the garbage. Yet he could not recall them ever pulling cans out of the pile, and several of the sacks that had been dragged out onto the floes were far too large for birds to move.

Then it hit him. Seals. Of course. Occasionally, leads would open in the pack ice, and several times he'd seen seals swimming and diving for fish in briefly open fingers of seawater near the ship. That had to be it. He'd been robbed by seals.

Nothing unusual occurred for the next two days. Then, just after dark on February 5, as he was heating up the last of his mutton, Bonkers Brian heard the banshees again. This time, standing in the galley wide awake, he knew it was no dream.

The howling started as a faraway cry carried to the ship by the wind. Brian turned and peered out the small porthole next to the stove. Perhaps, after all, it had only been the wind, for he could see nothing in the moonless black night beyond the icy deck.

He returned to his cooking, chiding himself not to let a breeze whistling across the ice stir the fears of his youth. *Take hold of yourself, Brian, you're no longer a boy quivering before a peat fire in your old grandmother's thatched cottage.*

Then the howling came again, closer now, louder, echoing off the near steel side of the ship. The hairs on his arms stood straight up, and he dropped the pot of boiled potatoes in his hand, the water hissing on the hot stove as the pot clattered to the floor.

Brian's heart thundered against his chest as reason fought with fear. He stared down at the potatoes in a puddle on the steel deck. There's no such thing as banshees. What he was hearing wasn't real. It was all—

What was that? Wood creaking. Something was climbing up the wooden stairs from the ice. There was silence outside for a moment, the only sound the faint crackling of mutton fat in the oven. Then something began to pad forward along the deck plates.

Brian's hand shot out for a butcher knife on the side of the sink. Banshees were spirits. Whatever was out there had a body. The sound of the footfalls got closer. He felt his throat constrict. Then the muffled approach suddenly stopped. Directly outside. Whatever had boarded the ship was on the other side of the galley door.

Brian felt his knees buckle at the sight of a haze of vaporized breath rising up past the porthole. He fought for control of himself and inched forward toward the small round window. He had to see what was out there.

He was inches away when the face suddenly sprang up from below, filling the circle of glass with its snapping, saliva-flecked teeth and great yellow eyes.

Brian screamed and fell backward, away from the terrible wolf face, slamming into the stove behind him. His hand fell on the red-hot metal and he screamed again, flinging reflexively back across the galley and into the door. As he banged against the handle, the galley door clicked open and a blast of freezing air shot into the overheated room.

Oh, dear God, no. A huge wolf paw had come in with the numbing blast. He reached forward to shove the paw out, feeling the coarse fur and sharp claws between his fingers.

Then, in a blur, a snout and slashing teeth shot through. Brian felt a terrible pain, and jerked his hand back.

Only there wasn't any hand at the end of his arm anymore. Blood spurted into his face as he stared at the bloody stump sliced as cleanly as if by a knife. He felt the door being pushed inward against his back. His feet skidded on the wet floor as he tried frantically to fight it back closed.

It was no use. His head slammed into the near bulkhead as the door flew inward and the immense wolf sprang into the galley. Brian raised the knife, but the frenzied animal was on him before he could bring it down, his long fangs embedded in the human's gurgling throat.

In a moment it was over. Bonkers Brian lay dead, blood flowing from his throat and handless wrist. The panting wolf straddled the lifeless body, then lowered his head and licked the staring human face, tasting the meal to come.

In an ordinary time and an ordinary place, the huge wolf would not have stalked humans, for men were as dangerous to wolves as wolves were to rabbits. But this was not an ordinary time, and this was not an ordinary place. There was no other meat out on the floes but that on the bones of humans. The wolf had become a maneater not out of a lust to kill but a lust to live.

A long triumphant howl filled the galley, then the animal began to drag the corpse along the deck and down the stairs to the ice.

The hunt had been successful, and somewhere out on the barren floes the pack awaited the return of their daring leader and ever faithful provider, the great wolf Beelzebub.

Biosphere Britannia
●●●●●●●●●●●●●●●●●●●●●●●

11:15 a.m.—February 6
British Fuel Reserves—15 days

"Do you know what we remind me of, Ben?" Marjorie Glynn smiled at Benjamin Meade as they walked in shirtsleeves and shorts along the small sea beach in Biosphere Britannia.

"What?" Ben said, stepping around a green turtle dragging herself laboriously up the sand to lay her eggs high beyond the lapping waves.

"Two cerambycidae first meeting on a log."

"What the hell are cerambycidae?"

"Beetles with elongated antennae. When two of them meet in the forest, they stretch out their antennae to touch and feel, sort of size one another up before they risk getting closer."

"Is that what we've been doing the past twenty-four hours? Sizing each other up?"

"I think so. I mean, we've talked about the Biosphere, geothermal generators, the British general election, all we have to accomplish in the next few weeks. But very little about ourselves."

"You're right. All I know about your personal life so far is that you're into chastity belts."

"Poor boy, still stung that I called you out for leering at me yesterday?"

"I'll keep in mind you don't appreciate male attention."

"That's not true. Despite what you may think, I consider myself quite a passionate woman."

"I'll want affidavits, of course, from your legions of boy-friends."

"Hardly legions."

"But you do date?"

"Of course. Most of the time, I enjoy the company of men. From time to time I even find one I like enough to share his bed."

"Are you in a relationship now?"

"No, not for the past couple of years." Marjorie picked up a palm frond and twirled it absently in her hands. "Truth is, but for the scientists I occasionally go out with, most of my would-be swains have seemed cut from the same dreary cloth."

"Let me guess; they only want one thing."

"That's part of it. But what really turns me off are the arrogant budding tycoons that think money makes them irresistible. The type that swagger up to you at cocktail parties, pinstriped and clutching beakers of Scotch, half of them reeking of some cologne named Mountain Man Musk or Bull Balls, or one of those damn hairy, smelly names you men seem to love to attach to yourselves."

"I don't wear cologne."

"It's your most sterling attribute."

"Thanks."

"You do share one thing in common with the men I'm describing."

"Rabid lust?"

"Money. From what I hear, you're rich as Croesus."

"I've been successful, sure. But I didn't make my dough sitting in some office with my wingtips up on the desk manipulating the stock market. I earned it sinking geothermal wells, ass deep in the muck of New Guinea or freezing my ass off in Antarctica."

"I'll grant you, there is a difference."

"Were you ever serious about a man?"

"Once. Edward."

"I take it he wasn't a banker."

"Botanist, actually. I met him at Oxford. He was the son of a lord, with dark eyes, flashing white teeth, and the physique of a rugby player."

"And you were in love."

Marjorie looked out over the small sea. "I convinced myself it was love, or at least close enough to make it all right. Still, the night we became engaged I remember thinking there was something missing."

"So you broke it off."

"Not right away. It took me several months to finally realize he was far more style than substance. He had a streak of narcissism. And a massive ego. Worse, his wit was often at the expense of others; including, occasionally, myself."

"Sounds like the kind of guy that needs a kick in the ass."

"A kick in the ass would do Edward wonders. I wish I'd thought of it. Anyway, enough about my ex-beaus. Tell me about yourself. I'd like to know what makes Ben Meade tick."

"What do you want to know?" he said, stopping to pick up a coconut lying in the sand.

"Well, as a for instance, those scars on your neck and right arm. From burns, aren't they?"

For a long moment Ben stared down at the coconut in his hands. "Yes," he said finally.

"Look, Ben, I didn't mean to pry. Obviously I'm making you uncomfortable. I've told you a bit about myself, but that doesn't mean you have to reciprocate."

"I went over a cliff in a Jeep. It caught fire."

"Good Lord. It's a wonder you weren't killed."

"Yeah, especially since that's probably what I was trying to do, kill myself."

Marjorie stood staring at him, suddenly uncomfortable. "You can't mean that."

"Oblivion was definitely what I had in mind. Not that my mind was functioning at the time. I was drunk."

"We all have our vulnerable moments. Times when we wonder what's the sense in going on."

"You've felt that way?"

"More than once when I was young and wounded to the quick. You know, my parents didn't understand me, or some cad used me in bed. I used to have dramatic visions of myself in a casket, draped in white lace, beautiful in death. How sorry the world would be."

"Crazy, isn't it, the way our minds warp when we've been hurt real bad?"

"How were you hurt, Ben?"

Ben went into a shot-putter's stance, his left arm straight out toward the small sea, his right hand cradling the coconut back behind his ear. "I came home and found my wife making love to my brother."

"Good God."

Ben spun to his left, hopped in the air, and let the coconut fly toward the water as he whirled around to land.

For a moment the two stood silently watching the ripples spread twenty meters from the beach.

"Not as good as I used to be," Ben said.

"Finding them like that must have been horrible."

He looked up and down the shore, avoiding her eyes. "What is this, a one-coconut beach? The Olympics are coming up, you know. How the hell am I supposed to practice?"

Marjorie stepped around to face him. "We don't have to talk about it."

"I want to talk about it, damn it. Unless you'd rather I didn't."

Marjorie could see the pain in his face. Perhaps it would be a catharsis for him to tell her. "No, I'll listen," she said softly.

"Ten years ago, I was just getting Meade International off the ground. My life was nothing but work. Eighteen, twenty hours a day I was either in my laboratory or sitting in front of a computer."

"This was out in Wyoming? Richard told me you have a ranch there."

"Yeah. I hired a lab assistant. Elizabeth. It wasn't long

before she started staying after work to cook dinner and help around the house. She quickly became a lot more than a lab assistant. I figured she cared."

Marjorie knew what was coming next. "And you started sleeping together."

Ben looked up. "Yeah. We were different in a lot of ways. She liked to watch game shows and go to shopping malls. I preferred reading and riding horses. But in bed we liked the same things. And we spent hours in bed."

I'll just bet you did, Marjorie thought.

"After we'd lived together for a few months, she started bringing up marriage. I wasn't wild about the idea. Who needed it? But, well, I wasn't dead set against it either. She'd become a big part of my life. And I wanted to make her happy."

"So you married her."

"A year after she arrived at the ranch."

"Did you love her?"

Ben was silent a long time and Marjorie didn't think he was going to answer her.

Finally he said, "No. I was playing house. I'm not even sure I know what love is."

"How long did your marriage last?"

"Two years. Then Charlie showed up."

"Your brother?"

"Yeah, my brother." Ben spat out the words as if they were venom. "All his life, Charlie's been a fuck-up. He's never held a job more than a couple of months, never owned anything but an old truck and the clothes on his back."

"He sounds the opposite of you."

"He is. When I headed off to college, Charlie hit the rodeo circuit. A year later I got a phone call from him. He'd killed some guy in a knife fight in a bar. He was doing five to ten in the Wyoming state pen."

Ben looked out over the small sea for a moment. "Still, he was family. When Charlie got out of the slammer six years later, I picked him up at the gate. By then Elizabeth and I had been married a couple of years. I brought Charlie to the ranch, gave him a job, moved him into a spare cabin I had."

"How did your wife feel about Charlie being there?"

"Hell, they hit it off right from the start. They used to watch those damn game shows together while I worked in the lab at night. He'd take her shopping and out for a couple of beers, all that fluff stuff I never could stand."

"How long did this go on?"

"Six months. Then I had to go to a business meeting in New York. I was already at the airport when I got a call my meeting had been canceled. I drove back to the ranch. The TV was blaring some soap opera in the living room. They didn't hear me come in. They didn't see me either; they were too busy screwing each other's brains out on the couch.

"I yanked Charlie off her by the throat. We had a knock-down, drag-out fight, Elizabeth standing there naked, screaming. It ended with Charlie throwing a chair at me and running out the front door, Elizabeth right behind him.

"Outside I could hear Charlie starting his truck. I ran to my den and got a rifle. By the time I got to the front door they were in the truck doing fifty down the ranch road, both of them still naked as jaybirds."

There was a wild look in Ben's face now and Marjorie knew she shouldn't pursue the subject. But she couldn't help herself. She had to ask him. "You said you got a gun. Would you have killed them?"

"I would have killed Charlie. Maybe her too, I don't know. But they got away. I started drinking. Water glasses full of Scotch, one after the other. The next thing I knew I was behind the wheel of my Jeep. I remember the fence posts going by in a blur. A mile before the main road I went over a cliff and the jeep caught fire. My ranch foreman found me on his way in to work an hour later. I spent a month in the hospital."

Ben kicked viciously at the sand, making Marjorie jump. "The bitch had probably been cheating on me with Charlie for months."

"Ben, perhaps we'd better change the subject," Marjorie said, nervous at the way the muscles were bulging in his neck.

"You wanted to know."

"I didn't realize it would upset you so."

"I'm not the first guy it's happened to. Of course, most men don't get cuckolded by their own brother, the son of a bitch."

"Ben, if I'd had any idea, I wouldn't have asked."

"You're a biologist, Marjorie. You should be used to turning over rocks and exposing slimy things. Well, you just turned over my rock, and now you don't like what's crawled out."

He was shouting now. God, she was sorry she'd started this. He'd be tearing up trees by the roots in a minute.

"Ben, you're working yourself up into a froth. I'm two feet away. There's no need to yell."

"I'm not yelling," he yelled.

"If you don't lower your voice, I'm leaving."

"The subject gets a little unpleasant and your first instinct is to flee in terror. Just like you hauled ass when the geothermal debate in Parliament got too hot for your delicate hide."

"How dare you!" Marjorie exploded, smacking him in the face with her small fist. He had a jaw like granite, and she jumped around the beach shaking her hand in pain. "Owww, you bloody bastard, you've broken my hand."

Ben stared at her dumbfounded, his rage obliterated by the unexpected blow. "I don't believe you did that."

"You drove me to it, you great ill-tempered baboon. I was only trying to get to know you, to be friends, and you respond by insulting me."

"Look, that crack was out of line. I—"

"I've already apologized for giving in to MacTiege. What do you want from me, blood?" She looked down at her skinned knuckles. "Blood! See what you've done."

Ben reached out to take her hand but Marjorie jerked it away. "Don't you dare touch me, you oversexed lout."

"Oversexed lout?"

Marjorie stomped down to the water and knelt to immerse her hand. "You have the bone structure of a Neanderthal. I think I've broken every knuckle in my hand."

Ben went and crouched beside her. "Please. Let me see your hand."

"The hand's all you get."

"You've made your point." He took her wet fingers in his and gently probed the bones. "I don't think you've fractured anything. It's going to be sore for a while, though. You really slugged me."

"You had it coming."

"You're right, I did. Look, Marjorie, we got on the one subject that can really turn me loose. I apologize. Will you forgive me?"

Marjorie looked at him. She could see in his eyes he was genuinely sorry. And, despite his temper and his bumptious sexuality, there was something very right about the touch of his hand.

"I suppose it was partly my fault," she relented. "I egged you into talking about what happened."

"Friends?"

"Friends."

"Ah, Anglo-American unity in full flower," Richard Booroojian said, descending a path from the savanna. "Hands across the sea and all that."

Marjorie and Ben untwined their fingers and stood. "It's hardly what you think, Richard," she said.

"Why, I don't think a thing at'll. I am merely the bearer of tidings. Ill tidings, I'm afraid."

"What's happened?" Marjorie asked.

"I've just had a call from a meteorologist in Plymouth. There's a gale blowing in from the Atlantic. The winds have almost doubled in velocity over the past few hours."

"That means the ash clouds will be here sooner than we thought," Ben said.

"The gale will present us with another problem, Ben. It's pushing more icebergs up the Channel. Within hours there'll be an impassable barrier of huge bergs between England and France."

"Jesus, my men and equipment landed in Paris six hours ago. They're already on their way to Calais."

"I'm afraid they'll be stuck there, Ben. There's no way to get an icebreaker across the Channel now."

Marjorie sank down on the sand. "The Chunnel gone, the

airports shuttered, and now our sea approaches blocked by bergs." She looked up at the men. "We're cut off from the world. Sixty million people marooned on this bloody freezing island."

BIOSPHERE BRITANNIA
• •

2:05 p.m.—February 7
British Fuel Reserves—14 Days

BENJAMIN MEADE PUT DOWN the phone in Marjorie Glynn's office in the human-habitat wing of Biosphere Britannia and pounded a fist down on the desk before him.

"Goddamnit, here I've got the best geothermal exploration team in the world and tons of state-of-the-art equipment ready to go to work and we can't even get them across the Channel, much less up to North Channel where they're needed."

"Even if we somehow got them to England, they'd end up sitting in London," Marjorie said. "When I talked to the railway people, they said there was no way they could transport your equipment up by rail. The tracks north to Scotland are buried under snowdrifts forty feet high in places."

The intercom from the entrance station buzzed insistently and Marjorie crossed to the desk and stabbed angrily at the button. "Yes?"

"The prime minister's lost in the desert," the panicky voice of Mickey at the reception desk burst out from the receiver.

"Good Lord," Marjorie said. "I haven't seen the papers. I didn't even know he'd left the country."

"No, no, our desert."

"What?"

"Yes, he popped in unannounced twenty minutes ago. I was off in the loo and when I came back there were two policemen standing here. They told me the PM had gone in to see the desert, and now I can't find him."

"I'll be right there."

Ben laughed. "He's not the first politician lost in the wilderness. Usually it's a desert of the soul."

"You'd think they'd let us know he was coming," Marjorie said, frowning down at her work-stained coveralls. "I look a fright."

"I don't think he's here for a fashion show."

"Men. Come along, then."

"Me?"

"You. I was going to try to arrange a meeting before you left for the ice. You *are* the bloody world expert on geothermal, you know. The PM will undoubtedly have some questions for you."

"What sort of questions?"

Marjorie opened the door. "Oh, nothing weighty. Probably just a few offhand queries on how you intend to save the country," she said, starting down the corridor.

"So long as it's nothing serious," Ben said, following her out. They were just about to walk through the tunnel to the main area of the Biosphere when the policeman's voice stopped them in their tracks.

"Hold it right there."

They turned as one of the prime minister's bodyguards approached from the entrance desk. "May I ask where you're going?"

"Into the Biosphere," Marjorie said. "I'm Dr. Marjorie Glynn, director here."

"May I see some identification please, ma'am?"

Marjorie fished out her photo ID. "There you are."

The policeman looked it over. "Quite right." He turned to Ben. "And you, sir."

"I'm afraid I left my passport in my street clothes."

The policeman cocked a brow at Ben's accent. "An American, are we, sir?"

"We are an American."

"So he keeps saying." Marjorie couldn't resist. "Still, with that twang when he pronounces vowels, one might wonder where he's from."

"That's a Western twang. When you're raised on a cattle ranch, it comes as natural as carrying a gun."

"Carrying a gun." The policeman took a new interest in Ben.

"I'll get you for this, Marjorie."

"Are we threatening the Biosphere director, sir?"

"You bet your ass."

"Perhaps we'd better straighten this out at the Yard."

"Marjorie!"

A detective in plain clothes came up the corridor. "What's going on here?"

"I'm not sure, sir," the policeman said. "This is Dr. Glynn, the Biosphere director. There seems to be some question who this chap is. Doesn't have his passport."

"My name is Benjamin Franklin Meade. I'm an American."

The detective took a packet of papers out of his pocket. "Meade, hey. If I'm not mistaken—"

"He really is who he says," Marjorie said, retreating.

The policeman threw her a dirty look.

"A little joke."

"Yes, here it is," the detective said. "Dr. Benjamin Meade. American geophysicist. You were cleared by our security people two years ago when you were here working on the North Channel project."

"Thank you." Ben gave the policeman a triumphant look.

"How's everything in your wonderful state of Colorado?" the detective asked casually.

"Wyoming."

The detective grinned. "Right you are. Pardon our precautions, Dr. Meade. Can't be too careful where the PM's involved."

"Of course."

"We'll just go find him, then," Marjorie said, leading Ben toward the tunnel again.

"Twang, huh?" Ben said under his breath as they passed through the first screen door.

Marjorie laughed.

When they found him five minutes later, Prime Minister Aldis Butler was deep in a sagebrush thicket staring up at a large columnar cactus. Clad in a three-piece heavy woolen dark blue suit, starched white shirt, and maroon silk tie, Butler looked incongruous against the desert terrain around him.

"Good morning, sir," Marjorie said, resisting the impulse to chide the prime minister for wearing unsanitized street clothes into the Biosphere.

"Morning, Marjorie," the prime minister said, without lowering his eyes. "Biggest bloody cactus I've ever seen. Hate to brush a horse up against that. These nettles would shred a hide good and proper."

"That's what they're for, sir."

"I beg your pardon?" The prime minister looked at her.

Marjorie smiled. "I mean they keep animals away, from feeding on the pulp."

"Oh, yes, of course. You must be Dr. Meade," he said, extending his hand to Ben. "Welcome to England."

Ben shook hands with the tall, thin, silver-haired Butler. "Thank you, Prime Minister."

"Shall we walk?" Butler said. "I hope you don't mind my wandering about in here, Marjorie. When I was here for your dedication ceremony, I didn't get to see much of your miniearth, what with the press and the photographers all over the place. I trust I haven't put you out."

"Not at all, Prime Minister," Marjorie said, following along with Ben as Butler strode out of the thicket and headed down the side of an arroyo. "After all, if you hadn't backed the Biosphere bill in Parliament, this would all still be just a dream."

"Your dream, Marjorie. And, if I might say, a vision for England as well."

"May I show you around, Prime Minister?"

"I'd like that." Butler waved his cane over the sand. "Where did you take all this from? Originally, I mean."

"We brought in most of the biome from the Vizcaino coastal fog desert of Baja, California. The area down near the sea of Cortez."

"Absolutely smashing. What's that plant there, Marjorie?"

"A creosote bush."

"And that?"

"Greasewood. If you'll look closely, sir, there's a Gila monster hiding just behind it."

"It's all terribly exotic. What a job you've done, Marjorie. Why, it looks as if the desert's been here a thousand years. Do you know, I saw a tarantula just before you came up."

"You want to be careful of those, Prime Minister," Marjorie said. "We've brought in life-forms as they exist in the wild. The tarantulas in here can give you a nasty bite."

"Rather like my opposition in Parliament. I can't wait to see the faces on some of those Labor MP's when we bring geothermal power on line. Tell me, Dr. Meade, when will that be?"

"I've looked over the plans your electrical engineers drew up two years ago," Ben said. "Once we've tapped into the geothermal reservoir and hooked up the steam generators, we can tie into the existing British power grid. We should be able to begin producing power in a couple of weeks."

The prime minister stopped walking and looked at Ben. "A rosy prediction, Dr. Meade, but your face tells me all is not well."

"I have two problems, Prime Minister. First of all, I got horsed around the last time I was over here. I was led to believe the geothermal reservoir at North Channel lay entirely under British territorial waters. It doesn't."

"You're quite right. Half the field belongs to Ireland. I apologize if you were kept in the dark."

"I don't like being conned."

"I assure you, we had a very good reason for keeping the extent of the geothermal field secret."

"Damn right you did. You've discovered a bonanza of energy and you don't want to share it."

"Ben!"

"It's all right, Marjorie, he has a right to be put out. Still, Dr. Meade, you are wrong about our motives."

"Then why don't you tell the Irish about the geothermal field? From what I've seen of the satellite data, that reservoir's big enough to supply both countries with energy for the next century."

"We have no quarrel with sharing the geothermal field. Our concern is time. As you know, our diplomatic relations with Ireland have completely broken down. Negotiations over the geothermal reservoir could take years. We don't have years. We need that energy now."

"When do you intend to tell the Irish the truth?"

"As soon as you bring in that first well. I promise you, we won't ask you to drill again until talks with Ireland have been satisfactorily concluded."

Ben shook his head. "I don't get it. One well can only produce enough energy to supply a medium-sized city. You're going to need twenty or thirty wells to power all of Britain."

"It's the symbolism that's important, Dr. Meade. Once North Channel actually starts producing electricity, I'm convinced Parliament will vote to fund full development of the reservoir. More importantly, it will take the wind out of the sails of the Labor Party's plans for a coal-based economy."

"So it's a political thing."

"Of course there's politics involved, Ben, that's the real world," Marjorie said. "But bringing in that first well will also give the nation something to believe in. As it is, the people have no heart to fight back against the blackmail of the radical unions."

"Marjorie's right," Butler said. "Bringing geothermal on line could break the back of the general strike MacTiege has engineered."

Ben stared silently at Marjorie a moment, then turned back to the prime minister. "I want to be sure I understand this. As soon as I bring that first well in, you'll open negotiations with Ireland over sharing the field."

"That is my intent." Butler held out his hand. "Agreed?"

Ben shook hands. "Agreed."

"Splendid. Now, shall we resume our walk?"

Marjorie and Ben fell into step beside Butler.

"You said you had two problems, Dr. Meade," the prime minister said as they approached a flat rock shelf. "May I know the second?"

"It's a matter of logistics," Ben said. "I've got tons of equipment and seventy-five of my engineers and roustabouts cooling their heels in Calais."

"Roustabouts?"

"Equipment handlers and drill-platform workers."

"Stop!" Marjorie yelled, grabbing the prime minister's arm.

"What?" Butler looked at her.

Marjorie pointed out the snake coiled under an edge of the rock shelf two steps ahead. "Diamondback rattlesnake, Prime Minister, highly poisonous."

"Wait till Mrs. Butler hears of this," the prime minister beamed, his light blue eyes sparkling. "Near done in by a rattler in the dead of winter not thirty minutes from London."

"Everything one would find in the Baja we've included in the desert ecosystem here in the Biosphere, sir," Marjorie said. "Perhaps I'd better walk ahead. I'd hate to lose the best friend we Biosphereans have in England."

"I wouldn't hear of it." Butler grinned, walking around the snake. "Why, I haven't had this much excitement since I put two fish into the *General Belgrano*," he said, referring to his service in the 1982 Falklands War. As captain of the British submarine *Conqueror*, he'd sunk the Argentine cruiser *General Belgrano* with two wire-guided torpedoes.

Marjorie looked at Ben and shrugged.

"We were talking about your engineers and equipment, stranded in France, Dr. Meade. If I might suggest, we could send military helicopters over to fetch the lot."

"We could use choppers to ferry my men up to North Channel," Ben said. "But a good deal of the equipment, the generators and the drill towers for instance, are far too large for helicopters to lift."

Butler bent and scooped up a handful of sand, letting the grains trickle through his fingers. "Warm as the beach at Brighton used to be. Have you ever had to drill under adverse winter conditions before, Dr. Meade?"

"Yes. In Antarctica."

"How did you transport your rigs?"

"Snowcats. They're sort of a combination tractor-snowmobile designed for polar work. We unloaded the rig sections from ships onto sleds at the edge of the ice shelf, and then the snowcats pulled the sleds across the snow to the drill sites."

"I see. So the situation is, we have vital men and equipment trapped in France and no ready way to get the whole show back across the Channel to Britain where it's desperately needed. Rather reminds me of Dunkirk."

Marjorie stopped dead in her tracks, her face animated. "Dunkirk! That's it!"

The two men stared at her. "Don't you see?" Marjorie said excitedly. "When our army was trapped on that French beach by the Nazis during World War Two, how did we get them back to England?"

The prime minister folded his hands behind his back. "Why, every private vessel between Ramsgate and Portsmouth crossed the Channel and brought them home. Everything from fishing boats to tugs."

"Exactly!" Marjorie could hardly contain herself. "Britain pulled off the impossible sixty years ago, we can do it again."

"How the hell can we use boats?" Ben said. "The seas will be frozen solid until late spring."

"No, no, not boats; I'm thinking of those snowmobiles that mechanics have been making out of old cars and lorries. Why, there must be thousands of them in England now."

"What, those contraptions with treads they use out in the country?" Butler said.

"Oh, I know they don't look like much, Prime Minister," Marjorie said, "but some of the larger ones are enormously powerful. I saw a picture of one in the paper last week pulling a boxcar on sleds."

Ben's face lit up. "By God, Marjorie, it just might work. We could build sleds big enough to hold the tower sections. Then hook up, I don't know, four, five snowmobiles to each sled."

"Exactly. The return trip from France up to North Channel will be the hardest part. The equipment will have to be pulled across both sea ice and snow covered land. Still, I'll wager snowmobiles could make it in three or four days. What do you think?"

"I think you're brilliant." Ben grinned.

"I agree with Dr. Meade," the prime minister said. "It's an ingenious idea."

"We'll need your help, sir," Marjorie said. "Would you be willing to make a national address? Call for volunteers?"

"I'll do better than that. I'll ask King Charles himself to make an appeal over the BBC."

"I'll call Calais and start the roustabouts building sleds," Ben said.

"What other support will you require, Dr. Meade?" the prime minister asked.

"I could use helicopter transport to fly my engineers and a small research submersible I need up to North Channel, sir," Ben said. "Most of the roustabouts can travel with the equipment."

"Anything else?"

"Yes. The captain of my research vessel is stranded in Reykjavik by the air controllers' strike. I'd appreciate it if you could send a military plane to get him."

"I'll see to it straightaway I get back to Downing Street."

Marjorie's face was animated. "We're going to do it, by God. We're bloody well going to pull this off."

"We British still have the stuff it takes," Butler said. "Our people have survived attacks on our island from Caesar to Hitler. We shall come through this assault of nature as well."

The plainclothes detective from the tunnel approached across the sand. "Beg pardon, sir, but the snow's getting quite heavy," he said to the prime minister. "Even running a plow before your car, we'll have a job getting you back to London."

"Very well, Keser. I'll be along directly."

"Yes, sir," the bodyguard said, and turned to alert the detail they'd be leaving.

"Dr. Meade, I believe I speak for all of England in saying how grateful I am you've come over to help us in this our hour of need. I wish you Godspeed in the great endeavor ahead."

"Thank you, Prime Minister."

"Marjorie, I shall ask the king to call for volunteers with snowmobiles this very evening. I trust I know our fellow countrymen well enough to promise you will have your 'Dunkirkers,' if I might coin a word."

Marjorie smiled softly. " 'Dunkirkers.' It's a good word, Prime Minister, a fine brave word."

"I have to caution you both not to expect a great deal of help from our armed forces. I can supply you with helicopters and certain other equipment and men, but for reasons I cannot tell you, the military assistance I can offer you is finite."

"The first Dunkirk expedition was a civilian show, Prime Minister," Marjorie said. "We can do it with volunteers again."

"There's a final thing," Butler said. "It's going to be a hellish trek from Calais four hundred and fifty miles across the sea ice and snow covered land to North Channel. We must expect there'll be times the expedition will falter. The Dunkirkers will need a strong leader along."

"I suppose that means you, Ben," Marjorie said. "It's your equipment."

Ben shook his head. "If you're going to call for English volunteers, you'll need an English leader. You."

"Me?"

"He's right, Marjorie," Butler said. "You're one of the most respected scientists in England. You have the intelligence, the authority, and the courage to lead the expedition."

"I don't know about the courage, Prime Minister. I've never considered myself a terribly brave person."

"Nonsense. You fought tooth and nail for the Biosphere bill in Parliament. You survived vicious personal and professional attacks, and gave as good as you got. You're the one to lead the Dunkirkers, all right."

Marjorie looked at Ben. "I didn't fight as hard when it came to funding the geothermal project. There is some sentiment I caved in to MacTiege."

Butler shook his patrician head in annoyance. "Twaddle. The votes simply weren't there. If you hadn't compromised with MacTiege, he would have killed the Biosphere appropriation"—he pointed his cane over the desert toward the distant savanna and the jungle beyond—"and all this would have been lost."

Marjorie stared past the two men at the snow lashing the glass slope of the Biosphere. "Perhaps, Prime Minister, but my battles in Parliament involved moral courage. Leading an expedition across hundreds of miles of ice and snow will require physical bravery as well."

Ben rubbed his jaw where she'd punched him yesterday. "You're tough enough to handle anything that comes your way, Marjorie," he said dryly. "I can attest to that personally."

Marjorie was silent for a long moment, then she nodded. "Very well. I'll do it," she said, looking first at Ben and then at the prime minister. "I'll lead the Dunkirkers to North Channel."

"Splendid, splendid." Butler beamed. He extended his hand. "I shall be in touch with you both."

Marjorie and Ben shook hands with Butler and watched him start back toward the Biosphere entrance. He stopped suddenly after a few steps and turned.

"You know, Marjorie, when it's not snowing, you can see the great pyramid of the Biosphere from London during the day. Yet, at night there's nothing visible but a huge black void. In the original design, don't I recall the plan called for the glass to be floodlit?"

"Yes, sir. But with coal so dear, we've never been able to afford the energy it would take to turn the lights on."

"We shall remedy that," the prime minister said. "On the day geothermal power first flows south from the ice of North Channel, we shall turn on the floodlamps. And it will not be just Biosphere Britannia we light, it will be a beacon for all of England."

DUBLIN
• • • • • • • •

8:30 p.m.

THE SNOWBANKS TOWERED TWENTY feet on each side of Dublin's Lower Bridge Street as General Sean McCormick trudged ahead through the blizzard, then turned right under a low archway at number 20 and passed into the dark tunnel beyond.

On the other side was the small, half-buried Brazen Head Hotel, Ireland's oldest inn, named, according to legend, after a notorious redheaded lady of the evening who'd leaned out a window to watch the siege of Limerick and lost her head to a Williamite cannonball.

McCormick crossed the cobbled yard, brushed the snow from his coat and hat at the threshold, stamped his boots, and opened the door.

Inside, he climbed a rickety staircase with beautifully carved banisters to the landing above, then walked down the dark corridor to the low-ceilinged barroom redolent of countless pints of stout.

For centuries past, the rebellious heart of Ireland had beat against these barroom walls. Here had gathered Wolfe Tone, Robert Emmet, Daniel O'Connell, and Michael Collins, among the many revolutionaries who'd sought out the Brazen Head to plot against the British usurpers of the Emerald Isle.

As always when he entered the room, McCormick glanced toward Emmet's writing table, still in the gloomy corner where he'd left it in 1803 before being hung by the British. The sight of the table never failed to stir the Irish officer's wrath, not that the hot embers of his anger needed a poker, and put him in the mood for the business ahead.

"General darlin', you're here at last." The thick brogue cut through the haze of tobacco smoke from the back of the room.

McCormick frowned at being so informally addressed. He was, after all, Irish minister for defense, not some lorry driver come to spill Guinness down his gullet in headlong flight from a nagging wife.

He swallowed his displeasure and headed toward a table against the rear wall where the redheaded leader of the IRA in Northern Ireland sat with his hands around a pint of dark ale, three days' growth of whiskers stubbing his hollow-cheeked face.

He needed Paddy Gallagher, and if Paddy were a bit rough around the edges, one couldn't expect Etonian manners from a man who threw bombs for a living.

Paddy was an integral part of McCormick's plans to drive the British out of Northern Ireland. Bernadette O'Fiaich knew many things about her lover, but the one thing she didn't know was that General Sean McCormick was not only Ireland's minister for defense, he was also military commander of the Irish Republican Army.

Ever since the day they'd met, he'd tried to convert Bernadette to the cause of Irish nationalism. Yet as fierce an Irish patriot as Bernadette was, she abhorred the violent tactics of the militant IRA. She believed that if Ulster were to be reunited with Ireland, it would have to be through negotiation and not terrorism.

Sean had finally given up, realizing Bernadette's politics of peace would soon become irrelevant. With the Sinn Fein gaining more seats in Parliament in every election, it wouldn't be long before the IRA's political front came to power and Sean McCormick was given the green light to lead the tanks of his powerful First Armored Brigade north across the border.

He had no illusions the battle would be easy. The British forces in Northern Ireland were well trained and heavily armed. McCormick would need Paddy Gallagher and his IRA terrorists to harass and sabotage British forces from the rear.

As for Bernadette, he would see to it that she retired from politics with the dignity befitting the Irish Joan of Arc. She would be terribly hurt when she learned he'd belonged to the IRA all these years. Indeed, it was likely she'd feel betrayed, and cast him out of her life forever.

There was nothing he could do about that. Though he be shunned by Bernadette, by his brothers and sisters and every friend he had, it was a sacrifice he was willing to make. His personal happiness didn't matter one whit measured against the holy crusade to reunite Ireland.

McCormick took off his coat at the table, pulled out a chair, and sat down across from Gallagher.

"What'll ya be havin', General?" Paddy asked, poising a hand toward the barmaid.

"I don't want a thing." McCormick glared at him. "I'm not here to drink. And I'll thank you not to use my military title. We can't be sure there's not an informer about."

"Informer, me ass," Paddy scoffed. "It'd be hard to find an Irishman not with us these days."

"Damn you, Paddy, because things are going our way, it doesn't mean the whole country's behind us. There are still them that would sooner talk to the Brits than fight them."

"You mean your girlfriend then, the once-nun paradin' in prime minister's clothes?"

McCormick bristled. "Leave her out of this," he said between gritted teeth, although he knew himself there was no separating Bernadette from the upheaval to come. He could protect her as a woman, but not as the prime minister.

"Let's get on with it," he said, fixing Gallagher with a hard stare. "I want to know what's goin' on in the North."

Paddy took a slow pull on his stout to show he was in no

awe of McCormick, despite the fact that the man had gained high position, and the bedroom favor of the prime minister.

"Me and a dozen of the boys from our Tyrone Brigade have been watchin' the Brit barracks in Omagh, like you asked us to, General. It's been a month now, ya know, and not a minute we wasn't freezing our arses off."

McCormick looked at the IRA man impatiently. "Did you get a count?"

"In a way of speakin'."

"And what do you mean by that?"

"They don't come out no more, ya know. Not a bus through the gate in weeks. It's the snow, of course, that and we haven't been usin' the bombs. Not that we haven't been tempted."

"I'll tell you again, no bombs. There'll be the right time soon enough."

"Aren't I just after sayin' we haven't? Not since that Dungannon job."

"Omagh. How many?"

Paddy wiped a froth of stout from his moustache. "There's not a brigade in there, as they have it in the press. A company, maybe; two, three hundred men, no more than that."

McCormick leaned back in his chair, his eyes skeptical. "Tell me how you know."

"Garbage."

"Garbage?"

"Brit garbage. We know they had a full brigade in there last summer. Then, they'd haul out forty barrels a week from the kitchen for the local carter to take off. We're sure because for a while we fancied tapin' a little present to the bottom of one of the empties goin' back."

"How many barrels now?"

"Five, six a week."

McCormick nodded. It fit with the information his regular army intelligence had been gleaning from the phone tap on the lines between England and Northern Ireland; in the past six months, there had been only a quarter as many individual phone calls coming out of the British barracks at Omagh.

"What about the SAS in Belfast?" McCormick asked about the British soldiers the IRA terrorists most feared, the ruthless crack troops of the Special Air Service.

Paddy slowly shook his head. "You know how they are, never a breach in security. They don't even throw out their garbage. Maybe they eat it, the bastards are tough enough," he said, respect in his voice for the elite and secretive British force.

"Nothing?"

"There's one thing."

"Yes?"

"We have a woman at the main post office. She says she's not seein' much mail addressed to Hereford these days. Half or less of what it was back in 'ninety-eight when there was that flap over the fishin' boats takin' potshots at each other."

McCormick chewed on that. The SAS had their headquarters at Hereford in England. "Interesting."

"Yes, I thought you'd think so," Paddy said. "Millie, another pint here, there's the girl."

"What's the mood up there?"

"The mood?"

"Our people. Are they ready if the balloon goes up?"

"That's a hard question. Most of us are just trying to keep alive these freezing days. Half the lads are burning peat to keep their families warm, and glad to get that. Thanks, Millie," he said as the barmaid delivered a brimming tankard.

"I'd have thought all those new mortars and shoulder-fired missiles I've been sendin' you would've raised the lads' spirits."

"Ya can't eat mortars, General."

"You sound tired, Paddy."

"I am tired, damn it. I been two days on a snowmobile gettin' down here. And for a week before I was out every night scrounging petrol. A cup here, a half pint there. I might as well tell you, all the lads up north are tired."

"There was a time you were all tired of British tyranny."

"Don't you wag a patriotic finger at me, General, sittin' here in your warm woolens. You don't know what it's like in the north these days, choppin' out frozen peat with an ax

and tryin' to decide whether to give the last of the stirabout
to old Granddad or the kid."

Millie approached across the barroom and handed
McCormick a note. "The boy brought it up, sir."

He glanced at the folded paper and rose. "I'll be right
back."

"Take your damn time," Paddy said, still indignant. "Millie, another."

McCormick threw him a withering glance and headed
along the corridor and down the stairs. A young lieutenant
from Irish Army Intelligence was waiting outside in the
snow.

"I thought it best not to come in, General, bein' in uniform," he said, nervously shifting a small cardboard box
from one hand to another.

"You did right, Lieutenant. What is it?"

"You know we haven't been able to raise Major Finigan all
day on the radio."

"Did you finally reach him?"

"No, sir. When the storm blew up after you left, Colonel
Heagerty thought it was a good chance to send a helicopter
out. Not likely the British would be up in such weather."

"Well?"

"He's not on board the freighter, sir."

"Did they search the whole ship?"

"Yes, sir."

"And there's no sign of Major Finigan?"

Even against the white snow, the young officer was visi-
bly pale. "Only one, sir. This," he said, holding out the small
box.

McCormick bunched his eyebrows quizzically and took
the container. He opened the lid and gagged violently, his
eyes bulging in their sockets at the bloody sight of the severed human hand inside.

BIOSPHERE BRITANNIA
• •

8:55 a.m.—February 8
British Fuel Reserves—13 Days

AN HOUR AFTER DAWN, the Royal Navy EH-101 helicopter banked sharply over Biosphere Britannia, and began its descent, its three Rolls-Royce Gem engines sending up a vortex of swirling snow from the small park fronting the glass pyramid below.

"What did you say was the name of your head geologist up at North Channel?" Ben Meade asked of Marjorie Glynn as they stood inside the front entrance of the Biosphere watching the chopper descend.

"Abbot, Reginald Abbot," Marjorie said. "If I know Reggie, he'll be there waiting on the ice. He's quite put out, you know, that an American's going to run the show."

"Great. Professional politics at thirty below."

"Oh, Reggie'll be all right, once he's circled you a few times and sniffed out that you're entitled to be top dog."

Ben picked up a bulging briefcase from the foyer floor. "I'll do the calculations for the equipment sleds on the way up, then call them in to my drill superintendent in Calais. It shouldn't take them more than a couple of days to build the sleds we'll need."

"Prime Minister Butler sounded terribly optimistic when

he called last night. Did I tell you Downing Street has had calls from hundreds of volunteers with snowmobiles since King Charles made his speech? We'll have our Dunkirkers, all right."

"And they'll have a hell of a leader."

"I hope I'm right for the job, Ben. I've led teams of scientists, but this expedition across the Channel is something else."

Ben put a hand on her shoulder. "Look, we all have our self-doubts, Marjorie. The trick is to trust in your own experience, your own ability, despite the qualms inside."

"Do you ever have self-doubts, Ben? You seem so sure of yourself."

"Christ, I've got cracks in my foundation that could bring me down tomorrow. Some of them scare the shit out of me."

"You, frightened? Of what?"

"My temper, for one. You witnessed that yourself. I tend to keep things in until the pressure builds and I explode."

"Like the time you wanted to kill your brother?"

"Yeah. I could be sitting in a prison cell right now, my brother dead and my life a meaningless shambles."

"Is temper your only fault, Ben?"

"No."

She waited. "Well? Are you going to tell me?"

Ben looked out at one of the helicopter pilots crossing the snow toward the entrance. "I don't know that this is the time, Marjorie."

"Will there ever be a time to tell me, Ben?"

He looked at her a long moment. More than once the past couple of days he'd berated himself for lusting after her their first time together at Tranquility Falls. He'd seen in her eyes how vulnerable he'd made her feel, alone out in the goddamn jungle with this panting man she'd just met. Maybe now he owed her a glimpse of his own vulnerability.

"I drink, Marjorie. More and more the last few years."

"But you haven't had so much as a glass of wine since you've been here."

"Too much work to do, too much at stake."

"Then you can control it."

"No, that's the point. I don't think I can control it any-more. I can keep away from it, just barely. But if I have one, I don't stop until I'm falling-down drunk."

Marjorie reached a hand up and touched his cheek. "Thank you for telling me, for trusting me."

"I do trust you, Marjorie. I never thought I'd say that to a woman again, not after Elizabeth."

"I won't let you down, Ben."

"I know you won't, Marjorie. And you won't let Britain down either. You've got the brains and the guts to lead those Dunkirkers."

The helicopter crewman opened the Biosphere door, a blast of freezing air swirling snow around his olive-drab flightsuit. He brushed himself off and crossed the foyer to Ben and Marjorie. "Dr. Meade?" he said to Ben.

"Yes."

"Lieutenant Perkins, sir. I'm your copilot for the flight to North Channel."

Ben extended his hand. "Glad to meet you, Lieutenant. This is Dr. Glynn."

Marjorie smiled as the young officer brought his fingers to his cap in an easy salute. "Ma'am."

"How's the flying weather, Lieutenant?" Ben asked.

"As long as we keep our flight altitude below the ash clouds, we shouldn't have any problem, sir. Still, we should be off as soon as possible. We lose what light there is early these days, and we've a fair piece to go."

"Ready anytime you are," Ben said.

"May I take your case, sir?"

"Yes, thank you," Ben said. "I'll be right there."

"You'll be careful out there on the ice, won't you, Ben?" Marjorie said as the copilot recrossed the foyer and headed back to the helicopter.

Ben nodded. "You take care too, Marjorie." He hesitated a moment. "Look, before I blew up and made a perfect asshole out of myself the other day, you said you wanted us to get to know each other. Do you still want that? Or do you know more than you care to already?"

She smiled. "We didn't get off to a very good start, did we?"

"It was my fault, nothing you did. Christ, my temper, and before that ogling you with my goddamn tongue hanging out."

Marjorie laughed. "I don't mind you wanting to get into my knickers, Ben. Just, it has to be a time I want that too."

He grinned. " 'Knickers.' I love the way you English put things."

"The irony is, I've always dreamt of making love by Tranquility Falls. There on the bed of moss beside the pool."

"But not with me."

"Not with a stranger, which you still were then."

"And now. How do you see me now?"

"As an interesting, if occasionally unpredictable man I've rather come to like."

A loud whine penetrated the glass walls around them and they turned and stared out at the helicopter blades beginning to whirl.

"I guess I'll have to settle for that," Ben said, squeezing her hand. "Goodbye, Marjorie."

She stood on tiptoe and softly kissed his lips. "Goodbye, Ben."

Ben held her gently for a moment, then turned and pushed out through the glass doors. He dashed across the snow, ducked low beneath the whirling helicopter blades, then paused at the open door of the craft to wave at Marjorie standing just inside the entry.

The copilot slid the door shut and buckled Ben into his seat. Ben leaned to the window beside him as the helicopter rose. From above, he got a new perspective on how huge the Biosphere complex truly was; acres of glass covering an entire miniworld. Once again, he marveled at Marjorie's achievement.

The helicopter flew north at 3,000 feet and Ben looked down at London blanketed in snow. The river Thames was a snaking ribbon of ice, and the drifted Westminster and Waterloo bridges were barely visible but for the thin shadows cast on the ice below them by the weak blue sun.

The Houses of Parliament and Westminster Abbey came into view across the frozen river, their ice-capped towers dwarfed by the cold rectangular blocks of the Department of Trade and Industry off to the left behind. St. James's Park was an azure expanse of drifts and leafless, ice-shrouded trees. Beyond, the snowy Mall looked all but lifeless from the Queen Victoria Memorial down to Admiralty Arch.

He could make out Buckingham Palace off to the left, its roofs buried under what looked to be several feet of snow, as were the tops of the buildings in Mayfair and the City of Westminster ahead. Most of the sporadic street traffic was lorries and buses, for there was precious little petrol available to private car owners these days.

Ben turned to the papers and charts in his briefcase as the helicopter flew out over the suburbs and headed north toward Birmingham. He had a lot of work to do before the flight got to North Channel.

It would take a couple of days more for the government to select volunteers, and organize the logistics of fuel and food supplies for the Dunkirk expedition. Meanwhile, plans had been laid for the volunteers to assemble at the English Channel port of Dover for the dash across the ice to Calais.

Ben worked on the dimensions for the sleds that would be needed to transport his heavy derrick sections and cranes as the helicopter droned north over the icy beechwood forests and open, deeply drifted Berkshire Downs of the English Home Counties.

Using a laptop computer, he calculated the 142-foot derrick could be transported with one 26-foot sled under the front, and another 18-foot skid under the smaller top section toward the rear. His revolving crane, with its 250-foot boom, would require four sleds, each almost thirty feet long.

Ben whistled softly to himself at the dimensions, and at the number of snowmobiles he figured would be needed to pull the sleds. Most of the larger equipment he'd ordered flown to France could be broken up into smaller loads and dragged over the ice by two or three treaded vehicles. But the derrick and crane, those babies were going to need up to twenty snowmobiles apiece to pull them across the Channel and up to North Channel.

He stared down at the countryside of the South Midlands now passing beneath the helicopter. To the southwest were the snowy Cotswold Hills, while to the northeast rose the icy uplands of Northamptonshire and Leicestershire. Before the warm Atlantic current began to change course, sheep had grazed in the uplands, and the countryside beyond was verdant with fruitful fields and orchards.

Now, the only signs of life were the dormant branches of thousands of tall hedgerow elms blowing in the wind, and smoke from the chimneys of one of the few inhabited larger villages.

A cloud of black soot hugging the northern horizon told him they were approaching Birmingham, England's second-largest city. He noticed the snow below getting progressively darker from the residue of the thousands of coal furnaces burning in the industrial metropolis.

The year temperatures in England began to plunge, three million people had lived in Birmingham and the West Midlands County. The lack of food and fuel out in the surrounding snowbound countryside had now forced two million more into the city, straining social services and housing, and adding hundreds of thousands to the burgeoning number of unemployed. Birmingham had become a stronghold of political support for Seamus MacTiege and his Labor Party radicals.

Ben shook his head sadly as they flew over the Bull Ring, the once bustling city center. Huge snowdrifts climbed the sides of all the buildings save the tall, cylindrical Rotunda tower. The millions sheltering in the city were all indoors, crammed into basements and attics and hallways, men, women, and children filling every nook and cranny they could find.

Birmingham was once the center of England's motorway and rail systems. Now the city's Gravelly Hill interchange, a tangled maze of roads motorists called Spaghetti Junction, was almost empty of vehicles, and the rail tracks leading to the half-buried New Street Station were undisturbed corridors of blue-white snow.

He turned from the depressing vista below and tapped the pilot on the shoulder.

The Royal Navy officer took off his headset. "Yes, sir?"

"I want you to call the Meade International office in Paris and have them patch me through to my drill superintendent in Calais," Ben shouted above the throbbing sound of the engine.

The captain nodded. "Take a few minutes, sir."

"Right. Thanks." Ben sat back again with his computer and began estimating how many snowmobiles would be needed to pull the huge generators waiting in Calais.

Several minutes later the call came in from his superintendent and Ben gave him the dimensions of the sleds that would have to be built in France before the Dunkirkers arrived.

"You're talking about moving a hell of a lot of dead weight, Ben," the superintendent said. "We going to have enough men and equipment to do the job?"

"Over nine hundred people have volunteered for the Dunkirk expedition," Ben said. "They'll be bringing two or three hundred snowmobiles with them. If you have any problems, give me a call. I'll be at the drill site in North Channel."

As he hung up, the shore of the frozen Irish Sea appeared below and he looked down at the horizonless expanse of snow-covered ice. Here and there long pressure ridges rose high above the surrounding floes, evidence of the way the icefields were relentlessly expanding and pushing in against the land.

Once the waters below would have been crisscrossed with the wakes of dozens of ships carrying goods from Bristol, Liverpool, and Glasgow in Britain, and from Dublin and Belfast in Ireland. Now there was only a huge expanse of dead blue-white ice, as lifeless as the glaciers of Antarctica.

Ben leaned forward to the pilot. "Do you know if my research submersible and drill pipes have been flown up from Paris yet?"

The pilot nodded. "I believe your sub and the other equipment were brought in last night, sir."

Ten minutes later, the pilot handed a pair of binoculars back to Ben. "There's the Isle of Man coming up on the port side, sir. Singular place. Thought you might like a look."

"Thanks," Ben smiled, taking the glasses. He turned to the window and focused on the tiny 32-mile-long, 227-square-mile independent country in the middle of the Irish Sea. He had flown out here for a week's vacation about ten years ago, and he remembered the island's neolithic monuments and tiny, sixth-century chapels called keeills.

Now, both the hilly country to the south and the plain in the north were buried in deep snow. The towering cliffs that made up much of the island's hundred-mile coastline were vertical sheets of ice. From the air, Ben could see coal smoke rising above only a handful of towns, and he guessed most of the isolated island's sixty-five thousand inhabitants had by now been evacuated to Britain.

Ben settled in his seat for the final fifteen-minute leg of the flight to the British drill site on the ice of North Channel. They were almost there when he spotted the lone ship frozen into the floes below.

He tapped the pilot on the shoulder. "What's that?" he yelled above the noise of the engine and rotors above.

"Irish freighter, sir. She's been locked in the ice since last summer. Believe it or not, the captain's still on board."

"What? All alone out here?"

"Yes, sir. It's a great joke with air-sea rescue up here. He's quite daft, of course. They call him Bonkers Brian."

Several minutes later the huge drill platform came into view perched fifty feet above the floes. Ben swept the work area with the glasses and counted several dozen men busy at various tasks.

To the far left, another Royal Navy chopper was just lifting off from the bull's-eye of the helicopter pad. He could see his research sub, *Yellowstone*, up on chocks near one edge of the platform, and several racks of drill pipe were stacked nearby.

Suddenly, out of the corner of his eye, Ben caught a distant, blurred movement behind a high-pressure ridge to the north, and he brought the binoculars up. By the time he'd focused on the far-off spine of jagged sea ice, there was nothing there. Just the wind blowing wisps of powdered snow off the top of the ridge.

Then he caught the movement again, several gray-black shapes passing along the other side of the comb of ice. Animals of some kind. The one in the lead climbed toward the crest of the line of broken floes, and Ben swung the glasses over. He refocused, then suddenly lifted up out of his seat as the animal's head came over the top and filled the lens.

It was a wolf. The biggest son-of-a-bitching wolf Ben Meade had ever seen.

LONDON
• • • • • • • • •

4:20 p.m.

SEAMUS MACTIEGE STOOD AT the sixtieth-floor window of his London office staring at Biosphere Britannia as the setting blue-green sun turned the huge pyramid's panes of glass into ten thousand turquoise gems.

As he'd expected, Prime Minister Butler had flatly refused the demand from the Trades Union Congress for a 20-percent wage hike. By now, almost three million union workers had walked off their jobs. Manufacturing plants, mass transit, government agencies, and the critical coal mines had closed down all over the country.

The commerce of Great Britain had come to a screeching halt. MacTiege had ordered the TUC's general secretary to allow deliveries of food to stores and coal to private homes to continue. It was the government he meant to bring to its knees, not the working man.

At first, MacTiege had been confident the general strike would prove the final nail in the coffin of the Butler government.

Then the Social Democrats had struck back with the announcement that the American geothermal expert, Dr. Ben-

jamin Meade, had returned to start up the North Channel
project again.

Two days later, King Charles had gone public with his
support of geothermal power. His speech calling for "Dunkirkers" to bring drilling equipment back from France had
gotten the country all fired up, given people a cause to rally
around.

If Butler and his scientist allies could convince the British
people there really was a chance to fuel and heat the country
with geothermal power, it would cut the legs out from under
his own plans for a coal-based economy and a Labor government.

MacTiege turned from the infuriating sight of the Biosphere and walked toward his desk. His dog Alfie raised his
head from a throw rug next to the desk and studied his master's face.

"You can always tell when Daddy's fretting, can't you,
lad?" he said fondly, bending to scratch Alfie behind his
ears. "Not to worry, Daddy's not beaten yet."

He pressed the intercom button on his phone and his secretary came on the line.

"Yes, Mr. MacTiege."

"Send Malachy in here please, Mary."

"Very good, sir."

MacTiege took a key from his vest pocket, unlocked the
bottom left drawer in his desk, and withdrew a two-foot-
long, three-inch-wide tube. He slid out the map inside and
spread it on his desk.

It was an infrared satellite survey of the geothermal reservoir under North Channel. He had first seen the map two
years ago during Parliamentary debate over funding geothermal research. As leader of the loyal opposition, he had
been one of the few members of Parliament privileged to
view the chart.

MacTiege had disagreed from the start with Prime Minister Butler's decision not to tell the Irish the geothermal field
extended under their territorial waters, despite the PM's in-
sistence that British development of the energy reserve
would ultimately serve both countries.

MacTiege commissioned geologists from the coal industry to do an independent study of the huge heat reservoir that stretched from beneath North Channel southwest under the Irish Sea.

The scientists MacTiege called in drew up a report pointing out that the North Channel site was on the northeast fringe of the geothermal field. If the first drill site proved viable, further wells would have to be sunk to the southwest in the Irish Sea. And tapping into the field close to Irish territorial waters would inevitably draw off geothermal energy that rightly belonged to Ireland. He had briefly considered leaking the information, then dropped the matter when he'd made his deal with Marjorie Glynn to mothball the North Channel project.

Now that geothermal was once more a lethal threat to the coal-based economy he envisioned, it was time to use the map and the report to put North Channel out of operation once and for all.

"Come," he said in answer to a knock on his door.

A short, thin balding man in a cheap food-stained suit limped across the office, his right hand an atrophied claw he held tight against his chest.

"You wanted to see me, Mr. MacTiege, sir?"

Thirty-four-year-old Malachy Rushe had lost most of the muscle functions on the right side of his body in a coal mine cave-in twelve years before. His young wife, overly fond of short dresses and all-night parties, had taken one look at her crippled husband and promptly divorced him, leaving Malachy to rot in a miners' rehabilitation center in Belfast.

Six months later, MacTiege had been touring miners' facilities as president of NUM when he came across Malachy alone and depressed, staring out a window from his wheelchair.

MacTiege took the crippled young miner under his wing, just as he'd taken in dozens of stray cats and dogs over the years. Within six months, Malachy had learned to walk again, although he would always limp. He was now the Labor leader's most trusted assistant, totally devoted to the person of Seamus MacTiege.

"Sit down, Malachy," MacTiege said.

A look of surprise crossed Malachy's face. He wasn't used to sitting in the presence of his boss. He lowered himself awkwardly into a chair before the desk, the fingers of his good hand digging his collar away from his neck. If he lived to be a hundred, he'd never get used to a shirt and tie.

"Do you remember when we first met, Malachy?" MacTiege began, allowing himself a small disarming smile. "You were in that convalescent hospital."

"It was more like a prison, sir. I hated it."

"Have you been back to Ulster?"

"Yes, sir, two summers ago. I still have a sister there, you know. And some friends from me mining days."

"You're Catholic as I recall, are you not, Malachy?"

"Catholic? Yes, sir, born Catholic, though I don't go to church but Christmas and Easter."

"But you were raised in West Belfast, the Catholic section."

"Aye. Out in Davis Flats."

"So your sympathies are with the Republicans there."

"I've no love for the Protestant vigilantes, the murderin' bastards."

"As a matter of fact, didn't you once tell me your brother-in-law belonged to the IRA?"

Malachy's face became guarded. "If it got out, they'd throw Aidan in Crumlin Road prison, sir. Me sister has six kids to feed."

"It's not going to get out, Malachy, not from me."

MacTiege rolled up the geothermal map and slid it back into its canister. "I assume Aidan has contacts in the Tyrone Brigade," he said, naming the IRA's principal paramilitary organization in Ulster.

"The Tyrone Brigade? Yes, sir, I daresay he has."

MacTiege reached in a drawer and took out a copy of the report warning that British geothermal wells in North Channel would siphon off Irish energy reserves.

He rolled the report inside the map, screwed on the top, and handed the canister to Rushe. "You're to give these to your brother-in-law and tell him to bring them to the commander of the Tyrone Brigade."

The simple miner's eyes widened. "You want me to go to Ulster, sir?"

"Yes. I'm sending you over in the union helicopter."

Malachy's Adam's apple bobbed. "Me? Me flyin' in your personal helicopter, Mr. MacTiege?"

"It's an important mission I'm sending you on, Malachy. I believe I can trust you to see it goes right."

"You know you can, sir. After all you've done for me, I'd do anything for you, I would."

"Would you commit treason for me, Malachy?"

The crippled miner stared across the desk at MacTiege. "Treason, sir?"

"Did I ever tell you how my father died, Malachy?"

Malachy nervously licked his lips, at a loss as to where the conversation was going. "I believe you told me once he was killed in the war, sir."

"At El Alamein."

Malachy shook his head sadly. "We lost thousands there."

"True, Malachy, but few died as my father did."

"How's that, sir?"

"He burned to death, roasted alive inside a tank."

Malachy winced. "That's 'orrible, sir."

"Yes. I found out the year the war ended. My father's old sergeant stopped by to tell my mother what a stalwart friend and sterling soldier my father'd been. I remember how proud I felt. Then he whispered something to my mother and they sent me from the room."

"The war ended in 'forty-five, sir. You couldn't have been more than a boy."

"Six. An age of unbounded curiosity. I listened at the door. I've wished to God ever since that I hadn't."

MacTiege sank back in his chair. "The sergeant described how the Germans had shelled their tank battalion one night. My father was a tank driver, you know. The shelling was incredibly precise. A phosphorous round pierced the turret of my father's tank."

"Phosphorous is evil stuff. If it gets on your body you can't put it out. It keeps burnin' through to the bone."

"That's what it did to my father. The sergeant went into quite some detail about what he looked like before they buried him in the sand." MacTiege closed his eyes. "Hideous detail."

Malachy could see the pain working in the Labor leader's face as he silently remembered his private hell.

"The reason the shelling was so precise was the Germans knew exactly where my father's tank was dug in," MacTiege said finally. "They knew where every tank and gun in the battalion was."

"How could they know that, sir?"

MacTiege tented his hands and peered over his fingertips at Malachy. "The Germans had captured a young corporal from the battalion. He betrayed the battalion's position. The bastard even drew the Nazis a map. When our troops retook El Alamein, they found the map. The traitor was shot."

"He got off light," Malachy said.

"That tube in your hands also contains a map. I must warn you that turning it over to the Irish could be considered an act of treason."

"A map of what, sir?"

"It's a top-secret satellite survey of the geothermal field at North Channel."

Malachy's head whirled. "North Channel? That place where the Dunkirkers is goin'?"

"Yes."

"Why do you want to do it, sir? I don't understand."

"Have you considered, Malachy, what will happen if Prime Minister Butler succeeds in bringing geothermal power on line?"

"A thing like that's well above my head, sir."

"It will be the end of coal mining in the UK. All your friends in the pits will be out of work, reduced to begging on the streets."

Malachy's face registered his alarm. "Men can't live on what they collect in a tin cup. How would they feed their families? How'd they keep a roof over the kids' heads?"

"Shuttered pits aren't the only threat we face, Malachy. Without miners to support our programs, the Labor Party will also vanish. There'll be no one to defend the working class, no voice for the poor."

"Let me round up some of the boys, sir. We'll go up to North Channel with a couple of cases of nitro and blow that bloody well to kingdom come."

"They'd have it rebuilt in a month. No, only the Irish can stop that geothermal project now. That's why I'm sending them the map. Are you with me?"

"Aye, sir, I'm with you."

"If we're found out, we could be shot, Malachy, like that scum who betrayed my father and his mates."

"I don't care, sir. We can't let them shut the coal pits and destroy the Labor movement. I'd sooner take a bullet through me head than see that happen."

MacTiege rose and came around his desk. He put his hand on Malachy's shoulder. "That map has got to get to the Tyrone Brigade."

Rushe cradled the canister as if it were the Holy Grail. "You can count on me, Mr. MacTiege."

"I know I can. The helicopter will be waiting for you when you get upstairs."

The miner turned to leave.

"One other thing, Malachy. I want you to stay at your sister's until you're sure the tube has been handed over to the IRA, then ring me up. Don't say anything specific over the phone, simply, 'It's done.'"

"'It's done.' I'll remember, sir."

"Good. Off with you now. I'll be waiting for your call."

Malachy dragged his right leg toward the door and twenty minutes later MacTiege heard the whine of the helicopter lifting off the roof of the union skyscraper. He was confident that within forty-eight hours the geothermal map and report would be in the hands of the Irish government.

Dublin would be up in arms over the British usurpation of Irish energy reserves. MacTiege had no doubt the volatile Sinn Fein leaders would demand that the North Channel project be shut down until Ireland's rights could be guaranteed.

Prime Minister O'Fiaich was a moderate, but her Fine Gael Party held only seventy-nine seats in the 165-member Dail Eireann. She held office only with the acquiescence of the Sinn Fein party. The Irish PM would have no choice but to insist that Britain abandon North Channel.

With relations between the two countries one step from war, Prime Minister Butler would be forced to bow to the Irish demands. That would be the end of geothermal power for Britain, and the death knell for the Social Democrats as well.

MacTiege felt Alfie nuzzle his leg and he bent to pet the dog. "You and Daddy shall be moving soon, Alfie. Would you like that? We'll bring Mildred and the other cats as well, of course."

Alfie whined and wagged his tail at his master's soothing tone.

A sudden thought struck MacTiege and he grinned into Alfie's liquid brown eyes. "It will drive the nobs up the wall, you know, Alfie," he said. "Oh, they'll have a fit all right, all us mongrels living there on Downing Street."

DUBLIN
• • • • • • • •

2:00 p.m.—February 9
Fuel Reserves—12 Days

IRISH PRIME MINISTER BERNADETTE O'Fiaich stared down in horror at the bloody human hand in a plastic bag Sean McCormick had just thrown on the desk before her.

"In the name of God, Sean, what is that?"

"The hand of an Irish patriot, Taoiseach. I've shook it many a time. Only then it was at the end of the arm of Major Brian Finigan."

"Finigan? The intelligence officer you had out on that ship frozen in the ice."

"The same."

"What happened?"

"Oh, I haven't every detail to give you, Taoiseach. Brian being the only Irishman on board that vessel, there are no friendly witnesses to say what occurred. When we find a soldier's hand, and none of the rest of the man, I have only me Irish imagination to fill in the blanks."

"Damn you, Sean. I want to know."

"The bloody British done it, of course, who else? Brian hadn't a single visitor the past four months but RAF helicopter crews." McCormick's face darkened with hate. "They couldn't just murder him, no, they had to torture

Brian first. They tore off his hand, and only God knows
what else."

"You've made your point, Sean. Take it away."

McCormick reached forward and picked up the hand with
elaborate slowness, making sure to hold it in front of Bernadette's eyes a moment before putting the human part back
in a container and returning it to his large briefcase.

"I can't believe they'd do it." Bernadette shook her head.
"The Lord God knows the British have committed grievous
sins against Ireland. I can't count the killings over the years.
But I thought the barbarous times had passed. I can understand the British Army in Ulster shooting IRA terrorists;
after all, the IRA is shooting at them. But this; to torture a
man . . ."

"The British have been usin' torture for years up in their
Crumlin Road Prison in Belfast. I've told you that, not that I
ever once had your ear."

Doubt clouded Bernadette's face. "I met Prime Minister
Butler back in ninety-five when I went over to London about
the reparations. He was still the leader of the opposition
then, and he was one of the only members of the British Parliament who would listen to me. I thought him a humane
man. I can't believe he'd condone this."

"I'm not sayin' Prime Minister Butler has his signature on
every outrage," Sean said. "But there's no denyin' Major
Finigan was murdered."

"But why, Sean, why?"

McCormick pulled a packet of photographs from his briefcase and threw them on the desk. "Because he knew too
much about this."

Bernadette squinted at the photographs. "Where's my
glasses? I can't make out what those are."

"They're satellite pictures of a British geothermal drill
platform in North Channel. At least that's what they claim it
is."

"Sean, for God's sake, that drill platform's been out there
for over two years. King Charles was just after making a
speech about it on British television, calling for volunteers to
bring equipment up there from France."

"I believe that Major Finigan discovered it's not a geothermal project at all but a staging area for an invasion of Ireland."

"And that's why the British murdered him?"

"I'm convinced of it. Perhaps he intercepted a Brit radio transmission. Or an RAF crew let something slip. Whatever it was, he knew. And the British knew he knew. They had to kill him to cover up whatever it is they're really doin' out there."

"Sean—"

"Before you tell me again it's all a fantasy I've conjured up, I'll ask you to hear me out," he interrupted heatedly. "Or was the severed hand of Major Finigan only more of my wild imaginin'?"

Bernadette sighed. He had a point. Certainly, she had no ready explanation of what had happened to poor Major Finigan. "Go on then, Sean. I'll listen. I'm not saying I'll believe your every word, mind you, but I will listen."

"I've known about Major Finigan for two days. I've delayed comin' to you until I had these pictures."

Bernadette put on her glasses and picked up the photographs.

"Those first shots were taken last month by that private Brazilian satellite firm we have a contract with."

Bernadette looked at the photos one by one. In the first and second pictures, the platform looked almost deserted, with only three or four figures visible on the deck.

Bernadette squinted at a rectangular structure with a thin curl of smoke rising from a chimney at one end. "What's that long building there?" she asked.

"Our photo analysts believe it's a barracks and mess," he said, handing her a magnifying glass from his briefcase. "Now in the third shot there, you'll see a helicopter on the landin' pad. Would you be good enough to take a peek at the name on the side?"

Bernadette squinted through the glass. She could just make out the lettering. "British Geothermal Research," she read off.

"Thank you," Sean said, too elaborately for her taste. He was leading her, where she didn't know.

"Now, that fourth shot you have was taken yesterday. I think you'll find there've been some changes."

The photograph did indeed show a different scene below. There was a much larger helicopter on the platform's circular landing pad, and another equally big one in the air, either coming in or taking off. On the deck were what looked to be several four-man teams carrying long tubular objects toward a three-sided shed.

Bernadette looked up at Sean. "Is that drill pipe they're shouldering about?"

"It could be a drill pipe, Taoiseach. Then again, could be rockets. There's no doubt what that thing is," he said, pointing at a squat, cylindrical object near the edge of the platform.

Bernadette studied the photo. "It looks like a small submarine."

"That's exactly what it is. Now, have a look at the rest of these."

The next four pictures showed increasing activity below, with people and machinery all over the deck, and individuals clustered in small groups down on the surrounding ice. In the last shot, there were three large helicopters circling simultaneously above the platform.

"There's no doubt they've suddenly gotten busy out there," Bernadette allowed, "but I'd expect that with them starting up drilling again. I've yet to see a single gun."

"Puttin' aside that submarine, and what's in them tubes, I'd like you to take a closer look at the markin's on them 'whirly-whirlys,' as you're after callin' helicopters."

Bernadette bristled. The condescending way he'd said "whirly-whirlys" was his way of putting her down for a silly, soft woman who had no business in this military man's game.

She glowered at him, then bent over the photographs. A moment later she straightened, chagrined by the magnified lettering on the side of the helicopters. "Royal Navy," she said, more to herself than Sean.

"What was that, Taoiseach?"

"Royal Navy, you insufferable bastard. Shall I scream it in your ear, then?"

"There's no cause to lose your temper."

"You've made your point, Sean. They've replaced their small research craft with large helicopters from the Royal Navy. Next, I'm sure, you'll be telling me what it all means."

He could sense he'd come up against a brick wall if he kept pushing. It was time for another tack. "Do you think me a fool, me Bernie girl?"

She looked at him out of the sides of her eyes. He was up to something with the "Bernie girl" stuff. Still, as always, she softened at his words. No matter how furious he made her, she loved him, and that had a way of being that.

"No, I don't think you're a fool, Sean. It's just . . . sometimes you do get carried away with this business about the war-mongering British."

"I'll admit I view the bastards with a jaundiced eye, and you know the reason why. But this time, I caught 'em with the goods. Even you, with your kind and trustin' heart, even you can't dismiss what I've shown you here today."

Bernadette drummed her fingers on her desk. "What do you suggest, Sean?"

"I want to send a reconnaissance patrol out to have a look. The satellite photographs can't tell us what them long tubes are, for instance. Are they pipes for drillin'? Or do they hold rockets to bombard our coast to the north before they send an invasion force across the ice? If it's a military base they're settin' up out there, we've got to know."

"Sean, if they're so dead set on invading, why wouldn't they simply come across the border from Ulster?"

"Because there's a million sets of Catholic eyes in Ulster. We'd know they was comin' weeks before. No, if it's an invasion they're plannin', they've got to mass their forces somewhere off our coast."

Bernadette took off her glasses and pinched the bridge of her nose. If ever there were a moment she wished she were a simple nursing nun again and not the prime minister of Ireland, this was it.

A military patrol out on the ice of the Irish Sea might be taken as a provocation by the British. The way things were since that gun battle between Irish and English fishing boats nineteen months ago, the least spark could set off a war.

Still, she was prime minister, and she had a duty to protect Ireland. Perhaps, after all, she was too trusting, too willing to give the British government the benefit of the doubt. She could hardly just brush aside the torture and murder of an Irish intelligence officer.

Although she was almost certain the British were indeed only drilling a geothermal well, as the media were reporting, still the platform was uncomfortably close to Irish shores.

Unfortunately, history had proven the English all too willing to spill Irish blood, and she had no right to let her own pacifist inclinations jeopardize the lives and freedom of her countrymen.

Sean was asking to send out a reconnaissance patrol, no more than that. Surely, she must allow him, and Ireland, an innocent look at what the English were up to out on the frozen ice.

She looked at Sean and forced a smile. "All right, Sean, I'll approve your patrol."

"You've made the right decision, Taoiseach," he beamed, reaching for his briefcase. "It'll take me a couple of days to arrange it."

"I have two provisions," she said as he made to leave.

A wary look replaced the smile on his face. "And they are?"

"I intend to make an inquiry about that drill platform through the American Embassy here in Dublin. You are to take no further action beyond a single patrol until we hear back from them."

"Agreed. What else?"

"The patrol is for the purpose of reconnaissance only. They are to go unarmed."

"Taoiseach."

"Unarmed, or not a single soldier sets foot on that ice. If it is to be war, despite all I might do for peace, it will not be an Irishman fires the first shot."

Sean bowed his head and she could sense the battle within him.

"Very well, Taoiseach. They go unarmed."

"I have your word?"

Sean looked at her a long moment. "You have my word."

"I expect to hear as soon as the patrol returns."

He snapped his briefcase shut and drew himself up straight. "You know, Taoiseach, Major Finigan was also unarmed. If the twenty-four young soldiers in that patrol meet the same fate as him, I'll have to buy a bigger case."

"What are you talking about?"

"Why, to hold all the parts, don't you see?" He thumped the leather bag as he turned for the door. "Two dozen severed hands would never fit in here."

DUNKIRK
•••••••••

7:25 a.m.—February 10
Fuel Reserves—11 Days

THE ASH-VEILED EARLY morning sun turned the white cliffs of Dover blue as King Charles walked to the edge of a hastily built platform atop the palisades and gave the Churchillian "V" for victory sign to the nine hundred Dunkirkers assembled on the ice of the English Channel below.

A wild cheer went up from the volunteers and the king turned to Marjorie Glynn beside him. "I wish I were going with you, Dr. Glynn," he said wistfully. "They're a brave and spirited lot."

"We shall need their spirit, Your Majesty," Marjorie said, her eyes sweeping the spectacle of men and machines out on the vast foreboding floes. "And their bravery."

The king motioned toward the huge crowd lining the cliff tops on both sides of the platform. "Just look at the thousands that have come out in this freezing weather to see the Dunkirkers off," Charles said. "Britain is united as she was sixty years ago when the first volunteers went over to rescue our army from the Nazi legions."

Marjorie smiled fondly at the enthusiasm in the king's voice. Lord knew he hadn't had much to cheer about lately, and the strain of the past few years showed in his gray hair and deeply lined face.

He had assumed the throne under the terrible cloud of his mother's assassination in the fall of 1996. The radiation deaths of thousands of Irishmen during the Windscale meltdown the spring before had brought demands of an eye for an eye from the IRA.

Despite unprecedented security around the royal family, vengeful terrorists had slipped into Scotland and blown apart seventy-year-old Queen Elizabeth's limousine with a shoulder-fired rocket as she was chauffeured south from Edinburgh.

His own coronation two months later had been the most tightly guarded event in the history of London, with tanks ringing Westminster Abbey and helicopters hovering overhead. The tight security continued to this day, and Marjorie could see dozens of Scotland Yard detectives ringing the platform, their eyes scanning the crowds.

Charles did not even enjoy peace within the secure confines of Buckingham Palace. There had been constant rumors about Queen Diana and that Swiss ski instructor in Gstaad. Then the king's personal valet had defected and sold a story to the tabloids about Charles's own romps with a twenty-two-year-old chambermaid.

Perhaps the deepest wound inflicted upon the newly crowned king had been the growing clamor for his abdication. As the aftermath of Windscale and the worsening weather continued to batter the economy, more and more jobless British men and women saw the maintenance of the royal family as a needless drain on dwindling state funds.

Although a majority of the people still supported the king, a rapidly rising number felt the royal role should be pared back. Many agreed with Seamus MacTiege that most of the palaces should be shut down and the several princes and princesses who lived useless lives in baronial splendor booted off the public dole.

The king's aide-de-camp approached Charles and Marjorie. "We'll be ready for your address to the Dunkirkers in ten minutes, Your Majesty."

"Very well."

The aide turned to Marjorie. "I have a helicopter waiting to take you down to the ice, Dr. Glynn."

King Charles extended his hand. "Good luck, Dr. Glynn. All of England will be cheering you on to Calais and back."

"Thank you, Your Majesty. I'm most grateful for your support of Biosphere Britannia these past years, and for coming here to Dover to see us off. We Dunkirkers shall do our best."

"I know you will. Be assured I shall be following your progress closely."

Marjorie curtsied awkwardly in her outfit of thermal underwear, insulated clothes, and fur-lined parka, then followed the aide to the helicopter fifty yards away.

The aircraft lifted off in a swirl of snow and Marjorie looked down past the edge of the cliffs at the odd assortment of vehicles scattered across the ice floes below. Almost all the half-tracks and ski-equipped lorries in the skeletal British Army were already assigned to the critical delivery of food and fuel to isolated English towns.

Only a dozen track-driven communications vans had been available for the convoy to France. As Prime Minister Butler had made clear to Marjorie and Ben, the Dunkirkers could expect little additional help from the armed forces beyond resupply by military helicopters.

Of the 275 vehicles clustered on the ice, only a hundred or so had been manufactured in a factory. Most of the machines had been built by hand, assembled from the parts of dismantled automobiles and tractors, vehicles made useless six months out of the year by snow-covered roads and frozen fields.

Almost all were fitted with skis in front instead of wheels, and the majority were driven by ridged conveyor belts in back that resembled tank treads. Perhaps a quarter were powered by old airplane engines, reversed to drive the craft in front forward. They varied in size from converted automobiles to a dozen former buses with huge tracks underneath and stoves and kitchens inside.

As the helicopter lowered toward the ice, Marjorie could

see trucks with sides reading "Applewhite's Pudding Shop," "H. Smirke & Son Chemists," and, most incongruous of all, "Stainer Bros., Upholsterers, House Furnishers, Funeral Directors."

The chopper settled on the floes and a moment later a Royal Marines officer popped the door and saluted Marjorie smartly. "Captain Walt Grady, Royal Marines, Dr. Glynn," he shouted above the din of the rotating blades above. "I'm to be your military liaison."

"Good to meet you, Captain," Marjorie said, accepting a hand down to the ice.

"Your command vehicle's over here," Grady said, leading Marjorie toward a Royal Marines communications van outfitted with skis in front and half-tracks behind. The officer popped the door in the rear of the vehicle and Marjorie looked into the eight- by twelve-foot space within.

One wall was almost entirely taken up with radio equipment and a television monitor. A hinged foldout desk and chair occupied the opposite wall. Up front, a sliding glass window gave access to the cab. In the middle of the van, a small metal table and four chairs were attached to the floor.

The loudspeaker mounted on the roof of the van crackled to life. "Attention on the ice. Please stand by for an address by His Royal Majesty, King Charles."

The Dunkirkers tinkering with their snowmobile engines and loading last-minute supplies began to gather around the van and the other communications vehicles in the convoy. The nine hundred volunteers stood expectantly, their eyes raised to the tiny figure stepping before a battery of microphones on the cliff high above them.

For a moment there was only the sound of the wind whistling through the pressure ridges stitching the ice. Then the king began to speak. "My fellow countrymen of the Dunkirk Brigade," the king began, his precise, aristocratic inflections familiar to everyone listening.

"I am confident I speak for the entire nation when I say that today Britain sends her finest men and women forth to do battle. Make no mistake, we are engaged in war, a mighty conflict to repel the cruel deprivations of the ice and snow that grip our British Isles."

The king's voice rose with emotion. "Britain must have geothermal power. It is you who, by your personal bravery and striving, will bring to North Channel the means to pierce the floor of the sea and bring that life-saving energy to our suffering land."

For fifteen minutes more, King Charles spoke of the grave energy crisis facing the British Isles, then ended his speech by wishing the Dunkirkers a heartfelt "Godspeed."

A cheer went up from the throngs atop the cliffs, and several hundred schoolgirls tossed red, white, and blue paper flowers off the palisades to blow out over the Dunkirkers standing by their snowmobiles below.

Circling overhead, news helicopters from the BBC and the international media sent live pictures of the intrepid expedition into homes and workplaces all over England, and the world.

Marjorie Glynn turned to Captain Grady and pulled a folded Biosphere Britannia flag out from under her parka. She handed it to the officer. "Run this up the radio antenna," she said.

Grady unfurled the twenty-four- by thirty-six-inch cloth to reveal a stylized white pyramid of glass with a fruit tree in the center stitched into the green cotton fabric.

"Most appropriate." He grinned, reaching up to pull down the long whip antenna.

Marjorie watched the wind take the flag straight out. "I think we're ready now, Captain. Let's get this show on the road."

Grady smiled widely and saluted. "Very good, Ma'am."

Marjorie climbed into the cab of the command lorry next to the young driver while Grady got in back and powered up the communications equipment. The engine started and the van spun in a tight turn and headed east, its tracks throwing up twin plumes of snow.

The 275 other vehicles fell in behind and the convoy roared off across the broken floes toward France. The squadron of media helicopters followed the expedition for the first several miles. Then a snow squall blew up the Channel and the aircraft peeled off one by one and returned to the English shore.

An hour into the crossing, Captain Grady slid open the glass window between the cab and the radio room. "I've just had a call from one of our communications vans in the middle of the convoy. A lorry's broken down. The driver wants the expedition to stop while he makes repairs."

Marjorie would have none of it. "We can't stop," she said. "If that snow squall traps us out here on the ice, we could lose the whole convoy. Have one of the vehicles behind pick the crew up."

A dozen more snowmobiles broke down over the next two hours as metal parts cracked in the intense cold and skis were snapped by the latticework of fissures and waist-high pressure ridges the expedition crossed.

Still, the Dunkirkers managed to make ten miles before the scout vehicles out ahead were suddenly stopped by a massive iceberg frozen into the floes. Other bergs ran east and west, forming a towering barrier of ice bisecting the English Channel.

Marjorie got out of the van and stood surveying the wall of ice as Captain Grady came up. "Looks like a job for the sappers," Grady said.

"Sappers?" Marjorie said.

"Explosives experts, ma'am. When I was assigned as your military liaison, I ordered an aerial reconnaissance of the Channel. I knew we'd have to blast our way through this line of bergs. I brought along a squad of sappers from my outfit. They'll have us through in under an hour."

"Very well, Captain. Carry on."

The Royal Marine officer nodded and put in a radio call. Ten minutes later Marjorie and her crew sheltered behind the lorry as the Marine sappers set off the charges they'd placed against the berg.

A huge explosion shook the floes, showering the van and the Dunkirkers with pulverized ice. The sappers advanced into the cavity left by the blast and set another charge. Again the floes reverberated with the sound of disintegrating ice.

Half an hour and three explosions later, the sappers had opened a canyon through the berg and the command lorry led the convoy through and out onto the clear ice beyond.

The falling snow began to lighten and the expedition made steady progress for the next several hours, the surviving vehicles now strung out across the ice in a line almost two miles long. The convoy was only ten miles from Calais when a message came into the command lorry that a supply van had turned over behind them.

"Apparently the relief driver is rather badly hurt," Captain Grady said.

"Turn around," Marjorie ordered the driver.

A quarter mile back, they could see a converted delivery truck over on its side at the base of a five-foot-high pressure ridge, a shattered front ski obviously the cause of the accident.

As they came up, the lorry driver was kneeling in the snow cradling the head of a man lying half under the toppled truck. The driver rose as Marjorie jumped from the van and hurried across the snow.

She winced at the sight of the victim. The man's crushed face was a mask of blood, his jaw horribly mangled and pushed to one side.

"He got thrown out and the lorry rolled over him," the driver said. "He's in a bad way."

Marjorie turned to Grady. "Get back to the radio and order the ambulance up here."

By now several more vehicles had pulled up and a small knot of Dunkirkers was standing around staring in shock at the grisly scene.

Marjorie grabbed the arm of the man nearest her. "C'mon you, all of you, let's get this bloody truck off the poor bastard."

The relief driver withered in pain as the truck was lifted off his legs and the blood coursed through his crushed arteries. Yet he hadn't screamed out, and Marjorie knelt by his side with a terrible suspicion.

Up close, she could see his skin turning blue beneath the blood. She put her ear against his torn lips. Nothing. He wasn't breathing. She pried open his mouth with her fingers. His palate was crushed down against his bottom teeth. There was no way for air to get to his lungs.

Captain Grady came running back across the snow from the command van, an emergency first-aid kit in his hands. "The medical team is at least two miles back. It will take them ten or fifteen minutes to get here."

Marjorie took the kit from the officer and pulled out a roll of gauze. "He'll suffocate by then," she said, swabbing the blood off the unconscious driver's neck. "We've got to do a tracheotomy, get his windpipe open."

"Thank God you're a doctor," Grady said.

Marjorie had a sinking feeling inside. She had a medical degree but she'd spent her entire professional career as a molecular biologist doing DNA research. She'd never treated a patient.

"Look, Captain, I don't practice medicine. I'm a pure researcher, double-stranded RNA, that sort of thing. I've never done a tracheotomy."

She suddenly realized the dozen men standing around were all staring at her.

"I don't know what that double RNA stuff is," said a bearded driver in a greasy plaid coat, "but I know ya got more training in these things than the rest of us, ain't that right?"

"The last time I made an incision it was on a cadaver in an anatomy class," Marjorie protested. "And that was eight years ago. I'm not qualified to operate on him."

"All's I know is if you don't open his windpipe, he's going to die right here in front of us," the driver pressed. "Make up your mind, miss."

"Doctor," Marjorie said automatically, immediately regretting it.

The men stared at her.

"Jesus, all right, then. I suppose I'm it."

She ripped open the relief driver's jacket above his throat. "I'll need a knife."

The burly lorry driver snaked a hand into his pocket and withdrew a ten-inch-long switchblade. He leaned over and held out the closed knife to Marjorie. As she reached for it, he hit the button in the handle and the blade flicked out an inch from her outstretched fingers.

She jerked her hand back, bringing a smirk to the driver's face. For a moment, the two locked eyes. Then, in a blur of movement, she snatched the knife from his fingers with one hand and with her other yanked a leg out from under him.

The driver let out a loud grunt as he came down hard on his ass on the snow-covered ice. For a moment he sat there stunned. Then his face twisted in rage and he pushed himself up and started for Marjorie.

"I wouldn't do that, old chap," Captain Grady said, his right hand resting easily on the holstered pistol at his belt.

"Anyone got a match, a lighter?" Marjorie looked around the circle of drivers.

A round, ruddy-cheeked little man with a briar pipe clenched in his teeth pulled a dented Zippo lighter from his pocket and handed it to Marjorie.

She flicked it on and ran the knife blade back and forth several times through the flame. Satisfied, she leaned over the injured driver and spread the skin taut against his neck. For a long moment she hesitated, the sharp tip of the knife an inch above the man's windpipe. Then she took a deep breath and pressed the blade down into the white flesh.

Several of the men watching blanched and averted their eyes as blood began to flow freely from the four-inch-long incision that opened under the knife.

Marjorie stared at the wound, then cursed under her breath. "Shit." She hadn't cut deeply enough. She gritted her teeth and fitted the blade back into the bloody trough on the driver's neck, pressing down harder this time. Suddenly she felt the knife tip sink through into the windpipe.

A loud gurgling sound erupted from the driver's chest as his bursting lungs sucked in great gulps of air. Then he exhaled and a violent spray of blood shot up over Marjorie's face and clothes. The driver took another breath, then another. Within minutes, his color had returned.

Marjorie stayed at the injured man's side, stemming the flow of blood from his face and neck with gauze and keeping his windpipe open with her fingers. Five minutes later the ambulance raced up and a doctor and nurse leaped out.

"I'll take over now," the physician said, kneeling in the snow.

Marjorie stood and stretched the kinks out of her back from bending over the injured driver so long in the intense cold. "He's lost a lot of blood," Marjorie said as the doctor inserted a tube in the driver's windpipe and began to bandage his head.

"We'll give him a transfusion in the ambulance. Did you do the trach?"

Marjorie nodded.

"Damn fine job. You saved his life."

"Bit of all right, Dr. Glynn," the pipe-smoking driver said, the new look of respect in his face reflected in the eyes of the other drivers as well.

Score one for the Oxford anatomy course, Marjorie thought, peeling a frozen rivulet of the driver's blood from her caked face. "Can he be moved?" she asked the doctor.

"Yes, we can make him comfortable enough in the ambulance."

"I hate to hurry you, Doctor, but we must get going," Marjorie said. "There are too many deep fractures in the ice to risk crossing the floes in the dark. If the sun sets before we reach France, we'll be trapped out here all night."

"There's not enough fuel to keep all the lorries running until morning," Captain Grady said.

"That's what I'm worried about, Captain. Half the expedition could freeze to death."

The doctor nodded. "I understand. We'll get him into the ambulance straightaway."

Ten minutes later the relief driver was bandaged and safely strapped to a bunk in the ambulance. Marjorie waved the crowd of Dunkirkers back into their lorries and climbed into the cab of her command vehicle.

"Crank it up," Marjorie ordered the driver, pulling off her bloody gloves and bending to warm her freezing fingers over the floorboard heater.

"Aye, ma'am," the young driver said, shoving the shift lever forward with a loud crunch of gears.

The rest of the track-driven trucks resumed their place in line and the expedition headed east again toward France, the eerie blue sun sinking ever lower over the shadowed ice floes behind them.

NORTH CHANNEL
• • • • • • • • • • • • • • • • • •

9:05 a.m.—February 11
Fuel Reserves—10 Days

A TREMENDOUS EXPLOSION BOOMED out over the floes of North Channel, and a moment later a shower of ice and freezing seawater rained down on the British geothermal drill platform suspended fifty feet above the ice.

As the air cleared, Benjamin Meade turned from his vantage point at a window in the operations center. "C'mon, let's go see if we've got a hole big enough to get the *Yellowstone* through," he said to Captain Mel Sanderson, sprawled on an old leather couch set against the far wall.

Sanderson had arrived by helicopter the night before and he was still tired after his long trip to Britain on an RAF jet. The old sea dog cocked one eye open. "I haven't gotten my beauty rest yet."

"The only thing that would make you beautiful is a head transplant."

"Yeah, well, there's a certain little dancer in Boston happens to think I'm the handsomest devil she's ever seen."

"I've seen you operate, Mel. When you get finished pouring champagne into women, they think a moose is handsome."

Sanderson yawned. "You're just jealous of my sexual prowess. I'm practically a legend in my own time."

"You're going to be an unemployed legend if you don't get your ass off that couch. We've got work to do."

Sanderson swung his feet to the floor and grabbed his arctic parka off the arm of the couch. "I'll never get used to this weather. Here we are ten miles off the coast of Scotland and it's thirty below zero."

"It's been this cold here before."

"Bullshit. When?"

"During the last ice age," Ben said, opening the door to the freezing deck.

Sanderson looked up at the sky as they stepped out onto the snow-drifted platform. "That damn blue sun gives me the creeps," he said, his eyes adjusting to the surreal aquamarine glow through the ash clouds above.

"It's going to be that way for a long time," Ben said. "The latest satellite scan of R-Nine shows magma still rising up into the cone."

The two walked over to the edge of the steel deck to peer down at the huge hole the Royal Navy explosives crew had just blasted in the ice below the west side of the platform.

"What are you going to do down there, Ben?" Sanderson asked, eyeing the jagged chunks of ice bobbing violently in the pocket of black seawater below.

"I've got to inspect the well head," Ben said. "While I'm down there I might as well check out the platform legs."

"We'd better pump some antifreeze solution into that hole or it'll ice back over while you're submerged," Sanderson said.

"Yeah, you're right," Ben said. "There's a tank of marine antifreeze beside the supply hut. Get a couple of men and pump in a thousand gallons or so. I'll have the launch crew ready to lower the *Yellowstone*."

Sanderson nodded. "Should take about twenty minutes."

Ben was walking toward the *Yellowstone* when Reggie Abbot, the chief British geothermal scientist on the North Channel project, hailed him from the top of the iron stairway leading down to the ice. "I say, Ben, half a mo."

Ben stopped and waited for Abbot to cross the platform, annoyed that the Englishman had obviously been down on the floes despite Ben's orders that everyone stay on the platform while the ice was being dynamited.

"You could have gotten yourself hurt down there, Reggie," Ben said as the scientist walked up, a thick, yard-long length of electrical cable in his hands. "Didn't you get the word we were going to blast?"

"Not to worry, Ben, I was safely away on the other side of the platform," he said, giving Ben an insouciant grin that communicated he didn't consider himself bound by the orders of the American newcomer.

"Look, Reggie, I don't want to lecture you, but ice is tricky stuff. That blast could have fractured the floes like a plate of glass. You're lucky you didn't find your English ass bobbing around with those chunks of ice down there."

Abbot stiffened. "Conjecture is so often the plaything of idle minds, isn't it, Ben?" he said, flashing a crocodile smile.

"In any event, my English ass, as you put it in your inimitable Americanese, is quite dry, thank you. I went down to check on an electrical problem, and found this," he said, handing Ben the section of line.

"What is it?" Ben asked, shaking off his annoyance.

"An electrical cable."

"I can see that."

"Can you also see it's been chewed?"

"Chewed?"

"If I'm not mistaken, those wolves we've been seeing out on the floes the last couple of days paid us a visit after dark. That cable was fine the last time I checked it late yesterday afternoon."

Ben stared out over the ice. "I thought that howling sounded closer last night. But what the hell would they chew up a cable for?"

"There are salt compounds in the insulation. This time of year, animals crave the stuff. I've seen wires nibbled away by foxes and badgers before. This is my first experience with wolves."

"Damn," Ben swore. "I've got to start running new drill

pipe down tomorrow. There'll be work crews all over the ice. It's going to be dangerous enough without having to worry about wolves attacking."

"My thought exactly, Ben. We can't have our chaps traipsing about the floes with a wolf pack snapping at their heels. We're going to have to get rid of the beasts."

"What do you suggest?"

"The Scots Guards, I should think. They're the ones chased the bloody wolves out here on the ice in the first place."

"All right, Reggie, I'll leave it up to you. I've got to dive in the *Yellowstone* before that hole freezes over."

"I'll buzz the military. Until the Guards arrive, I'll mount sentry duty with a target rifle I have in my quarters. I used to pop tin cans off the platform to while away the time before you Americans and your poker games arrived."

"Just make sure you take your potshots from the platform," Ben warned. "I've hunted wolves. Believe me, a target rifle will wound one just enough to piss him off real bad."

"Are you advising me on hunting now, Ben, in addition to your geothermal tutoring?"

"Oh, for God's sake, Reggie, do whatever the hell you want. I've got to get the *Yellowstone* over the side," Ben said, stalking off to ready the submersible. Marjorie had been wrong about her friend Abbot accepting his secondary role. The bastard was determined to keep up his internecine sniping to the bitter end.

For the next half hour, Ben went through a systems check on his research sub. The eighteen-foot-long *Yellowstone* had two compartments. At the cylindrical bow, a five-and-a-half-foot-diameter clear plastic bubble bulged like a match tip from the front of the craft.

The acrylic sphere was surrounded by searchlights, exterior sonar gear, and long, remote-control manipulator arms that could use tools on well-head machinery and retrieve objects from the seafloor.

The twin seats in the bubble allowed the pilot and observer to see 360 degrees around them as they steered the craft through the depths. On small panels before each seat were rows of pressure and air gauges, systems switches, communications gear, and the navigation control that looked like a car's steering wheel with the top and bottom thirds cut off.

Behind the sealed pilot sphere was a metal pressure chamber large enough for two divers, with a sea lock in the floor. During normal operations, divers lowered the pressure in the aft compartment until it matched the ambient pressure of the seawater outside, then went out through the hatch in the deck.

Ben checked the battery packs, making sure they held a full charge, and finally the cylindrical oxygen tanks mounted on the exterior hull. As he was finishing his inspection, Mel Sanderson approached across the windswept deck.

"We've pumped in enough solution to keep the hole open for about three hours," Sanderson said. "You ready to go down?"

"All set. You take over as launch chief, Mel."

"Right. Watch yourself under that ice, Ben. You get your ass in trouble, I don't know how the hell we'd ever get you back up."

"I'll be careful. See you in a couple of hours, Mel."

Sanderson turned for the operations center as Ben lowered himself through a manhole atop the transparent sphere at the front of the *Yellowstone*. As he strapped himself into the cramped pilot's chair, he could hear a crewman dog-shut the hatch above.

He put on his communications headset. "*Yellowstone* to launch chief. Hatches secure; oxygen on; all electrical systems up; motor-drives ready. Let's go, Mel."

"Launch chief to *Yellowstone*," Sanderson's electrified voice came back. "Stand by to launch."

Ben could hear Sanderson giving orders to the operator of the huge deck crane that towered above the *Yellowstone*. Then he felt a jolt as the crane lifted the submersible off the deck and swung the craft out over the hole in the ice below.

Ben had a clear view of the blue-white floes of North Channel as he was lowered toward the sea. Far off to the west, he could see what looked to be a half-dozen blurred shapes moving along the shoulder of a pressure ridge. Wolves, he realized uneasily.

For a moment, he debated calling Abbot to warn him not to let anyone down onto the ice. Then he shrugged to himself. Abbot was a big boy. He knew the goddamn wolves were out there. He wouldn't be stupid enough to let anyone off the platform before the Scots Guards arrived.

Ben turned his mind back to the dive, his eyes sweeping the instrument gauges before him as the submersible settled into the pocket of freezing seawater beyond the west side of the platform.

Satisfied the *Yellowstone* was ready to submerge, he reached up and hit the cable disconnect switch that freed the craft from the steel umbilical cord of the crane. There was a loud hissing sound as he flooded the ballast tanks with seawater, then a numbing drone as he turned on the electric motors.

A moment later, the slushy waters of North Channel frothed up around the bubble of the pilot's compartment, then everything was suddenly still as the submersible sank slowly into the depths.

Although he'd made over five hundred dives in the *Yellowstone*, Ben was struck by the silent beauty around him as he descended into the submarine world. The light was diffused through the ice above, but there was enough illumination to bathe the inside of the sphere in a radiant sea-green glow.

Even Ben's hands looked green. The only other colors visible were the orange faces of the instrumentation dials, and the trail of silver bubbles rising slowly upward as the *Yellowstone* sank toward the seabed.

The light began to dim, first to a deep blue-green, then to indigo, and finally to a blue-black twilight as the submersible neared the seafloor 415 feet beneath the ice. Ben turned on the exterior lights and gazed out at the gently sloping bottom stretching off into the murky distance. But for an occasional small fish attracted to the lights, there was no sign of life, and he switched on the sonar.

The electronic pulses of the sonar soon located the well head off to port, and Ben turned the *Yellowstone* through the depths. Several moments later, the submersible's lights picked up machinery ahead, and Ben began a slow inspection of the geothermal well.

The drill pipe protruded upward from the top of a room-sized pressurized compartment called the cellar. The cellar was designed to house technicians while they were making well-head repairs.

The men were brought down in a submersible service capsule that docked against the cellar. While the technicians were inside, the work compartment was served by an umbilical line that provided fresh air, electricity, and telephone and television connections to the platform above.

Ben was relieved that the cellar and drill pipe looked intact. He slowly circled the well head for the next thirty minutes, making notes on the condition of pipes and valves, then swung the *Yellowstone* around to have a look at the platform legs.

All four of the huge steel support jacks also proved to be in good condition, despite the pressure and pounding the rig had taken from the shifting floes. Finally, two hours after he'd begun the dive, Ben called the platform and told Sanderson to ready the crew to retrieve the submersible.

He was at the two-hundred-foot level and rising steadily through the gradually lightening depths when his earphones crackled.

"Launch chief to *Yellowstone*," the high-pitched, excited voice of Mel Sanderson came through.

"*Yellowstone*. What is it, Mel?" Ben said.

"It's Reggie Abbot, Ben. He went out hunting those wolves. You'd better get up here fast."

"Damn it," Ben fumed. "I told the son of a bitch to leave it to the Scots Guards. Where is he now?"

There was a long pause, then Sanderson's voice came back, his tone pained. "All over the ice, Ben. The wolves have torn him to pieces."

CALAIS
• • • • • • • • • • • • • • • • • •

3:00 a.m.—February 12
Fuel Reserves—9 Days

MARJORIE GLYNN YAWNED AS she started across the floodlit convoy assembly area in a snowy field a mile inland from the French port of Calais.

She was bone-tired. Dark circles rimmed her green eyes, her hair and skin felt greasy and every task now seemed to require a Herculean effort.

But for an occasional catnap on a bunk in one of the dormitory lorries, she had been working continuously since the Dunkirkers had reached France just after dark two days before.

It was now 3 A.M. and there were still several loose ends to attend to before the Dunkirkers would be ready for the dash across the ice back to England. The wooden sleds designed to carry the tons of geothermal equipment were huge. Building them had required emptying every French lumberyard within fifty miles of their stock of large beams and planks.

Thank God, the French authorities had been exceptionally cooperative, for once casting aside all Gallic bureaucracy and quickly providing Marjorie with whatever she needed to get the work done.

A radio and television appeal for French carpenters had

succeeded beyond anyone's expectations, and over a hundred volunteers had been hard at work on the sleds within hours of the first broadcast.

Perhaps it was the new spirit of regional unity brought about by the formation of the European Community earlier in the decade, Marjorie mused, or maybe French solidarity with Britain against the suddenly hostile climate. Whatever the reason, the citizens of Calais and the surrounding region had opened their hearts to the Dunkirkers, furnishing the expedition with everything from hot meals to warm beds.

Marjorie spotted Captain Grady supervising a loading party ahead and she worked her way toward the Royal Marine officer through the busy roustabouts and crates of machinery.

"How's everything going, Captain?" she asked as she came up.

"We're almost ready to go," Grady said, his own fatigue showing in his deeply lined face and red-rimmed eyes.

"Do you think you've got enough lorries hooked up to pull that thing?" Marjorie said, surveying a 142-foot-long derrick that was linked by chains to a motley collection of tread-driven trucks ahead of it.

"Yes, if Dr. Meade's calculations are right, a dozen lorries should be able to manage it." The officer turned and pointed to an immense drill tower stretching 260 feet across the snow. "It's that big bloody bastard I'm worried about. It weighs fifty tons."

Marjorie looked past Grady's shoulder at the huge tower. It had taken thirty-five French carpenters nearly a full day to build the four separate sleds that would be positioned along the length of the steel monster. Another three hours had been required for derrick operators and roustabouts to hoist it into place on the wooden sleighs.

"I've assigned the biggest lorries, all large diesels," Grady said, pointing toward a line of twenty ski- and tread-equipped trucks lined up in front of the tower. "Still, it's an incredible weight. I shouldn't be surprised if we blow a few engines on the way."

"Engines we can replace," Marjorie said. "It's the Dunkirkers I'm worried about. Everyone's exhausted, and we haven't even started back to England yet."

"Yes, tempers are beginning to fray," Grady said. "I've had to break up several fights already this morning."

"The loading's taken every hand, but we can rest our people in shifts on the trip back. There are enough bunks in the dormitory lorries to handle a third of the expedition at a time."

Grady grinned tiredly. "As played out as everyone is, I doubt even bumping across those bloody floes will keep anyone awake."

"What about the two turbine generators? Have you loaded them yet?"

"We finally finished packing them away about an hour ago. They're so huge, we had to break them almost completely apart to fit them on the sleds."

"I hope the men were careful stowing them. Those turbine blades are rather delicate."

"The chaps handled them like eggs. I also had the carpenters insert special springs between the sled runners and the cargo platforms to cushion the equipment on the trip."

"It appears you've thought of everything, Captain," Marjorie said, glancing at her watch. "Hurry the loading along as quickly as you can. I want to be well out on the Channel ice by dawn."

Forty-five minutes later, Marjorie was checking equipment manifests at the table in the back of the command lorry when Grady knocked once and opened the door.

"We're ready, Dr. Glynn. The men are warming up their engines now."

Marjorie stepped outside and looked toward the assembly area. The idling motors of the Dunkirkers' snowmobiles were sending clouds of steamy exhaust into the glow of the vehicle's headlights.

Along a ridge top bordering the floodlit field, several hundred French carpenters and workers had gathered to see their British comrades off. As they waited, the tired workers stomped their feet in the snow and flapped their arms across their heavy jackets to keep warm.

"Give me ten minutes to thank them," Marjorie said, looking toward the French volunteers. "Then we go."

Marjorie searched out the harbormaster and the head carpenter and exchanged Gallic hugs and kisses. Someone pressed a bouquet of roses into her gloved hands and she felt a lump in her throat as the grizzled workmen gathered around her, thumping her back amid cries of *"Bonne chance, bon voyage."*

The chivalry of the French volunteers renewed her spirit and Marjorie was smiling as she made her way back to the command vehicle. "God, what magnificent people," she said to Grady.

"The next time someone says anything about the 'bloody frogs' I'm going to punch his lights out," Grady said.

"We have a long way to go, Captain. Signal the convoy we're moving out."

Grady radioed the communications vans spaced through the long column of trucks, and runners fanned out from the vans to pass the word down the line. The sounds of grinding gears and straining engines rose to a crescendo as the track-driven lorries started slowly ahead, yanking taut the chains that stretched to the sleds behind them.

As Marjorie watched, the teams of hybrid snowmobiles moved out one by one, pulling the long wooden sleighs behind them like mechanical huskies hitched to huge dogsleds.

The French workers cheered and waved small Union Jacks as the long column snaked slowly west out of the assembly area, the powerful lights high in the work towers playing over the equipment-laden sleds as they bumped and swayed across the snow.

There were forty sleds altogether, some pulled by a single lorry while others required the horsepower of up to twenty snowmobiles chained ahead of them. Satisfied the trucks and sleds were all in their assigned places, Marjorie climbed into the cab of her command lorry.

The light was on in back and she could hear Captain Grady advising British Army headquarters in London that the convoy was starting back across the Channel.

Marjorie turned to the driver. "Let's go home," she said,

then closed her eyes and sank against the worn seat. She was asleep before the driver had the truck in gear.

Twenty minutes later she awoke again as the convoy of Dunkirkers crossed the French coast, the headlights on their snowmobiles reflecting off the white ice floes layering the English Channel. The expedition retraced its route of two days before and by dawn they were already a third of the way across.

As the blue sun rose above the horizon, the news helicopters returned. Marjorie waved through the windshield as a large chopper with the letters BBC on the side hovered low overhead, matching its speed to the command lorry as a television camera focused on the cab of the truck.

Five minutes later Captain Grady slid open the window in the rear wall of the cab. "Radiophone call, Dr. Glynn."

Marjorie took the receiver from the officer. "Hello."

"You look tired. What have you been doing in France, partying all night?"

"Ben," she said, surprised to hear his voice. "How on earth do you know what I look like?"

"I turned on the news a couple of minutes ago and there was your command lorry on live television. I could see the circles under your eyes right through the windshield."

"Not from partying, you bloody bastard. I've been collecting your rotting equipment."

"I saw the derricks being towed behind you. Jesus, how on earth did you get those sleds built in two days?"

"I had a lot of help from some wonderful Frenchmen."

"You're doing a hell of a job, Marjorie."

"It's the Dunkirkers who are doing all the work. I'm just along for the ride."

"Bullshit. I got a call from my chief engineer in Calais. He said your leadership had earned the respect of every man and woman in the expedition. He told me that you'd even performed a medical operation out on the ice."

"Yes, well, had to be done. It was that or watch one of my drivers die before my eyes. Enough about me. How's everything at North Channel?"

"I'm afraid I've got some bad news, Marjorie. Reggie Abbot's dead."

"Reggie? Good God, what happened?"

"He tried to take on a wolf pack with a single-shot target rifle. They tore him to shreds."

"Wolves? Where did they come from?"

"Apparently they're the same animals that escaped from the Glasgow Zoo last spring. After what happened to poor Reggie, the Army's flying two hundred Scots Guards out here today to hunt them down."

"They'd better get on with the job. We should be up there in three or four days and I have no intention of exposing my Dunkirkers to attack by wolves. Not after all they've been through already."

"Have you got a route mapped out?"

"Yes. We'll cross the English shore at Brighton, then continue on to Reading. From there we'll push north through Worcester, Shrewsbury, and Wrexham. I plan to cross onto the ice of the Irish Sea at Rhyl on the coast of Wales."

"I got a call from the prime minister's office that a hundred more crews with large track-driven trucks will rendezvous with the expedition sometime late today. With that extra horsepower pulling in the sleds, it shouldn't take you more than a day to cross the Irish sea to the drill platform."

"It depends on the condition of the floes, Ben. We've run into several large pressure ridges out on the Channel. If we encounter rough ice on the Irish Sea, it could delay us."

"I'll see if I can talk the army into sending a helicopter out to scout the best route up from Rhyl."

"That would certainly save us some time." Marjorie yawned.

"You're exhausted, Marjorie," Ben said. "Try to get some sleep during the crossing."

"I haven't been able to sleep for more than twenty minutes at a time for the past three days. Too many worries chasing themselves around my mind."

"Promise me you'll at least try."

"Perhaps later. Goodbye, Ben."

"Goodbye, Marjorie."

As Marjorie handed the receiver back to Grady, she noticed he'd turned on the television monitor. The BBC channel was showing live shots of a huge crowd of people, the red, white, and blue colors of hundreds of British flags vivid against the snow around them.

"Where's that coming from?" she asked.

"Brighton." Grady grinned. "According to the BBC, there're over thirty thousand people already gathered to greet us."

Marjorie stared at Grady incredulously. "Thirty thousand!"

"Yes, and more on the way. The commentator predicts a hundred thousand will be waiting by the time we cross the coast."

Marjorie turned on the seat and stared through the windshield for a moment at the ice floes ahead, her tired mind stunned. A hundred thousand men, women, and children braving the freezing cold to cheer their countrymen home from France. A soft smile slowly formed on her face. King Charles was right. The British people were still indomitable.

There were tears in her eyes as she turned to the young driver. "See if you can find one of the dormitory lorries," she said. "I think I can sleep now."

LONDON
• • • • • • • • •

2:45 p.m.

BRITISH SECRETARY OF STATE for Energy Nan Dupont handed the file of computer printouts across the desk of Prime Minister Butler and sat back in her chair as he pored over the figures.

Butler rifled through the pages, then raised his eyes, a look of exasperation on his angular patrician face. "I'm at an absolute loss with this computer mumbo jumbo, Nan. Boil it down for me, will you?"

"We have barely nine days' supply of fuel left, Prime Minister."

"I take it your survey didn't find any reserves squirreled away."

"Here and there a small coal dump or a few thousand gallons of oil we'd missed before. Not enough to make much difference."

"What about flying in fuel? The Allies airlifted coal into Berlin when the Russians cut off the land routes fifty-odd years ago."

"I've run a computer calculation of that possibility," Dupont said. "It's not even remotely feasible. Berlin was a single city. We must supply the entire country, from the northern tip of Scotland to the Channel coast."

"I've had offers of help, air tankers, that sort of thing, from the leaders of virtually every country in the European Community," Butler persisted. "I've also gotten a call from President Allen volunteering whatever American Air Force planes we need."

Dupont shook her head. "An airlift would require round-the-clock snow removal at our airports, especially the fields in Scotland and Wales. Even if the snowplow operators hadn't gone out on strike, still we wouldn't have the manpower and equipment to keep even a quarter of the airports open."

Butler shook his head wearily. "Give the devil his due, MacTiege has us by the throat. He's infiltrated the Trades Union Congress with his own radical people top to bottom. They'll drag the general strike on until the government falls."

"Even the strikers must feed their families and keep their homes warm, Prime Minister. Surely the unions must relent at some point."

"It's an open secret that NUM and some of the other labor movements have been stockpiling their own food and fuel for months, Nan. While the rest of us are eating rotten potatoes and burning the furniture to keep warm, the strikers will be able to carry on for weeks longer."

Butler turned at the sound of a knock on the door. "Come."

The prime minister's personal secretary stuck his head in. "Beg pardon, sir, but you asked to be told when the Dunkirkers reached England," Smythe-Bruce said. "They're just coming into Brighton now. It's on the telly."

"We can use a spot of good news. Thank you."

"Shall I turn your set on, sir?" the obsequious functionary asked, his compulsion to be part of things at Downing Street urging him a step into the room.

Dupont rose and started across toward the television cabinet facing the prime minister's desk. "You needn't bother, Smythe-Bruce. I'll tend to it," she said, determined the ever-

hovering secretary not join them. The man's endless fawn-
ing made her skin crawl.

"Very well, ma'am," Smythe-Bruce said, his disappoint-
ment evident in his thin face as he withdrew.

Dupont switched on the BBC channel and returned to her
chair, angling the seat so she could see the television.

The TV was showing an announcer holding the tip of a
pointer against a map of the British Isles. "The Dunkirkers
will be coming off the ice here at Brighton," he said, indicat-
ing the resort city on the shore of the English Channel.

He moved the pointer up the map to a location due west
of London. "Once ashore, the expedition will push on to
Reading where they'll be joined by a hundred more large,
track-driven lorries that will help hasten the journey to
North Channel. After a night's rest, the Dunkirkers will head
north through Worcester, pass to the west of Birmingham,
and cross into Wales near Wrexham. They plan to keep on
twenty-four hours a day, with relief drivers spelling each
other every four hours."

The announcer looked off camera a moment and nodded.
"I've just been told the Dunkirkers are approaching the
beach. We're going to switch now to live coverage from a
BBC helicopter over the Channel."

"Good Lord, look at that," Prime Minister Butler said,
coming forward in his chair as the aerial view from the helicopter flashed on the screen. The expedition was strung out
over the floes in a column almost three miles long, the homemade snowmobiles with their odd tread drives looking even
stranger in the light of the blue-green sun.

In the lead was Marjorie Glynn's command lorry, her Biosphere Britannia banner whipping in the wind at the top of
the vehicle's long radio antenna.

Interspersed through the convoy behind came supply
trucks, canteen vans, several Red Cross ambulances, repair
vehicles, and dozens of flatbed trucks loaded with crates of
drilling equipment and sections of pipe. Toward the middle
of the column, ten decrepit buses bumped across the floes,
smoke rising from stovepipes jutting incongruously out of
their roofs.

"What are those buses for?" Dupont asked.

"They've been converted into dormitory lorries, I'm told," Butler said. "The relief drivers catch a few hours sleep in them between shifts behind the wheel."

The helicopter flew down the line of hybrid vehicles below and they listened as the BBC commentator described the scene. "Here come the workhorses of the expedition, the heavy diesel lorries pulling the derricks and the drill tower for North Channel," he said as the camera swept the convoy.

"Look at the size of that tower they're pulling," Butler marveled. "Good God, it must be almost three hundred feet long."

Dupont shook her head. "It would be a formidable task to transport that over normal roads. And here they are dragging it across a wasteland of ice."

The announcer's voice came back. "The sleds the Dunkirkers are pulling were built by French carpenters in under two days' time. An amazing piece of work."

Butler rose from his desk and came around to stand beside Dupont. "You can just see the steel runners there under the sleds. Did you catch that piece on the news about where those came from?"

Dupont shook her head.

"They're sections of rails the French high-speed trains run on," Butler said. "The French yanked up an entire mile of the line between Paris and Calais to fashion those runners."

"The French have been loyal allies all through the crisis, Prime Minister," Dupont said. "We owe them a great deal."

The BBC helicopter banked and the camera swung back to a shot of the command vehicle now only a few hundred yards from the beach. "The crowd's been waiting hours for this moment," the commentator said. "You can see hats being thrown in the air now."

Butler and Dupont watched as the throngs surged forward toward the wide avenue the police were attempting to keep open for the Dunkirkers to cross the shore.

"I shouldn't want to be one of those policemen trying to restrain the crowd down there." Butler grinned. "The last report I heard estimated over one hundred thousand people were waiting to welcome the expedition back to Britain."

"The Dunkirkers have fired the spirit of the entire country," Dupont said. "God, I wish I were part of it. I've half a mind to rush out to Reading and join them there."

"It's a worthy sentiment, Nan, but the truth is I need you here in London."

The commentator's voice grew excited. "The expedition's lead vehicle is coming ashore now," he said as the camera focused on Marjorie Glynn's command lorry crossing the beach beneath a shower of hats and paper flowers.

Everywhere in the delirious crowds, British flags were waving in the stiff wind off the Channel ice. As the BBC helicopter swooped low over the crowd, the camera showed people hugging each other, their faces radiant.

The rest of the convoy followed the command lorry over the shore, one equipment-laden truck after another rolling up the icy slope of the snow-covered beach. As the snowmobiles pulling the derricks and steam generators approached, the policemen pushed the throngs back to make room for the extra-wide sleds.

Finally, the immense drill tower bringing up the rear of the column lumbered over the English shore, long leads of taut chain stretching to the twenty straining trucks towing it from ahead.

"They're home, Prime Minister," Nan Dupont said softly, her eyes moist.

"Home, Nan, but with still a long way to go," Butler said. "There's over three hundred and fifty miles of ice and snow between Brighton and North Channel. And we're running out of time."

North Channel
•••••••••••••••••••

11:45 p.m.—February 13
Fuel Reserves—8 Days

"IN ALL ME LIFE, I've never been so cold," the young Irish paratrooper said to his buddy, barely visible in the moonless night beside him as they trudged over the dark surface of the frozen Irish Sea.

The night before, the patrol of twenty-one privates, a corporal, a first sergeant, and the captain commanding had boarded a helicopter at Dundalk on the coast. The Irish aircraft had skimmed low over the darkened floes and landed the soldiers on the ice fifteen miles south of the British drill site.

The captain had forbidden lighting even their small portable gas stoves that night for fear a British air patrol might spot the flickering flames. None of the troops had felt warm since leaving the helicopter.

"Colder than a witch's teat," the second young soldier said. "If I'd have known this is what we was volunteerin' for, I'd of kept me hand in me pocket, I would."

"A little stroll out on the ice, the captain said. It's quite a sense of humor that one has."

"Quiet in the ranks," the first sergeant hissed from behind them. "You'll bring the bloody Brits down on us."

"Brits, me arse," the first private threw back. "There ain't nothin' out here on the ice but us and the howlin' wind."

"Don't think in the dark I can't tell that's you, Sullivan. I'll have your stripe if you don't shut your flappin' mouth."

The private fell silent at the threat, and the patrol moved quietly on, the only sounds the crunch of boots through the crusted snow layering the ice and an occasional grunt as a paratrooper stumbled on one of the innumerable small fissures snaking across the floes.

Twenty minutes later, the captain called a halt, and the men fell out for a brief rest and a hurried meal of fortified chocolate bars and cold tea from their thermos canteens. While the men ate, the officer consulted his maps by the glow of a hooded flashlight.

Several minutes later, he whispered down the line for the first sergeant to come up.

"Yes, Captain O'Connell?"

"Near as I can make out in this trackless waste, we're within a mile of the drill platform. If it weren't for this blowing snow, we'd have seen the lights by now."

The sergeant's eyes swept the dark horizon to the northeast. "The wind's been dying down the past hour, sir. We should see somethin' soon."

"What's the name of that Signal Corps lad they assigned with the night camera?"

"Corporal Donovan, sir."

"Send him to the front as soon as we see the lights. I'll want pictures of the platform, whatever's on the deck, and any equipment the Brits might have out on the ice."

"The bloody tea's cold, damn it," the loud epithet rang over the ice.

"Quiet, I told you," the sergeant whispered furiously down the line.

"Who was that stupid bastard?" Captain O'Connell asked.

"Sullivan, sir. He's a malingerer and a chronic complainer. I wish we'd never brought him."

The two men froze suddenly at the sound of a far-off wail.

"What in the name of God was that?" the sergeant whispered.

The captain stared into the dark, listening intently.

"It must have been the wind," he said after a moment. "A gust moaning over a pressure ridge out there somewhere." In truth, it had sounded more like the howl of an animal to the captain, but he kept that opinion to himself. The sergeant and the rest of the men were jumpy enough as it was.

"Didn't sound like no wind to me, Captain."

"Whatever it was, it hasn't come again. Get the men ready to go. I want to reconnoiter that Brit platform and be well away before dawn."

Out on the deck of the British Geothermal drill platform a mile away, the young Scots Guards officer in charge of the sentries that night had also heard the primeval cry. Unlike the Irish paratroopers approaching across the ice, Lieutenant Sam Scribner knew exactly what had howled in the night, and he started nervously making the rounds of his men.

"Keep a sharp eye. It sounds like they're getting closer," he said to a wide-eyed private staring down his rifle barrel at the black floes beyond the reach of the searchlights.

The private licked his lips. "They say the leader of the pack is huge."

"Beelzebub."

"Yes, sir, Beelzebub. It means 'devil.' "

"He's only a wolf."

A long howl echoed across the ice again, nearer now, and both men instantly tensed.

"Only a wolf," the private repeated softly, his mouth like cotton now. "Only a wolf."

"Keep your nerve up," Lieutenant Scribner said, then hurried off to check his men posted on the other side of the deck.

Out on the dark ice two hundred yards beyond the reach of the lights, the great wolf Beelzebub passed among his pack. They had all fed on the meat of the human that had come out on the floes after them two days ago. The meal had cost the pack, for before he'd died the man had shot one of the younger females.

The bitch had lived almost a full day after the bullet passed through her haunches, and her far-off cries of pain as she lay dying near the drill platform had unnerved the pack. They had hidden far out on the broken floes for a full day, but now hunger had again driven them toward the only source of food within five hundred square miles of ice.

Satisfied the pack would follow, Beelzebub let out a great howl, and started toward the lighted platform ahead, making sure to keep low on the shadowed side of the pressure ridges as he went.

The wind was blowing from behind the pack, and the wolves did not catch the scent of the Irish paratroopers approaching the platform from the other side.

Yet the patrol had heard Beelzebub's piercing howl so near across the ice, and the Irish column froze in its tracks. The first sergeant felt the hair on his neck stand up. He went forward to the side of the captain, a breath held tight in his chest.

"That was no wind, sir," he whispered.

"I know," Captain O'Connell breathed back, the whites of his eyes large in the night.

"What then?"

"A guard dog, I'm guessin'. One of those German shepherds."

"Beggin' your pardon, sir, it didn't sound like a dog to me."

"You tell me then, First Sergeant," O'Connell rasped, fighting to keep his voice low.

"I been thinkin' as we marched, sir. Those stories on the British telly about them wolves in Scotland. Maybe the things came out here on the ice."

"God, I hope you're wrong. Damn the prime minister, sending us out here unarmed."

"We've got our camp knives, sir."

"Knives," the Irish officer scoffed in a hoarse whisper. "If it's wolves, we won't be stopping them with five-inch blades."

"What are we goin' to do, then, sir?"

"Keep quiet and lay low for a while. Maybe they haven't picked up our scent."

On the platform, Lieutenant Scribner ran across the deck to the north side where the last howl had come from. There was no question now the wolves were closer. The beasts were out there, just beyond the lights.

Both sets of iron stairs down to the ice were guarded, but there were several large crates of newly arrived American equipment stacked on the floes right below the deck. The sudden horrible thought flashed through his mind that the wolves might be able to scramble atop the crates, then leap to the deck.

"Steady, men. They'll be coming now. Safeties off. Put your weapons on automatic fire." There was a chorus of clicking sounds as the Guards readied their rifles. "Pick your targets. As soon as they're in the lights, fire at will."

Out on the floes, Beelzebub stopped behind a jumble of ice blocks. He'd heard Lieutenant Scribner shouting, and the metallic sounds of the weapons being readied. For a moment, he stared up at the armed men visible in the lights above. Then he turned, emitted a low growl at the pack, and began to circle the platform, the other wolves close behind.

The pack was fifty yards from the other side when the wind abruptly shifted. For the first time, Beelzebub caught the scent of the Irish paratroopers ahead. His huge snout quivered, testing the breeze. Then a growl started low in his chest and reverberated across the floes. There were humans down on the ice.

"Mary Mother of God!" Private Sullivan scrambled up the line and shot a hand out to grip the sergeant's shoulder. "I heard what you said to Captain O'Connell. There's wolves out here."

"Get hold of yourself." The sergeant shook him.

"Everybody take your knives out," Captain O'Connell ordered in a high-pitched whisper. "Fall in on me."

"Oh, Jesus God, I don't want to die," Private Sullivan whimpered.

Beelzebub crept steadily nearer, the rest of the starving pack close behind him. The tremor of desperation the great wolf had detected in the terrified voice of the private was as clear a sign of vulnerability as the bleating of an injured deer. The prey would not escape the pack now.

Lieutenant Scribner had broken into a sweat despite the subzero temperature on the exposed deck. The wolves were out there. But where? He prowled the platform railing along the north side, his eyes straining into the dark below. Around the perimeter of the deck, his men peered down through their gun sights, their fingers tight against the triggers of their weapons.

"Oh, my God, I am heartily sorry for having offended thee—"

"Shut up," the Irish sergeant hissed as Private Sullivan said the Act of Contrition.

"We've got to go home," the private cried, suddenly jumping up and running away into the dark before the sergeant could grab him.

Twenty yards away in the black night, Beelzebub had seen the panicked youth separate from the herd of humans. Instinct sent an adrenal surge through the great wolf. He let out a primeval howl and leaped forward. In three bounds he was on the man, his huge canine teeth sunk in the Irish soldier's neck.

The rest of the starving pack was close behind, snarling

and snapping as they began to tear the flesh off the still twitching body.

"God have mercy on him," the sergeant whispered, collapsing into the snow next to Captain O'Connell.

On the platform above, the British soldiers heard the sounds of the pack feeding in a frenzy beyond the lights below. "The wolves! They're over here, over here," several sentries began screaming out.

Lieutenant Scribner came tearing across the deck. "Open fire," he yelled as he ran. "Bring that mortar up."

A hail of automatic rifle fire splattered the floes, the rounds hitting indiscriminately across a hundred yards of ice facing the platform.

"We've got to get out of here," Captain O'Connell shouted above the din of rifle fire and ricocheting bullets. "Follow me, men."

The Irish patrol rose just beyond the lights, and began running in a crouch toward the southwest.

From his vantage point on the deck above, Lieutenant Scribner could just make out the blurred shapes moving hurriedly across the snow-covered ice. He spun to the mortar team setting up at the edge of the deck. "Get a shell in there. Range, sixty yards. Fire."

The *ra-whoomoph* of the shell leaving the barrel echoed across the deck, and a moment later the mortar round blew a large crater in the ice ten yards to the right of the fleeing Irish patrol.

"Correction, left two degrees," Scribner ordered. "Fire."

The round landed in the middle of the Irish patrol. Captain O'Connell, the sergeant, and twelve privates were killed outright. The surviving corporal and eight privates were all wounded with shell fragments. Moaning, they began crawl-ing across the ice, trying desperately to escape the deadly mortar spitting rounds at them from the platform above.

"Right in the center of the pack," Lieutenant Scribner yelled in triumph.

"Some of them wolves are still moving, sir." The Guards-man next to him pointed to the shadowed shapes moving away from the circle of carnage below.

"Finish them off, men," the lieutenant ordered, and an-other round of automatic rifle fire erupted over the platform. A minute later, all was still on the ice below, and the officer ordered a cease-fire.

Ben Meade had been sound asleep when the arms fire started from the platform. He had barely had time to throw on thermal coveralls and dash across the deck before it was all over.

Lieutenant Scribner turned and snapped a triumphant sa-lute as the American ran up to his position. "We got the wolves, sir. Every last one of them."

"Are you sure, Lieutenant?" Ben asked, peering over the rail.

"As you can see, there's nothing moving down there, sir. We must have put a couple of thousand rounds into them."

Mel Sanderson arrived out of breath, his arctic parka half buttoned over the thermal underwear he'd been sleeping in. "What the hell's going on?"

"The lieutenant here says he just finished off the wolves," Ben said. "I want to go down and take a look. Better bring a couple of men with rifles, Lieutenant. They may not all be dead."

"Yes, sir."

Out on the ice, Beelzebub and the pack were now a mile away. When the gunfire and terrible explosions had begun, the wolf had picked up the dead private in his great jaws and led the pack far from the platform. Now, safely away from the humans with guns, they stopped to feed.

Ben Meade and Mel Sanderson followed the British soldiers down the iron access stairs and across the ice, Lieutenant Scribner leading the way with a flashlight. The men were fifty yards from the platform when the young officer suddenly stopped in his tracks and emitted a small cry. "Oh, my God," he said, gagging.

Ben and Mel came up beside him and stared in disbelief. Scattered across the mortar-pocked ice were not dead wolves but dead men. Bodies with missing arms and legs and heads.

A few yards away were other men, these so riddled with bullets their thermal clothes were red with blood from neck to ankle.

"In Jesus' name, what have we done?" Lieutenant Scribner breathed, his face twisted in horror.

"Who are they?" Ben said, his voice barely audible.

The lieutenant stepped forward and turned over a headless body. For a long moment he stared down at the uniform, then his eyes met Ben's. "They're Irish soldiers."

Mel Sanderson shook his head. "Jesus, there must be twenty or more dead."

Ben's eyes searched the snow. "I don't see any weapons. There's not a rifle or a pistol among them." He spun around and confronted Scribner, his eyes blazing in the beam of the officer's light. "Do you know what this means, Lieutenant?"

The young Scots Guards officer stared back, his mouth working wordlessly.

"You have just massacred an unarmed Irish patrol," Ben said, a knot of corded muscles bulging from his neck. "There is no explanation we could furnish that will satisfy the Sinn Fein and the other militarists in Ireland. This means war, Lieutenant, war between England and Ireland."

DUBLIN
• • • • • • • • • • • • • • • • • •

11 a.m.—February 14
Fuel Reserves—7 Days

"THIS HAD BETTER BE important," General Sean McCormick said to Paddy Gallagher as the serving girl at the Brazen Head Hotel put two pints of stout before them and turned back for the bar. "I've got a patrol out havin' a look at them Brits on the ice. I'll want to be at the Ministry when they call in."

"Well, General darlin', curse me for takin' ya away from your important regular army business. I've got me gall thinkin' you might be interested in a piece of information from the IRA lads up north, us being irregular troops, as it were."

"You've made your damned point, Paddy. Now what is it couldn't wait till evenin'?"

Paddy reached down to his rucksack beside the table and withdrew the long tube Seamus MacTiege had sent to the IRA in Belfast. "This was waitin' for me when I got back to Belfast five days ago. A British report come with it. Both top secret, as you can see by the seals."

"If this stuff is so bloody important, why'd ya take so long gettin' it to me?"

"The British have had the border sealed tighter'n a drum the past week. I had to wait me chance. Four days in a freezin' barn, packed in with the goats to keep warm. You try it."

"All right, all right." McCormick took the tube from Paddy. "Who's it from?"

"There's no note. But the messenger that delivered it to one of our Tyrone Brigade lads works for Seamus Mac-Tiege."

McCormick unscrewed the cap at the end of the tube. "MacTiege. What's he want with the IRA?"

"He's got his reasons. Once you have a look at what's in there, you'll see what I mean."

McCormick drew out the map of the geothermal field that stretched from North Channel down under the Irish Sea and for a long moment stared wordlessly at the map.

"Interesting, ain't it?" Gallagher said, taking a long pull on his stout.

"You said you had a report. Let me see it."

"I'll have a drink first. Brogan's, if you please. The way things are up north, there's not a bottle of whisky to be had."

"Later."

"Now."

"You're pushin' it, Paddy. You're a wanted man in the Free State, you know. One word from me and you'll be cool-in' your heels in Dublin Prison."

Gallagher leaned back in his chair, letting his jacket flap open to reveal the handle of a long knife. "You sic your coppers on me, I'll hunt ya down and gut ya, General darlin'."

McCormick stared across the table for a moment. "Ya know, Paddy, you're just mad enough, I believe you'd do it." He waved a hand at the serving girl scrubbing glasses behind the bar. "Nel, a bottle of Brogan's over here."

Gallagher grinned and reached down into his rucksack. "It's a happy man you've made me, General. Here you go, then."

McCormick took the report from Gallagher, noting the now broken "Top Secret" seal on the cover, and sat back in his chair to read. He didn't look up when the serving girl brought over the whisky, nor the several times Gallagher clinked the bottle against the glass as he poured himself generous draughts.

Halfway through, McCormick understood why the leader of the British opposition had leaked the report. The information was political dynamite, explosive enough to blow Prime Minister Butler right out of office.

Finally McCormick finished the report and stared wordlessly at Gallagher.

"Speechless, are ya, General darlin'? You shouldn't be that surprised they'd do it. The brazen bastards have been rapin' Ireland for a thousand years."

McCormick let out a bitter laugh. "You know, Paddy, I've used the same words to the prime minister more'n once. Not that she's ever listened."

"For Christ's sake, she's been a nun most of her life. Her head's been soaked in God's own goodness so long, she can't believe what devils them Brits are."

"She'll believe this." McCormick thumped the British dossier. "This time it's not me warnin' her about some British scheme. This time I've got it in their own words. They're gettin' ready to siphon off energy reserves that belong half to Ireland."

"Do you think she'll act, then?" Gallagher asked. "Once she sees what I brung ya."

McCormick reached for the bottle of Brogan's and poured himself a drink. "She'll be forced to. I'm taking this report straight to the Sinn Fein leadership in Parliament. Once the Dail Eireann finds out the extent of British treachery, I've no doubt the government will issue an ultimatum to London."

"If fighting breaks out, us lads up north will be outnumbered ten to one."

"You won't have to go it alone this time, Paddy. Should it come to war, I'll be in Belfast with the First Armored Brigade within twenty-four hours. I promise you that."

Gallagher rubbed his hands together. "The lads are itchin' to use those new shoulder-fired missiles you sent us."

"Understand me, Paddy, there's to be no shootin' until everything's ready. We go too soon and we'll have the European Community all over our backs. The Americans too."

"The bastard Brits are stealin' our energy. For the love of God, General, what further justification do we need to strike back?"

"An incident, Paddy, a British provocation. The geothermal field's the bomb. Now we need a spark to light the fuse."

NORTH CHANNEL
••••••••••••••••••••

11:45 a.m.

"I WISH I HAD a goddamn drink," Ben Meade said as he stared hollow-eyed out the window of the operations center at the mortar-cratered ice below.

Bringing the remains of the massacred Irish soldiers up onto the drill platform had flayed his emotions, and he'd been up all night. The blood-smeared Irish faces were so very young, that is when the shell-shattered bodies had heads attached.

Ben's guts had knotted in anguish at the thought of the pain their senseless deaths would wreak on their mothers, fathers, wives, kids. He felt a hand on his shoulder and turned to look into the fatigued face of Mel Sanderson.

"The last thing you need is a drink. You're whipped, beat up physically and emotionally. So am I. What do you say we crash for a couple of hours?"

Ben blew out his cheeks. "Later, Mel. I've got to call Marjorie. I don't want her to hear about what's happened from someone else."

"Promise me, no booze."

"Jesus Christ, get off my back, will you? Do you see a bottle in my hand?"

"Take it easy, Ben. I'm not trying to be your conscience. After all our years bouncing around the world together, I care. You don't mind if I care, do you?"

Sanderson yanked his parka off a wall hook and started for the door.

"Mel, shit, I'm sorry. Seeing all those dead kids, God, I'm still shaking inside. No booze, I swear."

"I'm going to get some sleep. You coming?"

"Soon as I call Marjorie."

"Okay."

A blast of freezing air from the platform outside swept into the operations center as Sanderson opened the door and left.

For several minutes Ben studied aerial photos of the ice floes layering the surface of the Irish Sea. Then he picked up the phone and put through a call to Marjorie's command lorry. A minute later she came on the line.

"Good morning, Ben," she said, the sound of the truck's engine audible in the background. "How's everything up at North Channel?"

"Bad, Marjorie, about as bad as it can get."

For the next five minutes Ben told her what had happened. He heard her suck in her breath when he recounted how they'd spent hours searching the ice with lights for body parts.

"Dear God, Ben," Marjorie said, her voice catching in her throat. "There aren't words. So many young men dead for nothing."

"I talked to Prime Minister Butler last night. He wasn't optimistic that Prime Minister O'Fiaich could keep the lid on. General McCormick and the Sinn Fein are certain to use the massacre to stir up war fever in Ireland."

"I refuse to believe it will come to war," Marjorie said. "Surely the European Community will step in and mediate things."

"I wish I shared your optimism. Look, Marjorie, I'm worried about this last leg of your trip."

"That's thoughtful of you, Ben, but I shouldn't be concerned if I were you. The Dunkirkers have been magnificent, and those extra lorries we picked up in Reading have sped up our progress immensely. We've made twenty miles already this morning.

"It's not the crossing of the ice I'm worried about, Marjorie."

"What, then?"

"I've been looking at aerial photos. There are a half dozen huge pressure ridges stretching from the Isle of Man east across the Irish Sea to the coast of Cumbria."

"But that's directly in our path."

"I know. You're going to have to swing west of the Isle of Man. In places you'll be within a few miles of Irish territorial waters."

"Surely they won't attack us, Ben? We're unarmed."

"So was that Irish patrol, Marjorie. If General McCormick wants revenge, you Dunkirkers will be his number-one target."

DUBLIN
●●●●●●●●●●●●●●●●●

12:15 p.m.

THE TEACUP TREMBLED IN the hands of Irish Prime Minister Bernadette O'Fiaich as she sat at her office desk feeling numb and afraid.

Her heartbeat was rapid and irregular, as it had been since the call from Aldis Butler had woken her at home at 3 A.M. Errant strands of graying hair hung down around her deeply lined face from the hastily done bun on top of her head. When she'd looked in the mirror this morning she'd been shocked to see the reflection of an old and exhausted woman.

There had been deep anguish in the voice of the British prime minister as he told her how the Scots Guards had mistaken the Irish patrol for the wolf pack that had been plaguing the drill platform. Bernadette knew Butler to be a decent man. She was convinced that neither Windscale nor this latest atrocity had been his doing.

After she'd hung up with Butler, she hadn't been able to get back to sleep. Finally, she'd called her driver at 6 A.M. and gone to mass. By 9 A.M. she was in her office, working the phones, arranging a Cabinet meeting for 1 P.M.

Then she'd put the affairs of state aside and spent the rest of the morning composing handwritten letters to the families of the slain Irish soldiers. It was all she could do.

When she finished the last letter she sighed and sank back in her chair, dreading the prospect of telling her ministers of the massacre. Sean would scream for revenge, and he wouldn't be the only one. She could already hear the cries of outrage when the news reached Parliament.

The intercom buzzed on her desk and she reached forward and wearily pushed the button. "Yes, Kathleen?"

"The minister for defense is here to see you, Prime Minister."

She could feel her heart begin to palpitate. Had Sean somehow found out about his slain soldiers? She'd know soon enough. "Very well, send him in, Kathleen."

"Yes, Prime Minister."

When Sean came through the door a moment later, his face was impassive, devoid of the smile and warm eye contact he usually gave her. And instead of slouching into a chair as he normally did, he remained standing rigidly. "Good day, Taoiseach."

She looked at him. "A bit formal today, aren't you, Sean?"

"I must tell you, Taoiseach, I am here as the minister for defense, not Sean McCormick."

"I don't care if you're here as Mother Goose, take a seat. You make me nervous, standing there like a rootless oak about to topple over on me desk."

"I understand you've called a Cabinet meeting," Sean said, sitting down stiffly.

"Yes."

"There's a matter I must bring to your attention before you meet with the other ministers."

"And that is?"

Sean reached inside his tunic and brought out the British geothermal report. "This came into my possession earlier today."

Bernadette wondered for a moment if she should tell him about her erratic heartbeat. No, she decided, now was not the time for her to appear vulnerable.

She reached for the bound booklet. "What is this?"

"A top-secret report of the British Parliament."

"May I ask how you came into possession of a secret British document?"

"It was passed to me by the IRA in Belfast."

"They're terrorists, Sean. Outlaws. How many times must I tell you, I'll not have a member of my government consorting with bomb-throwers?"

"We can discuss my relationship with the IRA later. For now, I strongly suggest you look at the report."

Bernadette sighed. "Get yourself some coffee," she said, motioning toward the carafe on the side table. Then she opened the booklet and began to read.

It took her only a few minutes to understand the gist of the parliamentary report. The geothermal field under North Channel extended well into Irish territorial waters. The energy reserves the British were so intent on tapping belonged half to Ireland.

She was aware of Sean standing by the sideboard gauging her reaction over the rim of his coffee cup. In the name of God, why hadn't Butler told her?

"I can't believe it," Bernadette whispered. "There are Irishmen freezing to death, and they don't tell us there's a vast reservoir of heat and energy right at our doorstep."

"You should know, Taoiseach, I've already shown the report to the leadership of Sinn Fein," Sean said impassively. "At this very moment, an emergency decree is being prepared giving me the authority to use the armed forces to stop British geothermal operations in North Channel."

"You've gone behind my back."

"I had to. You would not act. I am confident that Dail Eireann will issue the British an ultimatum to withdraw from North Channel or face war."

"I need time to think."

Sean returned to his chair. "Can't you see, Taoiseach, Ireland has run out of time? Those Dunkirkers are bringin' high-tech drilling equipment back from France. Once that platform starts producin' electricity, they've got what they want. They can drag on negotiations for years while we burn peat moss and half the population freezes to death."

Bernadette emitted a short, bitter laugh. "Ironic, isn't it, Sean? It is a geothermal project out there after all, not the military staging area you supposed."

Sean studied his hands. "So it would appear."

"All those young soldiers dead for noth—" She stopped, realizing with sudden horror she hadn't told him about the patrol yet.

His eyes bored into her. "What dead soldiers?"

Bernadette's heart felt like a lead weight inside her.

Sean was on his feet now. "What dead soldiers?"

"The patrol you sent out. The British mistook your men for wolves. They've all been killed."

"Wolves?"

"The Scots Guards opened fire on what they thought was a wolf pack. Automatic weapons, mortars. It was pitch-dark. Prime Minister Butler assured me the whole thing was a horrible mistake."

"Wolves! He tells you the bloody British Army thought they were shooting wolves. And you believe him!"

"If you'll only listen."

Sean's mouth worked wordlessly for a moment, his ashen face a mask of disbelief. "You did this! You sent those young soldiers out there unarmed."

Bernadette felt a sudden spasm of pain in her chest. She went rigid, waiting for it to pass.

"I'm going to put the first armored division on full alert," Sean thundered.

The pain was worse now, gripping her chest like a monstrous vise. The room whirled before her as her heart stopped pumping blood to her brain. She brought her hand up weakly. "No, no. I forbid it."

"Forbid all you want. The emergency decree before Parliament will give me full control over the armed forces."

Sean turned on his heel and stalked across her office. "I'm sorry it has come to this, Taoiseach, but you gave me no choice. No choice at all," he said from the doorway, looking at her but not seeing her, not grasping she was dying at her desk.

"Sean, please, don't leave me," she said, but the words never left her throat. The door slammed. He was gone.

The horrible pain radiated out from her chest, numbing her arms and legs. Bernadette tried to reach the phone but her hand wouldn't respond. She was paralyzed. Although she was deeply religious, the cold panicky fear of the unknown that grips all life in the face of death swept over her.

Was there a God, an afterlife, a heaven and hell? Or had her whole life been a meaningless sham? Her eyes went to the large crucifix on her office wall. She'd never noticed before how bright red was the blood dripping from the nail holes in the hands and feet of the Christ figure.

Doubt tortured her. How could the blood of one man, even the son of God, wash away the sins of the world? There were too many sins, too little blood.

The face of Christ began to move in a circle. At first, she thought it was a sign. Then she realized the whole room was spinning before her eyes.

She could no longer control her muscles and she slid slowly down out of her chair. The drawers in her desk passed before her, inches from her face. Then she felt the rug against her cheek. *God, don't let them find me like this, sprawled across the floor like a common drunk.*

Suddenly the terrible pain in her chest was gone and she began to pass through a tunnel. She could see the curving sides arching around her. There was a bright light ahead. She was going faster and faster, like a speeding train. Then she was in the light.

An overwhelming sense of peace and joy flooded over her. She realized there were others there with her in the light; her long-dead parents, her first mother superior. They were smiling, welcoming her, telling her, somehow without words, that everything was all right now.

Bernadette O'Fiaich, Ireland's last great hope for peace, was dead.

LONDON
● ● ● ● ● ● ● ● ●

6:35 p.m.

THE BRITISH HOUSE OF COMMONS had not witnessed such
rancorous personal attacks and bitter recriminations since
the tumultuous debate over Windscale reparations to Ireland three years before.

For almost four hours, Labor Party members had been rising from their sea-green leather benches to flay Prime Minister Butler and the Social Democrats with accusations of
provoking Ireland to the brink of war.

The speaker of the House, James Marks, stood behind his
desk on a raised podium at the end of the paneled, church-
sized chamber. Perspiration was pouring down his face
from under his powdered wig as he banged his gavel down
hard several times.

The sound of the wooden hammer striking the speaker's
desk was barely audible above the heated voices shouting
back and forth from the five tiers of benches facing each
other on both sides of the rectangular room.

"Order, order," the speaker demanded, his exhaustion
after hours trying to control the angry members showing in
his lined face.

In the front row of the opposition side of the House,

Seamus MacTiege sat listening to the prime minister respond to the latest attack from a Labor MP from Wales. The slaughter on the ice of North Channel had played right into MacTiege's hands, and he had no intention of letting Aldis Butler off the hook.

MacTiege let the PM finish his remarks, then rose. A dozen other members who wished to be heard also popped up from their benches around the chamber.

"Seamus MacTiege." The speaker recognized the opposition leader, and the other members sat back down in their seats.

For a long moment MacTiege stood there without speaking, gathering the attention of the members as the hubbub subsided around him. Then he began. "Mister Speaker, for many hours now we have posed serious questions of malfeasance to the prime minister, and had back not answers but excuses."

A chorus of "Hear, hear!" went up from the Labor Party members behind him.

"We've asked the Right Honorable gentleman how could we come to the brink of war with Ireland."

"We've been at war with them for nine hundred years," a Social Democrat backbencher shouted down.

The speaker brought his gavel down. "Order, order. Let the gentleman speak."

MacTiege ignored the outburst. "We asked how the Scots Guards could open fire on an unarmed Irish patrol. And the answer? The incredibly lame and ingenuous excuse? Wolves. Our soldiers thought they were firing at wolves."

Catcalls from the Labor members reverberated through the chamber.

"Is the prime minister asking us to believe that our soldiers are so badly sighted they cannot tell a fur-cloaked wolf from a uniformed soldier?" MacTiege asked, his tone dripping sarcasm. "Did the Guards suppose the animals had paraded into some games shop and laid down a pound apiece for human masks to wear over their canine faces?"

Derisive laughter hooted down from the opposition benches. Several Social Democrats leaped to their feet, waving angry fists at MacTiege. He stood unflinching, his head back and his eyebrows arched imperiously at the infuriated members across the aisle.

"Order, order," the speaker shouted hoarsely, his wig askew on his head.

"Mr. Speaker," MacTiege began again, then waited while the Social Democrats sat back down and quieted.

"Mr. Speaker, is it not apparent to every member of this House that the chaos and incompetence that has characterized this government has now spread to our military? The Right Honorable Mr. Butler has lost control of our economy, lost control of our energy policy, and now he has lost control of the army as well."

As MacTiege sat down, Prime Minister Butler came to his feet, along with three dozen members on both sides of the House, all of them gesturing frantically to be recognized.

"Prime Minister," the speaker shouted. "Let the prime minister respond. Order, let him speak."

Prime Minister Butler leaned across the dispatch box toward the opposition benches, his face flushed and his eyes boring into Seamus MacTiege. "I find it incomprehensible that the leader of the opposition could accuse me of bungling our economic and energy policies when it is the unions that support the Labor Party that have brought this country to the brink of catastrophe."

"Call off the general strike," a Social Democrat backbencher yelled down, bringing on a chorus of angry rebuttals from the Labor side of the House.

Butler ignored the tumult, his voice rising above the shouting Labor members. "As to the Army, I informed this House some hours ago that I have ordered an investigation into why the Scots Guards fired on the Irish. That investigation is proceeding—"

Catcalls and indignant shouts interrupted Butler and he waited while the speaker once more gaveled the members to a modicum of order.

"That investigation is well under way. I must say before the findings are in, however, that it is not difficult for me to believe that nervous young soldiers could mistake humans crouched in the pitch-dark for the forms of wolves. What happened on the ice of North Channel was tragic, but the circumstances are understandable, whether or not members opposite agree."

Butler sat back down amidst a wave of boos and hisses from the Labor members.

Seamus MacTiege came to his feet. "Prime Minister, in the two years you have been in office, I have agreed with scant few of your statements. You are leading this country to rack and ruin. Indeed, you are leading us straight to war."

Members of Parliament shot to their feet on both sides of the House, the MP's waving their fists in the air and shouting accusations at the opposition across the way.

As the tumultuous shouting match raged on, a doorkeeper slipped into the chamber and solemnly handed the prime minister a message from his Downing Street office. Butler sagged in his seat as he read the folded sheet, his head shaking from side to side in stunned disbelief. Finally, he rose, his face pale and grave.

It was several minutes more before Speaker Marks could bring the body to order again. Butler waited with his head bowed, his eyes cast down at the floor.

"Prime Minister," Speaker Marks said. "Let the prime minister speak."

"I have just been informed . . ." Butler began, then lost his voice. He cleared his throat and started again. "I have just been informed of a tragic event, the consequences of which I can only imagine."

The House quieted, the members leaning forward in their seats expectantly.

Butler looked around the hallowed chamber and thought of Churchill standing where he stood, hand on his hip and bulldog face thrust forward as he told Parliament of Nazi victories. Had he the courage and wisdom of such a giant? Could he lead the country through the terrible times ahead?

Aldis Butler wasn't sure. He wasn't sure at all. He braced himself and began again. "I must tell you with deep personal sadness that Irish Prime Minister Bernadette O'Fiaich died earlier today in her Dublin office."

A collective gasp ripped the air like a serrated knife.

"I ask for a moment of silent prayer for a great Irish lady, and a great democratic leader," Butler said.

The members bowed their heads and for a minute there was quiet in the House of Commons, the only sounds the low murmur of members at prayer, and an occasional cough.

Seamus MacTiege sat with downcast eyes, but his racing thoughts were far from prayer. Now was the time to strike, he felt it in his bones. The pot had come to a boil even without the fire the leaked geothermal report had undoubtedly lit under the IRA.

With the pacifist hand of Bernadette O'Fiaich gone from the Irish helm, and Aldis Butler stained with the blood of the slaughtered Irish patrol, the bonds of trust between heads of state that had kept the tenuous peace had been shattered forever.

The prime minister had now become a detriment to peace, for the Irish militants would never forgive him for the massacre at North Channel. MacTiege was confident the members of Parliament representing the smaller minority parties would realize this as well.

It was vital that they did, for he would shortly need their votes. He bent to the Labor member next to him and whispered instructions. The MP nodded and turned to pass the word.

Satisfied he was ready, MacTiege rose from his seat. "Mr. Speaker, we are all stricken by this terrible news. Prime Minister O'Fiaich was not only a great leader of Ireland, she was a woman of uncompromising principle and morality. Ireland, indeed the world, is poorer for her passing."

A chorus of "Hear, hear!" reverberated from both the government and opposition benches.

"Unfortunately, as we mourn this great lady, we must also recognize the new dangers her death has brought about. Prime Minister O'Fiaich alone has kept the Irish militarists in check. I must ask the Right Honorable Mr. Butler, does the government now recognize that war is inevitable?"

Butler sprang to his feet. "We recognize no such inevitability. Yes, General McCormick and his Sinn Fein allies will undoubtedly now wield more power. But the Irish Parliament is a body of rational men and women. I cannot believe they want war with Britain."

MacTiege rose again. "The Irish Parliament may well be comprised of rational individuals, but these are irrational times. Millions in Ireland are freezing in their homes, barely able to feed their families. The Irish people blame us for Windscale. And now we have murdered twenty-four of their young men."

"What about the IRA?" an Ulster Unionist Party MP shouted from the opposition back bench. "Bernadette O'Fiaich was the only one who had the stature to hold them back. Now she's gone, the Sinn Fein are bound to seize power."

"Order, here, order. I haven't recognized you, Mr. Crosby," the speaker said.

Butler came to his feet to respond. "I have every confidence the Fine Gael and the other moderate parties in the Irish Parliament will keep the Sinn Fein in check."

Seamus MacTiege rose again as Butler sat down amidst a chorus of derisive shouts from the Labor benches.

"Mr. Speaker," he said above the uproar.

"Mr. Speaker, I must tell this House that if the Right Honorable Mr. Butler has every confidence in the Irish Parliament, we have no confidence in him. This government has brought Britain to the brink of war. This government cannot, must not, continue in office. I call for a vote of censure."

Across the aisle, Prime Minister Butler sat stiffly as the House of Commons erupted in tumult. MacTiege's motion didn't come as a complete surprise. He knew the Labor leader would make his move sooner or later. Still, the moment was a blow, both personal and political.

If the vote of censure passed, he would be forced to go to the king and tell him he could not form a workable government. He would then have to call a general election.

On the podium, Speaker Marks exchanged a brief whispered conversation with a civil servant in the box to the right of his chair, then straightened and gaveled the House to order. "A motion of no confidence in the government has been made," he said, his voice strained. "Is there a second?"

Fifty Labor members shot to their feet, their angry voices affirming their leader's motion.

The speaker looked toward the prime minister a moment, a great sadness in his face, then turned away and brought his gavel down hard. "Very well, then. The House will vote on the motion to censure."

While the members were being polled, Prime Minister Butler turned to his special assistant, the Social Democrat MP from Bexhill and Battle sitting beside him. "What's your estimate?"

"We're in trouble, sir. I've been hearing whispers. Many of the minority members believe the Irish will never negotiate with you now, not after the carnage at North Channel."

"Then they'll vote with Labor."

"Yes, sir. The question is, how many."

Butler turned his stone-faced gaze on Seamus MacTiege conferring busily with his cohorts across the wide center aisle. The thought that this rabble-rouser, this fascist opportunist might well replace him as prime minister was all but overwhelming. Finally, he sighed deeply and looked away.

Twenty minutes later Speaker Marks gaveled the members to order again, his face ashen beneath his long wig of tight curls. "On the motion of censure, three hundred and twenty for, three hundred and twelve against. The motion is passed."

Prime Minister Butler closed his eyes. "God save England," he whispered to himself as the triumphant cheers of the Labor members reverberated off the paneled walls of the House of Commons.

IRISH SEA
• • • • • • • • • •

2 p.m.—February 15
Fuel Reserves—6 Days

"UNIDENTIFIED AIRCRAFT COMING IN fast from the west," British Marine Captain Walt Grady said, poking his head into the cab of the command lorry from the communications room behind. "From the size and speed, I'd say it's another Irish fighter."

Marjorie leaned forward toward the windshield and searched the sky toward the west. In a moment she caught sight of the tiny black dot approaching from the direction of the Irish shore.

"I see him," she said. "How many does that make?"

"Five in the past day," Grady said. "They're keeping close tabs on us."

Seconds later the Irish jet slashed low over the command lorry, banked and flew down the column of half-tracked trucks, buses, and homemade snowmobiles strung out for three miles across the floes.

"Are you sure we haven't strayed across into Irish territory?" Marjorie said.

"I have a direct feed from our global positioning satellite," Grady said. "We're five miles our side of the border. It's those bloody bastards that are violating British sovereignty."

"After what the Scots Guards did to their soldiers, I don't think Prime Minister Butler is prepared to complain," Marjorie said.

The Irish jet made a second pass over the convoy, then turned west and disappeared back toward Ireland.

Marjorie sank back against the seat and rubbed her red-rimmed eyes. "How long before we reach North Channel?" she asked, deep fatigue in her voice.

"We're about twenty-two miles from the drill platform," Grady said. "Providing we don't run into a pressure ridge or a deep fissure and have to detour, we should be there in a little over two hours."

Ben Meade was looking over the latest infrared scan of the geothermal reservoir beneath the seafloor when he heard a loud cheer go up from the men on the platform outside. He knew it could be only one thing; the Dunkirkers were in sight.

He grabbed his parka and went out onto the platform. The roustabouts had all dropped what they were doing and rushed over to the south side of the platform. As he started across the snow-covered deck, he spotted Mel Sanderson standing at the rail with a pair of binoculars up to his eyes.

Sanderson lowered the glasses at Ben's approach. "Jesus, what a magnificent sight," he said, handing Ben the binoculars. "You know, when those Dunkirkers left for France, I wouldn't have given ten-to-one odds they could haul all that son-of-a-bitchin' equipment back across four hundred and fifty miles of ice."

Ben shielded his eyes against the bluish glare of the ash-veiled sun and looked toward the lead vehicles. "Never underestimate the British, Mel. Especially when they've got leaders like Marjorie Glynn."

Sanderson stole a look at his friend. Ben had talked a lot about Marjorie Glynn the past few days. "I got a feeling you have more than a professional interest in Dr. Glynn."

"A man could do worse."

"So you've proved the past few years."

"What the hell's that supposed to mean?"

"Just that since you and Elizabeth split, you've seemed determined to avoid any woman that came remotely near being right for you. I've lost count of your one-night stands."

"This from a man whose idea of a long-term relationship with a woman is to take her out to breakfast the next morning."

"It's different with me. My life is the sea. I'm married to the *Abyss*. But you, you were meant to have a family and kids. It's time you got around to it."

"Jesus, Mel, I just met Marjorie a couple of weeks ago and already you've got us walking down the aisle. Besides, I may have screwed up the relationship already."

"What'd you do, make a move on her?"

"Not exactly."

"You dumb bastard."

"You don't understand. I got in this situation where . . . well, I guess I kind of salivated a bit. It put her off."

"Salivated? That's all you did?"

"Yeah. Now drop it, will you? We've got work to do. Those extra supplies come in?"

"That cargo chopper dropped them off last night. Steaks, chops, vegetables, enough to feed the Dunkirkers for a couple of days while they rest up."

"What about provisions for their trip back?"

"They should be coming in tomorrow, along with three helicopter tankers with enough fuel to get them to their homes in Britain."

Ben surveyed the approaching convoy. "If there's anything else we need flown in, it'll have to be in the next couple of days."

"Why the time limit?"

"There was another major eruption from R-Nine yesterday. The debris will be over us in about sixty hours. The ash clouds will be so low it will be impossible to put any aircraft up."

"How long you figure we'll be socked in?"

"At least a week, maybe as long as a month. I'm going to

ask the Dunkirkers to leave fifty or so of the large diesel lorries here for us to use to haul supplies out from Scotland."

"Good idea," Mel said. "If the eruptions continue, there's no telling what the flying weather will be like this winter."

"Speaking of flying, did you arrange for a chopper to take Marjorie back to London?"

"Yeah. Tomorrow morning. I figured she could use a night's sleep in a bed that wasn't bouncing up and down. I assume there'll be nothing else bouncing up and down in her bed tonight."

"You've got a dirty mind, Mel, you know that?"

"I'm not the one that was salivating all over her."

"I didn't . . . goddamn it to hell, don't you have anything better to do than stand here speculating on my sex life? Get the mess crew cracking. Those Dunkirkers are going to need some hot food."

"All right, all right, I'm going."

"Leave me those glasses."

Sanderson tossed the binoculars to Ben. "I expect an invite to dinner," he said, starting for the mess hall. "I want to meet this lady of yours."

Ben turned to the rail and focused on the column of Dunkirkers approaching across the floes. "She's not my lady," he mumbled to himself.

For the next twenty minutes, Ben watched the expedition draw closer. Finally, Marjorie's command lorry was within a few hundred yards and he turned and crossed the drill platform to the stairs leading down to the floes.

As he stood on the ice waiting, a gust of freezing wind whipped up the snow around him and for a moment he had a mental picture of what it must have been like for the Dunkirkers crossing the floes of the Irish Sea in the fierce wind and cold.

A moment later the noisy lead vehicle ground to a halt opposite the stairs and he walked around to open the passenger door. "Welcome to North Channel, Marjorie. God, I'm glad to see you."

For a long moment Marjorie just sat there looking out at him, her exhaustion written in her sunken eyes and lined face. "Hello, Ben," she finally said, her voice hoarse and weary.

Ben handed her down from the cab. "You all right?"

"No, she's not," Captain Walt Grady said, coming around the side of the half-track. "She hasn't closed her eyes since we left Reading almost forty hours ago."

"Have you met Captain Grady, Ben? He's a Royal Marine. Walt, this is Dr. Meade."

Ben extended a gloved hand. "Captain."

"How do you do, Dr. Meade."

"We've emptied out our warehouse and heated the place up, Captain. You'll find enough cots and sleeping bags in there for all your people. It's not exactly the Ritz, but at least everyone can stretch out and rest."

"Personally, sir, all I want is a bed that doesn't reek of diesel fuel."

Ben laughed. "The mess hall will be serving meals around the clock. Your Dunkirkers can eat any time they want to."

"Thanks. I'll pass the word."

"We'll start unloading the drilling equipment in the morning," Ben said, "after your people have had a good night's sleep."

"We'll be ready, sir."

"I'd better see everyone gets settled," Marjorie said as the rest of the half-tracks in the column began pulling up around them.

"I think you should leave that to Captain Grady," Ben said.

"No, it's my job."

Ben put his hands gently on her shoulders. "Let go, Marjorie. You've pulled off the impossible leading the expedition up here. But you're ready to collapse. We still have a lot of work ahead of us. You won't be any use to anybody if you end up in a hospital bed."

"He's right, Dr. Glynn," Grady said.

Marjorie looked at them both a moment, then let out a resigned sigh. "I suppose you're right. I am tired. Very, very tired."

"You need food and sleep," Ben said.

"Do you know what I need even more?"

"Name it."

"A cup of tea. Did you know it's completely impossible to make tea in a lorry careening over sea ice?"

Ben grinned. "C'mon, I'll make you a pot myself."

He stayed one step behind Marjorie as they mounted the steps, afraid she'd topple backward in her deep fatigue. They reached the platform above and he led her across the deck to the operations center.

Inside, he helped her out of her parka and pointed to a worn armchair by the heater. "Make yourself comfortable. I'll be right back."

Ben went to the small kitchenette and put water on to boil, then returned and sat down across from Marjorie. "Your tea will be ready in a minute. Then I'll order you a steak from the mess hall."

"Steak. That does sound good, though I'm not sure I've the energy to chew it."

"I've ordered a helicopter to take you back to London in the morning. You need a week's sleep in your own bed."

"I'm not going back. I'm staying here until you bring that well in."

"This is no place for a woman."

"What?"

It was the wrong thing to say to Marjorie Glynn; he knew it the moment the words were out. "Jesus, I didn't mean that the way it sounded."

"Yes you did, you chauvinist bastard."

"There are seventy-five horny roughnecks out here, that's all. You'd be, well, more comfortable in London."

"Screw your horny roughnecks. I've handled sex-crazed men before. You're one of them."

"You do know how to hurt a man."

"You'll get over it. That's the last I want to hear of me leaving. Besides, if I went back to London now I'd only get embroiled in politics. After what happened in Parliament yesterday, I don't think that would do the prime minister any good."

"You mean MacTiege would use you to flog Butler?"

"Exactly. He's always contended that our geothermal operation up here would prove a source of friction with the Irish."

"Turns out the son of a bitch was right," Ben said.

"Yes, tragically, and he won't miss an opportunity to point that out to the press. If I went back to Biosphere Britannia now I'd have the media all over me. I'd end up a lightning rod for Labor attacks on the PM."

"What a fucking mess. Prime Minister O'Fiaich dead and Butler censured by Parliament. All the polls show the Social Democrats losing the general election Butler's been forced to call."

"Don't count the prime minister out yet. If we can start generating energy before the election, the voters could return the Social Democrats to office. Making any progress?"

"Yeah, we're getting there. A cable crew from Scotland has laid lines across the ice. Once the turbine generators start producing electricity, we can send it directly into the British power grid."

"What about the well?"

"We've installed new pipe down to the depth I reached two years ago. As soon as we get my laser drill in place, we'll start down again."

Marjorie yawned. "How long will it take you to set up the laser drill?"

"Eight, ten hours. It's going to be a son of a bitch getting that huge tower up here from the sled, but once that's done the drilling itself should go pretty quickly. That laser burns through rock like butter."

A silly grin spread over Marjorie's lined face. "Funny. The past week, I've been eating cold butter hard as a rock, and you've got rock soft as butter."

The tea kettle began to whistle and Ben rose and crossed to the kitchenette. "You're so tired you're getting punchy," he said, his back to her as he poured the steaming water into the teapot.

He turned to get a cup and saucer from the cupboard. "You can take my room. I'll bunk in with Mel. He's anxious to meet you, by the way."

Ben put the tea things on a tray and carried them back in. Marjorie's chin was resting on her chest and she was breathing rhythmically. He put the tray down on a side table and knelt before her. She was sound asleep.

He smiled gently, slipped his arms under her back and legs and carried her to the small bedroom he'd been using. He untied her shoes, then wondered for a moment if he should undress her. No, he decided, after what happened in the Biosphere, she might wake up and slug him.

Instead he loosened her collar and covered her with a blanket. For several minutes he stood staring down at her. Her auburn hair was spread across the pillow and her full lips slightly parted. So this was what she looked like when she slept.

Despite the dark circles under her eyes and the fatigue lines creasing her skin, he could see the vulnerable young girl in her face. It made him feel warm, protective. He wished he were lying beside her, his arm cradling her against his chest.

He was suddenly very glad she was staying. He wanted her near, wanted to see her, talk to her, touch her hands, her face. "Admit it, asshole, you're nuts about her," he mumbled to himself. "The woman's gotten under your skin."

The thought suddenly scared the hell out of him. He'd allowed Elizabeth to get under his skin, and her betrayal had torn him to pieces. If Marjorie turned out to be a wrong number, he'd probably end up drinking himself to death.

He let out a long breath. Too late now. He couldn't change the way he felt about Marjorie. The longer he looked at her sleeping face, the more he was certain of that. Besides, Marjorie wasn't anything like Elizabeth. Marjorie wasn't like any woman he'd ever met.

He bent and kissed her lightly on the forehead, then turned to leave. For a long moment he stood at the threshold looking back at her. Then he closed the door quietly behind him.

DUBLIN
• • • • • • • • • •

4:15 p.m.—February 16
Fuel Reserves—5 Days

GENERAL SEAN MCCORMICK WEPT openly as he stared down
at the dead face of Bernadette O'Fiaich. The death of the Taoiseach had left him shaken and guilt-ridden. When they'd told
him the time of her heart attack, he'd realized with horror
she'd been dying even as he left her office two days before.

Some artless mortician had rouged her chalk-white cheeks
and applied a too-red lipstick to her bloodless lips. In life,
Bernadette had shunned cosmetics and to McCormick the
makeup made her look like some huge hideous china doll
with stiff-lashed eyes that would pop open if he sat her up.

"What have they done to you, Bernie girl?" he sobbed.

Bernadette O'Fiaich had been the only person who ever
understood him. She forgave him his excesses, his milita-
rism, his enmity toward everything British. She alone realized his burning hatred of England was but the mirror of his
passionate love of Ireland.

And she had loved him. He knew that. Her love had been
so total, so strong that it had often scared him, at times almost smothered him. She was like a brimming pitcher con-
tinuing to pour even though the too-small glass was already
full and overflowing.

In his own inadequate, stilted way he had loved her back. Who but the devil could not love a woman of such saintly goodness and compassion? Yet, he knew in his heart, his had been more the love of a spoiled boy for his nurturing mother than the love of a man for his mate.

Undeniably there had been times in bed, especially at first, when her virgin innocence and her awakening passion for the unknown joys of sex had aroused his carnal desires. And there had been the perverse allure of her being an ex-nun, the fantasy partner of ten million Catholic schoolboys.

Looking down at her in death, he felt a consuming shame of his licentious secrets. He had been unworthy of the love of Bernadette O'Fiaich. For a long terrible moment he looked into himself and knew he'd been given a great gift his hollow heart was incapable of accepting.

The sight of her cheapened by the hideous makeup suddenly infuriated him. He would not let the morticians dishonor her in death as he had dishonored her in life.

Oblivious to the roomful of mourners sitting on folding chairs behind him, Sean took out his handkerchief, dipped it in the water of a flower vase beside the coffin, and began wiping the makeup off Bernadette's face.

A gasp went up from several women in the front rows.

Sean paid no attention, diligently scrubbing Bernadette's cheeks and eyelids and lips until he had all the rouge and mascara and lipstick off her face.

Finally, he straightened. "There, me Bernie girl, it's the last thing I can do for you, and little enough it is. You would have hated it, going to your grave painted like a clown."

Sean crossed himself, said a last prayer over her body, and bent and kissed her cold lips. Then he turned and marched out of the funeral hall, his back straight and the row of ribbons on his chest flouncing against the tunic of his dress uniform.

Outside, a line of mourners stretched out of sight down the snow-covered street, tens of thousands of men, women, and children waiting patiently in the freezing cold to pay their last respects to the Irish Joan of Arc.

A wizened old woman spotted the minister for defense

and approached as he was about to get into his car. "What's to become of us now she's gone?" the old woman said in a broken voice, her liver-spotted face barely visible behind a hand-knitted muffler.

Sean gently gripped her arm. "God will watch over Ireland. As He always has."

"But who's to lead us here on earth? Who's to fill the shoes of the Taoiseach?"

Sean looked at her for a long moment, seeing the suffering soul of Ireland in the tears frozen to her cheeks and the terrible fear in her eyes. "I am, old grandmother," he said softly. "I am."

Half an hour later he was behind his desk in the Defense Ministry. For several minutes he looked over the photographs of the Dunkirkers expedition his reconnaissance jets had taken, searching for any sign of heavy weapons aboard the huge sleds.

He didn't spot anything suspicious, but still one could never trust the Brits. He called the Air Force chief of staff and ordered surveillance flights over the British drill platform.

He had just put down the phone when the intercom on his desk buzzed.

"Yes?"

"George Connors is on line two, sir," the sergeant said.

"Put him on," McCormick said. Connors was the head of the Sinn Fein Party in Parliament.

"The Dail Eireann just finished voting, Sean. That British geothermal report swung two of the minority parties over to our side. We've got what we wanted, all of it."

"An ultimatum to the British?"

"Yes, and it's unequivocal; withdraw from North Channel or the Irish Army will go on the march."

"How much time did you give them to respond?"

"Forty-eight hours."

"You've done a splendid job, George. When the Sinn Fein forms a new government, no doubt you'll be the next prime minister of Ireland."

"A united Ireland, eh Sean, once we've driven the bloody Brits out of Ulster."

"That'll be my job, George, and I'd best be about it. Goodbye."

McCormick hung up and encoded a shortwave message to Paddy Gallagher in Belfast ordering him to have his IRA terrorists ready to strike in forty-eight hours. Then he wrote out a command transferring six Irish Army divisions to staging areas just south of the border with Ulster. Finally, he ordered the 1st Armored Brigade to move east immediately to an assembly point on the coast of the frozen Irish Sea.

As the Signal Corps corporal left his office with the messages, McCormick sat back in his chair and looked at his watch. If the British hadn't withdrawn from North Channel by 5 P.M. the day after tomorrow, his tanks would roll east across the ice.

North Sea
•••••••••••

7:45 p.m.

MARJORIE GLYNN HAD NEVER known such terror in her life. The ice fields of the Irish Sea were cracking beneath the weight of the Dunkirkers' huge sleds and all around her snowmobiles and people were being swallowed up by huge crevasses yawning open in the floes.

She could see the 260-foot-long drill tower sliding down base first through a gaping fracture. Men were clinging to the pyramid top, screaming for her to help them. She leaped out of her command vehicle and started running across the ice.

A terrible roaring sound began to build in the distance. It grew nearer and nearer. A huge crack was opening in the floes, its arrow tip racing toward her. The sound grew louder and louder until it filled her head.

Then suddenly the ice split open beneath her boots and she was tumbling down between the glistening white walls, down toward the freezing black water below.

She threw her head back and screamed, her hands scratching at the empty air above her.

"Marjorie. Marjorie, wake up." Ben shook her, kneeling beside the operations center couch. "It's all right. You're having a nightmare."

Marjorie sprang awake and threw herself into Ben's arms, gasping for breath as she buried her head against his shoulder. Despite sleeping sixteen hours straight, she was still plagued by exhaustion and she'd lain down on the couch for a nap after supper.

For a long moment, she gasped for breath and clung to Ben. "God, it was awful. A huge crevasse opened in the floes and I was falling. I can still hear the ice cracking."

"Easy, easy," Ben said softly, stroking her auburn hair as he held her against him. "What you're hearing is a jet going over."

"A jet?" she said against his shoulder.

"Irish fighter. It's the third one in the last hour."

As her heart slowed, Marjorie suddenly realized she was in Ben's arms. His embrace was strong, yet tender. There was no mistaking that he cared; she could hear it in his voice and feel it in the caress of his fingers through her hair.

So often when men held her she'd sensed their need to dominate; her body, her independent spirit. In Ben's arms, she felt wanted, nurtured, a person instead of a prey. It felt good, right, and she lingered a moment against his chest.

Finally, she eased her head off his shoulder and looked at him. "I suppose you think me an awful baby, frightened by a dream."

"If you're a baby, I am too. I have nightmares all the time."

"You do? What about?"

"Dying alone. It's always the same dream; I'm in a coffin being lowered into my grave and there's no one there I know, no woman I love, no friends, just some indifferent funeral director and two guys with shovels. Then the dirt comes in over my coffin and I'm food for the worms."

For a long half awkward, half tender moment they looked at each other. Then Marjorie swung her feet off the couch and sat up. "You know, before I met you, when I knew you only as this rich American scientist I'd read about in magazines, I imagined you had everything you wanted in life. Including women."

"There've been three or four women in my life since Elizabeth. But, with every damn one of them, I always had this gut feeling they were more interested in what I had—money, access to the power brokers—than in me. It was always show time; evening gowns and limos and state dinners at the White House."

"That's not an unattractive picture you're painting."

"I'm not saying it wasn't fun. What the hell, I grew up poor twenty miles from the nearest store. I liked the limelight and the money and the glamorous women. For a while. But I'm thirty-four now. That bullshit's paled for me."

"What is it you want out of life, then?"

Ben blew out his cheeks. "Truth?"

"Truth?"

"I've got all the dough I'll ever need. When I bring this field in, I'm going to sell Meade International and go chase a dream back in Wyoming."

"What's your dream, Ben?"

"To teach the earth sciences, to get kids excited about geology and oceanography and climatology, to teach them to love learning about our planet the way I did when I was young. There are so many scientific discoveries yet to be made. Somewhere out there are kids who will unlock secrets of nature unknown to you and me. All they need is the inspiration to search for the keys."

"It's a wonderful dream, Ben."

"It will be once the most important piece is in place."

"And what's that?"

"A family. I want a wife to share my life and my love with. A woman who laughs a lot and likes animals and mountains, and the way aspen leaves look shivering in the wind. A woman who'd rather wear jeans than evening dresses, and doesn't give a shit about money. And kids. I want towheaded boys and freckle-faced girls. A house full of them."

Marjorie smiled softly. "I like your dream, Ben. I wish I had my own to share with you."

"Surely you've thought about the future, what you want out of life."

Marjorie slowly shook her head. "It's strange, I suppose, but I haven't thought much beyond Biosphere Britannia.

There's always been so much to do, I haven't had much time to plan my own life."

The Irish jet made another pass over the platform and Ben rose and walked to the window, watching the plane streak low over the floes toward the west.

Marjorie came unsteadily to her feet and crossed the room to Ben's side. "What do they want?" she said, catching a glimpse of the jet disappearing back toward the Irish shore.

Ben shrugged. "Who knows? After what we did to that Irish patrol, that bastard McCormick may intend to harass us for a while."

The phone rang on the communications console behind them. Ben continued to stare morosely out over the floes toward the west, making no move to answer.

"Want me to get that?" Marjorie said.

"Yeah, thanks," Ben said.

Marjorie turned and crossed to the phone. "Operations center."

She listened a moment, then nodded. "Hang on, I'll tell him."

"It's Mel in the drill hut," she said to Ben. "The laser drill's broken through to some sort of cavity."

"How big?"

Marjorie repeated the question into the phone.

"He says there's no way of telling yet. He's lowered the drill head two hundred feet and still hit dead space, so it's at least that deep."

Ben turned from the window. "Tell him I want to look over the satellite imaging again before I come over. There may be a cavern or a fracture down there I missed before. Meanwhile, have him pull the drill out. We'll send a TV camera down."

Marjorie repeated the message into the phone. As she hung up, Ben crossed the room to the large IBM computer linked by cellular modem to his laboratory in Wyoming.

"Anything I can do to help?" Marjorie said.

"Yeah. I could use an extra set of eyes going over the satellite images. We'll be looking for an anomaly in the rock strata beneath the seabed."

"What sort of anomaly?"

"A vertical fracture or hollow in the rock. It won't be easy to spot."

For the next hour, Ben and Marjorie sat side by side studying hundreds of infrared satellite pictures of the earth's crust deep beneath the seabed of North Channel. It was almost 9 P.M. before Ben pointed to a thin shadow on the screen. "That could be it. Let's get over to the drill hut."

A freezing wind was whipping the deck as they crossed toward the floodlight drill hut. The hut was fifty feet on each side, with the new laser drill tower jutting up almost three hundred feet above the work area. Both the tower and the hut had been enclosed in thermal plastic panels to keep out the intense cold.

Inside, the building smelled of diesel fuel and machine oil. They spotted Mel Sanderson near the well head.

"How's it going, Mel?" Ben said.

"Okay. We've brought the drill back up and we're about to lower the camera now. You find anything on the satellite images?"

Ben shrugged. "Maybe. One of the shots shows a narrow vertical shadow at the depth we're drilling now. Could be a fracture."

"How long before you can get the TV camera down there?" Marjorie asked.

"About an hour," Mel said, watching two roustabouts maneuver the camera into the well head on the end of a long section of drill stem.

"I haven't been in here before," Marjorie said, looking around the cavernous space at the huge pieces of equipment and runs of pipe that made up the power plant.

"We've got some time," Ben said. "C'mon, I'll take you on a tour."

He led her across the hut to a sixty-foot-high steel tank. "With only one platform out here, we're cramped for space so we're using a single-flash power plant as our prototype. When we get other platforms built, we'll switch over to much larger double-flash units."

"Single-Flash, Double-Flash, I don't understand any of it."

"It's a relatively simple technology," Ben said. "This cylindrical piece of equipment in front of us is called a separator."

Marjorie studied the huge tank. "How does it work?"

"Basically, we lower the pressure inside and that causes about twenty percent of the hot geothermal water piped in from below to flash into steam."

"And that drives the new generators we brought from France?"

"Eventually, yes, but first the steam is passed through those bus-sized devices over in the corner there. They're called scrubbers, and they remove most of the vaporized gases, metals, and minerals before the steam hits the fan blades in the turbines."

"I think I know the rest; the mechanical energy from the spinning turbines is converted into electrical energy inside the generators."

Ben grinned. "You got it."

Marjorie wrinkled her nose. "What is that bloody awful smell?"

Ben pointed to an immense vat against one wall. "Drilling mud. That tank contains about ten thousand gallons of the stuff."

"Mud? You're kidding."

"No, we couldn't drill without it. We pump it down the pipe and it flows out through the drill bit at the bottom. Pressure forces it back up between the outside of the drill pipe and the well wall."

"What on earth for?"

"Several reasons; it lubricates the drill bit and brings the rock chips back to the surface. It also cakes the sides of the well to keep it from caving in until we can get pipe in place."

Mel Sanderson approached across the steel-plate floor. "If you two tourists can tear yourselves away, we need the TV monitors set up in the control room."

"I figured you had that taken care of already," Ben said.

"Yeah, like I've had time. I've only got two hands, you know."

"Relax, Mel." Ben grinned, steering Marjorie for the small control room. "We'll hook up the monitors. Let us know when you have the camera in position."

"Yeah, yeah, I'll be over as soon as I'm done."

For the next forty-five minutes, Ben and Marjorie connected fiber-optic cables to a TV screen and hooked up the camera's remote-control switches. The TV eye had both a close-up and wide-angle lens. A small spotlight mounted on the camera would illuminate the dark depths below.

Mel came in and crossed the control room. "The camera will reach the dead space in another five minutes or so," he said.

"Okay, let's see if the remote controls work," Ben said, sitting down before the television monitor. Marjorie and Mel pulled up stools on either side as Ben flicked on the switch activating the camera and spotlight. The three watched as the screen filled with the blurred gray image of the inside of the eighteen-inch-wide drill pipe.

"What are those wide scratches in the metal?" Marjorie said.

"Abrasions left when the drill head got off line going up or down and rasped against the pipe," Ben said.

"I thought a computer kept the drill straight as a string."

"Normally it does. But the computer can't anticipate an eighty-mile-an-hour gust of wind knocking the tower off center. When that happens, the pipe bends a degree or two."

Several minutes later the end of the last pipe section appeared below, then the camera was through and into a dark void. Ben reached forward and hit a button to stop the camera's descent.

Slowly, he began to rotate the camera. For several seconds the screen showed only black space, then the turning light picked up a perpendicular rock face descending down into the depths.

"There's one side of the fracture," Ben said. "Let's see how wide across it is."

He rotated the camera 180 degrees and a second subterranean cliff appeared directly opposite the first.

Marjorie glanced at the calibration marks on the edge of the screen. "Looks to be about twenty-five, thirty feet wide," she said.

"Yeah, but how deep?" Mel said.

"Let's find out," Ben said. He flicked on the wide-angle lens so both cliffs were in view on the screen, then started the camera down.

"The depth gauge is over to your right, Mel," Ben said. "Call out the readings as we go down."

Mel glanced at the gauge. "We're down thirteen hundred feet . . . thirteen twenty-five . . . thirteen fifty."

The monitor suddenly showed the facing cliffs flaring back away from each other as the camera descended and Marjorie came forward in her seat. "Lord, look at that, the bloody fracture's getting wider."

"Could be we've just gotten lucky," Ben said. "The deeper that bastard goes, the less rock we've got to drill through."

As the minutes passed, the descending camera twice showed the cliff faces flaring in, then out again. At one point the gray-black rock walls came within ten feet of each other, then once more drew apart into the darkness.

At the nineteen-hundred-foot level, a thin stratum of smooth black rock appeared in the cliff face on the left of the screen.

Mel tapped the monitor with his finger. "What's that dark-colored band there? Looks like the frosting in the middle of a layer cake."

"Shale bed," Ben said, stopping the camera's descent.

"What the hell's shale?" Mel asked.

Ben switched the camera to the close-up lens. "Sedimentary rock formed from mud or clay."

"Will you just look at all the fossils scattered through there?" Marjorie said. "There must be dozens of them."

"I wonder what that little beastie was," Ben said, pointing at a small oval of scalelike indentations in the cliff face.

Marjorie peered at the screen. "God, I haven't seen one of

those since my paleozoology course at Oxford. It's a wiwaxia."

"A wi-what?" Mel said.

"Wiwaxia. It was sort of a small marine porcupine with chain-mail scales and sharp spines. Lived during the mid-Cambrian period about five hundred and forty million years ago."

Ben scanned the cliff face with the camera. "What's that fossil down at the six-o'clock position on the screen, Marjorie? You see it? That sucker that looks like a chunky worm?"

"Cute." Mel made a face.

Marjorie laughed. "Five hundred million years ago, that little bastard was one of the terrors of the seas. It had a muscular, toothed proboscis that it used to reach out and swallow its prey whole."

"Not your typical garden-variety worm," Ben said.

"We're looking at some of the earth's earliest life-forms," Marjorie said. "When those animals lived, shallow seas covered much of the continents and land animals hadn't even begun to evolve."

For several more minutes Ben panned the shale stratum with the TV camera, while Marjorie pointed out fossilized mollusks and flat oval trilobites that looked like armored cockroaches.

"Back to work," Ben said finally, hitting the descent button again. "Let's find out how deep this fracture will take us."

Several minutes later, Marjorie suddenly craned her neck toward the monitor. "Do you see that? There at the bottom of the picture. It looks like vapor coming up from below."

Mel squinted his eyes at the screen. "Yeah, I see it now. Steam, I think."

Ben said, "There's a vent somewhere deeper down. What's our depth here, Mel?"

"Coming up on twenty-five hundred feet."

Now both opposing cliff faces came back in view.

"Looks like the fracture's closing again," Marjorie said.

"I think you're right," Ben said. "The walls are only six, maybe eight feet apart through here."

The three watched the monitor tensely as the camera continued its descent into the depths of the narrowing fracture.

"Twenty-six hundred feet," Mel read out.

Another minute passed. Suddenly the picture on the TV monitor jerked up and down several times, then tilted at a crazy angle.

"What's happening?" Marjorie said.

"The camera just bounced off one of the cliff faces," Ben said, flicking a switch to stop the descent. "That's as far down as we dare go."

He rotated the camera lens directly downward. For several moments the monitor showed only dark billowing vapor. Then suddenly the smoke swirled to one side and they could see a furious column of gray-black steam jetting violently up from the V-shaped bottom of the fracture.

"There must be enormous pressure below to send up a geyser like that," Marjorie said. "We've got to be close to the geothermal pool."

"What's the final depth reading, Mel?" Ben asked.

"Twenty-seven hundred and fifty feet," Mel said.

Ben said, "If our calculations are right, the geothermal reservoir's less than two hundred feet below."

"And the laser can drill down at twenty feet an hour," Mel said excitedly.

Ben nodded. "Unless something goes real wrong, we'll punch through early tomorrow morning."

LONDON
••••••••••••

10:45 p.m.

AN ALL BUT PALPABLE sense of dread and looming defeat permeated the Cabinet Room at Number 10 Downing Street.

The ultimatum from Dublin had stunned Prime Minister Aldis Butler. He had expected a harder line from the Irish nationalists now that Bernadette O'Fiaich was gone. Still, the flat threat of war that had arrived at Downing Street three hours before was beyond his worst nightmares.

He looked down the long Cabinet table at his exhausted ministers and felt an overwhelming despair that he had the strength and the resolve left to rally them.

"You have all had a chance to read the Irish demand. I should like your individual assessments," he said.

"Certainly the tone of their letter is bellicose," Secretary of State for the Home Department Ralph Merriweather said. "Yet we have had threatening communiqués from Dublin before. I question whether they actually mean it. Would they go to war over North Channel?"

"There is no doubt in my mind that they would," Chancellor of the Exchequer Malcolm Fulbright said. "General McCormick has been searching for a reason to use his new tanks against us since Windscale. Our drill platform up there on the ice is merely an excuse for him to attack."

"I don't entirely agree, Ralph," Butler said. "Yes, McCormick is vehemently anti-British; undoubtedly the deaths of his family at the hands of our Ulster forces has much to do with that. However, the ultimatum passed the Dail Eireann."

"The Sinn Fein doesn't have a majority in their Parliament," Secretary of Energy Nan Dupont said. "That means the ultimatum needed the support of several of the moderate minority parties to pass."

"Exactly my point," Butler said. "One wonders what swung those votes to McCormick and the Sinn Fein."

"I think that's obvious; the massacre at North Channel did it," Merriweather said. "Good God, how would we feel if twenty-four of our unarmed soldiers were gunned down by the Irish Army?"

Butler peered down the table at the home secretary, his face contemplative. "Perhaps, but I think there's something more to all this. After all, opening fire on that Irish patrol was not a premeditated act. Prime Minister O'Fiaich understood that when I called. I believe the other Irish moderates would also believe it was nothing more than a terrible mistake."

Fulbright threw up his hands. "Then why the ultimatum? You don't threaten war on a whim."

"Their letter demanded we pull out 'until sovereignty over the energy reserves may be resolved,'" Butler said. "That tells me they've somehow found out the geothermal reservoir extends under Irish territorial waters."

"How could they know that?" Dupont said. "Our chart of the reservoir and the parliamentary report are both tightly held secrets. No one but those present and the leaders of Parliament have seen those documents."

Butler shrugged. "I could be wrong, Nan. Or there might have been a leak. Whatever the case, our paramount concern at the moment is how do we respond to the Irish demand."

"We tell them to shove it up their bloody arses," Merriweather blustered angrily. "That drill platform is within British territorial waters."

"That's true, Ralph," Butler said mildly. "However, the geothermal reservoir the platform is tapping extends under the border. We are not entirely within our rights."

"If they had asked we stop drilling, that would have been one thing," Merriweather said. "But they are demanding we abandon the platform. I say again, most strongly, it is British territory."

Malcolm Fulbright puffed out his cheeks. "If we accede to this demand, what's next? Do the Irish order us out of the Inner Hebrides islands off Scotland? Where does it end?"

"I take your point, Malcolm," Butler said. He turned to Secretary of State for Defense James Litchfield. "It comes down to our military capability, doesn't it, James? In a word, can we defend the platform?"

Litchfield drew his lips into a hard line, the wrinkles bunching on his square chin. For a long moment he stared down at the highly polished table. Finally he raised his eyes toward Butler, "No, Prime Minister, we cannot."

A collective gasp went up from the ministers around the table.

"What the bloody hell do you mean we can't defend North Channel?" Merriweather demanded angrily. "I should think if General McCormick sends his tanks across the ice they'd be sitting ducks for the RAF."

"Under normal circumstances, yes, the RAF could take them out, though we'd suffer high losses. Our intelligence people tell me the Irish First Armored Brigade has state-of-the-art ground-to-air missiles."

Merriweather stared at Litchfield. "Normal circumstances?"

"There was a second huge eruption of R-Nine several days ago, Ralph. Surely you're aware of that."

"Yes, yes, but what does that have to do with the RAF?"

Litchfield looked across the table. "I think the secretary of state for the environment might best answer that."

Sir Geoffrey Tanner sat back slowly in his chair. "The volcanic clouds from the second eruption will arrive over the

British Isles tomorrow night, Ralph. The air will be saturated with ash and volcanic debris that would clog a jet engine within minutes. Any aircraft that attempted to fly under such conditions would certainly crash in flames."

Merriweather's mouth worked wordlessly for a moment. "How long will the RAF be grounded, then?"

"A week at least," Tanner said.

Malcolm Fulbright slammed his fist down on the papers before him. "Then send our tanks across the ice, as the Irish intend."

Litchfield threw up his hands. "What tanks? The service-wide demobilization we put into effect two years ago has left us with only skeletal active forces. We have several thousand tanks, but ninety percent of them are mothballed. The crews have been disbanded. It would take a minimum of six months to retrain and reequip a tank army."

"Surely the European Community and the United Nations will not stand for blatant Irish aggression," Nan Dupont said.

"I'm afraid we can count on only lukewarm support from the EC, Nan," Butler said. "Spain, Portugal, and most of the former Eastern Bloc nations, Hungary, Romania, and that bunch, all backed Ireland's demands for reparations after Windscale. No doubt they will side with Dublin again over North Channel."

"Our position is not much better within the UN," Merriweather added. "Half the bloody third world still sees Britain as a colonial bully boy. Our war with Argentina back in the eighties made us anathema to a dozen nations in South America and Africa. We've too few friends in the General Assembly."

"What is the American position, Prime Minister?" Malcolm Fulbright said. "Have you talked with the President?"

"Yes, an hour ago."

"Will he support us?"

"He has promised to call in the Irish ambassador to Washington and communicate his deep concern."

" 'Communicate his deep concern'?" Geoffrey Tanner

scoffed. "That doesn't exactly sound like a ringing endorsement of Britain."

"This is an election year in America, Sir Geoffrey. With the economy a shambles over there, the President already trails in the polls. Our confrontation with Ireland presents him with a special problem."

"He's afraid of alienating fifty million Irish American voters," Fulbright said.

"Yes, Malcolm, and who present can blame him? We've all run for office. We all understand the realities of politics."

"Still, surely President Allen intends to do more than simply call the Irish ambassador on the carpet," Fulbright said.

"He's assured me privately that he'll be working behind the scenes as well," Butler said. "He's going to ask old Teddy Kennedy to call some of the members of the Dail Eireann he knows personally. Yet, beyond twisting a few arms and issuing a call for peace, there's little Washington can do."

"Britain is alone, then," Nan Dupont said morosely.

"Quite alone," Butler said. "And alone we must decide our course. Do we give in to the Irish ultimatum and withdraw from North Channel? Or do we stand and fight?"

"Knowing the Scots Guards cannot possibly hold the platform?" Secretary of Defense Litchfield said. "Knowing we must lose?"

"Knowing we must lose," Butler said quietly.

"What bloody choice have we, really?" Ralph Merriweather said. "If we abandon the geothermal field, the only source of energy left for Britain is coal."

"And coal is Seamus MacTiege," Malcolm Fulbright said.

"He'll win the coming general election in a landslide," Merriweather said.

Nan Dupont's face was pale. "And turn Britain into a fascist state, isolated from the world, our people shivering in their cold homes and hovering on the brink of starvation. To me, even war with Ireland is a less frightening prospect."

"We must defend North Channel, Prime Minister," James Litchfield said. "No matter the odds, we cannot surrender the future of this nation without a fight."

A chorus of agreement rippled through the ministers.

Aldis Butler looked around the table. "I have come to the same conclusion. Nevertheless, I wanted to hear it from the Cabinet. I will order the civilians on the ice to evacuate to Scotland. The Guards will stay and defend the platform."

The prime minister's voice was thick with emotion. "To the last man."

North Channel
•••••••••••••••••••

BEN MEADE FROWNED AS he sat at the operations center's control panel reading the latest meteorological report from the SEASAT probe in geostationary orbit 542 miles above the North Atlantic.

"Problem?" Marjorie Glynn said, crossing the room from the kitchen with a pot of coffee and two cups on a tray.

"Nothing unexpected. The ash cloud from that latest series of eruptions on R-Nine is nearing the west coast of Ireland. It will be over us by tomorrow night."

"At least it will ground those Irish jets that keep buzzing us," Marjorie said.

"Yeah, with all that volcanic debris in the air, I doubt if even the seagulls will go up."

The long-distance radiophone rang and Ben reached for the receiver. "North Channel Operations."

"Dr. Benjamin Meade, please."

"Speaking."

"The prime minister is calling, sir," the Downing Street operator said. "One moment, please."

Ben put his hand over the mouthpiece. "Marjorie, it's the prime minister."

"Put it on the speakerphone, will you?"

Ben hit the speaker button and a moment later the two heard the tired voice of Aldis Butler.

"Hello, Ben."

"Good morning, Prime Minister. I was going to call you shortly."

"Oh?"

"We got lucky last night. Our laser drill burned through to a vertical fissure almost fifteen hundred feet deep. It will save us three days of drilling. We should punch through to the geothermal reservoir within the next hour or so."

"That's wonderful news, Ben. Under different circumstances, I daresay the church bells would soon be ringing all over Britain."

"Different circumstances?"

"We are at the brink of war, Ben. By tomorrow night there will be four hundred Irish tanks advancing on North Channel."

"War? You can't mean it," Marjorie blurted out, her face a mask of stunned disbelief.

"Is that you, Marjorie?" Butler said.

"Yes, Prime Minister."

"I'm sorry to say there's no longer much doubt hostilities will break out." Butler told them of the Irish ultimatum and the British decision to reject the demands from Dublin.

"Satellite surveillance has picked up the movement of their First Armored Brigade out to the coast of the Irish Sea. Our intelligence people tell me they've brought in large fuel trucks from all over Ireland. That means they need enough petrol to take them a long distance, and that can only mean North Channel."

"May I ask what your government intends to do, Prime Minister?" Ben said.

"The platform is British territory, of course," Butler said. "The two hundred Scots Guards will stay and defend it. However, I must ask that you and Marjorie and the other civilians up there withdraw to Scotland immediately."

"We can't abandon all we've done here," Marjorie said, a

desperate passion in her voice. "It's not just the geothermal field at stake; it's the very future of Britain."

There was a pained resignation in Butler's voice now. "I know that all too well, Marjorie. The loss of North Channel will insure the election of Seamus MacTiege and doom Britain to a future of hopeless privation. I have beseeched my God for an answer, a shred of hope. I have received neither."

Marjorie and Ben looked at each other, gloom in their faces.

"My military aide tells me the Dunkirkers left enough transport there to get you and the roughnecks safely across the ice to Scotland," Butler said. "He is on the phone now instructing Lieutenant Scribner to ready the vehicles for your evacuation."

"I'm not going to turn tail and run," Ben said heatedly. "I request permission to stay and fight alongside the Scots Guards. I'd be willing to bet most of my men will volunteer too."

"Thank you, Ben. It is a brave offer. But I cannot allow it."

"We have forty or fifty cases of nitroglycerin out here, Prime Minister. My boys are damn good with that stuff. We could take out a couple of dozen tanks with that much explosives."

"I am ordering you off, Ben. I'm sorry but that's final. I'll speak to you both when you reach Scotland. Goodbye."

The speakerphone went dead and for a long moment Marjorie and Ben stared at each other in silence. Then Ben suddenly swept a hand across the console desk sending charts and computer printouts showering to the floor.

"All our work, all our dreams, gone, shot to shit, ashes."

Marjorie put a hand on his arm. "Perhaps there'll be another time, Ben, another chance."

"You know better, Marjorie. With that goddamn IRA madman in power in Ireland and Seamus MacTiege prime minister of Britain, both geothermal power and Biosphere Britannia are finished in—"

Ben stopped in mid-sentence as the steel floor of the operations center began to vibrate. "Feel that?"

"Yes, what is it?"

The direct phone to the drill hut rang shrilly and Ben snatched the receiver off the hook. "Yeah, Mel?"

"I pulled the drill out to change the bit and all of a sudden there was steam jetting up the pipe. We must have been close enough to the reservoir that the pressure cracked open the last section of rock below the pipe."

Ben grabbed Marjorie's arm and pulled her down into the seat next to him as the operations center began to tremble violently. "Shut the seabed valve, Mel. If the granite cap above the reservoir is cracked, it'll only be a matter of minutes before the pressure blows the rock apart and we get a geyser up the pipe."

Marjorie held on to Ben's arm, her frightened eyes darting toward the table as the coffeepot and cups shook off the tray and crashed in pieces on the floor.

"Better clear the platform, Ben. If she blows before I get that valve closed, anyone out on the deck could get scalded bad."

"All right, Mel, I'll get everybody inside. Call back if you've got a problem."

Ben hung up and hit the button for the warning Klaxon outside. Instantly the shrill sound of the horn warning roughnecks off the deck reverberated across the platform.

"I've got to make sure everyone gets under cover," Ben said, starting for the door. "Do me a favor and take any calls from Mel."

"You shouldn't be long," Marjorie said. "The deck will be the wrong place to be if that drill pipe vents."

"Be right back," Ben said, yanking his heavy parka off a hook by the door.

Marjorie shivered as Ben opened the door and a blast of arctic air swept into the operations center. He pulled the door shut behind him and Marjorie turned and scanned the systems monitors on the control panel.

A repeater gauge hooked to the drill-hut systems showed the steam pressure in the pipe building rapidly. She bit a nail and stared at the round glass face.

Two minutes later, the phone rang again.

"Operations."

"Marjorie, let me talk to Ben."

"He's out herding everyone off the deck, Mel."

"Jesus."

"What's the bother?"

"The seafloor valve's sticking. I can't get the bastard shut. There's a jet of superheated water coming up behind the gases."

Marjorie's hand went to her throat. "Ben!"

"Get on the loudspeaker and warn him back inside. Fast."

"How much time do we have?"

"Minute, ninety seconds tops."

"Get that bloody valve shut!" Marjorie yelled into the mouthpiece, then dropped the receiver and snatched the loudspeaker mike off the panel. It was a wireless model, thank God, and she dashed across the shaking floor to the window.

The deck was clear. Obviously Ben had already gotten the roughnecks and Scots Guards into the shelter of the barracks building and mess hall. She wondered for a moment if he'd followed his men into one of the other buildings. Then she saw him far across the platform. Bloody hell, he was pulling a tarp over the *Yellowstone*.

Marjorie flicked on the mike switch. "Ben, get back here," she shouted. "Mel can't shut the valve. There's a geyser coming up the pipe."

She saw him suddenly drop the tarp and start running for the operations center. The deck was shaking violently now and Ben was having a hard time keeping his balance.

She watched him fight his way across the trembling steel plates. He was almost there, only twenty yards from the door. Then she spotted a patch of ice directly ahead of him. The fur-lined hood of Ben's parka was obscuring his view. She knew he couldn't see the ice.

Marjorie opened her mouth to warn him but before she could get the words out Ben's feet skidded from beneath him and he pitched headfirst onto the steel deck.

"Get up," she yelled into the mike.

Ben didn't move.

She whirled from the window and tore across to the door.

The wall of subzero air outside stunned her. She could feel the terrible cold in her bones the moment she started across the deck. When she reached Ben, he was moaning softly, a trickle of rapidly congealing blood seeping from a gash on his forehead.

Behind Ben, ice and snow were cascading down off the steel beams of the drill tower as the superstructure trembled in the throes of the pressurized gases and water surging up the pipe in its midst.

Any moment now, Marjorie knew, superheated water would jet out the top of the tower and shower the platform with a scalding rain. She reached under Ben and grabbed his arms, pulling him as fast as she could toward the operations center door.

They were ten yards away now, then five. The freezing air hurt Marjorie's lungs and the deep cold was fast sapping her strength. Ben weighed a ton.

At last, they were there. The door had blown shut. She turned the knob with her gloveless hand. The door opened, jerking her hand inward as it swung. *Jesus God,* her hand had frozen to the metal handle!

Tears of pain spurted from the ducts at the corners of her eyes, then immediately froze into ice pellets on her stinging face. A thunderous roar was building from the drill tower now. The thermal geyser would erupt over the deck any second.

Marjorie braced herself, closed her eyes, and yanked her hand off the knob. A four-inch-square piece of skin stayed frozen to the metal and she fell to her knees, screaming in agony as blood gushed from the raw flesh of her palm.

Suddenly her screams were drowned out by a titanic roar as a geyser of superheated water and steam erupted from the top of the drill tower. Instantly she forgot her pain and dove for Ben.

She felt an adrenal surge and found the strength to drag him across into the threshold into the operations center. Then she threw her shoulder against the door and slammed it shut again.

Marjorie collapsed on the floor next to Ben, fighting for

breath, the raw wound in her hand sending intense spasms of pain up her arm. Outside she could hear the boiling rain falling on the drill platform.

Her eyes darted toward the vaulted ceiling above as the deluge of superheated water pounded down on the metal roof. The operations center sounded like the inside of a beating drum.

Then she saw Ben move and she rolled over on her side and pushed the fur-lined hood back from his face. His eyes were open, trying to focus.

After what seemed an eternity, the deafening rain began to slacken. Finally the scalding downpour stopped, the only sound now the hissing of steam venting from the drill tower across the deck.

"Ben, are you all right? Can you hear me?"

"Yeah, Jesus, what happened?" He tried to push himself up on one elbow.

Marjorie eased him back down. "Lie still a moment. You took a header onto the deck."

"How'd I get back inside?"

"I dragged you. You're as heavy as a horse, by the way."

Ben suddenly noticed her bloody palm. "What'd you do to your hand?"

"I grabbed the metal doorknob without a glove on. Tore the skin off."

Ben pushed himself up into a sitting position. "We'd better get you bandaged up."

Marjorie blew gently on the reddened flesh. "I thought I was going to die when it happened. Pain's eased a bit now."

Ben put a hand to his throbbing head. "Last time I had a headache like this I'd downed a bottle of Scotch the night before."

He rose groggily to his feet. "Where's the first-aid kit, do you know?"

"Yes, I saw it in the kitchen when I was putting away the flatware. Second drawer down, I think."

Ben found the first-aid kit and pulled out a tube of burn jell. Gently he applied the ointment to Marjorie's palm.

"Feel better?"

"Worlds. Thanks."

The phone rang as Ben finished wrapping Marjorie's hand with a gauze bandage. He picked up the kitchen extension. "Operations."

"You all right?" Mel Sanderson said. "One of the rough-necks was looking out the window and saw Marjorie dragging you inside."

"Yeah, I'm fine. Lost my footing on some ice and smacked my head on the deck. Marjorie's worse off than me. She tore the skin off her palm when she grabbed the knob outside."

"You want me to come over?"

"No. I just patched her up. We're okay."

"Jesus, I'm sorry, Ben, but there wasn't much I could do. The goddamn seafloor valve stuck and before I could get the bastard closed that geyser was up the pipe."

"It happens, Mel, forget it. You got everything buttoned down now?"

"Yeah, except I think the pressure gauges are off. We're measuring almost fourteen thousand pounds per square inch at the well head."

"The gauges aren't off, Mel. We're punched into a geo-pressurized zone. I suspected we were sitting on one when I saw that subterranean geyser last night."

"Geopressurized zone? What the hell's that?"

"Basically a pocket deep in the crust where the steam and water are trapped under extreme pressure. A normal hot-water field usually measures around five hundred pounds per square inch."

"No wonder I couldn't get that valve closed with that much pressure below."

"Look, Mel, we've had a call from the prime minister. I have to talk to you and the men."

"Something wrong, Ben?"

"Real wrong. I'll be over in about half an hour."

"Your turn," Marjorie said as Ben hung up, dabbing at the cut on his forehead with a disinfectant swab.

Her face was close to his, her fingers gentle against his skin. Her breath was sweet and warm, and a clean outdoor

scent wafted from her hair. He remembered her telling him
she melted snow to wash it.

"You smell good."

"I'm not wearing perfume."

"That's what I mean. Nothing to mask the natural you."

"Flatterer. Hold still."

Had she moved closer, or was it his imagination? Her
eyelashes were the same auburn shade as her hair. He hadn't
noticed her eyelashes before.

"There, that ought to hold you," she said, putting down
the swab but not moving away.

"I thought for a moment when you smashed into the deck
you were badly hurt," she said softly. "Or worse."

"I didn't think you cared. Personally, I mean."

"You silly man, of course I care. You do wear well, you
know. Oh, you've got your rough edges. Still, you're a damn
fine man, Benjamin Meade, and I shouldn't like to lose you."

"I don't want to lose you either, Marjorie." He stroked her
cheek gently with the back of his fingers. "Come back to Wyoming with me. That dream I've got, you could share it, you
know."

"Ben, I can't. My work's here with Biosphere Britannia."

"You heard what the prime minister said, Marjorie. It's
over. We've lost the battle here in Britain. Let's go where we
can do some good. Hell, at the rate the volcanic clouds are
spreading, within the next year every country in the northern latitudes is going to need biospheres. You build your
miniearths and I'll find the energy to power them. We make
a great team. We've already proved that."

"Perhaps you're right," she said, squeezing his hand
against her face. "I doubt there'll be any place for me in a
Britain ruled by Seamus MacTiege."

The two turned as the door to the operations center
opened and Lieutenant Scribner came in, a worried expression on his face as he pushed back the hood of his parka.
"We've got rather a problem," he said.

"What is it, Lieutenant?" Ben said.

"Everything's encased in ice out there. All the equipment

on the platform, the forklifts, the stairs down to the ice. The deck itself is like a skating pond."

"That's to be expected," Ben said. "In temperatures like this, when superheated water hits cold steel it freezes solid in seconds."

"Yes, well, unfortunately the tracked lorries the Dunkirkers left were parked on the ice beside the platform. There's no chance you civilians can use them to get to Scotland. They're entombed under a foot of ice."

Ben whirled and grabbed Marjorie by the shoulders. "That's it! Son of a bitch, that's it."

Marjorie looked at him in bewilderment. "What's it?"

Ben tore across the room and surveyed the ice-encrusted platform outside. "The well! It couldn't have vented for more than two or three minutes and there's a foot of ice wherever the thermal water hit steel."

"What possible difference does it make?" Marjorie said. "Everything out here on the floes freezes solid eventually."

"Don't you see, Marjorie? It's a way to stop them."

"Stop who, sir?" Lieutenant Scribner said.

"That Irish brigade, damn it," Ben said, turning to stare out over the dark ice fields stretching west toward Ireland. "We're going to stop those tanks with cannon fire from the center of the earth."

NORTH CHANNEL
••••••••••••••••••

1:05 p.m.

THERE WERE HUMANS DOWN on the ice again and the great wolf Beelzebub watched them intently from the top of a pressure ridge a mile from the drill platform.

The wolves had now eaten three men. Still, the pack would have returned to hunting deer, rabbits, and game birds if their normal prey were available. It was not their instinct to stalk humans. There was hunger, not hatred, in Beelzebub's eyes as he stared at the two-legged forms in the distance.

That morning, the humans had come down the ladder from the distant platform and used axes and small objects that spit out fire to melt the ice from one of the machines they rode in. It had taken them hours, but the humans had finally gotten the machine started.

Then they'd begun lowering what looked to the animal like long branchless tree trunks down to the ice. There was now a large pile of trees on the surface of the floes. As Beelzebub watched, the men on the ice began wrapping the end of a chain around several trees.

The wolf growled low in his chest at the sight of the chain for he had been tethered to a stake by such a cruel device when the humans first captured him in Canada.

The men then attached the other end of the chain to the machine they'd freed of ice. This one did not look like the other such machines that Beelzebub had seen, for in front it had a derrick that tapered up and out like a long snout. A moment later, four of the men got into the machine and began dragging the trees out onto the floes.

A short distance from the platform, the machine stopped and the men got out. They were on foot now, and Beelzebub sensed they were vulnerable. Keeping to the back side of a pressure ridge, he moved quickly across the ice toward the humans.

Every hundred yards or so he would raise his eyes over the spine of ice and make sure the men were still there. They were, turning a stick that corkscrewed down into the ice. Each time he looked, the stick had penetrated deeper into the frozen surface of the floe.

He was only fifty yards away, the adrenaline surging through him, when the men stopped turning the stick, pulled it out of the ice, and put something small down the hole they had made.

The wind changed, blowing toward him now, and he could smell the humans for the first time. Mixed in with the odor of their sweat and urine was the scent of fear. It was unmistakable to the huge animal.

When he detected this smell in the animals he hunted, he knew their fear was of him, their stalker. But the humans did not know he was there, he was sure of that. Their fear was of something else.

Unconsciously, he stored the fear fact among the other hunting information in his canine brain and watched as the men got in their machine and pulled the trees several hundred yards away, a wire trailing out the back of the machine to the hole.

Beelzebub was sitting on his haunches puzzling over what it was the men were doing when a tremendous explosion blew him head over heels down the back of the pressure ridge. He was running before he finished rolling, not stopping until he was again almost a mile away.

He licked himself all over, checking his body for wounds.

Finding none, he turned his attention back to the hunt. Between him and the men was a small berg trapped in the floes and he climbed the sloping side and looked back toward the place where the ice had exploded.

There was now a huge hole in the floes. The long snout of the machine was pointed out over the hole, lowering the trees on a chain into the dark churning water below.

Beelzebub would have retreated then, leaving the dangerous humans to their frightening tasks, but his hunger would not let him. At night, the temperature out on the floes often fell to 40 degrees below zero, and an animal his size needed thousands of calories a day to keep warm.

He had not eaten in three days, nor had the pack, at that moment hiding through the day in a jumble of ice slabs several miles away. His instinct told him that in another day or two starvation would begin to set in. If they did not find food by tomorrow, they would have to return to the land where men hunted them from terrible flying machines that attacked the pack like huge screeching eagles.

For the next three hours, the great wolf watched the humans as they worked their way down a long narrow valley flanked by high-pressure ridges running out over the floes toward the west.

Five times the humans blew holes in the ice, five times they lowered trees into the black water, five times the holes froze over and disappeared again beneath the blowing snow. Beelzebub recognized the pattern, but it made no sense to him, just as he did not comprehend most of the things that humans did.

When the men finished lowering the trees into the last hole, one of them pointed toward the west and they all stood for several moments looking out across the broken floes.

The wind brought their scent to Beelzebub and again he smelled their fear, stronger this time. Standing there stock-still, staring toward something they couldn't see, the humans looked to the wolf like deer intent on some threatening noise they had heard in the forest.

Suddenly Beelzebub understood that whatever it was the

men feared, it was coming from the west, from somewhere across the vast plateau of sea ice.

Finally the men got in their machine and drove back to the platform. The great wolf watched them climb the stairs up to the deck. Neither he nor the pack would go near the human structure again, for they had lost two yearling males during the terrible night of the guns three days before. The dead yearlings were now buried beneath the quickly drifting snow too close to the platform for the pack to risk dragging the bodies away to eat.

The great wolf turned and headed across the floes toward the icy lair where the pack waited, the fear in the humans stored in his brain. Animals that were afraid were easier to panic, to cut from the herd.

Tomorrow the hunting would be better.

NORTH CHANNEL
••••••••••••••••••

9:15 a.m.—February 18
Fuel Reserves—3 Days

"I'M AFRAID WE'VE NO choice but to remain here in North Channel, Prime Minister," Marjorie Glynn said into the operations center phone. "There is simply no alternative."

"You say the lorries the Dunkirkers left there are completely useless?" Butler questioned.

"They are encapsulated in ice, sir. It took us over five hours yesterday just to chop a pipe-setting machine out and get it started again. It would require days to free enough lorries to get us all out."

"We haven't any large snowmobiles anywhere near the coast up there," Butler said, "but perhaps we could send helicopters out to take you off."

"That's out of the question, Prime Minister. The ash cloud is barely a hundred yards above the ice out here. Some of the pressure ridges rise almost that high. Helicopters could not get through."

"As hard as it is for me to say this, Marjorie, the wisest course may simply be for you and the other civilians there to allow yourselves to be taken prisoner. At least it would spare you facing those Irish tanks."

"It may be the Irish who are taken prisoner, Prime Minister," Marjorie said, telling him of Ben Meade's plan to stop the Irish tanks.

"What are the odds this geyser cannon of Dr. Meade's will work?" Butler said, his voice skeptical.

"We don't know, Prime Minister. But what does it matter, really? We have no other chance."

Butler sighed wearily. "I suppose you're right. Still, you'll be gambling the whole show on one throw of the dice."

"Have you an alternative, sir?"

"No, Marjorie, I don't. I'll advise the Cabinet of your situation. Perhaps one of my ministers will have an idea how to get you out of there. I'll ring back later."

"Goodbye, Prime Minister."

As Marjorie hung up, the door behind her opened and Ben and Mel Sanderson came in, a blast of freezing air swirling in past them.

Their faces were barely visible beneath layers of hoarfrost that had formed each time they'd exhaled on the subzero deck outside.

"Lord, you two look half frozen," Marjorie said, crossing the room to help them off with their parkas. "Let me get you some coffee."

"Thanks," Ben said, blowing on his hands.

"You can put a shot of brandy in mine," Mel said.

"Right you are," Marjorie said, turning for the kitchenette.

"Did you get through to the prime minister?" Ben said.

"Yes," Marjorie said, pouring two coffees and adding a generous dollop of Hennesey to Mel's cup.

"What'd he say?" Ben asked.

Marjorie brought the coffee back in and handed the cups to the men.

"What could he say? There's no way to get us out of here."

"I mean about my plan to stop the Irish tanks."

"He wonders will it work."

Ben sipped his coffee. "Don't we all? It looks good on paper, but who the hell knows if we can actually pull it off."

"I heard you blast the dive hole," Marjorie said. "Is the *Yellowstone* ready to go down?"

"She will be as soon as the deck crew finishes charging the batteries," Ben said. "About ten minutes."

"I hope to hell you can find all that pipe we put down through the ice yesterday," Mel said. "Odds are those sections didn't sink straight down."

"The bottom's almost dead flat," Ben said. "The sonar should pick up the pipes easily enough, then we'll zero in with the sub's searchlights."

"How long will it take you to weld the pipes in place?" Marjorie asked.

"Four or five hours," Ben said. "I've got twelve hundred yards of pipe to string together to bring the mouth of the geyser cannon up under that ice valley."

"Why did you decide to aim the geyser cannon at that particular valley?" Marjorie asked.

Ben turned to the control panel and picked up a satellite photo of the ice floes surrounding the drill platform. "That Irish brigade will come at us from the west. There are several large pressure ridges running north–south in that direction. Most of them are too high and steep for tanks to cross."

Mel jabbed the photo with his finger. "That valley is the only way through those pressure ridges. They've got to come that way."

"Exactly," Ben said. "And that's where we'll be waiting for them." He put down his coffee cup. "You two have any questions?"

"One," Mel said. "How the hell are you going to hold the *Yellowstone* steady and do the welding at the same time? You'd better take someone down with you to handle the controls while you do the torch work."

Ben shook his head. "No. I wouldn't ask anyone to risk it with me."

"You don't have to ask," Marjorie said. "You have a volunteer. Me."

"Forget it, Marjorie. There's a million things that could go wrong down there. I'll be working a long way from the opening in the ice. If the *Yellowstone* suddenly springs a leak or loses power, there'll be no way to surface."

"This is a British show, Ben. You don't think I'm going to

let you risk your bloody neck while I sit up here twiddling my thumbs."

"Marjorie—"

"Must I remind you that I am head scientist here? You take me down with you or you don't go."

"I think she just pulled rank on you, old buddy." Sanderson grinned.

"Jesus, I don't have time to argue with you, Marjorie," Ben said.

"It would be fruitless in any case. I'm going."

For a long moment Ben and Marjorie locked eyes in a test of wills, then Ben turned and stalked angrily across the room, grabbing his parka off a hook by the door. "All right, all right, you go. But I hope you've got your little English ass insured to the hilt 'cause there's a real good chance we won't be coming back up."

He yanked the door open, then slammed it furiously behind him.

"A smidgen testy today, isn't he?" Marjorie grinned at Sanderson.

Mel laughed. "He'll be all right. He's just used to running his own show."

"So I noticed."

"C'mon," Sanderson said. "Let's get you two launched."

Ben was already on board when they reached the *Yellowstone* resting on wooden jacks at the lip of the drill platform. Sanderson gave Marjorie a boost up the ladder on the side of the small submersible and she peered down through the hatch.

"May I come in?" she asked Ben.

"Jesus, you don't come 'in,' you come 'aboard.' Got it? Aboard!"

"May I come 'aboard,' then?"

"Do I have a choice?"

"No."

"Welcome aboard."

"I don't think you mean that," she said, grabbing the lip of the hatch and lowering herself into the cramped cabin.

"Take the copilot's seat," Ben said, pointing at one of the

two contoured seats facing the clear plastic sphere that formed the front of the cylindrical sub.

Marjorie worked her way carefully forward and sat down. The floor-to-ceiling acrylic bowl before her afforded a 360-degree view of the floodlit deck outside. There was a butterfly-shaped control wheel directly in front of her. Six inches beyond the wheel was a small dashboardlike panel crowded with gauges, systems monitors, and electronic switches.

Behind her to the right and left, the *Yellowstone*'s curved walls were lined with rows of instrumentation. "Looks like a bloody spaceship in here."

"Actually, the design of the hull and several of the systems are very similar," Ben said, letting go of his pique at Marjorie. "Like a spaceship, the *Yellowstone* is built to survive in an airless, alien environment."

Marjorie watched through the plastic bubble as a forklift maneuvered a pallet of six-foot-long cylinders up to the front of the submersible.

"What are those things?" she asked.

"Acetylene tanks," Ben said, coming forward. "We'll need at least eight of them to cut and weld the pipes below."

As they watched, two roustabouts began carefully strapping the tanks to the *Yellowstone*'s hull on either side of the transparent pilot sphere.

Ben picked up a microphone and switched on the exterior conning tower speaker. "Make sure all the fuel lines are connected to the main torch feed," he said.

One of the men waved a hand in acknowledgment and began checking the stainless-steel lines.

"Is that the welding torch?" Marjorie asked, pointing through the plastic at a long, thick assembly of rods and pneumatic tubes extending out in accordion folds from the front of the sub.

"No, that's one of the manipulator arms. There are two of them," Ben said. "The torch is that wicked-looking bronze contraption near the acetylene tanks to your right."

The roustabouts finished loading and Ben went back and pulled the hatch shut. "Strap yourself in, Marjorie," he said. "We're about ready to dive."

Marjorie buckled her lap and chest restraints as Ben turned on the oxygen system and started the *Yellowstone*'s electric motor. The steady hum of the battery-driven engine was interrupted by the sound of Mel Sanderson's electrified voice coming through the cabin speaker.

"Launch chief to *Yellowstone*."

Ben handed Marjorie a set of earphones and throat mike, and put on his own. "*Yellowstone* to launch chief. Go ahead, Mel."

"You ready to go down?"

"All set. Drop us in."

"Good luck, you two. Lifting off."

Despite her brave front, Marjorie's heart beat wildly as the submersible lurched off its jacks and rose above the deck of the drill platform. A moment later, the *Yellowstone* swung out over the floodlit hole in the icepack and she blanched at the sight of the black water below.

Ben looked over at her dead-white face. "There's still time to get out of this. I can have Mel put us back on the deck."

"No, damn it," she said between clenched teeth. "I'm going down with you."

Ben shrugged. "Have it your way."

The lateral swing of the *Yellowstone* stopped. For several seconds, the small submersible twisted in a half circle. Then the craft shuddered once and started down as the crane let out line.

Marjorie stared straight ahead through the bubble, afraid to move, as the *Yellowstone* lowered toward the dark pocket of icy sea. A moment later the sub settled into the water and began to roll from side to side. Outside, she could hear choppy wavelets splashing against the hull.

"I'm casting off the line," Ben said, reaching up to hit the cable disconnect.

"Roger, cable free," Mel Sanderson replied.

Ben flicked several switches on the control panel to his left and a loud hissing sound filled the sub.

Marjorie started. "What's that?"

"Take it easy. I'm flooding the ballast tanks to dive."

"Oh."

"Turn on the lights," Ben said, wanting to give Marjorie something to do to relieve her anxiety. "That silver toggle switch to your right."

Marjorie searched the control panel before her, found the switch, and snapped the toggle to the on position. The *Yellowstone*'s powerful searchlights stabbed out into the water now flooding up over the plastic sphere in front of them.

Fascination replaced Marjorie's fear as the sub lowered into the inky depths of North Channel. As she watched, a froth of air from the ballast tanks rushed up in a cloud of luminous bubbles that spread out beneath the thick ceiling of ice ringing the dive hole.

Marjorie felt a soothing serenity come over her as they sank into the womb of the sea and slowly her body relaxed against her seat straps.

"Well, then, this won't be so bad."

Ben pushed the control wheel forward and the *Yellowstone* nosed downward into the depths. "Piece of cake," he said.

He reached over to his left and slipped his fingers into a device that looked like a fleshless metallic hand. Rings fitted over his upper fingers while the tips were snugged into five hollow tubes with sensor wires attached to the ends.

"What on earth are you doing?" Marjorie asked.

"Making sure the manipulator arm works," he said. "This thing I've got my hand in is the remote control. Every movement of my arm and fingers will be duplicated exactly. Watch."

He flicked a switch on the panel before him, then arched his hand up toward his face.

Marjorie yelped and pressed back against her seat as the arm outside mirrored Ben's movement, rising up through the water like a huge metal lobster claw about to smash through the plastic and grab her.

"Don't you dare do that again, you bloody bastard."

"A little robot humor."

"The next time we're in the Biosphere I shall introduce you to some zoologist humor. There's a particularly voracious species of carnivorous ants that would love dining down your pants."

Ben winced. "God, you're vindictive."

"Very."

He lowered his hand and moved it forward. Instantly the manipulator arm followed his movements, coming to rest on the welding torch.

Marjorie suddenly caught sight of a pencil-thin form rising from the depths at the outer range of the searchlights. "There's something out there. See it? Over to the left."

"To port."

"What?"

"You don't say 'to the left,' you say 'to port.' "

"Any other little nautical terms you'd like me to use? Ship ahoy, walk the plank, anchors aweigh? Perhaps I should address you as captain. How does Captain Bligh suit you?"

"To the left, you say?"

"To the left."

"Thank you."

Marjorie grinned. "You're welcome."

"Yeah, I see it. It's the main drill pipe coming up from below. What's our depth? The gauge is on the panel to your right."

Marjorie glanced over. "Two hundred eighty feet."

Ben nosed the *Yellowstone* toward the drill pipe ahead. "Let me know when we reach four hundred feet."

The *Yellowstone* slowly circled the huge steel pipe as the sub descended, the lights picking up colonies of barnacles that had found a home on the cylindrical steel.

Beyond the lights, the icy waters stretched through the dark depths toward the Atlantic Ocean in the north and the Irish Sea to the south.

"Three hundred and fifty feet," Marjorie said. "Three hundred and seventy-five . . . four hundred."

"Here's where it starts to get tricky," Ben said, leveling off the *Yellowstone* and nosing the small sub in toward the pipe. "Grab the wheel."

"Not bloody likely."

"C'mon, c'mon, I need you to hold the *Yellowstone* steady while I use the torch."

"Surely you intend to give me a bit of training first. Good

Lord, you don't put someone in a car and expect them to drive."

"I don't have time to run a country day school for well-bred lady submarine drivers. Just keep your eye on the depth gauge and use the wheel to bring us up or down. I'll run you through the rudder controls later."

"You really are a chauvinist bastard. Do you know that about yourself?"

"If you're not going to help me, why the hell did you come down here in the first place?"

"I'm beginning to wonder."

"Take the goddamn wheel or I surface and get someone else."

"All right, all right, I'll do it. But if I crash this bloody thing, you've only yourself to blame."

"The only thing you can hit is the pipe. And I'll be watching that."

"How terribly reassuring."

"Look, it's not that big a deal. Pull the wheel toward you to bring her up, push it forward to go down. To go left you turn the wheel left, right you turn right. Got it?"

Marjorie gingerly took the wheel. "I'm not sure I've got anything. I'll do my best."

"That's all I ask." Ben hit the switch on his throat mike. "*Yellowstone* to launch chief."

"Launch chief."

"I'm about to start cutting the top section of pipe loose, Mel. Get set to pull it up when I give you the word."

"Roger. I've got a direct line to the roughneck crew on the drill deck. Let me know when you're ready."

"Is the well-head valve shut? If we've got pressure in the pipe, it'll blow us right up through the ice."

"The valve's shut, Ben. All the same, there's bound to be some residual gases and steam trapped in there. Maybe I'd better open the topside valve and vent the pipe before you start."

"No, it will take too long, Mel. There can't be that much residual pressure. I'm going to go ahead and cut her open."

"Okay, but don't blame me if you get bounced around down there."

Ben maneuvered the manipulator arm over and grasped the acetylene torch. "Bring us in a little," he told Marjorie.

Marjorie bit her lower lip and eased the wheel forward. Slowly the tiny sub moved in toward the eighteen-inch-wide pipe rising through the icy depths.

"Okay, that's good," Ben said, carefully lifting the torch out of the equipment tray with the robotic hand. He extended his wrist straight out and the manipulator arm mirrored his movements, bringing the tip of the cutting tool up against the pipe fifteen feet away.

Then he turned and hit a button on the hull beside him. Instantly a tongue of orange-red flame spit out through the freezing seawater, biting into the eighteen-inch-wide cylinder before it. Within minutes, the torch had cut through the metal and a fusillade of steam and scalding water jetted out into the sea.

"I thought you said there wouldn't be much pressure in there," Marjorie said, fighting the jerking wheel as the *Yellowstone* rocked violently in the turbulence created by the escaping steam.

"We'll be all right. Just keep her back thirty feet or so until it all vents."

Several minutes later the last of the trapped steam hissed out of the wound in the pipe.

"Bring her nose back in," Ben said. "What I want you to do now is swing the stern slowly in a circle as I cut."

"Anything else? Perhaps you'd like me to put the bloody thing through some figure eights; maybe you'd fancy a loop or two?"

Ben laughed and took the wheel in front of him. "You're right, I'm asking too much without a demonstration. It's simply a matter of a little finesse with the wheel and the rudder pedals. Watch."

He repeated the maneuver several times until he was sure Marjorie was comfortable with the controls. "You want to practice it a few times?"

"No, I think I've got it."

"Let's get on with it, then. We've got a lot of work to do."

Marjorie nosed the *Yellowstone* in toward the pipe once more and Ben resumed cutting. She kept one eye on the depth gauge and the other on Ben's progress, swinging the stern of the sub in a slow arc as he circled the pipe with the torch.

Ben hit the switch on his throat mike as the tip of the torch neared the starting point on the pipe. "She'll be free in a minute, Mel."

"Roger, they're standing by in the drill hut, Ben."

The torch completed the circle and the huge drill pipe suddenly came free of the section below, its jagged bottom swinging out dangerously close to the *Yellowstone*'s plastic pilot bubble.

"Jesus," Ben swore. "Throw it in reverse. Fast."

Marjorie's hands and feet worked the controls, a sheen of sweat breaking out on her face as the sub backed quickly away from the twisting pipe.

"Well, Captain Bligh, I take it you didn't anticipate that." Marjorie cocked an eye at Ben.

"You just love it when I fuck up, don't you?"

"Not a bit of it. I just thrill to these occasional reassurances you are in fact human."

"I can't work with someone who doesn't regard me as perfect. I'm ordering you off my sub, Marjorie. Don't forget your purse."

Marjorie burst into laughter. "You know, at times you can be an insufferable, hard-headed, chauvinist son of a bitch. But you do make me laugh."

"Is that good?"

"Yes, Captain Bligh, that's good."

"I'm glad I'm doing something right with you." Ben grinned, then flicked on his throat mike. "Top's free, Mel. Tell the boys to take her up."

"Roger. Up she comes."

As Ben and Marjorie watched through the bubble, the top section of pipe lurched once, then began slowly rising. A moment later it had disappeared into the dark waters above them.

Ben said, "Okay, now all we've got to do is weld twelve hundred yards of pipe together."

"Have you done this before?"

"Yeah, half a dozen times, but never a section that long."

"Let me get this straight. You intend to angle the pipe up under the floor of that ice valley?"

"Right."

"How sharp an angle?"

"Eighteen degrees; that's less than the angle of stairs in a house. Head her back down, Marjorie. Those first sections should be within a hundred yards or so of the well head."

While the *Yellowstone* lowered through the depths, Ben flicked on the sonar and scanned the sandy bottom. As he directed the sonar beam toward the southwest, the sound waves began bouncing back off a mass of long, thin objects lying on the flat seafloor.

"There they are," Ben said, pointing at the jumble of cylindrical images on the sonar monitor. "Bearing one hundred and twenty degrees. Bring her nose around."

Five minutes later the *Yellowstone's* lights picked up the litter of pipe sections dead ahead.

"We'll need the angle section first," Ben said. "You see it?"

Marjorie reached for the searchlight control handle and panned the beam over the pipes scattered over the bottom. "There it is," she said as the light played over a section of pipe angled like a bent finger.

"Good. Bring us as close as you can and I'll pick it up with the manipulator arm."

As Marjorie held the tiny sub steady, Ben snared the section with the robotic arm. "Beautiful. Take us back up, Marjorie. We've got a geyser cannon to build."

At the four-hundred-foot level, Marjorie brought the *Yellowstone* close in to the section of drill pipe Ben had cut. As she held the sub steady, Ben used the manipulator arm to lower the angle section over the thermal pipe coming up from below.

He checked the *Yellowstone's* compass, making sure the

mouth of the angle was pointed west, then welded the two pipes together.

Over the next four hours, they located the other piles of pipe that had been lowered through the ice and one after another welded the two-hundred-foot-long sections together.

"What's keeping the pipes from breaking apart at the welds and sinking back to the seafloor?" Marjorie asked as the gradually lengthening steel column angled up toward the ice above.

"I had a couple of the roustabouts tear the solid foam insulation from the walls and ceiling in the recreation hut and stuff the pieces in the pipes. The foam is full of air pockets that provide just enough buoyancy to prevent the sections from sinking after they're welded together."

The last section was only seventy-five-feet long, and when Ben welded it in place, the mouth of the pipe had slanted up to within twenty feet of the underside of the ice west of the drill platform.

"That's it," Ben said, rivulets of perspiration running down to soak the collar of his shirt. "Time to go home."

"Thank God, I'm whipped," Marjorie said, turning the *Yellowstone* back for the dive hole twelve hundred yards to the east. "Can I ask you something? Personal, I mean?"

"Sure."

"Are you scared of what's coming? Tanks, soldiers." She paused. "Maybe death."

For a long moment, Ben stared out into the dark sea beyond the lights. "Yeah," he said finally. "I'm scared."

"Good," she said. "I was afraid I was the only one."

Ben and Marjorie fell silent as the *Yellowstone* neared the dive hole.

In the dark freezing sea behind them, the yawning mouth of the geyser cannon pointed up at the brittle ice above.

DUNDALK BAY, IRELAND
. . . .

4:15 p.m.

A DARK, EVIL-SMELLING cloud of diesel fumes hung low over the coast of County Louth as the 442 tanks, supply trucks, and armored personnel carriers of the Irish Army's 1st Armored Brigade idled their engines on the frozen lip of the Irish Sea.

In the tiny parlor of a commandeered cottage a quarter mile from the ice-covered beach, Lieutenant General Sean McCormick was staring at a map of the Irish Sea pinned to the rough plaster wall when there was a knock on the door.

"Come."

McCormick's aide popped his head in the door. "Mr. Connors is calling from the Parliament, sir. I put him through on your scrambler phone."

"Thank you, Lian," McCormick said, picking up the receiver of his portable field phone. "Hello, George."

"We've had a reply from the British, Sean."

"And?"

"They've rejected our ultimatum to evacuate the drill platform. They claim it's British territory. Prime Minister Butler insists that the Scots Guards will defend it with all means at hand."

"Well, then, it's the answer we expected, isn't it, George?"

"That it is. Nevertheless, the leaders of the Fine Gael Party are in an uproar. The scent of war's in the air and the cowards are near faintin' at the smell."

"I'll bring 'em a victory home. That's all the smellin' salts we'll need to revive the weak-kneed bastards."

"None of them liberals is long for the Parliament anyway, Sean. Once you've beaten the British, all of Ireland will rally behind our Sinn Fein Party."

"And Ulster will be reunited with Ireland at last, George. Don't lose sight of that."

"God bless you, Sean. And good hunting."

"Goodbye, George."

McCormick hung up and crossed to the door. "Get my battalion commanders in here, Lian."

"Yes, sir."

Five minutes later, Colonel Kevin Florence, commanding officer of the First Battalion, and Major Michael Fox, commander of the Second Battalion, came to attention before McCormick. "At ease. Are your battalions ready?"

"Provisioned and fueled, General," Florence said.

"Rarin' to go, sir," Fox echoed.

McCormick turned and jabbed his swagger stick at the wall map. "From here at Dundalk Bay we'll head east across the ice for fifty kilometers, then turn north and run midway between the coast of Ulster and the Isle of Man."

He tapped the map location of the British Geothermal project in North Channel. "It's a hundred and twenty kilometers to the Brit drill site. I want our forces in position by zero three hundred tomorrow morning."

"No doubt British satellite surveillance will pick us up out there on the ice," Colonel Florence said. "The bloody limeys will know we're movin' north."

"I remind you the ice floes we'll be crossin' lie over international waters," McCormick said. "We can bring our forces up to within two kilometers of the geothermal site without violatin' British territory."

"Still, General McCormick, we can't expect the British to just sit on their hands with an armored brigade comin' at them," Major Fox said. "Suppose they rush defensive forces out to that drill platform."

"They haven't a thing up there to stop us with," McCormick said confidently. "I have intelligence there isn't a single British armored battalion stationed in all of Scotland."

"Aye, but they've got near thirty thousand troops in Ulster," Florence worried. "What's to stop them from movin' those forces out to defend the geothermal well?"

"The IRA," McCormick said.

The two battalion commanders exchanged skeptical looks.

"At midnight tonight the IRA will begin a general uprisin' in Belfast," McCormick said. "There'll be coordinated attacks on police stations, army barracks, power plants, the works. The British will be up to their arses."

"And once we've taken the drill site, what then, General McCormick?" Major Fox asked.

"We'll leave a holdin' force and swing the brigade west to relieve the IRA lads in Belfast. At the same time, our remainin' Army divisions, totalin' near sixty thousand men, will pour north across the border from the Free State. When we've taken the city, we'll mop up the British Army in the rest of Northern Ireland."

Colonel Florence pointed toward the coast of England on the map. "They may not have any armored units in Scotland, General, but the Royal Air Force has over one hundred fifty Tornado F3 ground-attack jets stationed at Leeming in western England. Those planes have a combat radius of six hundred kilometers."

"They're armed with Skyflash and Sidewinder missiles," Major Fox added. "Radar-guided stuff that could chew our tank columns to bits."

"The RAF will not attack," McCormick said.

"Beggin' your pardon, General, but how do you know that?" Florence said.

McCormick turned to his briefcase on a small table beside him and pulled out a sheaf of papers. "I received this meteorological report from Dublin Airport not an hour ago," he said. "The volcanic ash from the latest eruption of R-Nine has grounded all flights between Iceland and Scandinavia for the past twenty-four hours. Those RAF jets wouldn't get fifty miles before the ash clogged their engines and they crashed in flames."

"How long before the ash clears enough for the RAF to fly again?" Major Fox asked.

"Accordin' to the meteorologists, at least ten days. By then, the Brit geothermal station will be in our hands." McCormick swung around and lashed the map with his swagger stick. "And the reunification of Ireland will be a *fait accompli.*"

"A *fait accompli,* you say, General McCormick," Colonel Florence said dubiously. "I wonder will the Brits think the same? They've ruled Ulster since the twelfth century. What's to keep them from sending in the RAF and armored units from Scotland once the ash has cleared?"

"Are you forgettin', Colonel, the British Parliament has just passed a vote of censure against the government of Prime Minister Butler? He's been forced to call a general election. Butler won't dare risk heavy military losses just before the country votes."

"What happens after the election, General?"

"All the polls are saying the Labor Party will win and Seamus MacTiege will be the next prime minister. I can tell you, Mr. MacTiege has no interest in usin' force to keep Northern Ireland a part of the United Kingdom."

Major Fox grinned. "Then we have only to take and keep Ulster until MacTiege assumes power."

"Exactly," McCormick said. "Any questions?"

The two battalion commanders shook their heads no.

"Then it's time to move out. Colonel Florence, your First Battalion will lead the column."

"The ice is crisscrossed with pressure ridges, General McCormick," Florence said. "I'll need a company of sappers to clear the way."

"That will take too much time. Use the cannon in your lead tanks. Blast a way through where you have to."

McCormick's face hardened. "Understand me, gentlemen, I'll brook no delays. If a vehicle breaks down or falls

into a fracture, leave it. We must be in position by three
A.M."

He grabbed his greatcoat off a hook on the wall and put on
his campaign cap. "When we arrive at the stagin' area, refuel
your tanks immediately. I want the brigade ready to attack
at dawn. Let's go."

McCormick led his battalion commanders out of the cottage. Florence and Fox saluted and turned for their vehicles.
The general watched them speed off, then walked across the
snow to where his command tank waited with the engine
idling against the subzero cold. He pulled open the entry
hatch in back, climbed in and yanked the steel cover closed
behind him.

"Go," he barked at the driver.

The thirty-ton Centurion tank lurched forward, its 120-
millimeter cannon bobbing like an angry finger as the steel
monster clanged nosily across the furrowed farm field toward the distant beach.

McCormick took the gunner's seat in front and leaned
forward to peer through the periscope eyepiece. As the Centurion cleared a low rise, he could see the 1st Brigade's machines of war bivouacked along the ice-crusted coast below.

Most of the brigade's eight thousand troops were inside
their vehicles, with perhaps a hundred men outside checking equipment or smoking in small groups. Here and there,
individual soldiers were out urinating into the snow.

The Centurion rolled across the beach and out onto the ice,
coming to a stop near the center of the brigade's massed
tanks. McCormick turned to his radio operator. "Get me the
First Battalion command tank."

A moment later the operator handed McCormick the field
phone. "Colonel Florence, sir."

"Are you in position, Colonel?"

"Yes, sir, ready to roll."

McCormick looked at his watch. It was 4:45 P.M. Time had
run out for the British. "Move your tanks out, Colonel."

He put down the radiophone, popped the turret hatch,
and raised his head and shoulders up into the bitterly cold
air. From his perch, he watched Florence swing his lead tank

in a half circle, his battalion pennant whipping in the arctic wind as the steel behemoth headed out across the floes.

Behind Florence, the massed tanks, supply trucks, and personnel carriers of the Irish 1st Armored Brigade maneuvered into their assigned places in the column.

For several minutes General Sean McCormick watched, the adrenaline surging through him as his attack force started east across the frozen Irish Sea.

Buckingham Palace, London
•••••••••••••••••••••••

8:30 p.m.

"GOOD EVENING, YOUR MAJESTY," Prime Minister Aldis Butler said, bowing from the waist as he entered the Buckingham Palace study of the English monarch. "It is good of you to see me."

King Charles rose behind his desk and crossed the walnut-paneled room, cupping a hand beneath Butler's elbow. "Good evening, Prime Minister. Thank you for coming round. Do sit down," he said, leading Butler toward a large couch facing a bay of leaded windows.

The Prime Minister sank wearily into the deep maroon velvet cushions. For a moment, Butler's eyes wandered around the room, taking in the priceless English antique furniture, the worn but still exquisite Persian rugs, and the oil portraits of British royalty stretching back six centuries.

The room bespoke tradition, power, and wealth. The sense of history within these walls was almost palpable and Butler wondered how many past prime ministers had come here to tell their kings of terrible tidings.

"Will you have a drink? Scotch neat, as I recall," King Charles said.

"Thank you, not tonight. Stomach's on a bit of a rumble."

"Of course." The monarch eased his lanky frame into a patterned armchair, crossing one long pin-striped leg over another. "These are perilous times, Prime Minister."

Butler nodded his gray head tiredly. "Never more perilous, Sir."

"I've been briefed by the military chiefs, of course, but I've asked that you come here tonight because I want to hear your personal assessment of our situation. Are we facing war?"

"I don't see how it can be avoided. Our satellite intelligence has confirmed that the Irish First Armored Brigade has crossed onto the ice of the Irish Sea. Their tanks are at this very moment heading north toward our geothermal platform."

"When do you expect their attack?"

"Tomorrow morning. Once they fire their first salvo, the die is cast."

King Charles closed his eyes and for a long moment said nothing. Finally, he pinched the bridge of his nose and looked at Butler. "Damn them."

"Damn him, Sir. General McCormick. He and the militant Sinn Fein clique have been spoiling for a confrontation with Britain since Windscale."

"I understand his wife and children died at the hands of our Ulster forces. That has no doubt left him a bitter man."

"I believe him to be both bitter and ambitious; a vengeful megalomaniac. There is no question in my mind he is behind the Irish ultimatum."

"I read the document very carefully. The Irish demands give specific map coordinates for the geothermal reservoir. Can you tell me, Prime Minister, how this top-secret information came into the hands of General McCormick?"

"Not with any certainty, Sir. I have my suspicions, of course."

"Do you see a link to the vote of censure Mr. MacTiege pushed through Parliament?"

"There is an obvious parallel. After all, if we bring geothermal power to Britain, that is the end of our dependence on coal."

"Quite. Looking back, Mr. MacTiege had always viewed the advent of geothermal power as a direct threat to his own power base."

"It would destroy his entire platform. Mr. MacTiege has called for a coal-based economy and the abandonment of scientific solutions to the problems of the cold."

"I recall his vehement opposition to Biosphere Britannia."

"The development of these miniworlds powered by geothermal energy would be the salvation of Britain. Yet, for entirely selfish political reasons, Mr. MacTiege would deny the nation the bright future Biosphere Britannia promises."

"I am expected to be beyond politics, of course, Prime Minister, but I don't mind telling you, I find both the man and his methods far beyond the pale."

"There's no question he's a threat to our democratic institutions. Once in power, he'd waste no time instituting radical measures across the board."

"Including the abolition of the monarchy," King Charles said, his face bemused. "I understand he has also proposed huge strip mines out in the country."

"The man would take us back to the grime and poverty of the Industrial Revolution." Butler shook his great head sadly. "The great pity is, we had won the battle between geothermal and coal. The American, Dr. Meade, brought the first well in yesterday."

"One well could not have come near supplying Britain's energy needs."

"No, Your Majesty, but the Dunkirkers brought two of Dr. Meade's high-technology generators up to North Channel. Together they can produce five hundred thousand kilowatts, enough power to supply ten percent of Scotland's energy needs. Within six months, we could have enough wells sunk and generators in place to power half of Britain."

"The advent of geothermal power would have been the handwriting on the wall for Mr. MacTiege."

"For the Trades Union Congress as well. I'm convinced that if we had been able to bring the energy on line from that one well at North Channel, the general strike would have collapsed overnight."

"Now the strike will go on. How much fuel have we left?"

"Three days' supply, Sir; not a ton more."

"You realize, Prime Minister, I will have to call the general election almost immediately. We don't have the traditional weeks or months. No doubt Labor will win, but it is that or allow the country to grind to a stop and the people to freeze in their homes."

"I understand. You have no alternative."

King Charles rose and crossed to the fireplace. He took an ornate bronze-handled poker from its rack on the marble hearth and stirred the crackling logs. "We will lose far more than our geothermal energy tomorrow, Prime Minister. Our defeat at the hands of General McCormick will mark the beginning of the end of our traditions, our democratic values, our very way of life."

Butler's voice was barely audible. "I would rather the Lord God take me tonight than live to see the morning."

The king replaced the poker and turned to face Butler. "Is there no way to stop those Irish tanks; no way at all?"

Butler stared down at his gnarled hands a moment. "Dr. Meade has a plan. In candor, I cannot tell you that I have great faith it will work."

King Charles looked increasingly incredulous as Butler explained Ben Meade's thermal cannon. When Butler finished, the monarch shook his head. "I'm afraid I share your view, Prime Minister. It is simply too farfetched."

"That is also how my Cabinet ministers see it."

"We must accept the imminent loss of the geothermal field, then."

"Ulster as well, Your Majesty. Our intelligence analysts believe General McCormick will turn his tanks on Belfast once he's seized the drill platform."

"What irony. What a bloody mockery of history," King Charles said bitterly.

"Your Majesty?"

"A century ago, at the end of the reign of Queen Victoria, our dominions stretched round the world."

"The sun never set on the British Empire," Butler said softly.

"Yes, Prime Minister. And now? Now the sun never rises. There is only a blue-green glow through the awful ash. And when we lose Ulster our empire will have shrunk . . ." The king paused, his voice choking.

"Shrunk to this lone island, this impotent outpost of Europe, this tiny, freezing empire of ice."

Off the Isle of Man
•••••••••••••••••••••••••

11:50 p.m.

IT WAS NEARING MIDNIGHT as the Irish 1st Armored Brigade
rumbled north past the Isle of Man, the 442 tanks, personnel
carriers, and supply trucks in the attack force strung out in a
column almost three miles long.

In his command tank near the head of the column, Lieutenant General Sean McCormick stared at the radar screen as
a white radius circled the softly glowing green tube. The radius swept past the three-o'clock position, leaving behind a
thin half-inch-long blip on the screen.

Whatever the radar was reading on the dark island in the
distance, it was at least a hundred feet high. And tapered. It
could be a rock spire, or a silo. It could also be a missile.

McCormick punched a code into the on-board computer
and a map of the Isle of Man appeared on a monitor next to
the radar screen. The chart showed coastal cliffs opposite the
position of the column, with a lighthouse on the promontory
the radar was scanning.

McCormick relaxed. He knew the British had their own
radar on the remote island outpost, and no doubt it was at
that very moment tracking the progress of the Irish brigade.
It didn't matter. With the RAF grounded, the only threat to

the Irish force was the British Army in Ulster. And if Paddy
Gallagher did his job, even this danger would soon be neu-
tralized.

McCormick looked at his watch. It was two minutes to
twelve. The IRA uprising was scheduled to start at midnight. He reached across the cramped tank cabin and tapped
the radio operator on the shoulder.

The young sergeant leaned toward McCormick, a hand
cupped behind his ear against the noise of the tank's big
Chrysler engine.

"Get the BBC on the radio," McCormick shouted over the
din of the diesel and the clanking of the treads on the ice
below. "And patch in my earphones."

"Yes, sir."

McCormick put on a headset. A moment later, he heard
the precise baritone voice of the BBC announcer. "Good evening, this is the BBC midnight news. Your newsreader tonight is Kenneth Forsythe. In London, the prime minister
has met with the king in Buckingham Palace as the crisis
with Ireland appears nearing the brink of war. A mech-
anized Irish brigade is reported moving north across the ice
of the Irish Sea toward the British geothermal site in North
Channel."

McCormick listened as the BBC announcer read the rest of
the news: "We have a report from Washington that President Allen has offered to personally mediate the Anglo-Irish
dispute over the North Channel geothermal fields."

McCormick swore under his breath as the huge Centurion
tank rolled over a high-pressure ridge, bouncing him painfully against the radar set behind him.

"Watch where you're goin', damn it," he barked at the
driver.

"Yes, sir."

McCormick readjusted his earphones and went back to
listening to the BBC news.

"Dublin has failed to respond to the American diplomatic
initiative. The Irish government has also refused to send rep-
resentatives to a meeting of the European Congress called to
diffuse the volatile situation in the north."

McCormick returned to watching the radar as the announcer went on reading the news for the next ten minutes.

The midnight broadcast finally ended and a gardening show came on the BBC band. For the next half hour, a woman with an irritating nasal voice droned on about the nutritional value of hothouse vegetables.

Then, at 12:41 A.M., the announcer suddenly broke back in, his voice excited and high-pitched. "Ladies and gentlemen, we interrupt this program to bring you a news bulletin from Belfast."

McCormick tore his eyes from the radar monitor. "Turn that up," he ordered the radio operator.

The sergeant bent forward and hiked the volume.

"Government sources report at least a dozen bombs detonated in the city. The central post office has reportedly been destroyed, along with several police stations. The Strategic Air Services barracks in Newton Abbey north of Belfast is under heavy mortar and grenade attack."

The sudden crack of distant cannon fire echoed sharply through the tank cabin, drowning out both the noise of the engine and the voice of the BBC broadcaster.

For a long terrible second, McCormick thought the brigade was under attack from British guns on the Isle of Man. Then a second cannon shot echoed through the Centurion cabin and he realized from the near thunder of the detonation that it was one of Colonel Florence's tanks blasting a passage through a pressure ridge ahead.

There was a third shot, then the normal sounds of the engine and the clanking tank treads returned.

"I've just been handed a statement from British Army headquarters in Belfast," the BBC announcer said. "The military is requesting civilian ambulances and blood donors to report to Belfast Central Hospital as soon as possible."

McCormick took off his earphones. He'd heard enough. The IRA uprising was obviously under way. The British Army in Ulster would be far too busy defending Belfast to come out on the ice and challenge the Irish tank force.

He punched a request for a location check into the computer. The Centurion's guidance system was being fed continuous data by an international navigation satellite east of Iceland. The satellite could tell the position of a ship at sea—or a tank crossing ice—within twenty meters.

The location of the Centurion flashed on the monitor and McCormick sat back in his seat. They were within fifty kilometers of North Channel. They would reach the staging area by 3 A.M. There, the men would be fed, the tanks refueled, and the guns armed.

There was nothing now that could stop them. At dawn, as the pale blue sun rose behind them, the 1st Armored Brigade of the Irish Army would begin the attack.

LONDON
•••••••••

6 a.m.—February 19
Fuel Reserves—2 Days

SEAMUS MACTIEGE FELT HIS pulse quicken, the blood hammering behind his ears, as he watched the 6 A.M. BBC TV news in his Labor Party office in London.

"Ladies and gentlemen," the newsreader said, "as those of you who have been watching for some time already know, our BBC station in Belfast fell to IRA forces shortly after midnight. Without the station's satellite feed, we have been unable to bring you live coverage of the battle for Belfast. However, the first videotapes of the fighting have now been brought across the ice to Scotland."

A picture of a convoy of British armored personnel carriers speeding through a snowy city street flicked on the screen. A burning building halfway down the block illuminated the street.

"The scene you're viewing now was filmed on Falls Road in the Catholic enclave of West Belfast, long an IRA stronghold."

As the camera panned the convoy, bottles with flaming wicks in their throats lofted out from windows on the upper floors of buildings on both sides of the street. Two of the armored vehicles burst into flames as the Molotov cocktails exploded against their sides.

The camera showed British soldiers scrambling out of the flaming carriers, firing their rifles at the terrorist positions above them as they dove for doorways along the street.

"Dear God!" the newsreader breathed at the sight of a soldier falling out of the last personnel carrier, his heavy winter uniform on fire from head to toe. Two medics with red crosses on their helmets and vests dashed into the street and rolled him in the snow.

As his comrades dragged the withering soldier back toward a doorway, the camera zoomed in for a close-up. MacTiege drew back in revulsion at the sight of the charred black noseless mask that had been the pink face of a teenage boy only moments before.

The camera suddenly pulled back as several shots rang out and one of the rescuers dropped like a stone.

A fusillade of small-arms fire erupted from the doorways where the British huddled and red tracer bullets laced the upper floors of the buildings along the street. From their high vantage points, IRA snipers fired back, their bullets kicking up the ice and packed snow in front of the doorways.

Then the scene changed and MacTiege leaned forward, his eyes boring into the screen as a grainy shot of the inside of a heavily fortified building came on. The windows had all been shot out and there were huge chunks missing out of the jagged frames.

"In the most brazen attack yet, IRA forces have mounted a missile and mortar assault on the barracks of the Royal Anglican Regiment in central Belfast," the newsreader said.

Young British soldiers were huddled behind sandbags hastily piled around the windows. Every few seconds, one of the soldiers would pop up, let go a burst of automatic rifle fire at the enemy somewhere off in the dark outside, then dive again for the cover of the sandbags.

"The Royal Anglican is reported to have suffered over fifty dead and nearly two hundred wounded since the attack began at midnight," the newsreader said over the staccato blasts of gunfire on the soundtrack.

The next second, an incoming mortar round exploded

against the outer wall of the barracks and a section of wall
and sandbags were blown suddenly inward. The BBC camera rocked crazily, then the picture tilted and went black.

The television coverage switched back to the newsreader
in London. "I'm afraid our cameraman was wounded during the mortar attack you just witnessed," the newsreader
said. "We'll continue our coverage of the fighting in Ulster
as soon as we're able to get more videotape out across the
ice.

"In related news, infrared heat detectors aboard one of
our military satellites have followed the engine exhausts of
the Irish First Armored Brigade to within three miles of the
British geothermal platform at North Channel. There can be
little doubt an attack is imminent.

"In a prepared statement delivered to the press an hour
ago, Prime Minister Butler has linked the advance of the
Irish tank column with the uprising in Ulster. Downing
Street expects the Irish brigade to swing west and join forces
with the IRA in Belfast once they have captured the geothermal field."

The newsreader looked somberly into the camera lens.
"The prime minister's statement also admitted that severe
cuts in the military budget in past years have left Britain
without sufficient forces to stop the Irish advance. The First
Armored Brigade is expected to begin their attack at dawn.
That is about one hour from now."

MacTiege hit the remote control on his desk and turned
off the television. The mounting casualties in Ulster had unnerved him. Undoubtedly, most were the sons of working
men, for who but lower-class lads went into the army nowa-
days?

Suddenly the self-doubt that had plagued him since he
was a small boy rose again to assail his conscience. He
wished no war, no young soldiers dead. Yet the social
upheaval he had worked toward all his life, the leveling of
wealth and power between Britain's upper and lower
classes, would extract a price. If he had not dwelt on the cost,
he had always known it would have to be paid.

If fifty young soldiers lost their lives, a hundred, a thousand, their blood would not be shed in vain. Their sacrifice would bring succor to millions of British men and women yet unborn. Those that came into this world like him, poor, ugly, unwanted—despised merely for being—would have the same chance as the sons and daughters of titled land-owners and rich financiers.

The Irish, too, had been victims of the English aristocracy. Who could deny that for a thousand years the bloodsucking, self-perpetuating English upper class, the hereditary elite, had been brazenly usurping Irish land and wealth?

It was still going on in Ulster, and under the ice of North Channel. The Irish had a right to take what was theirs, and he was justified in helping them. The Arabs had it right: "The enemy of my enemy is my friend."

MacTiege rose from his desk and started across the room. No matter his justification, if it were ever learned he had delivered the top-secret map of the geothermal field to the Irish, he would undoubtedly be branded a traitor.

He stopped in front of the fireplace. Alfie was lying with his nose toward the flickering logs and MacTiege bent to scratch his dog behind the ears. "I did what I had to do. You understand that, don't you, Alfie? You don't think Daddy's a traitor."

As the mongrel raised his head, the firelight was reflected in the dog's soulful brown eyes and for a hellish moment MacTiege saw again the young soldier engulfed in flames.

He jerked back his hand in horror. Thinking his master was about to strike him, Alfie whimpered and shrank back from the expected blow. MacTiege recognized the fear in the animal and lowered his hand.

"What's the matter with you, Alfie? Daddy wouldn't hurt you."

Despite his master's reassuring tone, the dog remained wary, his tail curled between his legs.

Stung by the mistrust of his closest friend on earth, Mac-Tiege straightened and walked quickly across to the window. Dawn was breaking behind the thick ash clouds and a diffused blue-green glow was visible on the eastern horizon.

He drew a deep breath and turned to stare out toward the north.

In little over an hour now, the Irish tanks would seize the geothermal field. If the British resisted, there would be heavy casualties. After the battle on the ice, General McCormick would turn his tanks on Belfast and hundreds, perhaps thousands, more would die.

How many of them would burn to death, like his father, like that young soldier on the television? His conscience tore at him, raising a bilious guilt in his gut. For a moment he thought he would vomit. Charred bones and noseless black faces swam before his eyes. No! He wasn't responsible. Englishmen and Irishmen had been knifing and shooting and burning each other for a thousand years.

MacTiege whirled, his eyes boring in on Alfie watching him suspiciously from the hearth. "I'm not a traitor. I only did what I had to do. For the people. The country."

The dog remained motionless but for his muscles bunching nervously beneath his quivering fur.

"Please, Alfie, please don't hate me. I only did what I had to do."

North Channel
●●●●●●●●●●●●●●●●●●

7:35 a.m.

THE ALIEN SUN ROSE blue-green to the east, its eerie rays slitting like an aquamarine knife between the horizon and the ash-laden sky above North Channel.

Benjamin Franklin Meade stood at the rail on the freezing drill platform staring out over the blanket of volcanic debris covering the floes. Here and there, the winds had swept the top of a pressure ridge clear and jagged edges of ice jutted up through the gray powder like crystal sawteeth.

Horizon to horizon, the frozen sea looked surreal, a lifeless gray-white world of ice and ash, an arena set for the deadly sport of war.

Growing up he'd loved reading history, especially the descriptions of the fabled armies of Alexander the Great and Hannibal and Genghis Khan conquering exotic lands. Sometimes he'd put down the book and wondered what it felt like to be one of the soldiers in those armies.

What thoughts had passed through their heads as they faced the enemy on a foreign field? Had they been excited, thirsting for blood, or scared, terrified of the arrows and sword blows that would soon rain upon their ranks?

Now he knew. They had felt disconnected, aloof, their

emotions hovering beyond their bodies like heat over a banked fire. There was no sense of victory or catastrophe to come; only a flat, spiritless vacuum of the soul.

Ben lifted the binoculars from the strap around his neck and swept the ice to the west. There, at the end of the long ice valley where he had known they would come, the Irish tanks were massing for the attack.

For several minutes he stared through the glasses as the machines of war maneuvered into position, pencil lines of dark diesel exhaust trailing them as they moved. A column of tanks cut diagonally across the valley and he could see the stick silhouettes of cannons protruding from their turrets.

It was getting lighter by the minute. They'd be coming soon. He turned and headed back across the icy platform to the operations center.

A mile and a half out on the floes, the great wolf Beelzebub led the pack to the side of a house-sized slab of broken sea ice. While the rest of the wolves waited below, Beelzebub climbed the steep flank of the berg and stared toward the approaching tanks.

There were men inside the noisy machines, he knew that, but unless they came out on the floes there was no way the pack could get at them.

The starving animal settled down in the snow to watch, gnawing on a crust of salty ice in a vain attempt to still his terrible hunger. If the pack did not eat today, they would have to retreat back to land where the deadly flying machines waited to kill them from the sky.

When Ben came into the operations center, Marjorie was sitting at the communications console staring down at a fax sheet.

"This came in from the prime minister about ten minutes ago," she said as he took off his frost-layered parka.

Ben crossed the room and took the paper from Marjorie. *I regret to tell you our military analysts are most pessimistic you*

an successfully defend our drill platform with your geyser can-
non, the message read. Accordingly, I advise again that all civil-
ians surrender to the Irish forces before fighting breaks out. His
Majesty's government has informed the United Nations that Great
Britain will declare war on Ireland immediately following the sei-
zure of the geothermal field by their tank forces. God keep you.
Aldis Butler, Prime Minister.

Marjorie looked at Ben as he put down the fax. "Well?"

"I'm not going to surrender."

"So you're going to ignore the PM's fax?"

"No, not entirely. The geyser cannon is my idea. I won't
ask the rest of you out here to risk your necks on the chance
it will work. Where's Mel?"

"When the fax came in, he called all the roughnecks together in the mess hall. He's over there talking to them
now."

"Do me a favor and get Mel and that Scots Guards officer
in here."

"All right, Ben," she said, reaching for the phone. "But no
matter what anyone else decides, I'm staying here with
you."

A few minutes later, Mel Sanderson came in, followed by
Lieutenant Sam Scribner.

"I understand you've been talking to the roughnecks,"
Ben said to Sanderson.

"No, they've been talking to me, Ben. They reminded me
of a few things."

"Like what?"

"Like that winter back in 'ninety-six when we were sinking that geothermal well in Antarctica. You remember how
that blizzard hammered us for three weeks?"

Ben nodded.

"We got through that together. And we survived when
that typhoon sent ninety-foot waves right over the platform
we were working in the China Sea last year. We stuck with
you then, Ben, and we're sticking with you now. No one's
going anywhere."

Ben looked at the grizzled sea captain a moment. He knew
it would be fruitless to try to talk him and the roughnecks

out of staying. Besides, he needed them. "All right, we make a stand together."

He turned to Lieutenant Scribner. "I'm putting the roughnecks under your command, Lieutenant. Come over to the window with me."

Ben pointed out over the floes toward the ice valley stretching to the west. "The Irish tanks will come at us down that valley. I want you to lead a combined force of roughnecks and Scots Guards out behind the cover of the pressure ridge on the north side."

"How far down that pressure ridge do we go, sir?"

"Fifteen hundred yards. Before you leave, have the roughnecks stop at the equipment shed and take along all the axes and pry bars we've got."

"Axes and pry bars? What on earth for?"

"To take prisoners."

"Sir, I'm afraid you've quite lost me."

"I'm going to fire the geyser cannon when the Irish are fifteen hundred yards out. Once I've stopped those tanks, you go in. Here's what I want you to do."

The young Scots Guards officer's expression grew incredulous as Ben laid out his battle plan.

"I hope you got all that, Lieutenant," Ben said when he'd finished, "because I don't have time to repeat anything."

"I understand, sir. At least I think I do."

Ben extended his hand. "Good luck."

"And to you, sir," Scribner said, shaking Ben's hand, then turning for the door.

Several minutes later Ben and Mel watched through the window as the roughnecks and Scots Guards descended the stairs to the ice below, rifles and axes slung from their shoulders.

Fifty yards out on the floes, the heavily bundled men climbed the pressure ridge on the north side of the ice valley and disappeared over the jagged brow of ice blocks at the top.

Mel Sanderson lowered his binoculars. "They should be in position in about ten, fifteen minutes."

Ben crossed the room to Marjorie at the control console. "What's the pressure at the seabed valve?"

"Fourteen thousand and fifty pounds per square inch. When the geyser cannon goes off, the Irish are in for a nasty surprise."

The minutes dragged by as Ben and Marjorie went through a dry run of firing the twelve-hundred-foot long cannon slanting up from the floor of the sea to just beneath the floes of the ice valley.

When they threw the first switch, it would start an electric motor at the well head. Activating a second switch would direct the motor to open the eighteen-inch-wide valve in the throat of the well head.

Once the valve was fully open, superheated water and steam from the geothermal reservoir below would jet up through the barrel of the cannon and stab into the ice above.

"Here they come, Ben," Mel suddenly shouted from the window, his binoculars focused on the far end of the ice valley.

Ben rushed across the room and lifted his glasses. The long U-shaped passage across the broken floes was less than a hundred yards wide, with pressure ridges on both sides. Only a dozen Irish tanks could advance side by side in the front row. The other tanks, missile launchers, and armored personnel carriers were bunched behind in ranks of ten or twelve vehicles each.

"How far out do you figure they are?" Ben said.

Sanderson studied the advancing tanks. "Mile and a half. Maybe a little less."

For several minutes the two men watched the Irish brigade draw closer. Then Ben swung his glasses toward the pressure ridge to the north. The Scots Guards had reached the ambush position fifteen hundred yards down the valley. He could make out the shapes of individual soldiers strung out in a line just below the crest.

He turned from the window and crossed to the communications console to check the wind and weather. Both would be critical when he fired the thermal cannon. He nodded grimly to himself as the digitized readings flashed on the monitor. It was 35 degrees below zero. And there was a 30-knot wind blowing toward the northwest, directly at the approaching tanks.

"They're slowing down, Ben," Mel called from the window, his binoculars tight against his eyes. "No, wait a minute, they've stopped."

In his command tank in the middle of the front rank, General Sean McCormick popped his head through the turret and brought his binoculars up to study the British drill platform rising from the ice floes ahead.

He knew there was a company of Scots Guards stationed on the platform but there was no sign of soldiers as he swept the deck with his glasses. "Raise the British on the wireless and patch me through," he ordered his radioman in the cabin below.

Marjorie started suddenly and came half out of her chair as the radiophone buzzed on the console before her.

"If I'm not mistaken, that's General McCormick calling," Mel said, his binoculars trained on the man with headphones and a throat mike in the turret of the lead tank.

"Pick it up," Ben said.

Marjorie reached for the receiver as if it were a live snake. Reluctantly, she brought the instrument up to her mouth. "Operations. Dr. Glynn here."

"This is General Sean McCormick. I wish to speak to whoever's in command there."

Marjorie put her hand over the mouthpiece. "It's him. He wants to talk to the person in charge."

"You're head scientist out here, as you reminded me yesterday."

"Yes, but our defense is in your hands. I suggest you speak to him."

"Put it on the speakerphone."

Marjorie depressed the speaker button and hung up the receiver.

"This is Dr. Meade."

"I wish to avoid any needless loss of life, Dr. Meade. I'm

orderin' you to surrender the drill platform immediately. I guarantee you and your people safe passage to Scotland."

"We're not going anywhere, General. This platform is British territory. If your tanks attack, it is an act of war."

"It is the British who are the aggressors. I have your own maps provin' England is siphonin' off energy reserves that belong to Ireland."

"The geothermal reservoir straddles the border, General. Withdraw your forces and let the United Nations work out a fair sharing of the energy."

"There is no guarantee England will abide by a United Nations mandate. Understand, Dr. Meade, I am not prepared to negotiate. You will either surrender immediately or my tanks will take the platform by force."

"We will not surrender," Ben said.

"That is your last word?"

Ben looked at Marjorie. Her face was stony, and he could see a flicker of fear behind her eyes.

"We will not surrender," Ben repeated.

"I have given you every chance to avoid bloodshed, Dr. Meade. What is to come now is on your head."

The radiophone went dead and for a moment Ben stared silently at the speaker, torn that he had made the right decision.

"Here they come again," Mel shouted from the window. "Rolling our way fast."

Ben and Marjorie rushed across the room.

"How far you figure, Mel?"

"Three thousand yards."

Ben lifted his glasses and studied the fast approaching Irish tanks. "Keep coming, you bastards," he said beneath his breath. "Just keep coming."

General Sean McCormick took a last look at the drill platform from his turret perch as the huge Centurion raced across the ice. Then he slid down into the cabin and yanked the hatch closed above him.

"Range?" he said to his gunnery sergeant.

"Twenty-nine hundred yards, General."

"Open fire at twenty-eight hundred yards. Target their communications tower."

He turned to the radioman behind him. "Signal to the brigade: the command tank will take out enemy communications; all other units are to hold their fire until further orders. When the Brits lose their radio, they may change their minds about surrenderin'."

"Yes, sir."

McCormick leaned forward and rested his brow against the headpiece of the periscope sight. They were now close enough that he could make out individual buildings on the deck.

"Range twenty-eight hundred fifty yards," the gunnery officer said.

"Prepare to fire," McCormick ordered.

From his vantage point three-quarters of a mile away, Beelzebub stared intently at the men he'd seen approach from the distant platform. They were now lying down in a row along the back side of a pressure ridge, watching the machines coming down the ice valley toward them.

The wind was blowing the ice from the southwest and once again he picked up the scent of fear coming from the humans. He could tell by the direction of their eyes and their body language that they were afraid of the machines. But he did not know why.

It didn't matter. The only thing that concerned the huge wolf was that once more there were men down on the ice. Vulnerable. Beelzebub watched them for a moment more, then made his way back down the side of the ice slab and loped quickly out across the floes, the rest of the pack close at his heels.

"Twenty-eight hundred twenty-five yards," the Irish gunnery officer said.

"Load and arm," General McCormick ordered.

The rasping hum of the automatic loader lifting a shell into the breech filled the cabin.

"Twenty-eight ten."

"Prepare to fire."

"Twenty-eight five . . . twenty-eight hundred."

"Fire!"

"Get away from the window!" Ben yelled as a puff of white smoke shot from the cannon barrel of the lead tank, followed a second later by the echo of exploding gunpowder.

The three flattened themselves against the wall as the 105-millimeter shell screamed low overhead. A moment later, a jagged circle of ice and snow exploded into the air on the other side of the platform.

Through the windows to the south, they could see a plume of ash and vaporized ice mushrooming into the freezing air fifty yards away.

"We're sitting ducks at this range," Ben said, darting back across the room toward the control console with Marjorie close behind him. "I should have run the mouth of the geyser cannon farther out."

"For God's sake, Ben, we didn't have time," Marjorie said.

"Correction left two degrees," the Irish gunnery officer said. "Range twenty-seven fifty. Ready, General."

"Fire!"

In the operations room, Ben, Marjorie, and Mel froze, rooted where they stood as the Irish shell screamed toward the platform. A second later the explosive slammed into a steel cross beam two-thirds of the way up the radio tower.

The thunderous sound of the explosion was followed by a high-pitched cacophony of screeching metal as the shattered tower beams twisted and tore apart. The entire platform shook as the top sixty feet of the tower plunged down on the steel deck below.

"There goes the radiophone," Marjorie yelled above the din, staring through the window at the tower wreckage smoking on the deck outside.

"Radio tower destroyed, General," the Irish gunnery officer reported.

McCormick swept the platform ahead with his periscope lens. "Range?"

"Twenty-seven hundred yards, General."

The Irish leader focused on the building below the shattered radio tower. It was obviously the operations center for the drill site. He studied the numbers on the periscope lens. "Target at one hundred and seventy-two point five degrees. Lock on."

The gunnery officer punched the numbers into the targeting computer and the barrel of the Centurion's cannon moved into position. "Target lock."

"Fire!" McCormick ordered.

"Incoming!" Mel Sanderson yelled from the window.

"Get away from that glass, Mel!" Ben screamed across the room, yanking Marjorie down below the control console and covering her with his body.

A half-second later they heard the shell coming at them, its passage through the air producing a shrieking roar that grew closer and closer. There was a millisecond of dead quiet, a heartbeat in a vacuum. Then the northwest corner of the operations center suddenly blew apart in a deafening eruption of exploding gunpowder, metal, and glass.

The impact destroyed one of the pillars supporting the roof and a steel beam crashed down on the operations center floor, bouncing off the back of the control console as it fell.

The sound of the explosion died away, only to be replaced by the hellish howl of the thirty-five-knot wind whistling in through the shattered walls. The wind sent a miniblizzard of snow and papers swirling around them.

Ben helped Marjorie up. "You all right?"

"Yes, thanks."

"Mel, Mel, you okay?" Ben shouted against the roaring wind.

Across the room, Sanderson shook off the blanket of debris covering his back and rose. "Yeah," he yelled back. "Still in one piece."

"I'll get our parkas," Marjorie said, the fierce air currents tearing at her hair and clothes as she started toward the coat hooks near the door.

General Sean McCormick peered through the periscope at the shattered corner of the operations center. "Direct hit. Good shooting, Captain."

"That should convince them to surrender, sir," the gunnery officer said, grabbing the sides of his seat as the sixty-ton Centurion bounced over a jagged crevice.

McCormick squinted into the eyepiece. "I don't see any white flags yet." He pulled back and looked at his watch. "I'll give them three minutes. If they haven't surrendered by then, we open up with every gun in the brigade."

Lieutenant Sam Scribner stared through his binoculars in horror at the shattered and smoking operations center behind them.

Suppose Ben and Marjorie had been killed or wounded. Suppose the controls for the geyser cannon had been knocked out. It would be up to the Scots Guards then.

He motioned over his first sergeant. "Pass the word down the line for the men to get ready. If the geyser cannon doesn't fire in two minutes, we attack with mortars and grenades."

Seven sets of ocher eyes watched the sergeant run down the line. Beelzebub and the six surviving members of the pack had circled in to within thirty yards of the men on the pressure ridge.

The starving animals continued to inch silently forward,

using the broken floes to mask their movements, their empt
bellies scraping the ash-layered snow. The men they stalke
were intent on the tanks approaching down the ice valle
before them. Not one human had turned around.

The air in the operations center was now as cold as the dec
outside and Marjorie shivered violently as she shucked int
her parka. Then she fought her way back against the whip
ping wind to the window and helped Mel into his coat
When she reached Ben at the communications console, h
was fumbling at the controls with stiff hands.

His lips were blue as he zipped up his parka. Marjori
held his gloves while he slipped his freezing fingers inside

"They're getting close, Ben," Mel shouted from across th
room.

"Fifteen hundred yards, Mel. "Tell me when they'r
there."

General McCormick looked at his watch, then turned to hi
radioman. "Signal to the brigade; commence fire in ninet
seconds."

"Yes, sir."

Eighteen-year-old Scots Guards Private Johnny Micha
crawled along the back of the ice ridge to Lieutenar
Scribner's position.

"Permission to leave the line, sir."

"What!"

"I've got to take a piss. Bad."

"Make it fast, damn it."

Mel Sanderson cupped his hands around his mouth
"They're about a hundred yards from the target area," h
yelled over the screeching wind.

Ben looked up at Marjorie. "Ready?"

She stared back at him a moment, then bit the inside of her lip and nodded grimly.

Ben reached toward the control panel and snapped the toggle down. The red light next to the switch remained off. He flicked the switch off and on several times. Nothing.

"We've got a problem," he said to Marjorie, hurrying around behind the console.

The beam that had crashed down when the Irish shell hit had left a jagged tear in the thin metal access panel covering the guts of the communications equipment. "There's a screwdriver in the tool drawer in front," he said to Marjorie. "Let me have it."

Marjorie fished in the drawer. "Which one?"

"Phillips head. Hurry up."

Marjorie found the tool and handed it across the top of the console. In a minute Ben had the panel off. He sucked in his breath as he looked inside. Several of the switch wires leading to the mass of computer boards beyond had been sliced apart when the beam tore open the panel.

Ben came back around the console and grabbed a roll of electrical tape and a pair of wire-stripping pliers from the tool drawer. "I'm going to need a few minutes to splice the wires back together. Get on the radio and tell Lieutenant Scribner to create a diversion. We've got to stop those tanks before they roll past the geyser cannon."

Marjorie looked hopelessly at Ben. "We can't."

"Can't what, damn it?"

"We can't contact the Guards. Remember? The radio's out."

"Range?" General McCormick said.

"Fifteen hundred seventy-five yards and closing, sir," the gunnery officer replied, a thin sheen of sweat on his forehead now.

McCormick looked at his watch. "Open fire in forty-five seconds."

"Yes, sir."

Beelzebub stopped, the rest of the pack flattening into the snow behind him at the sight of the human turning toward them. The man slid a short way down the slope of the ridge, then opened the middle of his clothes and began to urinate into the snow.

The smell of the urine sent an adrenal surge through the great wolf. Now was the moment an animal was most vulnerable. Beelzebub turned and made eye contact with the others. *Him. We take him.*

"Fifty yards," Mel Sanderson screamed.

The wind was gusting in stronger than ever now, drowning out Mel's voice. Marjorie put her hand behind her ear and shook her head she hadn't heard.

Mel held up five fingers on one gloved hand, and circled his forefinger and thumb on the other.

Marjorie nodded, then bent toward Ben's ear. "Fifty yards," she shouted.

Ben's hands flew as he stripped the plastic sheathe off a wire. "I need more time, damn it, more time!"

Private Michael was buttoning up his pants when he felt the eyes on him. He looked up, expecting to see the angry face of Lieutenant Scribner. Instead, he met Beelzebub's starving eyes, staring at him from less than ten yards away. Behind the leader, six more wolves were tensed to leap.

"Wolves, wolves," Michael shrieked, scrambling as fast as he could back up the pressure ridge. At the sound of the yells behind them, several dozen Scots Guards turned from watching the approaching tanks. The pack was already halfway up the slope behind the fleeing private.

"Jesus God, it's Beelzebub," a burly sergeant yelled, leaping to his feet and bringing his automatic rifle up to his shoulder.

Beelzebub caught Michael by the leg, his great canine teeth sinking deep into the soldier's calf. The young private screamed in pain as he felt his shinbone crack. "Get 'em off, get 'em off."

The sergeant sighted on the wolves around the panicked Michael and flipped off his safety.

Ten yards down the line, Lieutenant Scribner jumped up. "No, no, don't—"

A staccato burst of automatic fire from the sergeant's rifle drowned out Scribner's words. At the sound of the firing, the rest of the line of Scots Guards and roughnecks turned from watching the approaching tanks.

Beelzebub yelped and let go his grip on Private Michael's leg as a bullet grazed his skull. Dazed, he rolled back down the slope. At the sight of their leader falling wounded, the pack lost their courage and bounded down the slope after Beelzebub.

"Down, down, hold your positions," Scribner yelled at his men.

Too late. All along the spine of ice, men were rushing back toward the center of the line.

Other soldiers now opened fire on the wolves behind them and the snow around the pack erupted with the impact of bullets. A shot caught the largest yearling between the eyes and the wolf keeled over, dead before he hit the snow.

Blood seeping into his eyes now, Beelzebub regained his feet and dashed for the safety of a mass of ice blocks thirty yards away, the rest of the pack at his heels. Halfway across the open ice, a burst of machine-gun fire caught the last surviving bitch in midair as she leaped a crevasse, cutting her body in two. A last whimper came from her severed head as it hit the ice.

The driver of General McCormick's tank caught a movement off to his left and turned toward the pressure ridge to the north. His mouth fell open at the sight of the British soldiers running along the spine of ice, their rifles pointing at something down on the other side of the ridge.

The driver whirled toward McCormick. "British troops, sir."

The general yanked his head back from the periscope. "Where?"

"On that pressure ridge to the north. There's hundreds of 'em."

"Stop the tank," McCormick yelled, swinging his periscope around as the driver jammed on the brakes. Behind the lead tank, the rest of the 1st Armored Brigade screeched to a halt.

"They've stopped," Mel Sanderson yelled from the window.

Ben looked up from the back of the control panel. He only had two more wires to splice. "You sure?" he yelled across to Mel.

"Yeah," Mel yelled back, studying the Irish tanks through his binoculars. "They're swinging their turret cannons toward the north."

"They must have spotted the Scots Guards," Marjorie said, alarm spreading across her face.

Sanderson panned his glasses across the valley toward the pressure ridge on the north. "Son of a bitch, the Guards are up on the top of the ridge. The crazy bastards, those tanks'll mow them down."

Lieutenant Scribner raced along the pressure ridge, gesturing frantically. "Get down, get down."

On the floes below the ridge, Beelzebub and the yearlings reached the field of broken ice, bullets shattering the ice around them as they disappeared behind the jagged white slabs.

The wolves gone, the panicked soldiers ceased fire. Lieutenant Scribner turned toward the approaching Irish force. Jesus God, the tanks had stopped. Their guns had turned from their bead on the platform. The cannons were now pointed straight at the pressure ridge.

Ben finished splicing the last set of wires, wound a strip of electrical tape around the connection, and dashed back to the front of the control console.

"Jesus, hurry up, Ben," Mel shouted from the window, his glasses trained on the Irish tanks. "The bastards have turned their guns on the Scots Guards."

"They're trying to outflank us," General McCormick said, studying the British troops through the periscope. "Message to the first tank squad. Target British positions on the ice ridge."

"Yes, sir," the radioman said, repeating the order into his throat mike.

"Range two hundred ten yards," McCormick said.

Ben looked at Marjorie. "If this doesn't work, we're out of here. And I mean running. Got it?"

"Push the bloody thing, will you? You're driving me mad."

Ben rubbed his numbed hands together, then reached for the first switch. An inch away, his fingers hesitated for a second. Then he flicked the toggle down. This time, the red light went on next to the switch.

Marjorie grabbed Ben's arm. "It's working! It's bloody well working!"

"Surprise time, General McCormick, you son of a bitch," Ben growled, then jammed the second switch on.

Three hundred feet below the ice, the huge seabed valve sprang open and a maddened torrent of superheated water and gaseous steam jetted up into the eighteen-inch-wide drill pipe above.

Driven toward the surface by the titanic pressure and heat deep within the earth's crust, the scalding plume boiled up through the pipe at two hundred feet a second.

The incredible force of the erupting column shook the seabed for several hundred yards around the well, vibrating the legs of the drill platform extending down into the silt.

The operations center began to shake violently. The door to the deck sprang open, and tables and chairs hopped like palsied dancers across the trembling floor.

Ben grabbed the top of the console and pulled himself up, reaching back for Marjorie. "Hold on to me," he yelled above the tumult. "We've got to get over to the window."

Together Marjorie and Ben fought their way across the violently shaking room to where Mel stood braced against the wall, his binoculars fixed on the stationary Irish tanks.

"Any second now," Ben shouted above the wind.

Twelve hundred yards down the ice valley, the superheated plume of water, steam, and volcanic gases surged up through the last section of pipe and stabbed into the underside of the floes. Like a hot poker piercing butter, the scalding column began to bore a cone-shaped tunnel through the thirty-foot-thick ice above.

"First squad has target lock, sir," the Irish radioman said.

General McCormick studied the pressure ridge two hundred yards away. The British soldiers had disappeared back below the crest but here and there he could make out the thin black shapes of rifle barrels against the snow at the crest.

"Prepare to fire."

The radioman relayed the order, listened a moment, then said, "First squad ready to fire, sir."

General Sean McCormick felt the adrenaline surge through him. This was it, the first salvo in the Anglo-Irish War, the war that would free Northern Ireland at last and make him a national hero. Irish schoolchildren would be reciting the praises of Sean McCormick for centuries to come.

He raised his hand, the order forming on his lips. "Open fi—"

At that moment, the floor of the ice valley three hundred yards beyond the Irish tanks disintegrated upward in a titanic explosion of ice, steam, and superheated water.

"Mary Mother of God," the Irish tank driver screamed, yanking back from the viewport as the valley ahead disappeared behind a curtain of furiously steaming water and hurtling blocks of shattered ice.

The hellish roar of the geyser filled the tank. McCormick's senses reeled. What monstrous weapon could make such a sound? He looked toward the driver. The young Irish corporal stared back, his eyes wide with horror and his mouth working wordlessly.

From the window of the shattered operations center, Ben, Marjorie, and Mel watched the maddened geyser jet higher and higher, the 1600-degree water sending furious steam clouds billowing out into the freezing air around it.

Like the stream from a monstrous fire hose, the geyser arched upward through the freezing air. Three hundred feet above the floes, the head of the madly steaming fountain disappeared up into the ash cloud lying low over the ice.

Marjorie grabbed Ben's arm. "That's why you angled the pipe toward the west," she shouted above the tumult. "You were aiming it. You were bloody aiming it!"

"If my calculations are right, the geyser will arch back down three hundred yards to the west." He looked at his watch. "In about six seconds."

Hidden by the ash from the eyes of the Irish troops, the roaring fountain reached its apex at two thousand feet, its flaring mouth hovering over the blanket of ash like the hooded head of a cobra. Then the column of boiling water began its hooking descent toward the ice valley below.

Sean McCormick stood and reached for the hatch lock. He had to know what was outside, what was making that hellish roar.

The young driver snapped out of his shock at the sight of

McCormick pushing open the hatch. "General, no, don't open—"

McCormick never heard him. His head and shoulders were already out of the turret and he was deafened by the tumultuous roaring of the geyser erupting through the floes three hundred yards ahead.

He stared in disbelief at the monstrous fountain spewing up through the center of the ice valley. Slowly his eyes followed the scalding tower up to where it disappeared through the low layer of gray-black ash above.

Then, somewhere in the vestige of his primal brain, Sean McCormick sensed death coming at him. Jesus God, where! Frantically his eyes searched the pressure ridge. The Scots Guards were still down behind the summit. Where? Where?

Then he felt the hot air being pushed downward as the geyser descended through the volcanic debris. He looked up at the same instant the flaring mouth of the fountain broke through the ash cover above him.

He opened his mouth to scream but before the cry could escape his mouth his head was drowned in the scalding torrent from the fiery bowels of the earth. The outer rim of the geyser had begun to cool but in the center the water was still over 1600 degrees, almost eight times hotter than the boiling point.

In the instant before he died, Sean McCormick went blind as the superheated water melted his eyes to a viscous jelly that squirted from his empty sockets. Like a high-pressure hose stripping paint off wood, the hissing deluge scaled the hair and skin off his skull.

He was still alive as the rich blood vessels in his thick lips burst. A millisecond later the intense heat expanded the tiny gas pockets in his fillings and his teeth exploded up through the roof of his mouth into his brain.

In the tank cabin below, the Irish crew screamed as the scalding water rained down on them past McCormick's now lifeless body. The gunnery officer pulled his jacket over his head and reached up to yank McCormick down by the legs, then stabbed a hand at the lanyard hanging from the hatch and jerked the cover closed.

He shrugged his head free of the jacket and shrank back in horror at the sight of Sean McCormick's steaming pink skull protruding from his dripping parka, his fleshless jaws gaped open in a last eternal scream.

Behind the command tank, the deluge of superheated water rained down on the ranks of Irish tanks and armored cars. Water coursed into the angled cannon barrels and seeped into the firing mechanisms of the machine guns and rocket launchers.

Trapped inside by the scalding geyser, the tankers were blinded as the geothermal rain obscured their viewports and periscopes. Within minutes the deluge had turned the ice valley into a long narrow lake, steaming wavelets lapping up over the treads of the stalled machines of war.

Ben swept the Irish force with his binoculars. The personnel carriers and supply trucks behind the tanks had escaped the geothermal torrent. Most of these had now turned and were fleeing back up the ice valley.

Ben turned to Marjorie. "Shut down the geyser cannon."

"Ben, are you sure? Won't they just come at us again?"

"They won't be able to, Marjorie. Shut her down."

Marjorie hesitated a moment. Then she crossed to the control console, flipped the switch closing the seabed valve, and hurried back to the window.

As the geyser slackened, clouds of heavy white mist broiled up from the steaming lake surrounding the tanks, enveloping the Irish 1st Armored Brigade like a thick malevolent fog. The instant the billowing vapor hit the immobile Centurions it froze against the subzero metal of the turrets and tank bodies.

Rank by rank, the machines of war began to disappear beneath ever-thickening shrouds of blue-white ice, their guns and treads frozen in place. When the clouds of steam began to dissipate several minutes later, it looked like the valley had been strewn with hundreds of rectangular blocks of ice.

"Here come our guys," Mel Sanderson said as the Scots Guards and the roughnecks poured down into the ice valley from the pressure ridge to the north and surrounded the ice-covered tanks.

As the three watched from the window, the Guards stood with their rifles at the ready while the roughnecks used their axes to chop the ice from the hatches of the first row of tanks.

Ben lowered his binoculars. "As soon as we get those tankers out of there, we'll put them to work on the Dunkirkers' lorries. With all those troops chopping off ice, we should be able to send those Irish boys home in a couple of days."

"What about their tanks?" Mel said. "There're over four hundred of them out there."

"We'll bring the mouth of the geyser cannon up under them tomorrow and send the damn things to the bottom."

"It's over, isn't it?" Marjorie said, her arms around Ben's neck. "It's finally over."

"The fighting's over." Ben smiled into her eyes. "But our work has just begun. We've got to harness the geothermal power that stopped those tanks and turn it into warmth and energy for the thousands of biospheres we're going to build."

Ben hugged Marjorie against him. "For ninety million people in England and Ireland, life has only just begun."

EPILOGUE
•••••••••

A LOUD CHEER WENT up from the huge crowd assembled before Biosphere Britannia as Marjorie Glynn and Ben Meade climbed the stairs to a floodlit stage flanking the entrance to the pyramid of glass.

Although it was 9:30 at night and bitterly cold, tens of thousands of men, women, and children had turned out to welcome them home after their arrival from North Channel an hour before.

The last of the Irish soldiers had been chopped out of their frozen tanks by midday yesterday. The Dunkirkers' lorries were quickly thawed out, and by dusk the Irish tankers were on their way home.

Ben and Marjorie had started east across the ice soon after, reaching Scotland at nine that night. A convoy of army snowmobiles had been waiting on the coast to whisk them south to Leeds. There they'd boarded a special snowplow-equipped train for the trip down through the Midlands to London.

Ben grinned as he looked out over the sea of faces illuminated by the bright lights of dozens of British and international television crews. "A man could get used to this."

"Perhaps you'd fancy a statue," Marjorie said. "I could ring up the Arts Commission. Have a bronze of you erected in Trafalgar Square."

"Marble's more my medium. Nothing fancy. Two, three hundred feet tall, maybe. A globe of the world at my feet."

"There'll be no living with you now, I can see that."

"Then you have considered living with me."

"Only during my weaker moments. I'm more inclined to take in a cat."

"I could purr. Rub against your leg."

Marjorie laughed. "Get away from me before I fetch a broom."

Another cheer went up from the edge of the crowd and the two turned to watch as a motorcade of four police cars and a Rolls-Royce limousine edged toward them through the packed throng.

"Here come the king and the prime minister," Marjorie said. "I think we're about to lose center stage."

Several dozen policemen gently cleared a path to the stage and King Charles and Prime Minister Butler got out of the Rolls and climbed the stairs.

The king beamed as he extended his hand first to Marjorie and then to Ben. "Welcome home and well done, both of you," he said.

Prime Minister Butler shook their hands. "Truth be told, Dr. Meade, my military advisers didn't think your geyser cannon would work. The generals are still scratching their heads."

"The power within the earth dwarfs any weapon known to man," Ben said. "General McCormick forced me to use that power against him. I hope to God that from now on the geothermal energy beneath North Channel will only be used for peaceful purposes."

"Your hope is well on the way to being realized, Dr. Meade," the prime minister said. "General McCormick's disastrous adventure has turned the Irish people against the Sinn Fein and their IRA hoodlums."

King Charles said, "When word of General McCormick's defeat and death reached the Irish Parliament, the minority parties threw their support to the Fine Gael. The moderates are back in control of the Irish government."

"I spoke to the leadership of the Fine Gael not an hour ago," Butler said. "They asked me to express their gratitude to you, Dr. Meade."

"To me? For what?"

"For sparing the lives of their First Armored Brigade soldiers and sending them home."

"Several of the brigade's officers were interviewed on Irish television today," King Charles added. "They told the Irish people that if you'd wished, you could have fired your geyser cannon when their tanks were directly overhead. You could have drowned the entire brigade in the icy sea."

"I never intended to kill anyone, not even General McCormick," Ben said. "All I wanted to do was stop those tanks."

"All of Ireland knows that now, Dr. Meade," the king said. "By avoiding bloodshed, you've insured that instead of bitter enemies, our two nations can now be peaceful partners."

Prime Minister Butler said, "We've assured the Fine Gael leadership that the geothermal energy under North Channel will be shared equally with Ireland."

"What's the situation in Ulster?" Marjorie asked.

"Without the tanks of the First Armored Brigade to support them, the IRA have been surrendering in droves," Butler said. "The last pockets of resistance are being wiped up now."

"We'll hold elections when things settle down a bit," King Charles said. "If the majority in Northern Ireland vote to join the Free State, Britain will not stand in the way."

"Did you ever find out how General McCormick got that map of the geothermal field?" Ben said.

"Yes," Butler said, his eyes hard. "When our troops raided the Tyrone Brigade headquarters in Belfast, they found Seamus MacTiege's right-hand man cowering inside. He confessed that MacTiege had sent him to Ulster with orders to give the map to the IRA."

"What's going to happen to MacTiege?" Marjorie said.

"He's under arrest and facing a charge of high treason," Butler said.

"Were there any other Labor leaders involved?" Ben said.

Butler shook his head. "No, and neither was the Trades Union Congress. Nevertheless, MacTiege's treason has dealt a body blow to the more radical labor leaders. They've called off the general strike. If we conserve carefully, we shall have sufficient energy until you can bring geothermal power fully on line."

"The energy reserves under North Channel are even greater than we thought," Marjorie said. "We shall be able to heat and power several thousand biospheres."

"I hope you won't mind, Dr. Glynn," Butler said, "but I've volunteered you to build the first biosphere in Ireland."

"I'd be honored, Prime Minister."

"What about you, Dr. Meade?" King Charles said. "May we count on you to develop the geothermal field?"

"I'll be here long enough to train British and Irish geothermal teams, Your Majesty," Ben said. "Then I must return to America. A volcanic winter is descending on the Northern Hemisphere. Geothermal power will be needed in the U.S. and every other country north of the equator."

He turned to Marjorie. "I'm hoping that Dr. Glynn will join me once she gets her biospheres built over here. In the years ahead, her miniearths will have to house not only English and Irish but Americans, Canadians, Russians, and a hundred other peoples."

Marjorie took his hand and smiled. "I'll work with you wherever we're needed, Ben. As you said not long ago, we make a rather good team, one I shouldn't like to break up."

"Well, then, now that's decided, shall we fulfill our promise to the people to light the Biosphere?" King Charles said.

"Everything's ready," Ben said. "The generators at North Channel have been hooked up to the cables we ran across the ice to Scotland. When you throw the switch, power generated at the geothermal station will flow through the British power grid to London."

King Charles stepped up to the bank of microphones at

the front of the stage. A wave of cheers and cries of "God save the king" rang out over the snowy square.

The king waited until the hurrahs had died down. "People of Britain," he began, "God has led us back from the edge of the dark precipice. We have prevailed over the aggressor. The threat of war has lifted from our land."

Hats flew in the air as the crowd cheered, their faces wreathed in joy at the words of their monarch.

"Ladies and gentlemen . . ." The king paused again to let the cheers subside. "Ladies and gentlemen, I give you Dr. Benjamin Franklin Meade and Dr. Marjorie Glynn, the heroes of North Channel."

Ben and Marjorie joined the king to wave at the crowd, bringing a deafening roar that vibrated the panes of glass in the Biosphere behind them. Two young girls hurried up the stairs and presented Marjorie and Ben with large bouquets of flowers.

The two stepped back but the cheering continued without pause. Beaming his approval, King Charles beckoned Marjorie and Ben forward once more and the rejoicing went on in waves, thousands of Union Jacks waving in tempo with the clapping hands and shouts of hurrah.

Finally, Marjorie and Ben rejoined the prime minister and the king raised his hands to quiet the crowd. "I say to all of you here assembled, to all our countrymen—and, yes, to the people of Ireland as well—a new day has dawned in our cold and snowy islands," King Charles said, his voice ringing out over the thousands before him.

"There is much to do. It will take the will of the nation and the work of thousands of dedicated men and women to build the scores of miniearths we shall need. Yet build them we shall. Lift your hearts and trust in the Almighty, for in the years ahead we shall raise our children and pass our days within the warm wombs of Biospheres Britannia. Know you each and every one, this miniearth we light tonight is but the first beacon on our path to Eden. God keep you all."

As the crowd cheered, Charles stepped to the side and threw the switch. Instantly Biosphere Britannia burst into a pyramid of light visible for miles around.

From near and far, the sound of church bells began to pea
out across the ice-covered English countryside. Television
cameras panned the delirious crowd, bringing the trium
phant scene into tens of millions of homes in Britain and Ire
land, and around the world.

King Charles turned to Marjorie and Ben. "Britain ca
never reward you enough for what you have done. Never
theless, there are certain honors I may bestow upon you o
behalf of a grateful nation. I shall expect you both at the pal
ace tomorrow morning at ten."

Marjorie curtsied. "You are most kind, Sir."

Ben bowed from the waist. "Thank you, Sir."

"Until tomorrow, then," the king said, turning for the
stairs.

"I shall be announcing for reelection tomorrow morning,"
Prime Minister Butler said. "I hope I may count on your sup
port."

"I don't think there's the slightest doubt you'll be re
turned to office, Prime Minister"—Marjorie smiled—"bu
you'll have my support all the same."

"I can't vote for you, of course," Ben said. "But I can give a
speech or two, if that will help."

"Thank you both," the prime minister said, following the
king down the stairs.

"Well, there's only one thing left for us to do," Marjorie
said. "Come along, then."

"Where are we going?"

"You'll see."

The two waved once more to the crowd, bringing another
surge of cheers, then Marjorie took Ben's hand, leading him
down off the stage and through the throng to the Biosphere.

"Aren't we going to get sanitized and change into coveralls?" Ben asked as she led him down the Biosphere's central
corridor past the shower room.

"Just this once we're going to skip the normal procedure,"
Marjorie said, opening the door into the air lock. "I think the
smell of germicide on our bodies would be a bit too clinical
for what I have in mind."

Ben's eyebrows arched. "And what, pray tell, do you have in mind?"

Marjorie flashed him a mischievous grin over her shoulder, then turned without answering and passed through the second air lock door. Ben sighed and followed her out into the soaring pyramid of life at the center of the Biosphere complex.

A family of pudus grazing near the edge of the desert looked up curiously as they crossed the savanna. They passed along the shore of the miniature sea and Ben glanced out at a sea otter floating on its back in a patch of kelp.

"When are you going to tell me where we're going?" Ben said, taking off his parka in the humid warmth.

"Patience, we'll be there directly."

Ben stopped as a flock of ducks lifted out of the nearby marsh. His face pensive, he watched as the birds circled up toward the glass apex of the pyramid almost four hundred feet above them.

Marjorie turned. "What are you thinking?"

"About the wolves."

"The wolves?"

"Yeah. Ducks are one of their natural prey."

"Beelzebub and his pack are maneaters, Ben."

"That's not an instinct, Marjorie. Wolves normally avoid humans. Beelzebub killed Reggie and the others because there was no other food out there on the ice."

"I suppose that's true."

"We owe those wolves something. If they hadn't caused that diversion along the pressure ridge yesterday, those Irish tanks would have rolled right past the geyser cannon. And we wouldn't be here."

"You know, I've been planning a wildlife biosphere," Marjorie said. "We've got to get the human environments built first, but in a year or so we could put up a habitat for the wolves."

"They'll starve to death long before then."

"I have a thought," Marjorie said. "Suppose we organize some of the Dunkirkers and search out the pack. We can capture them with tranquilizer guns and hold them in a zoo until their biosphere's ready."

Ben grinned. "That's a great idea."

"I have another idea I think you'll like even better," Marjorie said, starting off again for the nearby jungle.

The look in her eyes sent a hot flash through Ben and he hurried to catch up.

They reached the trail through the dense foliage and now the sounds of the jungle became intense, the screech of monkeys high in the trees in concert with the chatter of hundreds of birds.

The pungent smell of decaying leaf litter wafted over them, mixed with the sweet smell of orchids and fruit trees. Halfway up the trail, Marjorie's hand found Ben's. They smiled into each other's eyes, no need for words, no need but the nearness of each other.

The gurgle of running water became louder and a moment later Marjorie pushed aside a tangle of banana leaves and led Ben down to the foot of the cascade.

"Tranquility Falls," Ben said. He smiled ruefully. "The last time we were here you almost chewed my head off."

"You deserved it."

"One stare does not a lecher make."

"You have the libido of an immense rabbit."

"Did you drag me up here to remind me of my past sins?"

"No, I brought you here to ask if you remembered what I said when you apologized for 'ogling' me, as you put it."

"You said you didn't mind me wanting to get into your knickers, but it had to be a time you wanted me too."

"The time has arrived."

For a long moment Ben looked at her. "Is this for me? Some sort of reward for North Channel?"

"You silly man. I'll leave rewards up to the king."

Marjorie reached up and touched his cheek. "You are not a perfect man, Benjamin Franklin Meade. You have your faults."

"Big-time."

"Perhaps. Yet far more you are a good and decent man. You've made me furious at times, but you've also made me laugh, and made me proud." She circled his neck with her arms. "And you've made me love you."

Ben cradled her head against his shoulder, the blood hammering against his ears as he inhaled the sweet smell of her snow-washed hair. "I love you too, Marjorie."

They took turns undressing each other—their hands caressing, exploring, their mouths searching out each other's lips and noses and ears. Naked, they sank slowly onto the soft bed of moss at their feet.

Marjorie ran her fingers through his hair as he drew her gently against him. "Your dream for the future, Ben, towheaded boys and freckle-faced girls. Is that really what you want?"

He kissed the dimple at the side of her mouth. "A house full of them."

She nuzzled his neck. "You'll help me build the biosphere, of course."

"Biosphere?" His tongue traced the folds of her ear. "I thought we were talking about kids."

"We are. With all those little Meades running around, we shall need a miniearth of our own."

Ben and Marjorie made love slowly, deliciously, their bodies and their passions one, the newness and joy of each other carrying them along on waves of ecstasy.

Around them Biosphere Britannia pulsed with life, the calls of birds and animals melding with the far-off sound of church bells ringing out over the empire of ice.

HIGH-TENSION
THRILLERS FROM TOR

☐ 52222-2 **BLOOD OF THE LAMB** $5.99
Thomas Monteleone Canada $6.99

☐ 52169-2 **THE COUNT OF ELEVEN** $4.99
Ramsey Cambell Canada $5.99

☐ 52497-7 **CRITICAL MASS** $5.99
David Hagberg Canada $6.99

☐ 51786-5 **FIENDS** $4.95
John Farris Canada $5.95

☐ 51957-4 **HUNGER** $4.99
William R. Dantz Canada $5.99

☐ 51173-5 **NEMESIS MISSION** $5.95
Dean Ing Canada $6.95

☐ 58254-3 **O'FARRELL'S LAW** $3.99
Brian Freemantle Canada $4.99

☐ 50939-0 **PIKA DON** $4.99
Al Dempsey Canada $5.99

☐ 52016-5 **THE SWISS ACCOUNT** $5.99
Paul Erdman Canada $6.99

Buy them at your local bookstore or use this handy coupon:
Clip and mail this page with your order.

Publishers Book and Audio Mailing Service
P.O. Box 120159, Staten Island, NY 10312-0004

Please send me the book(s) I have checked above. I am enclosing $ _____
(Please add $1.25 for the first book, and $.25 for each additional book to cover postage and handling.
Send check or money order only—no CODs.)

Name _____
Address _____
City _____ State/Zip _____
Please allow six weeks for delivery. Prices subject to change without notice.

THE BEST IN MYSTERY

- ☐ 51388-6 **THE ANONYMOUS CLIENT** $4.99
  J.P. Hailey Canada $5.99

- ☐ 51195-6 **BREAKFAST AT WIMBLEDON** $3.99
  Jack M. Bickham Canada $4.99

- ☐ 51682-6 **CATNAP** $4.99
  Carole Nelson Douglas Canada $5.99

- ☐ 51702-4 **IRENE AT LARGE** $4.99
  Carole Nelson Douglas Canada $5.99

- ☐ 51563-3 **MARIMBA** $4.99
  Richard Hoyt Canada $5.99

- ☐ 52031-9 **THE MUMMY CASE** $3.99
  Elizabeth Peters Canada $4.99

- ☐ 50642-1 **RIDE THE LIGHTNING** $3.95
  John Lutz Canada $4.95

- ☐ 50728-2 **ROUGH JUSTICE** $4.99
  Ken Gross Canada $5.99

- ☐ 51149-2 **SILENT WITNESS** $3.99
  Collin Wilcox Canada $4.99

Buy them at your local bookstore or use this handy coupon:
Clip and mail this page with your order.

Publishers Book and Audio Mailing Service
P.O. Box 120159, Staten Island, NY 10312-0004

Please send me the book(s) I have checked above. I am enclosing $ _____
(Please add $1.25 for the first book, and $.25 for each additional book to cover postage and handling.
Send check or money order only—no CODs.)

Name _____
Address _____
City _____ State/Zip _____
Please allow six weeks for delivery. Prices subject to change without notice.